Minstrels' Gambit

Book I

of

The Minstrels' Tale Mystery

Nance Bulow Morgan

Dreamer Books
Marston, NC

Dreamer Books

www.dreamerdesigns.net

Nance's Official Website

www.nancebulowmorgan.com

ISBN: 978-0-9915625-0-3

Library of Congress Control Number: 4600393

Nance Bulow-Morgan

Nance Bulow-Morgan and the Dreamer Books Logo are trademarks belonging to Nance Bulow-Morgan

CREATED AND PRINTED IN THE UNITED STATES OF AMERICA

In all my life I have lived in interesting times; it hasn't always been easy, but it has always been interesting. Through it all there have been loved ones near and far who have remained close in my heart. For all their encouragement and wry humor through those and all times; you know who you are, I love you.

To my husband with whom I have faced headlong all things interesting; we haven't always been easy, but we have always been interesting. My capacity to string pretty words together cannot touch the depth of love and respect that continues to grow in me for you. Through thin and thick we are invincible. Forever devoted, I love you.

·~· Table of Contents ·~·

·~· Chapter One ·~·

I knew that Behlanna was not going to be a good city for me. I told Andreas so when I first caught sight of the dark tower situated predominately at the highest point in the northwest corner of the sleek dark wall. At that point the arms of the dark rock face conjoined with the city wall and reached out around it to form a fundamental primary defense.

Maybe it was the dark buildings, or the sharp angles of the place, or the many barren peaks of the anchoring crag, or the jabbering soothsayer who insisted that my life was under a dark shroud that had followed me since birth and would bring darkness to us all. Even the blazing orange and red suns overhead could do nothing to brighten the scene. Why should I be uneasy? Maybe it was just that my witch mother and I had been thrown out of the city of my birth because of her practice of so called dark arts. I still shudder when I think of the things they threw at us as they shouted their vicious taunts. One man nearly ripped me from my mother's arms with the intent of killing me—"the devil's spawn," he called me. I was such a sweet naive kid, but he thought I was the devil's own. My mother snatched his arm off me and spat a curse at him. The man reeled and the crowd drew back. Mother ran then. They continued to throw their garbage at us.though, they were too afraid to follow after that. I watched over my mother's shoulder as we fled. The man clutched his arm as he swayed on his feet and spittle

1

dripped from his mouth as he watched after us. My mother drew my face back around and buried my face in her protective arm. She raised me after that in a hovel in the woods and I always felt somewhat out of place in cities ever since.

My mother loved and taught me well. I learned how to read and write, and when I refused to learn her ways with magic for fear of the trouble it would cause me, she taught me how to make music. I played in the woods for hours each day. When I was not playing on my little harp or wooden flute, I played at fighting. The music in my head played over the drama of my imaginings at hard fought battles with imaginary beasts and human foes alike. I never lost a battle in those woods; I slayed them all with long sticks and handmade bows. It caused me to wonder about the world.

When I was sixteen my mother sent me to live with a man and his wife, they taught me how to fight with real weapons and then sent me out into the world when I was eighteen. They were harsh and I did not love them, but they taught what I wanted to know. I went back to see my mother and say farewell, but when I arrived there was nothing but a burnt out shell left of our little home. I rummaged through the ashes made crusty by the weather but I could not discern what circumstances had befallen my kind mam. I could learn nothing of her, though I tried. I never saw her again. I was sure the city folk had found her and burned her. That was always the way of ignorant people, to burn things they didn't understand. I was certain that they did it to keep her from being magiked back. So I became a sad, yet hardened obstinate girl when I went out into the world alone.

My friend Andreas however is a city boy, born and raised. His parents were still alive, though he said little of them. He was well educated in the ways of a nobleman, but he had managed to keep his common ways. He had learned to play the harp as part of his formal teachings and picked up lute and mandolin along the way. Where I shunned magic for the anguish it could cause he had a natural gift for it and reveled in it. His parents forbid him to use his magic and his teachers preached its evil ways. So he hid it from them and wondered at his own leanings. The magic came to him untaught; as if a savant. He did not fear it; it was a part of him for as long as he could remember. He did not feel that he was evil, but if he used magic did it make him evil? It wasn't until he went out on his own and found that he could use his magic for good that he fully realized the limited thinking he had inherited from his parents and teachers.

His father caught him once playing at changing the level of water in a birdbath at the back of their garden. He set him out that night with one hundred pieces of gold. The money stayed in a sack inside a carpetbag. Andreas never touched it for personal gain, but many families had benefited from his charity of it. He made his way with his music and odd jobs, but he always regretted leaving the city. He loved the noise, the culture, and activity.

We first met in another land in a small hamlet. I had taken my spot on a low wall near a pub at the edge of the market square and neatly arranged my humble instruments along the wall with my tip hat at the far end. I began to play a lament on mandolin. At that moment Andreas strolled into the market with his carpetbag in hand and stood a moment to listen. He watched me, and I him, and we exchanged smiles.

Then he sat on the ground right there across the square from me and pulled his elegant harp out of the carpetbag and joined me. I know it is odd to say that we made beautiful music together, but we did. I fell in love with him first for that, no first his beauty, then that. My hat was full by the night's end, and he would not take a copper for himself. So I bought him dinner and we exchanged histories and stories of our adventures. I fell in love with him several times during those tellings. I wondeedr if he felt the same. We stayed in the pub until it closed and then walked out along the edge of town talking until morning.

A sneak thief made a grab for my money purse and we both reacted. I drew sword and brandished it deftly. The thief turned to run and Andreas made an incantation that sent the man sprawling face first into a mud puddle. Andreas laughed, but I pushed his hand down and asked him if he was crazy. He had forgotten my tale about my mother and her dark arts and how we had been run out for it. He apologized, as he retrieved my purse from the thief still flailing in the mud. Then he launched into a tirade about the wonders he had experienced upon discovering his gift and his trials to learn how to use it. He promised to never use it in town again if I would agree to travel with him and perform together; for equal shares from that point on. I could not have said no had I been commanded to do so. I was in enthralled.

***

We had come to Behlanna from Plano after traveling without horses for a week, having lost them to bandits. We'd had a successful, yet prolonged engagement in Duke Midewin's villa to the south. He had retained us to exterminate a nearby estate that had once been an old school for the teachings of magic. Now it swarmed with conjured beasts, which must have been the undoing of the Mages. The current Land Baron, Midewin was a kind old Paladin and the brother of a lesser King. He had been sent to bring the land around the estate back into shape and now had the makings of a successful vineyard. His brother rewarded him by giving him the vineyard and the rule of the lands around it.

His successful enterprise attracted people in need of work and a small town of tradesmen and crafters cropped up along the foothills and river that fed out of the mountains to nourish the valley in which the vineyards lay. But he alone could not control the beasties that continually threatened his people. He needed to have his lands cleared of them and the assorted magical traps still intact at the old school.

The Duke who was a kind man had heard of our music and our skill with blades and summoned us to take care of his problem. When our work around the villa was complete we stayed on for a while. The Baron and his people were so grateful of our songs and tales of far off places and heroic deeds that they rewarded us handsomely. The Baron was quite hospitable and we became friends of sorts. He learned of Andreas's personal quest to understand his magic abilities and bestowed on him a trove of ingredients used for potions and spell castings, some minor enchanted items that he himself had procured on a foray into the school. These were in addition to the rather substantial take of gems and jewelry; he had given us as a fee.

We were enroute to Behlanna, at the Duke's suggestion for a few days rest before plying our trade there. Our horses needed a rest so we were on foot.when we were ambushed on the road. Andreas carried the large carpetbag that we kept our clothes, weapons and instruments in. I had the small chest the baron had filled with our payment under my arm. It was only slightly larger than one of those tomes only intellects or religious zealots take the time to read. Suddenly two arrows sank into it and five unsavory men charged at us from out of the trees along the sides of the road. I drew my sword and moved to protect Andreas just as he let loose a blast of flame that sent two of the men to the ground to vanquish the flames that had ignited their clothes and hair.

I stood in front of Andreas and he took the chest from me to place it at his feet so that I could draw a second sword. Three men still approached, though somewhat less exuberantly. I brandished my blades about with the entire flourish I had acquired over the years. Another arrow shot out from the woods and caught me in my right shoulder.

"Andreas, have you forgotten the drill?" It had become a matter of our limited number that Andreas would use his magic to take out distant projectile assaults while I dealt with the close combat.

"No my dear, it was only that I had not pinpointed them until now." He replied, and then began his incantations.

I fought well enough with my left hand, and fended the best I could with my right, imbedded arrow and all. Andreas took out the bowman and I severely wounded two of the three on me before the two burned bandits got their bearings. They thought they could help their odds and charged at us again. I still smile when I recall the looks on their faces as

Andreas let loose another blast of flame. They turned to run, but their feet could not carry them fast enough and they were soon scampering upon the ground in an attempt to smother flames while still managing a clumsy retreat.

The fire blast gives off a percussion that can be felt when in a close proximity and this one was. The men that I fought felt it at their backs and they must have seen my hair tossed back from it. They began to spread out and then finally they broke and ran. I yelled and gave chase to the one and only healthy man, knowing that I could not catch him, but I wanted them to feel our ferocity even as they ran away. When I was sure they would not return I turned back to Andreas. That was when I saw two more bandits jump on our mounts and ride back the way we had just come.

I didn't care horses are replaceable. I allowed myself to collapse. I was wounded in several places and bleeding badly, but more importantly they had not gotten the chest or the carpetbag! The bag held all of our instruments; flutes, a lute, mandolin, and harp, and a miscellany of small percussion instruments. We each had our preferences, but we could both play them all. Our lively hood was in those two receptacles. We felt sure the bandits would not return anytime soon so we stayed about a bit longer to tend my wounds and rest.

That was how it was that we traveled on foot through a remote countryside. We traded music for a nights sleep in a barn at a few farmsteads along the way, but most nights we spent sleeping on the ground away from the road.

We saw the first sign for Behlanna on a post with other signs upon it. We had our choice of Plano, Behlanna, Sandhitch, or Ahnrye. Behlanna was the obvious choice. It was known far and wide for a thriving commerce and we felt sure that we would make good minstrel wages in the marketplace and pubs there. Andreas found the stark towers beautiful "Like a stone forest," he said. To him the culture alone was reason to visit. I always found city culture either seedy or haughty and I did not prefer one to the other. Lucky me, Behlanna promised to offer both. It turned out that Behlanna had more substance to offer than I will ever need again in my lifetime. This tale is about that. Parts of it are retold to you as they were told to me by many other players who became involved along the way. I have endeavored to avoid their exaggerations and present to you only the truth of the matter.

***

The road we traveled to Behlanna took us over the mountains of the Dinarian Divide into a valley that ran the western arm of the range that surrounded Behlanna. We wound through foothills until the road intersected another, which traveled north and south along the Storm River. We went south toward Behlanna just as Duke Midewin had directed.

The walled city was situated comfortably in a valley of wooded hills back dropped by the jagged spires of the surrounding mountains. The jagged skyline of the rooftops above the walls against the jagged spires of the mountains seemed forbidding against the lush green of the hills. The river Storm moved swiftly by outside the city walls cutting a deep split as it ran down out of the mountains, swift and crazy, on its way north to the ocean. The landscape rose sharply on the west bank. Two mountainous shoulders cradled the city on the north and east sides where the city was made to be a part of that natural wall.

The docks were situated outside of the west wall of the city and a small community of warehouses, fisheries and housing for the workers had cropped up there. The cold steel grey river kicked up a cold white mist against the sharp grey rocks that stuck out along the course of the river. I became quiet and apprehensive. The whole atmosphere of the place seemed cold and dark to me. In contrast Andreas became talkative and was excited to be heading into the bustle of city life.

By the time we reached the city gate my shoulder was healing nicely, but Andreas insisted I leave it in the sling another day or two. I conceded, not so much because of any pain, but because I thought I might look like less of a threat. It was known to be a peaceful place, and I didn't want to make a bad impression.

Had it not been for that reputation, I might have turned away from it that day. As we approached the dark iron gates I was not sure that my consideration was a good one. The guards above the gate looked more like hardened mercenaries than city guards. Perhaps this was a conscious effort by the prince to maintain the peace. Most of them were massive in stature and they wore no standard. These men made us uneasy. I could not imagine a common citizen having the bravado to cross them. They looked down at us as we walked through the gate. Once we entered they called down to us and we stopped to acknowledge them. I was soon sorry that we had. Their only interest in us was my female gender. They were not kind with their attentions and it mattered not that I had Andreas as a male companion. As strangers in town our only recourse was to turn and continue on our way without a word. We could not afford to set the guard against us from the very first moment that we entered their city. I loathed the sound of their laughter as we moved away almost as much as the vile things that they said.

Andreas felt my anger, literally. I accidentally hit him in the face as I gestured and cursed the men in the ramparts. The feel of it jolted me back to reality, but when I looked into his eyes I saw a smile there and we both laughed.

"Oh, Sadie, I love you when you're indignant." He said as he rubbed the feeling back into his cheek

"I'm sorry, Andy. What do you say we get a room and I'll buy you a whiskey to take away the sting?"

"Wonderful idea you fiery vixen of a sex night, or did he mean sex knight- with a k? With that bit of armor you wear I can see how…"

"Shut up Andreas, or I'll slap you again, all the way back to yesterday. And when we see those road signs again I'm heading to Ahnrye. I hear they openly pillory their citizens there. It is so much more appealing to know what I'm up against, not like this wholesome little burg."

"The guards sure don't live up to the city's reputation do they, you sultry fox?"

"It is my fortune that my parents blessed me with a right proper blend of features and physique. I just will never understand why my good fortune gives license to others to spew lewd obscenities my way simply because they feel some misplaced sexual urge."

Andreas only shrugged and led the way to an inn just ahead. A whiskey was sounding good— a whiskey, a bath, and then bed. I was so tired that food could wait until morning, but any old inn was not going to be good enough this time around. I saw a young woman on the street and asked her where we could find a nice quite place to stay a few days.

She gave us directions to Aunt Katie's Room and Board. We had to walk nine blocks, five west, toward the palace, one north and three back east toward the center of town. Andreas was foot weary, but obliged me the extra walk.

As we made our way through the reek of bowery and something else unsavory, an old crone shouted at us from her doorway. Her voice quaked as she spoke and we had to stop and listen hard to hear her. She motioned us to her. not wanting to disrespect the elderly, we moved closer. She came to the top of her porch steps as we came near and reached out a gnarled old hand to me. I took it and felt her frailness. She put her face close to my ear and whispered these words; "Your days will grow as dark as the parents who gave you life. A dark hand reaches out for you even now. Beware, for it is not far and it will find you. I felt you coming even before you passed the gate. The dark is in you but, you refuse to recognize it. You have made yourself blind! Beware, beware." She drew back from me then making signs of protection against evil with her frail hands as she went back to her house.

Her startling demeanor and her words caused me to back away, but more out of confusion and annoyance than fear. I had seen old fortunetellers put fear into strangers before. It was a kind of an entertainment they made in their old demented years. I had scoffed at the weak minds of the foolish then. I had felt an energy pass between me and this

11

old woman and I admit that it shook me up. I took Andreas by the arm and turned him around to be away from there. The woman continued her superstitious hexes and mumbled to herself from her door way. Her ways reminded me much of the charms and incants that my mother would make to keep us safe.

"Your reputation precedes you I see. What did she say to you?" Andreas wanted to know, having been unable to hear the woman's words. When I told him he whistled and shook his head in disbelief.

"Some welcoming committee, huh?" I said in response to that.

We made our way toward the boarding house. The streets were cobbled, not dirt and crushed stone. The bustle of tramps and peddlers carving out existence in squalor gave way to a calmer, cleaner residential section of town. Merchant shingles swung above the doors of a house here or there. The neighborhood was alive with the voices of children at play, and birds singing in the trees that lined both sides of the cobbled street. The peddlers strolled rather than lurked and hawked their handmade wares proudly. The homes had small front yards. Most were surrounded by low stone or wrought iron fences. They were neat and well-kept and sat in rows like soldiers at attention. You might even say it was charming, unlike the litter strewn alleys and dirty buildings of the commercial district we had passed through just inside the gate. I remember thinking that maybe this city wouldn't be so bad after all.

When we arrived at Aunt Katie's Rooms and Board the place was in an uproar. People stood about outside craning to see some activity on the porch. A group of the city's guard stood together in the street while a contingent of men who were not guards swarmed around the place. They seemed especially interested in the front porch. We stood amongst the onlookers unsure if we should approach or not.

As the men on the porch moved about we could see that there was a man slumped back in a chair there. One of the men examined him. If he was not dead he was comatose. "Great, just great." I muttered.

"Calm yourself, we are just here to rest"

"Do you mean that?"

"We don't have to do anything; if you don't want to that is," Andreas offered as counter to my disappointment.

"By that I take it that you want to."

"No, no. You should rest. I mean you are weak still."

"Weak?"

"Well, ya, you still need time to heal, you've always been kind of slow with that."

"Ya, ya. Talk it up. I know what you're about."

"I'm not about anything. It doesn't matter that these people need our help. Your health is more important; still, maybe we could help in an advisory capacity."

"O, simply advisory?"

"Sure, we can offer our expertise, you can rest."

"Simply advisory, really?"

"If they will agree to it."

"I really would like some rest, but if they want the help—simply advisory, mind you. I guess I can handle that."

"That-a-girl." Andreas said, and began to move through the crowd to the porch. I followed. At the porch Andreas spoke to one of the men there. They were constables. From this vantage point we could see that the slumped man was surely dead. Blood had drained from a deep gash at the right side of his neck. His jugular vein had certainly been cut judging from the large pool of fresh blood at his feet. His death had been harsh, but quick. Our assumptions about the men examining the porch proved correct when we were introduced to Sheriff Traylor. Traylor took us inside immediately. We were patted down and our weapons were taken from us. We were not handled lightly.

Aunt Katie, a plump middle aged woman paced anxiously, behind her check-in counter, wringing her hands the whole while. Traylor motioned us to a table in a far corner away from the door.

"Your offer interests, but not for the reasons you might expect."

"What reasons then?"

"Your names were the last words to cross our victim's lips."

We both started at that, shock and confusion crossed our expressions unchecked.

"We only just arrived in town; your gate guard will know that." I said.

"He was only just murdered." Traylor responded.

We fell silent a moment formulating what we might say that would prove our innocence. Andreas spoke first.

"What was the man's name?" he asked.

'Brilliant defense,' I thought, a bit cynically, but I remained quiet.

Traylor thought a moment, no doubt weighing the ramifications of a proper answer. Figuring it would do his investigation no harm, he answered. "Eindal."

We thought, going through our lists of friends and acquaintances in our heads. It is a long list for both of us, but we arrived at the end together and answered in unison. "Sorry, I don't know him."

"Well he knows you."

"That is not a first," again in unison. Then Andreas finished the thought for both of us. "We are more than just minstrels, and when called upon we have done some adventuring and investigating of our own. More than once we have enforced the law of the land. We are not entirely unknown.

"What was it the man; Eindal, said pertaining to us and who did he say it to?"

"He only said, 'find Saeede and Andreas.' He said it to the serving wench that was bringing him a glass of port to take on the porch as he enjoyed a stick of dragon. She screamed for help and Kate and the guard on patrol came to her on the porch. Eindal was dead by then, and the guard sent for me."

"Who is Eindal?" I asked.

Polk weighed my question against my demeanor and then weighing in my favor answered; "A merchant. He comes here often and always stays at Kate's. He gives money to the poorer folks here when he can, but that's all anybody really knows. He does his business and then moves on."

"What does he trade in?"

"Not really sure, but we'll be checking into that."

"We came into town for some rest. We just finished a job for Baron Midewin. He will vouch for us. Let us help you. In the meanwhile we will prove to you our innocence."

I found myself saying. *'Great, so much for relaxation,'* I found myself thinking.

"We were going to take a room here. You can keep tabs on us and if we find anything we will report it to you." Andreas added.

Traylor thought long and hard. "Let me see what's in your bags before I decide."

Andreas and I shared another look, but quickly nodded our approval.

Traylor called two of his men in to watch us as he searched.

Andreas fidgeted as his sword was examined and then put with the four daggers that Traylor had taken from us during his pat down. Traylor examined my swords and bandoliers next. I fidgeted then, this all was uncomfortable considering the circumstances. He dumped out our clothes and went through them as well. Andreas stood as his mandolin hit the floor with a snap of the wooden bowl. He was pushed back down mightily. Traylor found the box of reagents and the jewelry we had obtained from the baron. I wished that we had figured out what they could do. I wished we had sold it all when we first came into town.

Traylor turned his attention back to us. "His purse is missing, and I see you have a sizable bit of coin between you."

"Midewin pays well." Andreas countered.

Traylor seemed dubious.

"If we were going to kill the man why would we do it on the porch where anyone could see us? Why wouldn't we wait and do it in his room?"

"If he was only just killed would we have had time to clean the blood from our weapons? I saw you look for it, but there is none, because we did not kill him," I added.

Traylor's face did not soften, but he was silent and went out to the porch. What he did there we never knew. When he returned he had a private conversation with Kate. She glanced at us a few times and nodded favorably to Traylor. When he turned his attention back to us he agreed to let us assist his investigation. "I have sent a man to speak with Midewin. He rides now and should be back in the morning, when he is I will know better of you. I know Midewin. He will tell us straight. Kate has agreed to take you on at her usual fee. I will be watching you, of that you can be sure."

"We would expect no less under the circumstances. I have no doubt this will end favorably for both of us."

"I will talk with you again in the morning after I talk to my man. The mortician will be here soon. If I were you I'd start investigating. Then get yourselves settled in."

With that being the last he had to say for the time being he nodded to his men and they all left. They made their way through the crowd and the others who had been waiting on the porch followed. We gathered up our things and then went out and began our own examination of the porch and of Eindal himself.

He was taller than Andreas, and had been handsome for his age; somewhere in his fifties we figured. He was dressed more like a woodsman than a merchant. His jerkin was brown leather over black silks. His boots were brown as well and came to his knees. A bastard sword leaned against the right side of his chair, making him left-handed most likely. He had a neatly cropped beard and short white hair.

It was not hard to see that his attack had come from beside him. The angle of the slash and the spray of blood it had caused indicated that the attacker had been nearly behind him but off to the right. He must have been experienced to get so close without Eindal feeling him. To have gotten to that position the man could not have come up the stairs from the street. It was unlikely he crossed the porch from Eindal's left, because he would have had to pass either in front of or behind him in order to gain the position to the right of and behind him. He would have had to climb over the rail of the porch from the alley that ran along side Aunt Katie's building.

There was a small smear at the edge of the pool of blood away from the body as if something had been removed, but the pool had filled in any void that might have been there. There was no trail of blood to track the killer. He or she had moved quickly after the kill to stay out of the blood. What we did find was a trail in the dirt at the alley side of the porch.

We went inside and gathered our things. Andreas arranged our room. Kate had a twinkle in her eye now. "Can you really help find the bastard that killed Einey? He was a good man." We promised to do our best.

She gave us the once over about house rules: No excessive noise, no swordplay, she mentioned both of those a number of times, among other things but we didn't really listen. We assured her that we had only come for much wanted peace and quiet, and perhaps a warm place to perform. We had wanted to do some sightseeing, but that would have to wait. Current circumstances were beyond our control. We hoped for a quick resolution and then we would resume our vacation.

We signed in and she escorted us to a room on the second floor. She undid the lock with a master key from a ring she wore strung around her neck and then dropped our key into Andreas's hand. I believe she wanted us to know that she could get into our room at any time if it was necessary so we had better be good. I can't say that I blame her. I suppose we did look like trouble, and she was kind enough not to turn us away. Andreas asked about a place to get a drink and she told us there was a bar in the parlor downstairs.

We had settled on taking one room before we had arrived at Aunt Katie's. We knew that people would then assume we were married and that would give us more time to evaluate the enigma of this reputably wholesome town. If at some other time we wished for companionship of the opposite sex we would fall back on our 'no that's my guardian' story and set up schedules for the room.

We looked around the plain, tidy room. There was a simple large bed between two windows on the outer wall, a sitting area with two chairs and a small writing desk near the door. A copper clad wooden tub sat up on a copper brazier in a corner near a window. The entire contraption was set on wheels so that it could be pushed to the window and the water could be tipped out. A muslin curtain could be drawn around the tub for privacy and there was a little chair near the tub.

I looked out the window, not much of a view, just a dead end alley, but it was quiet, just as we had requested. It had taken some convincing to get a room on the alley side of the house, but Aunt Katie believed us when we said it would help us to watch, because killers often return to the scene of the crime and the alley gave us a better to chance to do that We had to show her the trails in the dirt leading to and from the porch to that alley, but that sealed the deal. The dead end alley and a two way trail in that alley made no sense. We were in a hurry to investigate.

We washed at a basin of cold-water set on the dresser, changed into clean clothes, and stowed our gear under the bed. We took only our most concealed weapons and I left my chain mail behind. We locked the room up tight, and climbed out the window.

When we hit the ground and looked toward the main road we could see a guard, one of Traylor's men stationed there. We moved along the wall and deeper into shadow and the alley. Our attempt to follow the killer of Eindal soon proved futile. We lost the trail quickly. The culprit must have taken to the roof tops. We attempted to do the same several times, but when we were finally successful in getting to the roofs, there was no trail to follow, and no obvious route. We returned to our window and our room aggravated and in foul humor. We wanted that whiskey we had promised ourselves and wanted it badly. We went immediately downstairs to find one and hopefully relax.

The parlor was formal, but comfortable. The warm glow of a fire emanated from a small fireplace on the outside wall across from the entrance. A sturdy oak bar stretched nearly the length of one wall. The mirrored back-bar was complete with the finest stock of spirits. In the center of the room two couches were set in an arrangement around the fireplace while still giving service access from the bar. A wooden tea table was set in front of the couches. Around the perimeter of the room high back leather chairs and round pedestal tables were arranged randomly.

The moment Andreas and I entered the room the place went quiet. I should mention that Andreas has a bit of the fox about him too. He cuts a strong silhouette in his black silks. He is tall with the type of musculature that makes a man chiseled, yet sinewy, not bulky. His skin is the color of crème chocolate, but his emerald green eyes belong in a fair skinned face. His hair is black as ink and falls in wild ringlets to his shoulders. I stand in contrast to him with a shorter, more muscular build. My blue silks strike against my olive skin, and auburn hair. When a room goes quiet at our entrance we both just smile. I have white teeth and a twinkle in these baby blues, but when Andreas smiles it melts even my heart, and *I* know what a cold bastard he can be.

We took two chairs near the fireplace. We could feel everyone's eyes following us, until they recovered and the clink of glasses sounded again. Soon we heard comments coming from a group near the bar. "I'd roll her in a second." A gruff looking scoundrel said. His voice matched his appearance. A young woman behind the bar spoke up. "Is that all you'd be able to manage with such a fine thing as her? I'd roll him I dare say, but I'd take considerable more time, to be sure." Guffaws followed and then the woman stepped from behind the bar and came to take our order. I assume she did not realize we were able to hear the comments from the bar, because she was comfortable and friendly. I suppose even in peaceful cities the locals need their entertainment, this night we were it. We ordered four whiskeys and she went away with a nod.

When the bartender returned I asked what arrangements could be made to have a bath drawn. She asked our room number and said she would see to it. I gave her a piece of silver for the drinks and the bath. She curtsied and went off. It wasn't often we went first class, but this place offered that kind of service and yet the rates were modest. We each had one whiskey down when she returned and confirmed that a bath would be drawn immediately. When she returned to the group of patrons at the bar she told them that we were roomed together. There was some disappointment among them, but then they turned to degrading me for my class, or lack thereof in their opinion. "A woman should know her place." They wondered what I was thinking, that I thought I could dress like a man. Perhaps I should have changed into my dress, but I just didn't really care just then. "And what is such an obvious gentleman doing with such a slut."

"Do you hear that, Andreas? They think you're a gentleman."

"Yes, I hear. What they don't know may very well come back to hurt them, but, you a slut? If only they knew how particular you are. That gruff old cad at the end there would die to know his chances of even a second with you are rotting in hell."

We laughed and in one of those odd moments where two people think alike and act at the same time we raised our glasses to the group at the bar and smiled.

"Idiots." I said.

"Curs." Andreas joined.

We laughed again when the bartender had mistaken our action as a request for another whiskey. She brought them to us and I paid for them. We took the drinks to our room.

Andreas lit the candles on the writing desk with a minor spell he used for such things. A pile of coals glowed red in the brazier under the tub; warming the water. A knock came at the door and Andreas answered. It was a serving maid with fresh bath linens, scented oil, and soap. We needed nothing else so she left. I stoked the coals and offered Andreas the first bath but he declined. I pulled the curtain around the little tub, undressed, and gingerly lowered my tired bones into the hot water. The heat felt wonderful on my aching shoulder. I poured some eucalyptus oil into the water and the heady aroma mixed with the warm water, the whiskey, and my exhausted state to create a sudden state of euphoria. I don't know how long I soaked there, but I was beginning to prune when the cooling water brought me back to reality. I pulled myself out and dried off. I took a dry towel, wrapped it around myself and crawled into bed. Andreas had already fallen asleep; he stirred, but did not awaken.

When I woke hours later it was to the sounds of someone just outside our door. It was Andreas; he had gone down for fresh linens and to order fresh water for his bath. He closed the door with his foot and locked it with his free hand. He went over and opened the window, then pushed the tub to it, pushed forward on the tipping lever and the tub spilled out its contents into the alley with barely a spill on the floor. Two housemaids arrived soon after with pails of water and a bucket of coal for the brazier. Andreas sat in one of the chairs by the writing desk and watched them work. I rolled over and went back to sleep.

I dosed off and on, but not soundly, so I got out of bed while Andreas was still in the tub. I pulled my proper ladies dress from our bag, smoothed out the wrinkles and got dressed. I do enjoy looking like a lady on my off time, and it has the added effect of putting me at a more respectable level with the common folks. I despise that people categorize others by the way they dress, but that is the world we live in. Sometimes I try to turn it against people and attempt to open their eyes to their own ignorance. Sometimes I can just forget all that, and enjoy a day out of the field feeling beautiful.

I brushed my hair up into a twist and secured it with a silver comb from the small trove of jewelry we had been given by the duke. The purple sash I wrapped around my waist had been my mother's, a parting gift when she had sent me away. I wore it with honor, in remembrance of her. It also served well to conceal two small daggers within the folds.

Andreas finished his bath, dressed behind the curtain, and smoothed the wrinkles against his wet skin as he came back into the room. We took the chest from under the bed and made room for it in the bag. My swords and Bandoliers slid in alongside the chest, and our clothes packed in around everything. With that done Andreas belted on his short sword, and hoisted the bag. We would find a money exchange and have our coins turned into gems, to consolidate the bulk. The other things came with us, because we had learned never to leave our gear behind for long periods. I took one last look around to determine that we hadn't left anything, and then draped our cloaks over my arm to open the door for Andreas. He handed me the key as he went by and I locked the door behind us. I tucked the key down into my bustier and we went down to breakfast.

The dining room was quiet. Only three people were seated for breakfast and they each sat separately. We took a table next to a window that over looked the front porch and the street. The carpetbag took the seat between us and against the window. We ordered the house special and soon a tray heaping with sausage, eggs with melted cheese, crackle berry muffins and sweet butter was laid before us. The serving maid poured cider from a pitcher.

"Which of you is Saeede and which is Andreas?" The girl was the one who had discovered Eindal on the porch. She introduced herself and told us her story. From the time she had left him to get his wine to the time she returned was no more than a few minutes she assured us.

We inquired about his demeanor. She told us, "He was always business like, but not rude. He was usually cheerful, and friendly. Yesterday though, he seemed nervous, anxious." She had even asked him if everything was okay. He told her he was simply worried about the transfer of an important delivery. "He was a merchant. Did you know? A purveyor of unique items, he liked to say." She continued to inform us. He had eaten his meal alone sitting at the same table we had chosen. She had noticed that he barely took his eyes from the window. Most mornings he had his head to business, tallying or writing in his log. The fact that he watched the window didn't strike her as odd at the time. She figured he was just waiting for that delivery.

"Did he ever mention who he was waiting for?" Andreas asked.

I poured us each another mug of the refreshing cider. The meal was fit for a king. We had been eating like kings rather often lately. We ate as the girl spoke.

"No, but I did hear him mutter something about names known to him by reputation only, paths crossed, songs and tales. He only said your names as he died. I really shouldn't talk to you about this now. I have to work. Kate can tell you where to find me if I can answer more questions for you. Eindal was good to us here."

"We will find you if we need to know more, but you have already been helpful. One last thing though, for now."

When we asked her where his log was she said she figured Traylor had it. We thanked her, paid for the meal, ate quickly, and went out into the town.

We left the quaint neighborhood of Aunt Katie's and found a rich business district only two blocks away. A window sign declared the Money Merchant in that area of tradesmen, mercantilism, and warehouses. It was easy to see why Eindal had chosen Aunt Katie's for his home base while he was in Behlanna. We made the exchange of money, keeping one hundred pieces of gold a piece for mad money. The rest stayed in a pouch in the carpet bag as an expense fund. We strolled around town looking in the windows, at fine merchandise of all sorts but we weren't buying, we didn't really need anything.

We discussed the possibility that Eindal knew we were coming. Merchants, especially purveyors of unique items often have intelligence networks of their own. Perhaps Eindal was one of those. If he was expecting us — why? If he had a business proposition for us, it would have had to be very lucrative to take us from our planned vacation, ironic that he had done that anyway, and for free.

"What type of proposition was it do you think?" Andreas asked.

"Whatever it was he didn't want to speak openly about it. Let's go see Traylor and see if he has learned anything from Eindal's log."

"Let's."

Traylor's constabulary was well situated between the business district and the residential district. We went inside and found Traylor at a table looking over a black ledger.

"Does that belong to you?" Andreas asked. He was playing disrespectful with the guy that could put us in jail, not a smart idea. I made sure the look I leveled at him showed my disapproval.

Traylor didn't seem to care and gave us only an acknowledging glance. "It's Eindal's— nothing but a list of transactions."

"Anything noted about upcoming meetings? Anything underlined or emphasized in any way?" I asked.

"Anything worth risking your life for, you mean? No." He flipped the book to Andreas. "Look for yourself; let me know if I missed something."

I stood close to Andreas and we went through the book page by page together. As we did Traylor informed us that his man had ridden day and night to return with a favorable report from Duke Midewin. We had free reign in the investigation as long as we reported to him daily. We agreed and concentrated on the ledger. It held nothing extraordinary. In fact for a purveyor of unique items it seemed just extra-ordinary. We both knew that merchants often kept separate ledgers for their more valuable, sometimes illegal transactions. We did not elaborate on our unsubstantiated thoughts with Traylor. We had no need of the ledger and left it. We thanked him and left the building.

We made our way out of the business district and found that most of the city was actually rather depressed and frightening. High stone fences, many with spikes or broken glass imbedded into the mortar, surrounded most homes up to the second level. Many shops had apartments above them and although they were open to the late spring air they could quickly be shuttered tight. Traffic at the inns or pubs was not light; in fact it seemed heavy for the time of day. Beggars hung around in the alleys and on the walkways of these establishments panhandling from the happy drunks or pilfering from the staggering ones.

We saw a few groups of the city guard in the same black piecemeal style of armor as the guards at the gate. They did nothing to stop the carousing or the pilfering. So what purpose did they serve? Some patrols were on foot; others were mounted and still others were combined. We came to know them by their black armor. No matter to the armor type, it was always black, and we discovered their real livery—a tattoo of a black scorpion. Most often the tattoo was on the right forearm, but one man had it on his thigh, another on his left breast, another on the back of his neck. The Black Scorpions never questioned us but we were given long looks, and sleazy taunts.

We managed to keep our distance and made it un-accosted to the plaza outside of the prince's palace . The wall of the prince's compound enclosed the northern end. Large stone braziers were built into the top of the wall. Guards with heavy crossbows sauntered the parapets keeping an eye on the streets below. The outer walls of the city enclosed the east and west sides of the plaza and the city itself bordered the south side, opposite the prince's residence.

We were near the western defensive wall. A few buildings jutted out from it, but the side streets dead-ended at the wall. The wall was easily four stories tall at this end of the city, and we could make out the root of the stone crag rising up just behind it. Our eyes followed it back to the peaks that loomed up dark behind multi-leveled spires of the palace. We didn't wish to hesitate too long and risk drawing the attention of the guards, so we moved through the plaza and continued our stroll. The establishments around the palace were mostly for entertainment. There were theatre houses, galleries, stages for street artists, and a variety of eating establishments with a few brothels thrown in for good measure. Vendor stalls filled the street and we browsed among them. The atmosphere was like a carnival. I bought a summer frock and Andreas purchased a fine new mandolin, while dancers spun us and food hawkers approached us.

Traffic at drinking establishments in that district was winding down. Artists tend to work at night and the time was coming around to mid-day. We made our way south toward the business district and street traffic began to pick up again. We stopped at an outdoor café situated between the districts and ate lunch while we watched the traffic.

The poor folks had been moved along and were being reabsorbed into the city. The Black Scorpions were prevalent in the artists sector of the city and pan handling came to a halt as the richer element of society made their way into the streets. An entourage emerged from the palace gates and made their way through the vendors. The Prince's people were out to get supplies for the palace. That work was usually supervised by the lord's consort, but an old woman was in charge of this entourage. When I commented aloud, a young woman nearby informed us that the Prince was a bachelor; a bit of a womanizer she said. We wondered if that might be useful if we would need to infiltrate to get close to the prince.

We made pleasantries with the woman and she freely gave us her political opinion of the shabby job the prince was doing lately—until a group of Black Scorpion guards began to wander through the area. She said her goodbyes then and melted into traffic. The guards, remembering us from Aunt Katie's, eyed us suspiciously for a long time, but finally moved on. When they did we left our money on the table and made our way straight back to the boarding house.

Katie was very curious about us. She was leaning in the door way when we returned. The entire porch had been scoured clean and she was resting from the hard work. She moved aside but followed us in when we entered.

"If you were just going shopping why did you feel it was necessary to bring all of your belongings with you?" She asked, uncaring if it was rude or not.

"It keeps our things safe. If they are with us then they can't be stolen. From the look of things here it seems we were right to want to protect our things. You just had a murder in broad daylight. What is to stop someone from stealing our things from our room while we are away?"

She did not like my reply and "humphed" her disapproval. Then thinking better of it offered a defense of her establishment. "When the serving girl served his port wine she saw him slumped in his chair. She thought he had taken ill until she saw the blood and the slash at his throat. She called out and I ran to her. The guards came just after that."

"What is it you want to say to us, Katie?"

She sighed heavily, "I beg your pardon. I don't know really. Just that I run a nice place here. How could I know that Eindal was into trouble? A murder on the premises will do no good for my reputation."

I stopped and turned to her. "Katie, when this is solved and no fault points to you, your business will thrive again. I know you don't know us, but I implore you to trust us. What motive do we have to kill a man we never met? Did you see any blood on either of us? A slit throat would surely squirt a lot of blood. Why would we risk coming back to the scene of the crime, when we could have just left the city and gotten clean away?"

Katie was speechless, and the people near us in the room were buzzing with their own doubts, though they had been quite sure of our guilt just moments before. Sometimes I wonder if brains were given to all of the Gods' children. If not, who was the experiment, those of us blessed enough to have brains or those without?

I continued while I still had the floor. "We will help you solve this case. We have experience in police matters and discretion in situations similar to this. It will get you off the hook socially, and we will bring your friend's killer to justice."

"Of course," Katie said. "I am out of sorts with all of this. Please excuse me."

"Dear, lady," Andreas put on his charm. "You are excused of course. This is a trying time for us all. If we work together we will put this matter to rest along with Eindal and life will return to normal. You need not fear us. We will seek to end this matter quickly." He took her hand in his and patted it. "Goodnight now. We need our rest to be sharp and on the case again first thing in the morning." We turned then and continued up to our room. A guard had beeen posted. He waited in a chair across from our door. These were not Scorpions. It seemed that even with Midiwen's favorable report that Traylor was not willing to trust us completely yet.

Once inside I checked the window. Our other guard was still at his spot at the end of the alley.

I flopped into a chair and Andreas flopped onto the bed. We needed to figure a way to get by our hall guard and into Eindal's room. We didn't have many options, but we did finally settle on a plan. Not one of our best, but it would have to do.

I went down and ordered a bath. Andreas stayed in the room and moved around inside making just enough noise so that the guard knew he was still there. After seeing to the bath, I went to the bar for a drink. I was not well received, but they did not refuse me service. I sat so that I could see through the lobby to the stairs that led to the rooms. That way I knew when the water was being taken up, and I could keep an eye on the guard keeping an eye on me. I saw him at the top of the stairs and took my drink to the dining room and sat at a corner table. If he wanted to keep an eye on me he would have to move down the stairs, and away from the upstairs hall.

After the water was in the tub Andreas would make bath noises for fifteen minutes. He was going to count it out in his head. When I saw the last of the buckets come down I was to count off twenty minutes. If the guard didn't come down, to keep an eye on me, in that time then I was to order two whiskeys and bring them back to the room. If that happened then the plan was a bust. If the guard did come down then I was to take my sweet time and give Andreas the opportunity to get into Eindal's room.

Several minutes passed before the last of the buckets came downstairs. The guard stayed at the top of the stairs, watching me and listening to Andreas and the bath water. Satisfied by the bath noises in our room, he came down the stairs to focus on me, but he had no line of sight to our room.

The plan was working and I relaxed a bit. I had three whiskeys and sipped them slow, while I watched the guard watching me. I was really beginning to feel good about things then. The guard must have been confident that if Andreas did venture out of the room he would hear him. He didn't know Andreas like I did. I timed each whiskey to five minutes, give or take, and then I walked to the bar to order two more and whiskeys and dinner delivered to our room. I wasn't hungry, and I doubted that Andreas was, but it was part of our plan to act as normal as possible. I paid for everything and took the whiskeys with me. They were both for Andreas, why should I have all the fun?

Twenty minutes had passed by easily and it was time for me to return to my room. I stopped at the bottom of the stairs, and offered to let the guard go first, I just couldn't resist. He declined, naturally, but I convinced him that it was ridiculous for him to follow me when we could just go together. He held the drinks for me as I removed the key from my bustier and unlocked the door.

I could hear Andreas as I turned the key. He came to the door with his hair wet and a towel wrapped around him and took the drinks from the guard. As he shut the door he said, for the benefit of the guard; "Thank you baby, but what took so long? You had a few with out me didn't you?" When he grabbed me and said; "c'mere" I was surprised, until he flipped a leather dossier into my hands. Then he whispered in my ear, "I think I scared someone out of there when I came in, I saw a shadow at the window and it was open. When I looked out I didn't see anyone. I was careful to stay in the shadows as I shut and relocked the window so if they were watching, they didn't see me."

"You're fast," I said waving the dossier. "Where was it?"

"Under the mattress."

I crossed to the bed and sat down hard because of my semi drunken state, and the bed squeaked. I remember thinking what good effect that sound would be to the guard just outside and bounced a couple times more. It was not hard to imagine what he would think we were doing. I laughed aloud at the thought of it, and I laughed again when I realized that even my innocent laugh was adding to the effect. Andreas must have understood my thoughts, as he often did, because he was soon standing on the bed and jumping lightly up and down. I stood up because I couldn't read the papers while being jostled so.

At first I didn't understand what I had.

There were sheets headed with the names of towns and the transactions Eindal traded in each. I found one for Behlanna, below the heading was a column of monetary amounts and beside that a list of people, and what they had bought, sold, or traded with him. Above the list of transactions, were the names of establishments in Behlanna; presumably the location where the transactions took place.

The next sheet was a group of ciphers, tallys of Eindal's money in several accounts. Eindal was a very wealthy man. The third sheet was another list of people by description and location, but no monetary amounts, some of the people were repeats from the first sheet, and some were not. The rest of the sheets appeared to be manifests of wagons coming and going from various cities. Some had the word collected and a date scrawled across them, perhaps these served as receipts. These sheets were really just standard vouchers and scrolls for a man in the import business. Then I noticed a page that had only four entries listed upon it, or perhaps it was one item listed four times because the entries were identical, except for a circled symbol at the end of each line that was different. The problem was that I could not read the entries. The script was meticulous like the rest of the entries, I was certain that the hand was the same. Below each entry was a name— none that I recognized.

Only two items remained in the dossier for me to examine. One was a slim, leather bound ledger that appeared to be payroll lists, by name, amount and date. Apparently he was a good employer, because the same names appeared many times, some for years back. The second was a scrolled up list of transactions. Some of the items were indeed unique, but unique or not they were all expensive. Next to each item were a name, town, and a notation if the purchase had been paid in money or trade. I assumed the blanks left in that last column meant the item had not been procured or at least not delivered and so not paid for. If someone could locate these items they could collect a large sum of money, and Eindal would be none the wiser in his condition. I tried to see on which wagon these items had been shipped, but I could not. It was obvious that Eindal was smuggling his unique items in with legitimate cargo.

I could draw no conclusions from the material, but I was most curious about the indecipherable entries. I stopped perusing the files to ask Andreas for his opinion. He was still jumping on the bed, like a child and answered with an uncertain shrug. "What are the Dark Minstrel Scrolls?" A knock came at the door. Andreas tensed.

"Just a minute," Andreas said and adjusted the towel he had managed to barely keep wrapped around his waist during his bed bouncing. I put the dossier under a pillow stripped down to my undergarments, tousled my hair, and went to the door. A serving wench held forward a tray; I took it and tipped the girl a silver piece. She went away and the guard turned to watch her go after I caught his eyes on me. I closed the door and put the tray on the writing desk.

Andreas came over, picked up his first glass of whiskey, and sipped it rather quickly. I went over to the bed and stretched out on top of the tousled covers. I saw Andreas's eyes move over my form. I looked Andreas once over. He was a wonder. It was hell sometimes being so close a friend to one of the opposite sex. We had managed to keep our boundries and honored the friendship. I flipped the covers over myself and reached under the pillow for the dossier.

"What was that you said about scrolls?"

Andreas moved to sit beside me and flipped the pages for me and jabbed his finger at the indecipherable script. "Four identical entries; each says "Dark Minstrel Scroll".

"What language is this?"

"Archaic."

"Taught only to the finest practitioners of magic?"

"Yes."

"How did you learn it then?"

"You know my family wouldn't teach me. I learned in a back alley, from a homeless old mage. I paid him in food from my mother's kitchen."

"Sorry. Tell me more."

"There is no more. That's all it says. No customer name, no price indicated."

Our lack of conclusion didn't sit right with me, but the effects of three glasses of whiskey were in full effect by then and trying to read the notes in a reclined position became too much. I set the dossier on the bed beside me. The next thing I knew I was waking to a dark room. It was sometime in the middle of the night. I could not see through the windows so I could not gauge the time. The Dossier was under the pillow beside me and Andreas had his head upon that pillow.

Andreas was my friend. It didn't take away from the fact that he was one of the most beautiful men I had ever seen in all my travels stretched out in all his glory, and I was a healthy woman. I knew that I could have him if I wanted, but sex has a way of mucking up relationships, and ours was just fine as it was. I slipped from bed and pulled my half of the blankets over him. He moaned sleepily and snuggled into the soft fabrics. I lit the candle beside the bed.

Andreas never lit the coals in the tub brazier, so I did. While the water was warming I went over to the food tray for a nibble, and lit the candle on the writing desk. Andreas had polished off one of the dinners and had started on mine, but left me about half. I cut off a slice of lamb roll and ate with my hands. Then I undressed and settled into the bath. It was still cool, but warming.

The water eased some of the tension I had been feeling since our unexpected predicament of the day before. I wanted to add the eucalyptus oil but it was too heady and I was nursing a slight hangover. I slid into the water up to my chin. The noises of the inn were augmented through the water and I heard footsteps moving up the hall. They slowed, and then stopped at our door.

Before I could alert Andreas the door flew open. I rose quickly, and grabbed the two daggers from my sash still draped over the chair where I had left it. Through the gap between the curtain and the wall I saw two beefy thugs bearing down on Andreas with blackjacks. They wanted no bloodshed. I personally didn't care. Andreas was awake and dove for his weapons beside the bed; there was no time for casting of spells. I threw the first dagger from cover at the man nearest me, but furthest from Andreas. The knife hit with the weighted end of the pommel at the man's temple. He went down without sound; we could talk to him later. Meanwhile Andreas dodged the first blow from the other intruder but that move kept him from his own weapons. I threw back the curtain and let go the second dagger. It caught the man in the back and he arched back with the pain. He turned and was surprised to see me. How he could have missed the sound of me rising from the water, I don't know. His eyes fell upon his partner stark still upon the floor. That hesitation allowed Andreas the opportunity to get to his blade. I climbed out of the tub and moved to close the door. I was obviously weaponless now, so I posed no threat to him. He turned back to Andreas too late. Andreas brought the hilt of his sword down upon the man's temple with the force of both arms behind it and the man slumped to the floor. I took a quick look up and down the hallway. The guard was curiously absent. I saw no one else, looked again more carefully, still didn't see anyone, and then shut the door. The entire melee had lasted only seconds. The noise of the inn continued down stairs so I was certain that no one heard any of this subdued disturbance.

I locked the door and moved to the man on the floor. He was gasping for breath and he had that look of shocked terror frozen on his face. I had hit him too hard in my excitement and cracked the side of his skull. A slow trickle of dark blood slid out of his ear. I told him that his skull was cracked and there was probably bleeding to his brain, and that might well mean his death, but that my friend was a skilled physician and if it was possible he would save him. I could have been more kind, but I have no compassion for criminals. I did not touch his body as I removed his weapons and laid them on the floor.

I moved to the window and standing against the wall peeked out to the end of the alley. Our two guards were having a conversation there. There was some motioning back toward our room and I hugged tighter to the wall. The alley guard looked up at the window, but then he shrugged his shoulders and they moved away together. They went into the street, crossed, and headed in the direction of the constabulary.

Andreas was tying the other man to the bedpost and I went to see to them. Andreas was untouched, but his hands were shaking as he tied the knot. We exchanged a worried glance. Neither of us recognized the men. "The guards have gone." I informed him. Our next exchange of glances held deep suspicions, but neither of us knew where they led.

Andreas removed the man's weapons and then searched him thoroughly. Nothing but his weapons, not even a coin. We shrugged. Once that man was tied securely we returned to the other. Andreas assessed the damage and shook his head grimly, but he stood and went to get his things.

I stayed with the man until Andreas returned. "Do you need me?" I asked.

Andreas shook his head, "No, let's get dressed."

I glanced over at the man tied to the bed. He was still out cold. We got dressed.

When I returned the man on the floor was dead. Andreas closed the blank eyes, as he said, "Nice move. There won't be much blood on the floor this way." He turned the dead man's head to keep the blood from spilling out of his ear. Then he stood and went to see to the other man. He was still unconscious. Andreas shoved one of his shirts in the man's mouth. I was amazed at how much of the shirt fit in. He took the blade out of the man's back. That woke the thug and he would have screamed from the pain but for the shirt shoved down his throat. He struggled with his bindings but the pain was too much and he settled down quickly.

"If you are through being foolish you can tell us why you have come to pay us such an unwelcome visit so early in the morning. If you do that then I'll see what I can do for your wound. Your friend did not co-operate and so there was nothing I could do." This was the cold bastard part of Andreas that I know so well. He had not let the man die, the wound had simply been beyond his experience, but he was not going to tell this thug that. He held my knife out to me and I took it and rinsed it in the bath water. There was not enough blood to discolor that volume of water. Andreas removed the shirt from the man's mouth, but kept a dagger at his throat. I kept my ears to their conversation.

They had been sent by a man they did not know who paid them five hundred pieces of gold up front to take us out. That was an amazingly hefty sum for the two of us, but "You were under paid my friend," Andreas retorted arrogantly. I looked at the man as I was drying my blade and I saw his nod of agreement and the look of embarrassment in his eyes.

The mention of five hundred gold had caught my attention. I finished drying the dagger and returned it to the bandolier where it belonged, then I went to the dead man and searched him again. Sure enough he had a silk purse tied to his leg inside his boot. I untied it and by the heft of it I knew most of the gold was there if not all of it. I tied it to my belt and the man let out a slow sigh. "For the inconvenience you have caused us," I said. Again he nodded in resolved agreement.

"Did the man give you a reason for wanting us eliminated? Do you know where this man is now? How were you to confirm that you had successfully completed your assignment? Whose idea was it to bring a black jack to a knife fight?" Andreas asked each question in succession and then leaned in close to await the answers.

"We weren't supposed to eliminate you, just subdue you. He gave us the money and told us where we could locate you. He told us that we could keep anything we got from you and that would be plenty. He was hard about it and it seemed easy enough, and even if we didn't do the job at all we still had the purse." He looked up at me and I gave him a 'what should I do about it' kind of shrug and he looked back at Andreas. "We did the job though because of what he said about us taking whatever we got from you. We asked around about you downstairs and were told you carried large sums of money, a bag full of weapons and armor, and that you seemed to pay close attention to it. We figured maybe there was more in there then those people knew about."

I wondered why they had both come so boldly into the room before knowing the whereabouts of both of their targets, but I did not ask. If he was, going to do this type of thing again I felt it was my responsibility to watch out for his future victims and not tell him where any of his weaknesses lay. They were not young men, but perhaps they were not ambitious and they simply lacked experience.

"Do you live in Behlanna?" Andreas was asking. The man gave an affirmative nod. "And you did not recognize the man who hired you?" The frightened thug gave a negative shake of the head. "Then what did he look like?"

"He was an old man with a hunched walk and a cane." By the gods, the oldest disguise in the books. Andreas did not pursue it.

"And why did he hire you? What purpose did our being subdued serve for him? You seem inexperienced at this sort of thing. Did this man have any identifying marks, you know, birthmarks, scars or tattoos? There seem to be an inordinate amount of shady characters roaming your streets. Surely he could have found some one more up to the task." I was watching the man closely as Andreas barraged him with questions, and I noticed a reaction when he heard the question about tattoos, but I kept quiet.

"We have a reputation for burglary and we have made a good living. Unser there keeps a wife and a mistress on his share."

I was suddenly outraged. "He has a wife?" I nearly shrieked, but immediately lowered my voice to a whisper. "What about children?" I was absolutely enraged that I had killed a family man. I could tell the man did not understand the source of my anger and he did not answer. I strode across the floor and grabbed him by the throat, forcing his head back into the mattress. "Did this man have children?" I whispered with all the scathe I could put into my voice.

"Yes, yes," He croaked.

"How many?"

"Three."

"So, I assume you are ready to support his family now that you have cost a father and husband his life?"

"I—well I never. I have to…"

"To what, you dog. You never considered what you would do about a family if one of you should be killed?"

"I don't have a family."

"But you chose a partner who did! So now his family is your responsibility. Have you ever had a lucid thought in your life? Gods! I can't believe you. You walk in here with your head in your ass thinking you could take us out? I've never seen such clumsy work by the way. And you force me to kill a man with a family. I have rarely killed and *never* a family man. I hold you responsible for this!" I took to pacing and went off on a tirade I still can't remember completely while Andreas continued to entertain our 'guest'.

"Now you've done it, Mister. You went and rose up her sense of honor. I pity you. I dare say though, as much as she isn't going to like it, you just saved your own skin. I better look at your wounds now while she is distracted. She means it when she says you are responsible for his family. Just between me and you, I think its just luck that she never killed a married man before, though it is true that she tries to avoid killing all together and so I guess the odds could be in her favor. She will come back and check to be sure his family is taken care of though. She is annoyingly tenacious about some things. You may not know she is there, but that is a tribute to her ability not your lack of awareness."

I returned to the man and stood over him. He was obviously shaken so I went in for the 'kill'. "Tell me about the man's tattoo? For instance where was it?"

"On—I didn't say he had a tattoo."

"You didn't have to. Your face reads like a scroll. You are in the wrong business with a face like that." I kneeled, straddling him, nearly sitting in his lap. I could sense his tension. I used one arm to force him into the bed so that it ground into his wound. He went to yell, but my other hand was over his mouth instantly and all that could be heard was a muffled gurgle. I forced him back even harder. "The tattoo?" I asked. He shook his head affirmatively. I eased up, but I left my hand over his mouth.

"Was it a black scorpion?" Andreas took up the questioning, leaving me to be the incentive to answer. The man nodded affirmatively.

"Was he going to meet you somewhere?"

Negative nod.

"So you were to go to him?"

Hesitation. I moved closer.

"So he was coming to you." Negative.

"In the city?"

Affirmative.

"You know; this would be easier if I had more lateral here. I'm running out of yes and no questions. I don't think our guest is going to call out. You're not going to call out are you?" This last question was asked as Andreas put his hand on the back of the man's neck. The man was panicked now. I could feel his breathing change. He nodded a negative response, many times very quickly.

I released his mouth, but I did not get off him.

"So where, exactly, were you supposed to meet him and when?" The man swallowed hard and thought carefully about his response. "Come on now, you are in more danger from us right now then that man can cause you in the future. If you give us the right answers you won't have to worry about him again. So, you see by helping us you do yourself a favor."

"I doubt that your bravado can undo The Scorpions." He said, defiantly. "I can see that you are very confident in your abilities, but there are still only two of you. No one knows for sure how many Scorpions there are, well except maybe their leaders who ever they are."

"Don't they work for your prince?"

"The prince is the son of a king, but he is so far from succession that his father gave him control of this holding. The Scorpions are a blend of the Kings men given to his son and, vicious adventurers and mercenaries who could not find a better offer at the time. The offer must be a good one, because they don't seem to leave. There are the city guards and then there are The Scorpions. The Scorpions are the Prince's elite men. The training is said to be extensive, but there are more and more Scorpions on the streets all the time."

"Do the Scorpions out number the regular guard then? I didn't notice any of these city guards while we were about in your fair city. I actually thought the Scorps were the city guard."

"Perhaps."

"What is your prince called, and who is the prince's father?"

"His name is Duadan. His father is Dune. Dune rules the lands from Leah Mar Abbey in the south to Jeulard in the north and from Walther in the west to Ahnrye in the east. The king himself sits in Ahnrye."

"Tell me why the prince would sic his henchmen on us. What interest could two complete strangers be to him?"

"We were not told that. We thought if we performed well that we might be given a chance to join their ranks. Then we would not have to worry about where our next pay was coming from anymore."

"You have no reservations about taking orders that infringe upon the peace and quiet of honest citizens? Aside from the townie gossip, who did you think we were? What did they tell you about us?"

He hesitated at that, but then he resolved something within himself and answered. "You are spies."

"You believe that then?" Andreas let out a little laugh. "Spies for whom, for what purpose?"

"If you are not spies then why were you rummaging around in Eindal's room last night when you were told to do nothing illegal?"

I saw Andreas tighten his grip on the back of the man's neck. I could read his thoughts in his expression. He wanted to ask the man how he knew that, but that would affirm that we had done it, so then he just wanted to choke the man for being such an annoyance, but he loosened his grip and patted the man lightly. "Is this information that you gathered for yourself? I've seen firsthand how incompetent you are." The thug hung his head and we knew that we had planted a seed of doubt. We would have to discuss it privately later in case we faced the accusation from someone else.

"Tell me your name." Andreas tried a more friendly tone, "Just what you go by. This conversation is getting too intimate for us not to know at least some tag to call each other by."

"I am called Moon." He must have noticed our quizzical glances, because he elaborated. "I once had a bit too much celebration and at the urging of some of the men I howled at the moon. It seemed funny at the time, but I've never lived it down. Now everyone calls me Moon. I bet a lot of people don't even know why 'ceptin' those that was there."

"Let me introduce ourselves then." Andreas began. "This is my wife." That story again. "You can call her Lady. I am the man of the family. You can call me Sir." Sometimes I actually admire the bastard side of Andreas's personality.

"Help me get back on track, Moon. Where was it that you were supposed to meet this man, the Scorpion that hired you?"

"Right here."

"In this room?"

Another affirmative nod. I got up, took my swords from our bag, and went to stand with my back against the door.

"You tried very hard to avoid telling us that didn't you? You lied actually. I guess you just forgot that you said you were to go to him? Stalling until your back up can arrive, ay?" Andreas looked up at me. I was listening at the door. I shook my head to indicate that I heard nothing. "Maybe you aren't as stupid as you first let on," He finished.

"We couldn't very easily haul your bodies through the street without rousing suspicion. He was making arrangements for your transportation and then would meet us here."

"Yes, with one murder here already hauling more bodies through the street would frighten the people—turn them against us even more. Maybe they would even turn on us." Andreas was thinking aloud and our captive was visibly anxious.

"Any thoughts on this new development, Dear?"

I know he knows how much I love being 'married' to him, I almost didn't answer, because I was thinking what it would really be like, but I was on a job, so I went along. "I suppose we could wait for him to arrive, ambush him and eliminate him, but then the trail goes cold. We could ambush him and then take his place. Still if he wants us subdued, maybe he just wants to talk. If he kills us then the Eindal murder is wide open for suspects again."

"Maybe he thinks we have the dossier." We both looked at Moon.

"I swear I didn't tell him." He did not look or sound convincing.

"He wants the dossier." We said to each other.

"Once he has it he knows we'll pursue him. He'll have to kill us. Or subdue us and kidnap us. He can't afford to leave us here. He has to make it look like we ran, otherwise the Eindal murder would be without suspects."

"No it already is, remember, Midewin vouched for us to Traylor."

"Ya, your right, but if this guy knows that Traylor hasn't fully trusted us yet, our death does not hinder him. Our two bodies would clear our names. How do you like that?"

I said, "It is really just a matter of eliminating the competition at the proper time. What do you think, Muffin?" Andreas hated being called Muffin; he thought it was a feminine endearment, and he made obscene gestures at me behind Moon's head. I smiled; it warmed the cockles of my heart to annoy Andreas so. I noticed that Moon was smiling also. I think he believed that we really were married. "What are you smiling at, Worm?" I asked. That wiped the smile off his face. It warms the cockles of my heart to strike fear into the lowlifes of the world.

"That or we could go investigating now," Andreas was saying, "while our guards are away from their posts. How did you manage that, Moon, bribery?"

The man hesitated, he was looking for some other answer beside the truth, but Andreas pulled his head back by his hair and put the dagger back to his throat. "We told them we were on prince's business and that they were relieved of duty until further notice."

"What is the Sheriff going to think of having his orders rescinded without prior notice? And how did our guards believe that you were on princes business?"

"What can he do? He takes his orders from Polk." He said this as if we should understand. Andreas no longer cared about his next question.

Andreas said, "Who?"

"Polk, the Captain of the Scorpions."

I moved toward him a few steps "So, what will the sheriff do when he finds that Polk didn't really give that order?"

"Send back his guards to check on you I suppose." The inevitability of all of these people converging on our room was really putting me on edge. I wondered how long it would be before the first Scorpion arrived, or would the constables be first, or Polk, or Moon's employer? Could Moon's employer be any of the afore mentioned players? Perhaps even Polk and the employer were one in the same person. My sense for flight was coming to the surface, but I fought it back, my curiosity was twitching.

"Then since you are currently working for the Scorpions, you must have some idea of their chain of command," Andreas was asking.

"No not really just that Polk is the Captain. Far as I know everyone reports to him. Except the Prince of course, and the Prince leaves Polk alone for the most part. He only knows that he is safe and so he doesn't question Polk's methods. Polk is an effective leader, and the streets are safer than they have been for years."

"That seems an odd thing to say in the face of a murder. Tell us Moon, what do you know about Eindal?" I asked.

That caused our captive to squirm. I had hit a nerve.

"She'll be much easier on you if you co-operate, Moon. You may as well tell us. I know you don't realize it yet, but we are your best allies in this crazy mystery. Your life isn't worth much anyway as long as you failed to apprehend us." Andreas said. Moon's eyes got wide. "I'd leave town as soon as you gather up your partner's family if I were you."

I moved closer as I slapped the flats of my swords against my boots. Moon flinched. "Relax, she isn't going to kill you, remember? You now have a family to feed. But she can be vicious when she is angry, so much so that you'll wish she had killed you." This wasn't true of course, but Andreas was setting a mood. Moon was getting more and more anxious about the situation he had created for himself, and it could get real quite soon, so we had to keep a high level of intimidation on him if we wanted to continue to get information.

"Eindal. Moon, let's have it."

"He is a merchant, with charitable leanings." That surprised us because we were looking at him as going to any length to procure items if the price was right. "He gave large amounts of money to the less fortunate in the city, not just once, he kept coming back."

I thought of the dossier, if he had donated money he had not noted it there; at least not in any obvious way.

"I saw Eindal on his last two trips looking through the streets as if he were looking for someone. He went to all parts of the city, rich and poor, clean or filthy. As far as I could tell he never found who or what he was looking for. I talked to some people I know on the streets and they said he was acting strangely, like he was afraid of something. Eindal has friends among the Stalkers Society, but he never went to them."

"And what is the Stalker Society?"

"A passel of thieves."

We were beginning to see the delicacy of the matter.

Eindal had been expecting us. If he saw us come into town and recognized us then he knew us from other towns we had been in at the same time. Whatever he had wanted to speak to us about was still unclear, what was he smuggling, or rather what was it he wanted us for? He had run his business quite well without us. What was it that had him frightened?

"So far all we have is Scorpions, a stalker society, and a dead importer. Any idea what he was importing, Moon?"

"None at all; I think that is what he wanted you for."

There was no more information we could get from him, and perhaps no more time. After a moment of silence Andreas spoke, "It is time that we get you back to your life Moon, and return the body of..." He was right.

"Unser." Moon interjected

"...Unser; to his wife for proper burial. The dark is still with us, but for how long. What time of night is it Moon?"

"About three in the morning, I'd guess." That surprised us both, but we were glad of the extra time.

"Will you take us to Unser's family? We will see that you are all safely away from the city and then we will investigate the information you have given us. I don't know what we can do with it, but you have peaked our interest. Isn't that right, Dear?"

"Definitely."

Andreas and I geared up in silence. We were pouring over the information in our heads and relating it to the ledgers we had obtained from Eindal's room. I pulled the ledger from under Andreas's pillow and put it in the bottom of our bag, wrapped in the dress I had worn earlier.

After tending to Unser and his family our first course of action would be surveillance, to get to know the players in the city, on both sides of the fence. We would have to play in the seedier parts of town, maybe we would hear something, but more likely we would have to buy information. It could be a long process.

Andreas came over to me and escorted me to the corner of the room furthest from Moon; he reiterated the thoughts I had just had. "But we don't have that kind of time," We said together. "I have an idea." Andreas continued, "When we leave here we need to make it look like a fight happened. The bit of blood on the floor will help with that, but we'll have to take the body with us. We need to disappear. For those in the know, like The Scorpions, or maybe even the constables it will confuse them to have their two men and us all gone with blood on the floor. I hope they will think we have the upper hand and that will make them nervous. To others it will look like we are digging ourselves in deeper, and that we killed the 'prince's men' and disappeared."

"I follow, it will get us out of here for good either way, and it may buy some time while we investigate. Let's get on with it." Andreas went around spilling things and setting things over in disarray while I finished cinching my armor and strapped on my weapon belts.

I splashed some water out onto the floor for effect. When I looked around to see what else I could do I could think of nothing. Andreas had already strewn the leftover food and the tray across the floor in front of the writing desk, and he had tipped over the candle there and let it roll onto the floor. The chair next to the tub was on its side and he had torn the curtain from the ceiling. I went to the bed and took off the blankets. I only needed one, to wrap Unser in, but I pulled at the others for effect. Unser wasn't as heavy as I thought he would be. I used the blanket as a sort of sling over my back and it made him easier to carry.

Time was fleeting and we had to get Moon and Unser home. Breaking the news to his wife was going to be tough. Andreas and Unser were roughly the same height and build so Andreas pulled Unser's cloak off him and threw it around himself. He pulled the hood over his head and got into the man's weapons belt. I gave him the purse to put in place at his back. I draped a dress over my armor and weapons. The nice thing about chain mail; it doesn't add much bulk; I wrapped my cloak around that.

I unbound Moon and helped him to his feet. Andreas drew his sword incase Moon had any ideas of bolting. I put the sling with Unser's body over Moon's shoulder and made sure that his face could not be seen. I took up our carpetbag and we were ready. Andreas grasped Moon tightly by the arm and we went out into the hall. We left the door open, but kept the key. I put on my best distraught look and we went down and moved quickly through the common room of the inn. At that early time we saw no one, but we could hear workers, so Andreas shoved me a couple of times for effect and told me to "move you murderin' bitch."

Once outside we went around the building to the alley where I could take Unser from Moon, and Moon would lead us via back alleys to Unser's place. I removed my dress and stuffed it into the carpetbag then I wrapped my cloak around my left shoulder and under my right arm. It left my sword arm open while still giving me warmth and concealment when needed. I hoisted Unser's body and situated the sling much as I had my cloak. Andreas picked up the carpetbag from where I had placed it.

Andreas still had Moon tightly by the arm and we moved out. What we had thought was a dead alley outside our room was a trick on the eyes. Two buildings came across the alley very near each other, and in the shadows the narrow alley between them was concealed. Moon led us along the wall of our inn and suddenly the turn in the alley was apparent.

We wound around the first building and then the second and we were in another alley. We were heading away from the boarding house and had entered another sector of the city. The street ahead of us was not busy, there was only foot traffic and that was sparse. The shadows were deep and plentiful enough for us to utilize if we needed to. We crouched at the corner where the alley met the street and waited for an opportunity to cross unseen. Andreas had the final say in this, so I was confident that we had gone undetected. We entered another alley directly across from the first. Not far down the length it branched off in three directions. We took the right, and came to a gradual turn to the left. We took the turn and the alley narrowed. Moon picked up his pace, but Andreas did not let go of him. I struggled under my burden to keep up, but I could not speak of it. Stealth was the name of the game, and that meant silence.

We came to another turn to the left. Moon and Andreas were there well before me. I hoisted Unser higher on my shoulders and lumbered into a quicker pace. When I made the corner they were not in sight, but there was another sharp left just one building away. Seeing no other way they could have gone I turned in there.

Andreas stood alone a few paces ahead of me. I could make out people among the shadows, and Moon was walking alone to the end of a dead alley. At least I thought it was dead. I stopped and instantly felt a blade at my chin. The wielder of the blade was just behind me and to my left. The blade rested lightly on the curve of my shoulder.

"Put it down." Another voice said; this came from my right. I did as I was told and let Unser fall with a thud on the dirt of the alley, and then I turned around to see my assailants. There were three, two men and one woman I could see no apparent tattoos on any of them. Unser's body laid at their feet in a tangle with the blanket.

"Back up." The wielder ordered and I complied. I watched all around me as I retreated and made out six men in the shadows and at least three perched along the roofs. That made at least twelve and I made no attempt to see anyone behind me, Andreas would have that covered. I stopped next to Andreas, facing opposite him. We exchanged a quick glance, but I could see that he had not formulated any plan, and neither had I. We were captured, by whom we were unsure, but we knew that somehow Moon had orchestrated this. I made a mental note not to be so trusting of thieves, city folk, or anyone for that matter. I wondered then if I would listen to myself.

I heard a voice from behind me. "Turn around, Dear. Don't you know that it is rude to turn your back on your host?" I attempted to turn but the blade wielder still had his knife firmly at my chin. I raised my hands and he communicated with his eyes that we were to move together. I let him lead. Once I was properly turned about, he pulled back a few steps but did not lower his blade. I heard an audible whistle of appreciation, at what I wasn't sure, but for the first time since entering the alley I was afraid; no longer just apprehensive. A large man slipped from out of the shadow. He was not large like a fit virile man, but like a decadent sloth of a man. Even in the bad light we could see the folds of his flab and tell that his skin was pasty. "What a lovely pair, beautiful, magnificently beautiful." He reached out to touch my face and I lurched back. The wielder nicked his blade against my chin and raised my face with the point of it, turning my head back and forth while the 'dough boy' stood by and assessed me.

I felt Andreas tense. He wanted to protect me, but he realized any move on his part could be my last. We were being patted down from behind and our weapons were stripped from us. They even took my cloak and searched it for anything concealed.

"Two lovely specimens and married I'm told. What beautiful strong children you must have. No, no, someone in your trade wouldn't have children, and yet if it is to be believed that you are married, how is it that you consummate without conception?" He took two steps back and went over both of us with his eyes. I think he admired Andreas a bit too long, but he ended with; "Tsk, tsk. How long have you been in our fair city? Tell me what brings you to our neighborhood? And what is your interest in my man Moon here? Oh, yes, and why is one of my men dead?" He shouted the last question, and then restrained himself.

I looked across Doughboy's shoulder and saw Moon, looking rather smug. I couldn't stand that and so I said; "Your boy Moon there is directly responsible for that. We were bringing Unser's body to his wife, or so we thought." At this point I shot Moon an icy glare. "We wanted Moon to take up the responsibilities for Unser's family since he was directly connected to the cause of death. He told us he would take us to her. We were even going to finance them leaving town." At my last comment Doughboy could not resist a glance at our belongings that now lay in a pile near a wall at the back of the alley; amongst those things was Unser's purse. "If you teach such deception to your people then he is a worthy student," I breeched, "but you obviously already know of us. I suspect that you had someone watching us, to know of our marriage. Why would you be watching travelers you don't know? I suspect that from Moon and Unser's ineptitude that you would not have sent them for such a task, and yet here we are, and I am as confused as you are, unless we are already known by word of mouth for the murder of the merchant, Eindal."

Doughboy looked at me dubiously, but then I could see the reasoning behind his eyes and he smiled. He made a motion with one hand and our guards backed off. I rubbed my chin and came away with a smear of blood on my fingers. The look I shot the wielder could not have conveyed the depth of disapproval I held for my treatment, but things were turning to our side again and I would deal with him when I had a chance.

Doughboy moved away and was standing beside an opening that had appeared in the alley wall, near the back corner. He motioned for us to go in. We could see people move out of the shadows and file in before him. We hesitated naturally, but we were not left unguarded and we were pushed from behind. We abided by the treatment and went in. I looked over my shoulder as we entered the building in time to see our belongings being gathered up and brought inside. This was not the first time, nor was it the last I remember thinking what a bad turn our lives had taken since entering the 'fair' city of Behlanna.

We were led down a straight hallway passing many closed doors. We heard the sounds of revelry behind one, but we continued by until we came to a long flight of open stairs. The climb was steep. At the top we walked another hall passed numbered doors to another stairs that led up to a landing and a single door. Doughboy opened the door with his key and we followed him in. It seemed apparent that this was Doughboy's apartment. He placed his keys in a fold of his frock and stood aside to allow us—Andreas and I, Moon, and our two armed chaperones, to enter. "Please have a seat," he said, and motioned through a small arch to a parlor near the doorway. "I'll only be a moment." Our impatient escort shoved us forward and Andreas nearly took a swing, but the unsheathed swords stayed his hand. We went in and sat.

I chose a comfortable chair across the room and near a door that seemed in an odd place for what I knew of the building layout so far. Andreas sat in one of two more comfortable chairs, but he took the one nearest the archway. Moon had been moving toward the other comfortable chair, but when he saw our selections he thought better of it and sat on a hard wooden chair near the fireplace. Most certainly he did not want to show disrespect to Doughboy. The positions that Andreas and I had taken were a strategy that we had agreed on long ago. Whenever we entered into unknown quarters with a client, a perpetrator, or in this case an unknown consequential player, we took up positions near to any apparent exits available. It offered both defensive and offensive possibilities if things became dangerous. At that moment things felt very dangerous. Doughboy was dangerous and he was interested in us for some reason.. If it turned out that I was wrong, he wouldn't have us killed in his apartment. When we were taken away from there then we would have to act.

Truth is I was curious about Doughboy too, but I was more curious about Moon's position in this group. I wanted to stick him back with his own stupid little ploy to trap us. I was sure it had been an impromptu action and that he hadn't thought it through to the end. Whatever played out when Doughboy returned was sure to be interesting.

When Doughboy did return he had changed into a blousy silk tunic over muslin trousers that gathered at his ankles. Over it all he wore a housecoat. These clothes allowed his ample form room to move. His feet were immaculately manicured and sat atop a pair of wooden platforms strapped to his feet by velvet cords. In his hands he carried a highly polished cherry wood box. I looked over his exposed skin for tattoos but saw none.

He passed Andreas and came to me while he opened the lid and offered a view of the contents. Inside was a stack of black dragon sticks. Black dragon, if you don't know is an herb that is smoked for its euphoric effects. I waved my hand as an indication of no, but he protested.

"Would you insult my hospitality, Dear One?"

"Oh, no, and please don't let my abstinence, stop you. I have no objection to the practice; I simply find that it does not agree with me."

"Very well then I suppose, if you are certain." He held the box before me a moment, but realized that I would not change my mind and went to make the offer to Andreas.

Andreas was not as gracious as I was. "Why would I take Dragon with a man who holds me captive in his home?"

Doughboy slammed the box shut and put it on the table next to the open comfortable chair, but he did not sit, he paced instead. We had ruined his plan to intoxicate us. He was formulating another approach. Perhaps Moon was not to be blamed for his lack of ability if this was the master that he had trained under.

"You really can't blame him you know." I said in an attempt to keep him off guard.

"What?" Doughboy asked, not understanding.

"Well we only just met, we've been brought her at knife point and we don't know your name. Under the circumstances I'm sure that you must see the wisdom of our decision. I believe that we have shown great restraint under duress. My husband is not a patient man. I'd say at this point he has kept his boiling temper well covered, but boiling pots often blow their lids, if left alone. He is an awesome fury when his lid blows. I venture that if it were not for his concern for my safety that you would have a few less men at your beckon call right now."

Doughboy stared at me slack jawed a moment. His eyes were fiery, but then a smile teased at his lips and his eyes twinkled.

"Bless my soul, but you are refreshing. I have you at my mercy, and yet you will not be towed along to appease me, and still you manage to be gracious about it. How is it that a lovely such as you ends up with a cad such as him?"

"Don't let his gruff exterior fool you. Behind all that raw magnetism, and savoir faire lies, well, the intellect of a serial killer and the bloodlust of a madman."

Andreas smiled at me from across the room, but Doughboy definitely did not find this humorous at any level.

He leaned in close and put one hand on each of my shoulders. His grip was surprisingly strong and I could feel my arms go numb as he pushed his weight down on me and forced me into the soft cushions of the chair. He took any attack I might have had away from me, by kneeling on my legs. I struggled not to cry out, under the intolerable pain. He had caught me with my knees in a locked position and my heels propped up against the base of the chair. I couldn't change their position had I wanted to. His weight had effectively locked me into position. I let slip a grunt when I was sure my knees would snap, and he smiled lecherously.

"Do you think that I do not recognize a threat when I hear one?" He spat, "Your beauty and charm are not lost on me, but there is a place for such things and I assure you that this is not one of those times."

I ventured a glance at Andreas who was held tight by both guards. The one behind him had his arms locked behind his back, the other had his sword in both hands with the sharp edge of it pushed across Andreas's throat. I looked back at Doughboy who had his face nearly against mine.

"Do you worry about your mate little one, even when I could snap you like a twig?"

I did not answer, and he screamed at me. "Answer!"

"Yes." My voice trembled. It had not done that for a very long time, but then I had not dealt with instability so closely before.

He leaned back, putting his weight on my ankles once again. I grimaced and he removed himself. The guards loosened up on Andreas. The one with the sword dropped it to rest in the hollow at the center of his collarbone.

Doughboy continued as if nothing had happened "My name is Kapit."

Doughboy, I thought to myself.

"I am the chief administrator of a vast enterprise. I have many resources at my fingertips; I could have you taken out on a whim, or followed to the ends of the earth so do not cross me. My enterprise has need of you; I think that if you will shut up and listen you will see that you have need of my enterprise."

I swallowed hard and said, "Go on." I had heard talk like that only once before, that man had been a spy. I knew from that, that we sat within the Stalkers headquarters,

"Eindal was a friend of mine."

Doughboy Kapit continued, "We often did business together and he never cheated me. We were, in fact, working together on a most intriguing and dangerous affair. But lately he had grown distant. I had just learned of his return, and had sent a man to meet him. That man returned with the news of his death. I understand that as he died he asked for you and that shortly after you were implicated in his murder. I also gathered that you had only just entered town and had no direct opportunity to do the kill. Still I wonder, did you pay someone?

"We did not kill him, or have him killed. We didn't even know of him until we came into town," Andreas explained.

"Is that so? Can you prove it?"

I saw my opportunity to bring Moon back into the mix and I took it. "We were attempting to do just that when your man here," I pointed at Moon, "barged in and upset our investigation."

"Is that so?" Doughboy said as if he didn't believe it, but then he spun, startling Moon when he went nose to nose with him.

"Moon. Moon, Moon, Moon. What am I going to do with you? By what right do you interfere with the investigation of our finest purveyor's murder? Were you ordered to do so by someone in this society?"

When Moon did not answer immediately, Doughboy simply said, "Hmmmmm?" He kept his face immediately in front of Moon and looked him eye to eye.

"No Sir, Kapit."

"No?"

Moon shook his head.

"Then why did you interfere with these people?" Doughboy shouted so loud that his breath caught and he had to suppress a cough.

Moon jumped and his whole demeanor was like that of a cowered pup.

"Tell me man, or I'll end your life right here."

Moon stammered, but he began to tell him the same story he had told us about being hired to abduct us by an old man who had heard of their as burglars. He said he did not know the man, but that he was supposed to meet him at our room at the boarding house. He left out the part about the tattoo.

Andreas pushed ahead on that topic but played it down for Kapit; "You told us the man had a scorpion tattoo." He turned to Kapit, "Is there any importance to that?"

Moon didn't have a chance to answer, before Doughboy had him out of the chair and up against the wall by his neck. "You took a job from a Scorpion without reporting it first?

We don't do business with the prince's men and you know that. You had better have a dire reason!"

He let go of Moon who fell to the floor in a slump knocking over the chair in the process. He whispered, "Tell me what that reason is," and turned his back on the man.

Moon pulled himself to a sitting position against the wall. He met Andreas's eyes and there was hatred there. There was hatred for me too when he looked my way. For Doughboy Kapit there was a conflict of emotions in Moon's eyes. Kapit stood with his arms folded over his wide belly, looking down at his feet as he rocked to and fro on the wooden platforms upon which he stood. He was waiting for his answer.

The room teemed with tension. Kapit had everyone on the brink of panic; even his own guards. I wished that I were near Andreas. Even this small distance between us made me feel vulnerable before this unstable man.

Kapit started to move toward Andreas, slowly, deliberately. My heart raced and I moved to the edge of my seat, preparing to jump on Kapit if I had to, but he turned slowly and moved just as deliberately back toward Moon. He noticed my change in position, and although I tried to look casual he wagged his finger at me. He spoke to Moon in soft tones. "Come now, Moon. You know you can talk to me. You had better talk to me, and soon, or I may feel that you have betrayed me."

"I would not dream of betraying you, Sir. It was, in fact, that I was trying to impress you."

"O? Do tell." Kapit replied.

"We thought that if we could not only bring in a good cache, but also get paid for an abduction that you would see we were able to take on difficult assignments. Your portion of the retainer alone would have been one hundred gold. Anything taken from the marks would have been extra for all of us." Moon was a fast talker. I got the impression that this was not his first time in this type of situation. He wasn't much of a thief, but an expert weasel.

Doughboy seemed to soften, "Tell me why you took a job from a Scorp."

"I didn't want to at first, but Unser pointed out that we hadn't gotten much work lately, and that as members of the society we were still obligated to bring in a fair share so as to contribute to the membership."

"How convenient for you that Unser is incapable of corroborating your story. You are more fortunate than you realize, Moon. Had you succeeded I would have killed you, this way you are just out of the society."

Moon opened his mouth to protest, but Doughboy talked over him. "Where is the retainer that you received? Since you purport to have been on society business than I am bound to take my cut off the top and I will collect Unser's for his widow. You may keep the rest as a severance fee."

Moon let his head fall back against the wall and he looked up at the ceiling. His jaw was clenched and we could see the muscles move as he ground his teeth together.

"What is it Moon?" Doughboy Kapit asked as he moved closer and knelt beside him.

"They have it." He choked.

"The Scorps?"

"No, they do." He pointed one outstretched finger at each of us. His eyes never left the ceiling. Kapit stood up and came to stand in front of me. I put my feet flat on the floor, but I continued to lean forward as I looked up at him.

"Is this true, cuteness?"

I did not get what made this man operate on so many unconnected levels. First he loathes you then he loves you; he wants to kill you, then he wants to flirt. I had no close assessment of what he might do with whatever I said. The truth might only make us five hundred pieces poorer. Then again I would not have been surprised if he kissed me for the lie and killed me for the truth. I told the truth. He threw up his arms and I flinched. Then I realized that he was laughing. He threw his arms up a lot when he laughed. I sat back to avoid being inadvertently slapped. He was wearing himself out, and flopped into the other comfy chair. When he gathered himself enough he took a thready breath and coughed. I caught Andreas's look of disbelief, and tried to convey the same without changing whatever expression was on my face at the time.

We sat in silence waiting for whatever happened next. After he finished coughing and caught his breath it came, in the form of a loud and abrupt order. "Get him out of here now, both of you!" He pointed at Moon, but looked at his men. Moon went willingly out the door, but we heard a fracas in the hall that was soon silent. I believe they killed Moon.

We sat in silence once more, alone with a mad man.

He heaved a heavy sigh as he looked back and forth at the two of us. "So you have Moon's money. What do you plan to do with it?"

Andreas answered. "We were going to give it back to him to take Unser's wife and family somewhere safe. I can see now that he is too weak to be expected to hold up his end of that bargain. I guess we'll just give it to her and she'll be better off for it, without dwindling the purse with the cost of moving her."

"How do you plan to give it to her, now?"

"I was hoping that you would tell us where to find her."

I still can't believe that Doughboy actually had to think about this, but he did, for a long time. He finally agreed and gave us directions to her place, but we had to take Unser with us, and he refused to pay funeral costs, because Unser was not on a sanctioned job. We stood to leave.

"Where do you think you are going?" He asked. "We haven't finished our business." I did not savor being close to this man any longer than we had to, but we were in a tough spot.

"We weren't aware that you had hired us." Andreas said harshly. That was great, harshness on a mad man. I was still standing and prepared to run. "Were you aware, Darling?" Even better; get me involved, easy for him. I was closer to the titanic lunatic.

"No, not at all, Hon." I managed in my smoothest voice. "Please tell us what proposition you have to offer, Master Kapit."

"Sit, please, and I'll tell you."

I was starting to wish I had taken a dragon stick from him earlier. My nerves were shot after this night, and I had a bad feeling it wasn't about to get any better. We sat, but this time Andreas came over and perched on the arm of my chair. I let him see the relief in my eyes, and he smiled. I leaned back and he put his arm across the back of my chair and leaned toward me. He was a good friend.

Kapit held his chin up with his two thumbs and laced his fingers together. He looked across his fingers at us, but said nothing for a few moments. He looked long at each of us; his gaze was unsettling, as if he could actually know what was in our heads and our pasts. Finally he said, "I think I will trust you. I have a delicate matter of importance to tell you about and then we can talk about fees.

"I believe what I have to say is the same matter which Eindal had wanted to speak to you about. Eindal was in search of a set of scrolls. I was financing him along with a few other interested parties. I believe that he had possession of one. The value of the scrolls is priceless. Their power is unfathomable. For centuries they have been kept in various locations, seats of power, bastions of good. One was kept locked away in the temple of Nauticus. Recently the Priest charged with the care of this one scroll discovered a breach of the temple. Believing that the scroll was about to be stolen he went to defend it, but he was too late. He has not been seen again and the scroll is also gone.

I hired Eindal as soon as I got word that the scroll was missing. He knows his way around the underground markets. The Priest remains missing and Eindal has been running for his life ever since. I got a message through one of my agents in Tiahn. Eindal had contacted him. The message just said: "I have a line on the scroll. Check on the others. I'll see you soon."

Doughboy stopped speaking and glared at me. I could not tell what his reason might be; perhaps he was making sure that I was paying attention. "Please, continue." Andreas said politely. I was still wondering what scrolls could say that would make Priests disappear and Black Marketers run for their lives. Who were the interested parties? Who held the seats of power, and what made them so good? Had the scroll been stolen from him at the time of his murder? Why were the scrolls disappearing, and who was behind it? I focused again on Doughboy Kapit.

He was saying, "My man was on his way to meet Eindal just after we became aware that he was back in town. That was about the same time we became aware of you. When my man arrived a slender young man slipped around the corner of the building and introduced himself to Eindal. Their conversation was brief and the man left as quickly as he came. When he did Eindal was slumped in his chair. A young woman came with a glass of wine for him; she let out a scream. It wasn't long before the place was swarming with Scorpion Guards and soon after; Traylor's men.

"My man watched as you joined the crowd outside of Katie's place. He did not know who you were yet and you weren't much concern until you moved forward and engaged Traylor. While you were still inside he left to bring me the news and then he found a place out of sight to sit and wait for a time when you were alone. He watched while you searched the porch. To see what you were up to and report it to me. You never gave him the opportunity to approach."

We did not tell Kapit that we had slipped out that night. His man must be good, because he was hidden at least as well as we were.

"And then when you did go out the next morning you were followed," That was something we did not know, and I wondered who had followed us. "So my man decided to have a talk with Katie's waitress. That was when he found out that Eindal had asked for you with his dying breath. You are unknown in these parts, but I believe Eindal was inclined to hire you. Why?"

"We wonder that ourselves. We are all well traveled, perhaps our paths had crossed in other cities. We are minstrel's by preference, but we have had some success with constabulary work. It is possible that he knew of that."

"I was having you followed soon after my men made me aware of you and your involvement with the matter. This person supports your plea of innocence in Eindal's killing, and reports that Midiwen has vouched for you as well. I know of him he has an honest reputation."

"Did your man see who the killer was?" Andreas asked.

"The Black Scorpions." I whispered involuntarily.

"We suspect so, yes." Kapit affirmed. "How do you know this?"

"My instincts serve me well, and often. I tend to trust them. It is nothing I can prove. It is just that I've had a bad feeling in the corners of my senses since arriving in this *peaceful* little burg. We've been on the streets, and from what we have seen there, and what Moon told us when we captured and interrogated him, it fit."

"Don't trust what Moon tells you. Tonight is not the first time he has moved against the vows of his passage into the society. He is an opportunistic prig and I'm happy to be rid of him."

"What is it that you want from us?" Andreas asked. "Surely your vast enterprise has the means to deal with this better than we do."

"Ah, so we come to the rub. The society has a very strict policy about dealing with politics. The Scorpions represent the palace, which is certainly a political area. I can not ask my people to go into action on this matter and change a long standing policy just because I want to."

"It seems to me that you can do whatever you want around here."

"Oh, certainly I could, but those types of things lead to a deterioration of my leadership and that affects my ability to command my intelligence contacts and so I won't have it. Politics are a delicate thing, care must be taken to maintain our appearance of neutrality."

"But you are not neutral?" I asked.

"Only as a position of negotiation." Kapit elaborated no further and I asked nothing more as a position of our neutrality.

Why was this man who was so maniacal earlier making so much sense now, and doing it calmly? He didn't seem worried about respect earlier when he was ranting in front of two guards. Perhaps that whole thing was a charade, played out to put us on edge. I found myself looking at him in a different light, reassessing. He noticed my attention and winked at me. I looked to Andreas who was looking at me and did not notice. When I turned back again Doughboy was licking his lips lecherously. I jumped up from my seat. "No." I shouted, "No! I won't do it."

"What?" Andreas was confused, "Why not?"

"I can't work for this man, Andreas. I know you didn't just see that, but I will not tolerate his crazy sexual overtures."

"What?" Andreas again.

"You heard me."

By the gods I didn't know what to do. Andreas hadn't seen what Kapit would surely deny and I knew damn well I wasn't going to be allowed to just walk out of that place without permission.

"Trust me, Andre," I pleaded. "I can't work for this man."

"Okay." He shrugged, but he stood up beside me. To Kapit he said: "You heard the lady. I guess we'll be thanking you for your very special hospitality and say good bye then."

"No." Kapit said pithily.

"What do you mean, No?" Andreas snapped.

"I don't believe that you will."

Andreas grabbed my arm and sent me toward the door. "Watch us," he said.

"If you wish, but I don't see how you will be able to prove your innocence without our help."

"We have gotten along fine without you in the past."

"Yes, but the present holds facts that you are as yet unaware of."

Andreas stopped. I kept moving and had my hand on the door when my curiosity overpowered my desire to be away from this prick. I have a need to know all the facts about a job that I'm involved with. Like it or not I was involved. This time our own lives hung in the balance. We had to know.

We stood with our arms crossed, and waited for him to speak, but he did not. "Well?" Andreas finally ventured on.

"Oh, so now you want to know."

"Look Dou...Kapit," It was my turn to be unbalanced. "I am tired of your crazy banter. It is perfectly obvious that now we want to know. So, tell us now, quickly and precisely, or you will find yourself without a team to do whatever dirty work it is that you brought us up here in the first place to tell us about!"

"The sheriff, Fedar Traylor, is dead."

Silence, gaping jaw, confusion.

"I said..." Kapit began again.

"We heard you." We replied in perfect unison.

"Care to sit down?" Kapit asked.

We sat.

"What happened, and when?" Andreas asked.

"His throat was slit. Word is that a man and woman were seen leaving his office about an hour before his body was discovered, which was about an hour before you entered our alley."

"Which was about the time Moon and Unser came along and dismissed our guards? What happened to them, did they report back?" I said.

"They are as yet unaccounted for, so we don't know for sure, but their absence is pointing to the two of you as well."

"Surely someone must have seen the guard at our door leave Aunt Katie's." I hoped aloud.

"The condition of your room has led many to believe that you fought with your guards there."

Andreas and I felt as if the world was upon our shoulders, little did we know then how accurate that was.

Kapit broke the awkward silence. "I should have thanked Moon for bringing you to me. I sent men to find you. We had only just learned that you were not in your room, when there you were. It seems that someone very much wants you out of the way."

"Then why haven't they just tried to slit our throats? Why set us up on Murder charges?" I wondered.

"And why kill Traylor when he is the one who would be locking us up, when these implications are made?"

"Both very good questions to which I have no answer."

"We should just leave town," I said to Andreas. "Then they can't touch us."

"I'm not so sure," Andreas began, "the timing is what gets me. With Eindal, we can figure it was about this business with the scrolls, but Traylor? That doesn't sit right with me. We can't avoid the implications that having someone of our general appearance at his office suggests, and just when Moon and Unser arrive to conveniently dismiss our guards. We left the room looking like a battle zone. We played into their hands. They've made more of it than we thought they could, because there is something deeper at play here. Whoever is against us here will help them to keep making something of it and you can bet it won't be good for us."

"We just wanted some rest. We had heard Behlanna was a quiet law abiding town."

"I am sorry for your misfortune, but your misfortune may prove to be the world's salvation." Kapit offered. Then he changed tact "You look tough. My reports tell me that you looked pretty beat up when you arrived here. So you are ruffians, and strangers. No one knows you or can vouch for you, except Eindal and Mediwin, one who is dead and one so far away that it doesn't really matter except to those few of us who know, or rather know of him. You make the perfect patsy, and the real murderer or murderers move freely through the city."

"More than one person is involved here, that is apparent" I said.

"Yes, and we must consider how this relates to all of the things we have learned from Moon and Kapit here." Andreas added.

"I have been, and I am concerned that you let Moon get away from us, Kapit"

"Moon was too weak to be knowingly involved in this; he didn't have the wits for such intrigue. He wouldn't have been able to keep it all straight." Was that past tense? So, Kapit had eliminated Moon.

"I'm not sure we can." Andreas said just what I was thinking.

"You still have not told us everything."

Doughboy leaned back and sighed. He was gathering his thoughts before he spoke. We waited a long time for him to speak again.

He sighed and then began; "Four scrolls; they are called the Dark Minstrel Scrolls, they are a tool for both evil and good, depending on whose hands possess them. Each Scroll is an epic musical score that only a well trained musician would understand."

"I have seen the instruments in your bag. It kept me from a grave error in the alley. Are you then trained to read music?

We each nodded affirmatively. "We write more than we read, but, yes." I replied.

"It must be why Eindal waited for you."

"But how did he know we would come here?"

"Perhaps he was having you followed."

I was beginning to doubt our stealthy abilities.

Kapit continued. "Three scrolls—collectively called the Symphony of Nine Hells and a fourth scroll, called the Rise of Darkness. Each is a flawless, beautiful piece, nearly identical, harmonious to the others, but in their harmonic differences a cryptic message lies." Kapit lowered his voice and paused dramatically. He hunched his shoulders as if he was about to be smote. "The messages reveal the location of three keys each key opens three of the nine gates to the Abyss. Each scroll locates three gates. Three scrolls, three gates each; so it is possible to unlock all of the hells and set them loose upon the earth.

"The fourth scroll combined with the other three gives the words of power that ignite the spell that binds A Dark Prince; one who is able to walk the earth. It also has the words and ceremony that freed him from his binding. It is the key to the knowledge of the first three scrolls. The information is hidden amongst the differences in the arrangements. Each keeper of a scroll has some deeper knowledge of how these encryptions work. It is probably why the Priest is still missing and has not been found dead. He can more easily unlock the secrets of the scroll for them. Any evil that seeks the knowledge contained within these scrolls would not be afraid to torture a God's man to receive it."

Kapit believed that the locations of the other scrolls were revealed within each, so having only one scroll would allow the knowledge of the locations of all three; if one knew how to decipher them.

So we knew why Eindal had chosen us. It would take a musician of sizable worth to master each piece, play them against each other and reveal the differences. That seemed the easy part to me. It would be the unscrambling of the emerging code that would tax us.

"What do you want from us?"

"I'm sorry, I thought it was obvious. I want you to find Eindal's murderers, retrieve the first scroll, and find leads to the others."

"Perhaps we should go after the Rise of Darkness scroll. Without the keythat lies within, no gates can be opened." Andreas offered.

I suggested that without the three scrolls that made up the Symphony of Nine Hells we could not know the location of the Rise of Darkness. He noted that the Rise of Darkness could unlock the gates of hell and let loose pure evil upon the world.

I reiterated, "Without the three scrolls, there is no Rise of Darkness; no master key."

"No keys at all in our possession—Hell unloosed."

He was frightened and tired and so, not thinking at his best, I let it go. I found it hard to comprehend that we were actually having a conversation about such things, let alone actually contemplating becoming involved.

Kapit brought us back to some logic, another fine moment; Kapit the lunatic was more logical than either of us. I reasoned this away by noting that he had more time to absorb this information. I felt better for it.

"I'm sure Eindal was killed because of his interest in keeping these scrolls from being found, or worse, being deciphered and used. We intended, still intend to round them up and lock them under the protection of other worthy guardians, somewhere they can be safe for many more centuries."

"Shouldn't they be destroyed so there is no risk of this happening again in the future?"

"We are dealing with artifacts of the Gods, we are only the guardians. If they are to be destroyed then the Gods will decide that."

"How do we know that the Gods do not want us to destroy them? Have they given some indication, some sign?"

"No, but if they do we will follow their commands, for now we proceed as ordained."

"Ordained? By whom?"

Kapit sighed; he was considering some dark secret, something he was reluctant to reveal. When he spoke his tone was hushed, even reverent. "There are those who are bound by blood oath to protect these scrolls through all time— a secret sect."

"The interested parties are a secret sect— Oh; this just keeps getting better and better." Andreas commented.

"Tell us more about them."

"I cannot do that. I am sure that from what I have just told you, that you can see that their protection is inherent to our success at retrieving the scrolls. Even I do not know all of the pieces. I am only their eyes and ears. Through my network I keep them aware of what is happening in all parts of the world. From that we evaluate the danger to the sites where the scrolls are kept. My network failed to warn Nauticus, or to protect Eindal that has never happened before. Great minds and power are at work against us I can assure you of that. My intentions are for the common good, I am well aware that my position gives you doubt. Sadly, it is the only thing I can give you to base your trust upon. I only hope that you will trust me.

"If you decide to help us I will pay your expenses and give you a safe haven from which to operate. If you can find a way to gather the master key first, then I will not stop you, but that seems impossible at this stage of the operation.

"I fear, as I said earlier that this will lead to the palace somehow and I cannot activate my members there, as it is against our protocols and their oaths. In fact, I am advising extreme caution to those inside. They have always been my eyes and ears. They are not to become my voice or my hands. It has been so since we came into existence. I cannot even notify the prince. If he were involved I would play into his hand. If he is not involved, and I have no reason to believe that he is, I might play him into the hands of those around him who are."

"Is The Society a branch of the sect?"

"No they are simply a cover under which I operate. The society is a viable entity of the culture of Behlanna and an interest I take seriously, but they do not know of my oath to the Sect.

"I can offer you a sanctuary of sorts, and it will not be questioned. You can move on the palace and it breaks no oaths on my part to allow you to do that, since you are not an authorized agent of The Society, you will be acting on your own behalf, albeit under my protection to clear your names. Publically I will denounce you if you are caught. Privately I will do all that I can to keep you safe and protected.

"My protection offers you the hospitality of my house, access to whatever intelligence we can gather that concerns your task, and any aide that the Sect can offer without revealing itself. That is all that I can offer under the circumstances. Are you interested?"

Andreas and I studied each other long and hard. It was a minor empathy that we had developed after so much time spent together in highly emotional situations. We could read the others expression quite well.

"I think that is an understatement," I said.

"It seems we have no choice really," Andreas said. "But there is something that you have no choice in either. When we incur an expense or order something that seems unusual or even unnecessary to you, you must pay and you must obtain it as quickly as possible without questions. We are the ones directly in harm's way here and we cannot afford for our means and tactics to be questioned. We have no basis for your trust either, except that Eindal wanted us. If you trusted him you will trust us."

"I already said that I would."

"Good then."

"Is there to be a contract?" I wondered.

"Only verbally, written papers can be traced."

"Good then," we said together.

"Now remember," Kapit reminded us. "This city still holds allegiance to their prince. There have been two murders of highly reputed men. Whoever is running this show has made sure that you are suspect in both. Both men are known to be of good moral intent and highly honorable. They will want these murders solved. You will be hunted far and wide. The region that surrounds Behlanna is in the realm of the Prince's father. I would bet that handbills are being drawn up as we speak. Our prince's artist is a good one; some of those handbills will have your likeness on them. I'd say that by sunrise your faces will be all over town."

From my way of thinking it was hard to separate dilemmas, which was the most grave— clearing our names, or saving the world, either way the world looked very dark.

They were inextricably linked. I still did not trust Kapit, but in the course of things, to clear our good names, we had to stay to solve this new dire dilemma. Kapit offered the only protection we had so far. Still, if I didn't trust him could I trust his protection? It would be difficult to move through the streets even at night given that our descriptions would be well known. The constabulary would certainly be working overtime on the murder of their leader.

The unknown intent of the Scorps worried me the most. Perhaps we could find a few citizens of the city that would give us information, but they would surely be reluctant to talk to us and so their information might be false. Leaving seemed to be a way to survive for a time, but I had no doubt that this would follow us, and resurface at some later, most inopportune moment. I imagined an unloosed demon tapping me on the shoulder as I played a soft tune in a quiet village square. What use would my good name be then?

I was interrupted from my thoughts by the aroma of dragon in the air. Kapit had lit a stick of the heady leaf and he and Andreas were sharing it.

"Any way out, Andre?"

"I don't see any. Do you?"

"I'm afraid not."

"Will you do it then?" Kapit asked and offered me the stick. I took it from him, but I did not immediately partake.

"I will, but only if you keep your lecherous tendencies to yourself. One time, just one more time, if you even look at me funny, there *will* be a murder on my hands."

"That may be difficult. You are both so beautiful."

Andreas coughed out the smoke he had been holding deep in his lungs. "She— may not have— to kill you— if I get to you first, Dough—boy!" He spoke between coughs. That he called him Doughboy, when I had not had the chance to tell him that I had given him that name, amazed, but did not surprise me.

Kapit's face was like stone, but if our name for him bothered him, he did not say. "I will be on my best behavior," Kapit said, "if only you will do this thing. Eindal was a good friend, and I want to see some justice for him, the sect needs you, and the Dark Prince frightens me ever so much."

I looked at Andreas and he nodded, 'Yes.' I returned the nod and he gave the confirming word to Kapit. I took a long drag from the rolled leaf stick. I needed it.

"What about Unser?" I asked.

"I will see to him for you. I had intended to if you agreed to help us, but I couldn't waste time with him if I had to find another set of mercenaries." Kapit said. "You have no time for such things now. I will honor your intentions, if you will turn the money you had for him over to me."

Andreas and I looked to each other for some agreement on the matter. The truth was we were tired and didn't want to be bothered with it in light of this new information.

"You can trust me with the matter. Kapit said. "I know the hardships of growing up without a father and no money. I will see that they get it."

Andreas and I agreed.

Kapit stood and pulled on a bell cord in the ceiling. We had just finished the dragon stick when a man and woman we recognized from the alley came in with our things. They were unarmored, but armed with a sword and a dagger each.

"This is Sorrell," Kapit said making formal introductions, and the woman nodded; "and Argus," he continued, and the man nodded. "Sorrell, Argus, I would like for you to meet Saeede," I nodded; "and Andreas. They will be our guests for a time. I have offered them what protections my house has to offer." I noted that he did not say what protections The Society has to offer. Sorrell and Argus nodded again, and offered their hands in greeting. We shared handshakes as Kapit went on. "Give them the best I have to offer. Be sure that it is someplace quiet and show them the way in and out that best services them. I expect that you two will see to their needs while they are here so be sure that they know how to find you at anytime night or day."

With his orders to Sorrell and Argus complete he turned to us. "You are free to come and go as you please, but I would like you to apprise me of any developments as they occur. These two will know how to find me and I will make myself available as soon as possible from the time that I am notified. I imagine that you will want to rest for a time before you go about your business. If there is nothing else, then I will say goodbye for now." He extended his hand and Andreas took it, reluctantly I noted, but I doubted that Kapit could tell. I was just out of reach, fortunately, and when I nodded that seemed to be fine with him. Argus opened the door and Sorrel went out first. We followed to where she waited a few steps ahead. Argus closed the door behind us, and Sorrel led us away from Kapit's apartment.

We had to pay close attention to our surroundings. We were taken through doors we had not been through coming in. The interior walls and doors changed styles often, not unordinary, just different as we passed from building to building without ever going outside. Doughboy Kapit's vast enterprise was only beginning to show us just how vast it could be.

We were taken down another hall and waited while Sorrell reached up and flipped a concealed lever high up on the wall to our left. A panel slid open. Sorrell pushed it back a few inches, reached in and slid it into the wall to allow us access to another hall, and yet another building. There was thick carpeting on the floor here and we were taken passed one door. Sorrell stopped at the second. This door was a good distance from the first and another door was an equal distance from this one farther down the hall. The opposite wall was blank. Sorrell pulled a chain with many keys on it from around her neck and opened the door. She pushed it open and stood aside while we entered. Argus came in behind us and crossed to another door on our right and put our bag and confiscated items down just inside the door of a bedroom.

The place was an elegantly appointed. suite of three rooms. We stood in a large foyer divided from a rich parlor by three marble pillars. In the room beyond the pillars were three tall windows spaced across the wall and covered with thick velvet drapes. A large fireplace nearly filled one end of the parlor, near the bedroom. In the corner beside the fireplace an oak side bar nestled near one of the windows. It was stocked with various liquors, wine, and a keg of ale. Glasses appropriate to one type of spirit or another were stacked neatly on the far end of the bar. On the other side of the fireplace a scroll shelf rose from floor to ceiling. There were not many scrolls, but they were bound in rich leather wraps.

Argus returned and offered a tour. Aside from the stock of liquor we had enough firewood, for several fireplaces and the brazier below a marble tub, linens were in a closet in each room.. Water for the tub was available at the turn of a spigot and fed by gravity from a reservoir on the roof. The bedrooms had a huge bed upon a platform surrounded with a heavy drape. Across from the beds was another fireplace with a raised hearth. A stone shelf jutted out from the hearth to serve as a seat. The wood was stacked neatly below that shelf. One window identical to those in the parlor filled a space in the center of the wall beside the bed.

We had never stayed in such a place. When we had money we felt it was a waste too spend it so lavishly when more modest accommodations would suit us just fine. To have a place like that offered to us seemed very generous, perhaps Doughboy really did care.

Sorrell remained in the foyer while Argus showed us around. She removed a key to the room from the collection around her neck and handed it to Andreas who thanked her.

When she finally spoke she had one of those husky, but beautiful voices that some women are lucky enough to have. "Argus and I will move into the rooms on either side of you, so that you can find us easily. If you go to the end of the hall, not where we came in, but the other way, there is a stairway to the first floor. There is dining and a kitchen down there. I will let the cook know that we will have guests in this house and you will be accommodated during regular daylight hours, after that you will have to fend for yourselves." There were three bell cords in a corner of the foyer near the door. "If you prefer to be served in your room pull this bell cord," she indicated the center one, "and the cook will come see to your needs, again only during regular hours. If you pull this cord, it will ring in my room;" she pulled a cord to indicate which was for her, "or in Argus's room." She pulled the final cord to indicate Argus. "I will be available to you from midnight to midday, and Argus, from midday to midnight. If for some reason you would rather knock on our doors, I will be in the room to the east and Argus to your west, which coincides with the bell cords. If there is nothing else we will leave you so that we can get into our rooms and be ready if you should need us."

"That should be plenty for now," I said. "I really just want a good night sleep."

"Or day, as the case may be," Argus interjected.

"Yes," Andreas said.

Sorrell opened the door and our two guardian servants, went out. Andreas closed the door and locked it behind them.

I went over to the window and peeked out through the drapes. The light of dawn was making its way across the sky. I was surprised to see that the building where we were being housed faced the cobbled, tree lined street upon which Aunt Katie's Boarding House was situated. I couldn't tell where exactly that was, but I recalled from the buildings I could see that we were on the same side of the street with perhaps three or four buildings between us. It was then that I realized we had not been shown a safe way to exit or enter the building as Doughboy had instructed. It didn't really matter since we only wanted to sleep, but I couldn't help wondering if that was by design.

·~· Chapter Two ·~·

I woke up in the dark, not even remembering that I had lain down to sleep. I was fully dressed, even to my boots, having been too tired to undress. I felt Andreas breathing deeply, and sound asleep next to me. I rolled over and slept again. The next time I woke the parlor room was aglow with light of a fire in the hearth. I got up and pulled the blanket around me, to protect me from the chilly air of our spacious rooms and went to join Andreas where he sat cross-legged in front of the hearth.

"I didn't want to wake you by starting a fire in the bed room. Did you sleep well?"

"Yes, you?"

"Yes."

"Any idea what time of day it is?"

"After midnight." I took a chance and pulled Sorrell's cord. She came in. I told her we would be going out tonight after you woke up, so that when I next pull the cord she would have to show us the way out. Do you want to go down and see what we can find for breakfast?"

"Yes."

We went down stairs as we were, but I left the blanket behind. When we found the kitchen, Sorrell was there brewing tea. She offered some and we accepted. The strong herbal concoction was fresh and stimulating. I found some eggs and cheese and after starting a small fire under an iron covered stovetop; I scrambled up enough eggs for all of us and topped them with shavings from the cheese. Sorrell showed us where the breads and muffins were. I chose dark beer bread and cut some for each of us. We lathered it with sweet butter and stood quietly while we ate at the large butcher-block table in the center of the room.

When everyone was through Sorrell took the dishes and rinsed them in a pail of water on a wooden stand next to a copper tub.

"Have you worked for Kapit a long time?" Andreas asked her.

"Yes, I've lost count of the years," she replied, "He took me in when I was orphaned on the streets. Eindal brought me here. Neither of them is much of a father to me, but I am grateful for the life they gave me. I don't like to think of how it may have been with out them. Kapit keeps me close. I don't have to sell my body, or steal for him. I get jobs like this one I am doing for you now."

"What about Argus?"

"I won't speak for him. You will have to ask him yourself."

"Fair enough." Andreas replied.

"We will be ready to go shortly, Sorrel. Should we wait for you in our rooms, or should we meet at your rooms?"

"When you are ready come to me. I'll be there."

We agreed and went back up stairs to gear up for a night of stealthy shadowing.

Sorrell took us downstairs and through the kitchen to a basement below the house. In one corner, next to the food stores, a panel of stones that were once part of the foundation, swung out when the other side was pushed on with great effort. It allowed access to a low and narrow corridor.

Sorrell stepped in and took a hooded lanthorn from a ledge above the door. She lit this with a length of bound straws set afire with a spark from a flint she struck against the stone panel. She held the lanthorn high and showed us a pulley that would pull the door closed behind us the next time we came this way, and then she showed us the stone that would trigger the door to unlatch it from that side. She led us straight ahead down the corridor, which was expertly excavated and shored, with timbers at equal two-foot intervals. There were no turns or side passages and after about one hundred feet we came to the foundation of another building. Of course we knew there would be a door of some sort concealed there.

Sorrell moved forward and turned a piece of stone high up in the wall and the panel popped open. Just on the other side of the panel was a shaft about ten feet tall, only wide enough for one person. A ladder was attached to the wall across from the panel. She showed us how to open the door from inside the shaft and then explained the trapdoor at the top would open up behind a stack of crates and barrels in the alley outside of Aunt Katie's.

"There is no other way?" I asked. "We can hardly afford to be seen skulking around in Aunt Katie's alley."

"Nor can you afford to be seen anywhere in this city, so don't be seen." Sorrell replied with a little too much attitude, but she had a point so I let it drop.

"Very well then," I said and made my way up the ladder. Andreas was right behind me. Sorrel stayed in the corridor to lend us what light fell our way, but protected it from outside. We unlatched the door and climbed out into a space about two feet wide and twice as long. Once the trap door was securely shut again we rested our backs against the wall of Aunt Katie's, but remained in sitting positions. The crates were stacked amongst the barrels to allow viewing slits at random heights and angles to the alley. Our room had been further back into the alley. I turned my head to the left and I could see the street about fifteen feet away only dimly lit by the oil lamps hung from poles at odd intervals throughout the city.

We were well back in the shadows of the alley so we remained for a time to watch the street and saw that the traffic was sparse. There was no sound of cart traffic. Which meant the vendors and merchant trains were closed up for the night. The sound of hoof falls clomped far off; they probably belonged to the city constabulary or the Scorpions, either way was bad for us. We estimated the time to be around the second morning hour. That gave us nearly five hours to do whatever it was we were about to do.

We stayed to the shadows and moved casually to the street. Once there we looked out and saw an immediate opportunity to move onto the walkway that ran along that side of the street. We turned right, away from the boarding house and walked steadily but not quickly. We were out to get a better feel for the streets, if we moved too quickly we might miss something, if we moved too slowly we might be caught. Andreas had taught me long ago that to really know a city you had to see it at night, because that was how you got acquainted with the dark elements that lay beneath the surface during the day. Our search for dark elements was on.

We made a deliberate, decreasing concentric circuit of the city that would eventually bring us near the city's center. Lengthy placement of the oil lamps, the odd angles of the streets, and heftily constructed buildings made our way through shadow comfortable. We noted that every shop was shut with sturdy wooden shutters or iron gates; many of them brand new, a good indication of rising crime.

We wanted to find where the poor and homeless hid at night. They usually held no loyalties to anyone but those in the same situation; perhaps we could gather another insight of the players in this intrigue. We found a tavern that was just closing and huddled into an alley across the street to wait, hoping someone would pass by. We did not have to wait long. A middle-aged man wearing a ragged old blanket as a coat, belted around his waist, came out of the tavern. The proprietor called harsh words after the man and swung a leg around to kick him in the hindquarters. He fell short of his mark and settled on raising both his arms in a dismissive manner.

The shabby man's hair was long and ungroomed, and his beard was a grizzled patch of gray whiskers. He moved well through the streets and he was difficult to follow as he slipped through shadows. He came to an alley and slid in and out of sight. We slid in behind him. We lost him there, but we did not give up. This city had so much to reveal to us, so why not here in the alleys? A search revealed old barrels stacked like an inverted cone against a stone building. Upon closer examination I found a gap near the back where a person could slip through and under a small section of the barrels. Several building stones had been removed and were nowhere in sight. The low hole had been shored up with roughly cut timbers. A person could slide through on their belly if they weren't too wide in the girth. I am not too wide, but the hole was dark and not knowing where it lead I was not about to go in unprepared. I motioned for Andreas to come in under the barrels and I moved back as far as I could to allow him room.

It was cramped quarters, but Andreas had enough room to incant a spell he had named Vision. It allowed him to see into areas beyond our reach and see what was there. I sat watch quietly while he sat entranced. What Andreas reported after the spell had run its course was nothing we couldn't handle.

I went first and made my way through a low tunnel that had been dug into the dirt packed between two stonewalls of the building foundation. We arrived without mishap to emerge just under the lip of a porch landing and remained there in the shadow that it offered. The space around the edge of the porch opening was covered with a stack of firewood. It was camouflage and if one was careful they could make their way through a turn in the stack and make their way out from under the landing.

There was a cobblestone enclave beyond that. In the shadows of the buildings the homeless huddled. A few sat around small fires roasting potatoes or warming themselves. Most of them slept huddled together against the walls or near the fire wrapped in shabby coats or worn out blankets.

The night was not frigid, but it was cool enough to be uncomfortable. If we were to intrude on their hidden camp we might never gain their trust, but we had little time by which to gather information. We decided to make a stealthy entrance and get a closer look. Whether we approached anyone or not would depend on what information we gathered with our own four eyes.

There was a recessed corner created by two conjoined buildings to our left. If we stayed to the wall of the building we had just crawled from we could move just a few steps and melt into the shadows of that corner.

The location I'd chosen was the furthest from any people. Our surroundings had the feel of a courtyard entrance to a private dwelling, only here the walls were those of surrounding buildings and there was no roof. I knew we would be well hidden when I felt the temperature drop as I slid into position. This was one of those corners that never saw the sun. Andreas moved in beside me and we moved to my left as far as we could go and still be in shadow. This afforded an excellent view and we began our surveillance. We remained there two hours. Five more people came in through the woodpile. Three came in separately and moved through the enclave with some purpose and went to different spots along the walls to settle in for the night. Two came in together and one at a time they moved toward our corner. We didn't understand this; there was still plenty of room in the enclave close to a fire or other people that offered more warmth. Andreas nudged me to move, but I was still looking for a moment, and a location to move to. There was none available that afforded us any cover, but if we didn't do something we would surely be in direct contact. I pulled my hood over my head and motioned Andreas to move around me. He slipped around silently and when he sat back down he leaned his back against me using my dark form to block any view of his skin or eyes. I pulled my knees up and draped my cloak around them. I held it close from the inside and held my breath as the two men moved in and crouched no more than an arm reach away from me.

My heart pounded, and I knew that Andrea's did too, because I could feel it in my arm, through his back. We struggled to gain our composure as the man nearest me spoke in hushed tones. I jumped at the sound of his voice and silently reproved myself. This was a tight fix to be sure, but I'd been in others. The best thing was to sit silently and see what developed. What worried me most were the lack of a second exit and the awkward accessibility of the one we knew.

The man was asking the other what course they should take now that they were "in". That type of jargon indicated that they were either adventurers, like us, or thieves, or worse— cutthroats. While they talked I ventured a gaze from out of my hood and saw the black scorpion tattoo on the ankle of the man next to me. I tried to see the same identification on the other man, but I risked uncovering myself and so returned to my hiding position. We waited there, cramping and cold for what seemed like hours, but the sky remained dark. We would be safe until dawn moved in.

We didn't have to wait much longer for the men to make their move. A strapping boy of about eighteen years woke from his sleep and jumped about to warm himself. Stoked coals offered him little warmth. He came over to the wood pile and when he stooped to reach for a piece of wood the man nearest the corner stood and dropped a hard hit on the back of the boys head with a blackjack. The youth fell with a soft sound upon the ground. I tensed, to pounce on the two thugs, but Andreas stopped me. They maneuvered the boy through the woodpile to the opening below the stairs. I waited for Andreas's lead. It came as soon as the second man was through the pile and into the opening. He moved to the pile and listened, then he motioned me to move in and we were in pursuit.

I listened at the hole and heard them talking and shuffling through the narrow passage under the weight of their burden. I slid in and moved to the first corner as Andreas slipped in behind me. I saw them in the passage and we waited until they made the second turn, before moving in behind them. I took a second to look inquiringly at Andreas, but he just motioned me ahead. I wanted to save the boy and this seemed to be our best opportunity, but I trusted Andreas. For better or worse we were partners, so I moved on. I peered around the second corner just in time to see the second man hoist himself through the opening that led to the hiding spot below the barrels. I waited a second and then moved up to a spot just before the hole and listened. I could hear them moving around, presumably pulling the boy out from under the barrels. They spoke, but I couldn't make it out, then I heard the soft padding of someone running lightly through the alley. I hoisted myself up to where I could see into the space below the barrels. It was empty, but I could make out the form of a man standing just outside of the opening. I remained as I was, watching, until I saw the man stoop, put the boy over his shoulder, and walk away. At that moment I pushed myself up through the hole and crawled to an opening and looked outside. One of the men was at the alley entrance watching the street while motioning the other man forward. I could see a stock pony hitched to a wagon parked just inside the alley and the man with the boy made his way directly to it and hoisted the boy off of his shoulder to flop with a thud into the wagon bed. The man at the street heard the noise and ran to the wagon as the other man climbed aboard and took up the reins.

Andreas was behind me by this time and we moved into the shadows of the alley. The wagon turned right and headed up the street. We ran full stride to the street and stopped to check the traffic; there was none, aside from the wagon and us. We gave them a two-block lead and then trotted up the dark street, staying off the wooden walkways, but as close to them as possible for the shadow they offered. We were passing buildings we recognized from our stroll back to Aunt Katie's after lunch in the outdoor cafe. We were heading back toward the palace. We slowed our pace and pushed further in to the shadows as we approached the lighted plaza.

We stopped before the corner of a building and stooped low to peer into the square. The wagon had pulled up to the palace gate and was allowed to pass when the men showed their tattoos. I was right about them both having one. The other man had his on the inside of his left bicep. As I watched, the guards checked the street until the wagon was well inside, feeling comfortable they closed the gate. At this time Andreas clutched my shoulder. The touch was urgent and I looked over my shoulder at him. He was pointing toward the palace wall to a point where it joined the city wall. Another guard was there leaning back into the space he occupied. There was another door hidden from casual view by a root of the great crag that jutted into the city. He was calling over his shoulder to someone inside and never took his eyes from us.

We did not wait to see what transpired, but ran full speed at him. It was the only choice we had, given the situation and we made it immediately. I forced the guard inside and Andreas closed the door behind us. I fought the man aside, rather easily I thought, and ran across the room to stop the other man from retreating into the palace and calling an alarm. We disabled them without great noise or effort. Andreas was already undressing his man as I checked outside the second door. It opened on an hallway, empty of people at that time. The hall lead to a stairway and there was no one on it. There was a door near the stairs, but I neither saw nor heard anyone there. I locked the door. We donned the uniforms of our victims and then tied them up behind a stack of supplies. Andreas took pen and ink from a desk nearby and drew a black scorpion upon my breast. Andreas blew upon the ink to help it dry. If the scorpion tattoo upon a woman gave them hesitation, I would use my breasts as a distraction. Andreas then drew a scorpion on his left forearm and blew on it to dry the ink. We were ready. We felt confident that the gate guards had been distracted by their dark business and had not noticed us, since we had been undisturbed since our quick unplanned entrance. We were in it now with no intention of turning back. We wanted answers, so as long as we were there we weren't leaving without them.

I unlocked the door and peered out once more. We were within the defensive wall that ran around the palace and into the rocky crag. Two flights of stairs were straight ahead, running up on the right and down on the left. They were still unoccupied. The door I saw was between the two flights. I assumed it either entered into the courtyard or deeper into the palace proper. I looked to the left and there was the root of the crag at the end of the wall. We could only go to our right.

The dim light of torches set at even intervals along the inner wall afforded us a clear view. We had four choices; the stairs—up or down, the door, or to our right and deeper into the stronghold. We took the last choice. We would be closer to where they had brought the boy in. We might encounter more men, but we had no idea where the boy was being taken. We needed to close as much gap between us as we could.

We were in the first hours of morning; traffic was low when we started out, but we expected it to increase at the changing of the guards. Andreas took the lead. We stayed along the outer wall and in the shadows of the unlit intervals as much as possible. Each time we neared a lit section, we stopped behind wagons or barrels or just stayed to the shadows, and if there were people present we waited to move on. Each time the decision to continue toward the main gate was weightier.

The area within the walls was used as storage. There were wagons both loaded and empty. Under the tarpaulin of one wagon that provided us with cover we found weapons of all sorts. They were standard issue stuff and we each took a sword to add to our uniformed appearance. The occurrence of a wagon full of weapons was not unusual in an armed palace, but these weapons were new and keenly sharpened; perhaps the prince was expecting new recruits.

At the main gate, the wall swept out to accommodate the gatehouse. Three doors and another set of stairs presented us with another decision. Two doors could only lead out to the gate, one on the city side that must enter into the barbican and one on the palace side, the other could only lead directly into the courtyard The stairs lead up and down just as the first set we saw had. We decided to go up. From there we hoped to slip around the gate, get an overview of the palace grounds and then slip back into the wall at the other side of the gate.

I pulled my hood over my head. We had seen no women with the Scorpions yet, so I chose not to call attention to myself if we did encounter anyone. The entrance at the top of the wall was locked but I was able to remedy that quickly. I peered out to see the crenellated wall curve around the upper gatehouse. The gatehouse was a stout tower and the wall had been built out on either side. The top of the tower wall was also crenellated and two guards stood looking over the wall into the courtyard..

The yard was empty. There was no sign of the boy. What danger they expected from within their own stronghold I didn't know, but it told us that they were being ordered to watch for anything from anywhere. There was no way to get by unnoticed, and they had not seen us yet.

We would not be able to go unseen through the courtyard with the guards watching there. We went back and took the stairs to the basement hoping for a way past the gate from there.

We found it there, but we did not take it. We were given a tempting option beyond our ability to resist. Under the gate was a broad causeway running below the courtyard. The courtyard was built up on a great structure of stone arcades. We wondered how many people knew about this. It was part of the original structure, perhaps forgotten by the present day citizens of the city. Kapit had not mentioned it; perhaps that was beyond his protocols. It was in no way hidden from the guards of the palace.

We each took a side of the causeway and made our way toward the palace and away from the gatehouse foundation. We passed a few arched passageways on either side, but we only stopped long enough to insure that we would pass by unnoticed and then we left them behind. We saw no one and nothing until the causeway ended and branched off in two perpendicular arms. We assumed we had come to the main building of the palace and took the right hand branch in search of stairs. There were none leading up or down.

We had no idea when or if our victims from upstairs would be discovered and it made us anxious. At the root of the crag that formed a portion of the city wall we searched for a secret passage, but found nothing. That forced us to return along the same route but we went beyond the main causeway and stayed along the intersecting branch still in search of a stairway. We found a stable complete with three horses and tack, but there was no pony or wagon. We paid no more attention to it than that it was odd, and kept moving until we came again to a dead end at the root of the crag, and again we found no passage.

I rolled my eyes upward in exasperation. That was when I saw a heavy knot of rope against the ceiling. I could not jump and reach it, but if I had I been on horseback it would have been an easy task. Sitting on Andreas's shoulders I was able to reach. I gave a small tug and the knot pulled toward me followed easily by a length of rope as long as my arm. The rope stopped and I pulled to test the weight and to get a rough outline of the size of the door we were about to pull down. The distinct odor of hay and manure hit my nostrils and I suppressed a sneeze. The underground stable made a bit more sense now, and this seemed the only apparent way in or out of the palace grounds from the causeway.

The trap door was a counterbalanced weight mechanism, and since it was not coming down on its own I could reason that nothing or no one stood above us. I pulled down a little more and listened. Andreas struggled beneath me. I heard nothing, so I pulled down enough to get a grip and pull myself partially onto the inclined door. I was in a very vulnerable position, because I could not see all around me, and my weight was not enough to keep the door down. I scrambled to a standing position and balanced the swaying door long enough for Andreas to climb on. I moved slowly up to the floor to get a look around as I drew my sword. Andreas followed and the door floated to a closed position. I saw the locking mechanism in the floor, but left it alone.

We were in the stable and the animals were magnificent. They were spirited and our presence disturbed them in their stalls. We needed to be away from them before they gave us away. There were no stable masters in view so we moved straight ahead toward the sliding doors. It is so much harder to open a sliding door unnoticed. I did not like our prospects anymore than I did when we stumbled into this nightmare. We listened, and the horses snorted or stamped blocking sound from outside. I pressed my ear against the door to listen. Someone was opening the small service door within the big door. We pressed our backs against the second half of the sliding doors and waited. A stable master moved in and talked soothingly to the animals. We remained unnoticed as he moved to the nearest horse.

Andreas had the view of the outside. He grabbed my arm and we moved out onto the cobbled drive under the fore building on the inner ward. Across from us a stone building supported the other end of the roof above us. We were now safe from detection by the guards at the gate.

A door facing us stood wide open but the room beyond was dark and we couldn't make out the contents. A guard post jutted out from the wall next to that door. The door was open and it was currently unoccupied. We had to expect that the guard was doing his rounds around the courtyard.

The fore building was open to allow for traffic wide enough for carriage or wagon along the cobbled drive. To our right the drive ran to the gate. To our left it curved toward the manor house that was the prince's abode.

The wagon that had led us here was parked just off the cobbled drive next to the stone building. Andreas walked up to it and found it empty. They had taken the boy into the stone building or the wagon would have been parked near the manor.

I moved to the open door and found a garrison with all the complements, including rows of bunks and armed men. Most of the occupants were gone except four men standing guard near a set of stairs ran along the back wall that headed down.. The changing of the guard was in progress, we would have to move soon, before the men came back to their beds.

It would be nearly impossible to get by the men guarding the stairs. There was one way though, risky as it was. They were gathered at the top of the stairs, leaving the far end open for assault. If we could get there unnoticed we had only to drop over the side above the lowest stairs and drop down. We moved to the space between the wagon and the building to plan our moves in the dark and wait to see what became of the stable master. We didn't need anyone coming in behind us during our effort. As we whispered our exchange of ideas we lashed our weapons down so they would not move and give us away.

We had a plan in order quickly, and the stable master complied with a timely return. We followed him in and slid into the corner that offered the deepest shadows as the stable master took off his wrap and kicked the door shut behind us. He grumbled something about interrupted sleep and crawled into a bed not far from us. We hunched in the shadows until we heard the stable master snore, then we moved stealthily toward the stairs under cover of the center row of bunks. At the last bunk we squatted down to wait for our moment.

There was no rail on the stairs so it was a matter of speed and stealth. The men were bored and talked to pass the time. When they were all facing the speaker at the far end, and he with his face looking casually about as he spoke; we moved. I was first and leapt side long at the back wall to turn my body down the stairs and land on my feet. I moved to the right and unlashed my sword, but did not draw. Andreas landed just beside me and to my left. He unlashed his sword, but also did not draw. The conversation above us stopped, but then took up again. Our motion through the room might have been detected, but it was swift and silent. It was dismissed as fatigue or a trick of the bad light. I saw no movement toward the stairs from the guards so we turned our attention to our new surroundings.

Andreas had already moved up the narrow passage to an alcove between two closed doors. He stood facing me as I approached, his back pressed against the far wall of the passage. He had his finger before his mouth as a sign for quiet. As I moved closer I heard a sound I mistook for howling wind, but then I heard it for what it was— anguished cries of pain, fear, and sorrow. The sound assailed us from both doors. The hair on our necks and arms stood on end and our spirits grew dark from the sound. Our distance from the cries was indiscernible. Both doors were locked. We could not afford to split up to address both; we had to choose. We chose the door to my right. I pulled lock picks from my belt and in seconds the door eased open. I eased my swords from their sheaths. Beyond was another corridor that began at the door and ran in the same direction as the one we stood in. We saw no guards and so moved in and closed the door softly behind us.

Tallow candles, burning in sconces set near the doors along each wall, left oily rings of soot rising along the wall and onto the ceiling above them. The fat in the tallow left an acrid taste in the air. Andreas drew his sword and we moved purposefully toward the wailing.

We came upon two guards, one surprised us as he came around a corner from a side passage, but we recovered quickly. He too was surprised, but not as quick to recover. We killed him, almost instantly, without plan or intent. It was survival, he was dead and we were uninjured. We regretted the taking of life and said our private prayers over the body. Then Andreas pulled him into the shadows between the circles of candlelight and laid him against the wall with his cloak up over his face. We had a kidnapped boy and a world to save.

The second guard stood at the door that shut off the hall from whatever terror was being carried out beyond. Andreas moved ahead and showed the man his scorpion. The man opened the door a little, but then he saw my face as I came in to the light and pulled it closed. I pulled back my collar to reveal the scorpion drawn upon the curve of my breast. His hesitation was just enough time for Andreas to rap the man's temple with the butt end of his sword. The man slumped. We caught him and pulled him into the shadows where we bound and gagged him before covering him with his cloak.

Back at the door we walked right in and shut the door behind us. The room was a large chamber obviously for the purpose of torture. Two men were at one end looking out of an opening set low in the wall. One man was seated and chained to a chair. The other stood behind him forcing the man in the chair to watch whatever was happening through that opening. The sound of the wailing again pierced at our minds from the other side. The seated man squirmed and yelled defiantly, but his efforts were useless. One Scorp stood behind on either side. Four more stood amongst the various machines of torture scattered throughout the room.

The reaction of the four Scorps was casual at first as we moved into the room until they realized I was a woman and therefore we were not Scorps. Then their reaction was fierce and relentless. Andreas got off one blast of flame at those furthest from us. I took two wrenching hits to my shoulders before I could parry, and although my armor held, I stumbled and took two more hits. One fell hard to my chest and the other pierced my side. I remember thinking 'So much for saving the world' as I gasped for breath and scrambled away for a better defensive posture. Andreas was faring better, but was giving it his all just to deflect the blows being hailed upon him.

The other two guards were well aware of the situation, but they made no move toward us. It was obvious their duty was to protect the man standing behind them. That man if he had turned to see the disturbance was now refocused on the man in the chair.

I maneuvered myself between two torture machines and managed a cat and mouse game for a few moments. I was a clever mouse and was able to get in a couple of substantial hits upon each man. Just before I was about to lose my small advantage I tipped the table on one man and sent him stumbling. I jumped over the fallen table just as the other man thrust his sword toward me. I was not there to receive the thrust and his momentum caused him to stumble too. I ran and spun passed the first stumbling guard getting in two more slashing attacks across his midsection just below the fauld piece that protected his abdomen. He buckled over while he still stumbled backward. I stopped long enough to bring the butt of both swords down hard upon the crown of his head. His feet went out from under him and he fell motionless. I do not know if I killed him, there was no time to check.

My other adversary had regained his footing and was bearing down on me with great intent. I did not know how Andreas was faring at that point. The guard I faced was talented with a weapon, dexterous, and strong. He probably outweighed me by a hundred pounds. We were in an open area of the floor with nothing for me to use to gain any protection so I fought. I had to be faster than him to hold my ground, but I was feeling the pain of the pierce to my side and the arm I had wounded before coming to Behlanna was aching and beginning to weaken. A blood-curdling scream shook the air around us and I prayed that it was not Andreas, until I realized that it was from the room beyond the two men and the guards at the back of the room. Someone beyond that opening was being tortured as we fought! That gave me renewed strength and I went at my attacker with a flurry of spinning blades. I don't know how many blows I landed or missed, but he soon fell and begged for mercy. I did not give it.

I turned to see Andreas run one of his attackers through. The two guards at the back moved forward, but did not leave their posts. Andreas saw me and made a move that turned his opponent's back to me. I sighed, it was not honorable, but I saw the thick dark blood seeping from Andreas's side and I saw the weariness of his attack. I ran forward and thrust both swords into the man's back. He gasped his last breath and fell from my weapons. Andreas stepped back. We exchanged a glance. He conveyed great pain, but he was resolved to the task at hand.

I stepped in front of him and we both turned to see the two guards closer to us, battle ready, but not advancing. The man that stood behind the chair had turned and stood next to the chair with both arms raised before him. In his hands he held a silver bound scroll case of vast proportions. Great brass caps closed the ends and tooled steel clasped it all together. His muscular arms shook under the weight of it. In his belt he had a steel mace with a spiked head. I could not make out his features in the dim flickering of light. I heard

Andreas muttering an incantation behind me, and then the man spoke.

"Is this what you seek?" He heaved the scroll to land at the feet of the guard furthest from him. "Or this, perhaps?" He heaved the chair over backwards; we could now see the man chained to it. His face was wet from tears and contorted in fear and sorrow both. His breathing was wracked with sobbing. "Or perhaps it is me you want." He leaped through the opening and we heard his next words shouted back to us as he made his escape. "Or perhaps you seek what lies on this side."

The two guards leapt forward and Andreas let go his spell. Perhaps it was all the excitement, but I had never seen him release a blast of fire with such force before. The two men went down, burned, burning, and unconscious. I ran for the scroll to kick it out of the flames, but it was unscarred, even though the floor around it was charred.

I turned to show Andreas, but he was in a heap on the floor. My heart sank, and I nearly went to my knees. I ran to him and knelt beside him. He was alive and conscious, but just barely. "Go to him quickly." He said, and made a feeble motion to the man still chained to the chair. "Let me rest a moment."

I did as I was told, we had to be away quickly, and from the look of it I had three wounded men to see out. I found a hammer amongst the items hung upon the walls and used it to pound out the stake that pinned the links of chain around the man. "Bless you, bless you," He said, and then, "Please forgive me." It was then that I saw his tattered clothes were the robes of a holy man.

"Are you the Priest of Nauticus?"

"I am."

"Do you know where you are?"

"No idea."

"The palace in Behlanna." The priest shook his head in confusion. "I was not given your name. What can I call you?"

"I am Father Gan."

"We can talk later. Finding you is a bit of a surprise, but we have to get out of here. We can't go back the way we came now. Can you get us out of here?"

He nodded and picked himself up off the floor. "They killed him I'm sure; that evil bastard. I gave him what he wanted and they killed him anyway." He spoke through tears.

"You mean…" I motioned toward the opening. The Priest nodded.

"They made you watch?"

"They knew it would break me; to watch a child suffer. I could not let the child die to keep a secret. It was as if I held the knife myself. Then when you came in he signaled and his henchman killed the boy. It was my only chance to save the child, to absolve myself of a crime, but he killed him still. I knew it, but tried to deny it. I prayed God would stay his hand, but... Perhaps the retrieval of the scroll was the more important thing in God's judgment."

"Well we must deal with these consequences no matter what now. Can you get us out of here; away from the garrison?"

"I will try. I do not know the entire palace, but I was here as a dignitary once years ago, and with what I know of the dungeon—perhaps."

"See to my friend and I will bring the child."

"No, we will go through there. See to the child and I will bring your friend and the scroll."

The boy was dead and he was cut many places. Many had been healed, and cut again and again, just to sustain his misery, or perhaps to trick the priest. I broke the chains that bound him to the table with the hammer, and pulled him onto my shoulders. The Priest helped Andreas through the opening, and in turn Andreas gave a helping hand to the Priest. Andreas was white, and a cold sweat glistened on his brow.

"Can you fight?" I asked him.

"If need be. Father Gan will carry the scroll and fight too if he must." I looked at the father to assess his strength and noticed that he had a cudgel in his belt. Something he had retrieved from the other room.

"Who was that man, Father?"

"Polk, Captain of the Guard."

"Does he act for the prince?"

"I have not seen the prince since I was brought here, I don't know."

"I will lead, Father and you will follow me. Whisper to me the directions we will take and I will see that we are clear. Hold on tight to that scroll and fight only if you must. That scroll is the most important thing in all of our lives right now. Andreas will take up the rear and watch our backs. If we should fall you must try to get the scroll to Kapit at the Stalkers Society. I know you know him, do not pretend you don't. He will see to the protection of the scroll, and you will have some input as the keeper. So tell me now, which way we should go, we have delayed long enough."

The Priest's route took us out the door of that room and into another hall that traveled back in the direction that we had taken to arrive at the priest's rescue— back toward the garrison. When I questioned him he assured me he had seen other stronghold people go this route. We followed, passing many doors along the way. One was the door to Father Gan's cell. I was sure another was the door opposite the one we had chosen at the base of the garrison steps. We traveled beyond the garrison to a dead end.

"Father?"

"I know that others came this way."

"How do you know?"

"In all my time of listening to people pass through these halls I was sure that I had a lay of the place. I would have expected a door right here. I must have miscalculated and we are already passed it."

The father made sense. I was laid up once and was cared for in an abbey. I had listened to the passing by of the occupants for days, and when I left I found my own way out. "Look for us Andreas, will you? I'll stand watch"

Andreas took my place, and I moved to his place to guard our backs. Soon I heard a distinct clack and looked back to see a great stone slab pop open. Andreas looked through and then motioned us on. I passed through with Father Gan close behind. We moved along a wall in a dark corridor. Andreas closed the door, and sealed it with a spell he used for such things.

"Where to now, Father?" I asked.

"I'm afraid I do not know that, but we are beyond the garrison I think."

"Yes we are, Father, and though that makes me feel better we are not safe yet."

Andreas came up and stood beside me. "I think I know where we are. Doesn't this look like that passage we took off of that main causeway?"

"The one where we turned around. Yes, yes it does. So we missed a more direct way in. Let's not forget that should we have to return."

"I do not want to return to this place but I would like to know what this is all for. They must stage the horses here for defense, or parades or something; all along that causeway and up and down these wide halls."

"I can smell horse in the air."

"Why else would they have that door ramp from the stable? Where do you think all of those horses go in and out?"

"It could be anywhere from here."

"It could, but we didn't see anywhere obvious, and the garrison is just beyond that door."

"So you think that the way out would be close to the garrison?"

"Yes. They lead the horses up, the soldiers climb on, and away they go, but where? My guess is there." Andreas pointed at a dead end, the one that had turned us around earlier. The wall was about twenty feet wide, nearly twice as tall, and made of stone. I was doubtful, but Andreas had already moved to the wall to begin his search for some mechanism. We had searched before and been unsuccessful. I looked up, somewhat hoping to find another door like that that led us into the stable, but there was none. Father Gan clutched the scroll and looked anxious.

I put the body of the homeless boy on the floor and stretched to limber my shoulders. Then I went to Father Gan and tried to calm him. He was not a fighting man, and I took the moment to give him some advice. While we talked Andreas searched, but he found nothing.

"We go back the way we came then." I announced. Andreas and the Father lifted the boy back onto my shoulders and we fell into order and trotted along. I was growing nervous myself. Our escape had seemed too easy. I was expecting an ambush. To go back out the way we came in was risky. By now Polk must have alerted his men and in their search for us they were likely to find how we had gained our entrance. They would expect us to return by a familiar route, and would have guards posted there to await our return. "Back the way we came," I repeated under my breath. I thought to myself. *'I hate this town, I've been rustled around like a farm animal since I arrived and now I walk to my slaughter.'*

We came to the intersection of the main causeway, but we did not turn onto it until we had crossed it, staying in the shadows along the back wall. We turned into the shadows under the arcade of the main causeway and made our way to the stairs just below the main gate. I saw a sentry step off the stairs and peer in our direction. I pushed the father against the wall and Andreas knew what that meant and did like wise. I could not press myself into the shadows at the wall with the boy upon my back so I crouched low and watched. The sentry moved toward us. Why he did not call out I do not know. Perhaps he did not want to sound like a frightened boy if what he thought he saw proved to be nothing. Andreas and the Father were making a stealthy retreat behind me. I let the weight of the boy's body roll off my right shoulder and lean against the wall. I crawled backwards until I felt I was far enough away to stand and moved toward the nearest support pillar. I slid up along the pillar and looked around for Andreas and Father Gan. Andreas was also behind a pillar waiting for me to look his way. He motioned that he would be making his way around to the other side of the causeway. I had to strain to see Father Gan; he was further back along the wall. He held his cudgel in his right hand and tucked the scroll under his left arm.

The sentry saw the boy lying in a heap and trotted cautiously forward; weapon in hand. He stopped a moment to check the body and as he did I moved up three pillars along the outside of the walk that ran alongside the causeway. I was three pillars away when he stood up. I tucked away just in time and he did not see me. I looked for Andreas and to my surprise he was still moving up deep in the shadows of the other walkway directly across from me. He pointed at me, motioned with a finger across his neck, and then pointed toward the sentry. I could see from where he had pointed that the sentry must have moved closer to me; another move I had not expected. I risked a look around the pillar and saw him moving toward the causeway. I waited until I saw the tip of his toe come out from behind the pillar and I slid around to the other side of my pillar.

I thought he would have gone back for some support before moving on alone, but the sight of a dead boy didn't seem to intimidate him. He moved slowly, scanning both sides of the causeway. There was no way I could get up behind him to wrestle him down, or kill him as Andreas would like, without being seen. I had lost the advantage I was trying to gain when I slid behind the pillar rather than attacking right away. So now I waited until he moved out of sight behind another pillar and then I moved to the next one watching his moves until I saw an opportunity. When he took a hesitant step toward Father Gan's location, then another. I looked for Andreas but did not see him. The sentry took another step and was blocked from my view. I moved up a pillar. Father Gan was slowly raising his cudgel with a trembling hand. The sentry was determined now and walked straight to the father.

"I know you, what are doing here?" The sentry growled.

I moved into the causeway, and closed the distance of the final two pillars that separated us at a run. The man had Father Gan by the wrist, and the cudgel fell from his helpless hand. We needed quiet, so I had to dispatch the sentry swiftly. I moved forward, prepared to slit his throat, but the glance Father Gan leveled at me over the sentry's shoulder gave me away.

The Sentry reeled around yanking the good father with him. The scroll fell out from under Father Gan's arm. I swiped my dagger at his throat anyway, but he was quick and avoided it. He pulled Father Gan in front of him, and we had a stand off. No one spoke. My greatest fear was that he would call out before I could subdue or kill him. Then suddenly there was a rush of air and an invisible force rammed the sentry from behind. He fell into Father Gan and they both fell to the ground. I jumped upon the sentry and killed him with little more noise than his fall had made.

Andreas came up and together we dragged the man to the intersection and dumped his body around the corner. We took his weapons, a dagger and a broadsword to give to Father Gan.

"Nice Spell." I said quietly as we trotted back. "How long have you been working on that one?"

"I had the thought of it the day those bandits attacked us, and as you know I've had no time for practice. That was her maiden voyage."

"Nice."

"I had hoped to take him out with it, but I held back too much, not wanting to take you and the father with him."

"I'm still impressed."

"Nice of you to say so, now get us the hell out of here."

We gave the weapons to the priest who had already retrieved the scroll and was holding on tighter than ever. "No time for a lesson father, just do the best you can. We'll be right here with you."

We ran now, back along the walkway to the boy's body, but this time Andreas took him. Although we were both wounded I was the more able bodied fighter at that time and we could not afford for me to be hindered. We moved forward to just outside the stairway entrance. We saw no one so we moved into the stairwell and out of the causeway. I listened at the door at the top and heard two muffled voices. I held up two fingers and drew two daggers. They were not directly outside the door, the dirty buggers. I would have to move out and risk encounter until I made their position. I drew my hood up, but threw my cloak back so that the scorpion could be seen on my breast, Father Gan and Andreas stayed below in the stair well.

I opened the door and walked out as if I belonged. I was turning toward the voices, when one of them spoke again. "It ain't time to switch ye... Hey wait a..." I refused to wait and sank my first dagger between a rib and into his lung. The other guard was rushing me and I obliged him similarly. After finding no other occupants I pulled the daggers from them and put them out of their misery. The area was now well lit with additional lanthorns, so I only pulled the bodies out of the way of direct traffic, extinguished the lanthorns but left the torches, and then I went back for Andreas and Father Gan.

We took to the shadows as soon as we were away from the light. Under the guttering torches we trotted along as best we could. Andreas was struggling from pain and loss of blood. We saw two more Scorps approaching before they saw us and we were able to make it to the shelter of a supply wagon. We waited until they passed by and were lost from sight before we continued on. I took the boy from Andreas again and drew one sword instead of using my daggers. We ran. Those last two Scorps would soon find two dead comrades. Our luck was running low.

We made it to the supply room that was our first point of entry when a shout went up from down the corridor. There was no doubt they had found the bodies. I reached to open the door, but it was ripped open by a large Scorp with the guards we had overpowered directly behind him. They were coming to answer the shout that had just gone up. I lunged immediately with my sword, he still held onto the door, and I was able to stab him under the arm. Surprise and pain caused him to jump back into his partners. I beat them back and we gained access. Andreas locked the door behind us and then ushered Father Gan to the exit while I maneuvered our foes away from it. The quarters were close, and the battle did not go well. I kept the three Scorps away while Andreas worked to unlock the door, but I had been hit, slashed and stabbed too many times to number. It would have been worse had I not been carrying the boy. I prayed the gods would forgive me.

I felt cold blood streaming down my neck from a blow to my head. Then I heard a pop and a rush of wind. I knew it was Andreas's spell so I jumped back and they fell away from me. We sprang through the door. I pushed it shut even as Andreas muttered his spell to seal it. The closing and the sealing were simultaneous.

We stopped to catch our breath a moment. As I leaned forward the blood from my wounds and what was left to bleed from the boy pooled around me. Andreas was at the point of the crag root watching for any approach from the gate or the city. Father Gan came and took my arm, "Can you continue?"

"What other choice do I have?"

"The way is clear, but we must move now."

We moved; blood trail and all. Andreas was talking as we ran, but I couldn't make it out. I could only concentrate on moving, that is until I fell. I vaguely remember Andreas picking me up and Father Gan placing the scroll upon my chest. I remember only snippets of time after that, until I woke up on the cold cobbles of the homeless enclave.

It was morning. I was lying near a fire wrapped like a cocoon in many blankets. Chills wracked me nonetheless and I fought to suppress waves of nausea. I could not see Andreas, but Father Gan was nearby talking quietly to two men on the other side of the fire. He held the scroll under his arm; no one paid it any mind. It belonged there with the

God's man, so it was its own camouflage. A woman noticed me looking around and knelt down beside me. "Your friend has gone to cover your tracks, we sent some men along with him. They should be back soon." I thanked her and asked her to sit me up. She helped me to a wall, sat me against it, and wrapped the blankets around me again. The bandages wrapped on various parts of my body were blood soaked and stank. They needed changing, but I said nothing. These people had already done all they could for me.

Across the enclave a man and woman stood away from the main gathering of people. She cried inconsolably, the man held his arms around her and rubbed her back absently. I knew that it was their son that we had brought back. Father Gan came to sit with me, and told me Andreas had led us here, afraid that I would die if we had pushed on to Kapit's. The people had seen to our wounds and then Andreas went with two of the men who worked for the city cleaning the streets of manure. They had a wagon with a vat of water and each morning they began three trips around the city sweeping and hosing the city streets. The clumps of manure were shoveled into the wagon and used as fertilizer on the palace gardens. This morning their route began at the entrance to the enclave and wound through the city toward the palace.

The rising suns brightened the enclave and the air lost some chill, but still I shivered. Father Gan brought me to the fire and sat me down on an up side down pail. He gave me the scroll and I wrapped it in the blankets with me. An old woman brought me a potato cooked upon the fire but the smell of it turned my stomach and I lost my fight with nausea. Father Gan stoked the fire and was adding a third log when Andreas returned.

We were happy to see each other and we embraced. "We saw to it that our trail was removed, at least most of it," Andreas said.

"Father Gan told me."

"We are not safe here. The Scorps will know where the boy came from, and they will look for us here. These people are only safe if we are not here when they do. Sorrell is waiting outside to bring us back, apparently one of Kapit's people was aware of our situation and reported."

"Let's go then." I stood up and nearly swooned. "Where are all my things?"

"I have your weapons; your armor was not worth saving. I got rid of it in the city dump. Wrap a blanket around yourself and let's go. Can you carry the scroll?"

I nodded, "But I haven't thanked these people."

"Do it on the way out."

I did just that.

I had trouble keeping up with the pace that Sorrell set for us; the fever was in me and wouldn't let me go. I doubt that I could retrace our steps, but we were soon back in our suite. Andreas put me to bed. I kissed him; I think I said, "I love you." Perhaps it was just a nightmare. Andreas never said anything about it, and I certainly wasn't going to mention it.

When I woke Andreas was sitting on my bedside. I never saw him look so beautiful. He was tired but when I opened my eyes, his lit up and he stroked my cheek. "Welcome back, Sunshine." There was a fire in the room and it was dark outside, so I knew that I had slept through the day, but I was surprised when Andreas informed me that it had been two days and was approaching the morning of the third. I had some pain, but not what I had expected and my fever was gone. There had been poison on one of the blades I had been unable to fend off. Andreas, Father Gan, and Kapit's own physician had taken turns tending to me. Andreas told me that Kapit and Father Gan had been around quite often. Of course they didn't say it, but they were more impatient to know when we would go after Captain Polk of the City Guard on his quest to open the Gates of Hell than they were concerned about my personal pain. Looking back—I understand. They had fed me broth, tea, and tonic to revitalize my blood, but I remembered none of it. He told me that it was touch and go for the first day, but then my fever broke and it was just a matter of time. Andreas's own wounds were mending well, he told me, and I had no reason to doubt him.

Andreas briefed me on the intelligence that Kapit and his spies had gathered about our foray into the palace. "We already know that the man that got away from us was the Captain of the Scorpions. A man called only by one name; Polk. Polk has not been seen at the palace since that night. One of Kapit's men saw two riders riding away north from the city just before daybreak. One of them was Polk, the other was not known to him. It was learned they did not leave by the gate, since other Kapit men were there and never saw them."

"Are we sure that we can trust Kapit's men?"

Andreas shrugged, "These men were just on their regular assignments, and knew nothing of our foray. We now believe that Polk stole the scroll and was attempting to learn it's secrets by torturing Father Gan when Eindal played into his hands.

"Polk was the one who arranged the heist at Nauticus temple, or even performed it. Then Eindal acting as an agent for Kapit's secret sect heisted it from him."

"If that's true why would Eindal risk coming into town?"

"Do you remember what Moon told us? Perhaps Eindal didn't know it was Polk, perhaps it was an old man with a hunch and a cane, or perhaps, since Eindal seemed to have brains and Moon did not, the disguise was something more believable."

"Maybe a Nauticus Templar, someone strong enough, armored enough to get through the temple, and someone Gan would trust. Did anyone ask Gan about that?" I asked.

"He said a Templar got him out of the temple, and there was a face off with some men on the shore, but then he was hit from behind and ended up in the palace dungeons. He thought the Templar met a similar fate, or worse. But, how did you know?"

"Maybe I heard you all talking while I slept."

"Maybe it was that crazy instinct of yours."

"Maybe. Let's talk to Gan."

"Let's."

My speculation was confirmed and Gan was ashamed for having fallen so easily into Polk's trap. No one had any idea who the accomplice he escaped with was.

So we knew Polk and his partner had headed north. What did the prince know if anything? Kapit volunteered to find out, personally. Polk had access to the scroll we rescued for nearly two months; it was likely that he had gleaned information about the locations of the other two scrolls. Father Gan believed that Polk was more interested in the master scroll. Polk seemed to know that there was a faction against him, so if he had the master he could pick off the members of the faction one by one as they came to him and retrieve what scrolls they had or seek them out as it suited him. The torture that Father Gan had endured had been successful and Polk now knew where the master scroll was and was certainly on his way to obtain it.

We had a choice, follow Polk and hope he led us to the other two scrolls, or see what Gan knew and try to get the other scrolls first. Gan needed time to recall his teachings and how they related to the scroll and he wanted to study the scroll to confirm it all. I needed time to heal. This would all take time, and that was an expensive luxury.

In the mean time Andreas kept busy ordering the supplies we would need for such an extended quest. I sat near the fireplace and kept warm. Kapit fawned over me every waking hour with foods and drinks of every kind; anything he could think of to strengthen me from my loss of blood. I began to feel stronger on my second day. By then the parlor had become something of a warehouse. Piled in separate corners of the room was everything for cave delving: lanterns, ropes, spikes, and hammers. Another corner was piled high with rations, water skins, cheese, fruit and wine. Father Gan insisted on the wine; it was a blood tonic after all. Medicines and bandages were stacked in another corner, and a stack of hammocks and bedrolls was in another. In the center of the room was a pile of useful items: a new suit of chain mail for me, a new pair of boots for each of us, honing stones, daggers, a long bow for each of us, and six quivers with twenty arrows each, back packs larger than any I had ever seen, scribes and parchment with metal tubes to keep it all in, for maps, notes and messages, cold weather gear: fur coats, boots and mittens all in a trunk. Kapit saw to every delivery.

On the third day Sorrel and Angus came in and under Andreas's instruction the warehouse was cleared out. Meanwhile, Kapit was seeing to a staging point away from the prying eyes of the Scorpion Guard. He had seen to four horses for us. They were mountain bred horses, strong and agile.

Five days of inactivity left me stiff so Andreas helped me to gear up. I now had three swords, my old standards at each hip and a spare; the one I had taken from the Scorpion stronghold strapped on my back. Andreas made sure that my existing bandolier had any missing daggers replaced and he had ordered another so I was bristling with fourteen throwing daggers crisscrossed over my chest. Andreas now had two swords; his old standard and the one he had taken from the Scorps, but he had a new weapon strapped to his back, it was much like a staff— a weapon that Andreas loved and was quite good at, but it was made of iron and each end was fitted with a double edged sword blade. I smiled at his ingenuity. We strapped on new pouch belts, and filled them with a day ration of food, lock picking tools, flint and tinderboxes and a kit I had put together for each of us for the maintenance of our weapons. We had retained our personal packs and filled them with the tools of our trade. Andreas filled his with what he called med kits, little packets of medicines and bandages that he had put together from the separate components once stacked in a corner, and a change of clothes. My pack wasn't nearly as important as his. It held, only a change of clothes and my dress and sash for in town. I hoped to fill it with loot gained from our quest later.

We were checking each other's chinches and buckles when Kapit came to escort us to our staging area. As was usual in this compound of buildings we took a twisted way through many secret passages and ended up in the low basement of a stable against the North wall of the city. The basement and the stairs heading up were lined with Kapit's people, heavily armed and looking serious. Father Gan stood in the center of the room pouring over a scroll written in his own hand. Kapit moved to stand behind him and held the lantern high so that we could all see the writing on the scroll.

Gan spoke to us in hushed tones. "These are my own notes recreated from memory with help from the scroll we retrieved from Master Polk. I can only translate the music in my head, but I don't have a musician's ear. Our scroll is the Valkyries' Lament, one of the three scrolls. The fourth scroll, the master, gives the words of power that release the evil one's bindings. It also has the words that will reverse the spell and bind him. Gan's voice caught and he lowered his gaze. "That is the information I gave to Polk at my darkest moment. If he finds the fourth scroll he will have the words to unbind Malisgalar, The Father of Darkness —The Evil One. What I didn't tell him is that the music ignites the power of the words, or that the harmonies played together, but apart from the entire composition can destroy him.

We do not believe Polk can open that scroll without the musical keys hidden within the other three scrolls, but we don't know that for sure. If he does find a way The Evil One would be free but still locked behind the nine gates of Hell. He would be able to command the forces there once again, plotting and training until the gate keys were obtained— waiting for his time. Only three gates need be open. Three levels of Hell converge at each of nine gates. Opening only one gate will unleash dark forces upon mortal man. The march would be slowed, but they would march.

"These are our safe guards. The knowledge of the gates is only contained within the three scrolls. I don't see how anyone could know the locations without them. The master scroll must be unlocked, to take the knowledge from it. The key to unlocking the master scroll; Scroll Dominus is the musical codes found within the other three. Those notes, once they are revealed must be played precisely or the scroll will not open. We believe there maybe other musical codes within the scores that can be used to open, or if necessary lock the nine gates of Hell. The location of Scroll Dominus is hidden with in the three scrolls, so all scrolls must be obtained before gaining that knowledge.

"Assume that Polk gained enough knowledge of this scroll to reveal the first melody. He will prove a great adversary indeed if he could gain a battalion of demons from behind those gates. But, he needs the location as well as the melody and I don't believe he possessed the scroll long enough to determine both. We— that is, Kapit and I believe that you should go after the second scroll."

As Gan spoke a thought hit me. "Are we sure this scroll is not a fake meant to throw us off?"

"We—that is the sect, have examined this possibility and under every test we believe that it is authentic. Let me show you." He took the scroll from Kapit who had until now kept it hidden below the folds of his vast robe. He opened it and began to unroll a portion of it. "As you can see the decorative borders are very detailed and elaborate. It would take years to reproduce even one." The borders were indeed beautiful and we were sure that would be enough to help us identify the others.

"Within the border are the hidden pictographs that hold more of the secret that we are still trying to unravel. We are researching our options; trying to find a way to reseal any of the three gates should he succeed at opening them. What would escape we cannot be certain of. We are also— I grieve to say it— preparing our allies for the possibility of war should any of us fail."

"But Polk would still know the musical key and could return to open them again." Kapit added.

"Yes," Gan eagerly agreed, "but if we get the second scroll before Polk we can gain the melody of the second Key of Gates before him, and move to protect those three levels. If he is ahead of us now we would only lose time trying to find him first, and then he may gain the second scroll before we do."

"You said that you revealed what the master scroll is, he must believe that he has a way to open it, or at least he knows the location of the other two. Why else would he give up this scroll? Do we know if the master scroll is safe?"

"We do not, it is a great chink in our armor that we must call upon ancient memories and writings to recall it, and yet it is that very thing that keeps it hidden from Polk. We must protect the scrolls that we know." Kapit announced.

Father Gan's shoulders slumped and he shook his hanging head. "There is only this time; it is all we are given and we must act now or all is certainly lost. Your talent must carry the hope we have to keep evil from our world. We search for Polk even now, but he is still lost to us. Ahead of you, or behind— we need to gain some advantage and so

129

reluctantly this must be our course." He looked to meet our eyes and held our gaze until we nodded our agreement. "May your Gods be with you," he said. An odd comment from a man devoted to only one God. He took my hand in both of his and I knew that he understood the power behind his words.

"And yours with you," I said.

Kapit chimed in to hurry us along. "The pictographs of this scroll lead to the piece entitled, The One King." He took up the scroll, carefully rolling it and placing it back into its case. "It lies in a chasm deep in The Stormy Mountains on Winter Top Island. There is no access from below. The wind of the chasm is so strong it can blow a man skyward. It sweeps down around the jagged peaks and surges down the mountains to gather in the chasm, where it swirls around and gathers force against itself. This all creates an extraordinary updraft. It is a natural phenomenon and an incredible dilemma for anyone wanting to descend into the chasm. I have no advice for you as to how to get down, but your resourcefulness got you this job. I have every confidence that you will find a way. Once you have The One King in your possession you should be able to decipher the whereabouts of the next scroll.

"Look for a man called Egidio on the quayside in Sandhitch. Give him this medallion and he will take you to the island, and wait for you if you ask him. I saved his daughter from a compromising situation many years ago. He gave me this trinket and told me that should I ever need a favor in return that I should return this to him and he would do all he could, no questions asked. He is a good and peaceful man, and deserves respect so be sure that he gets it.

I never thought I would need the repayment. I'll probably owe him after this.

"When you get the second scroll, study them both at every chance. When you learn their cunning codes you will be able to find your way to the other scrolls, and have some idea what lies ahead. Now you must go. Our time is already short and we are wasting what we have. Godspeed to you." He hugged us each heartily then led us upstairs.

His people there opened the door and moved up to secure the stable. We moved in and found two horses saddled and stomping at the bit, two pack horses stood at the ready in a large stall. Each of the riding horses had large saddlebags and a pack across their rumps. One packhorse was laden with a trunk and one of the large packs strapped at each side. The other had a large pack strapped to each side and one across her rump. Each horse seemed capable of carrying rider or burden with equal ease.

Kapit wedged a leather bundle between the saddle and bedroll on the grey rider. "This," he said, "is the first scroll. Guard it well. The chest there is full of gold and jewels use it as you need to, but should you fall prey to bandits, the chest is your decoy, let it go."

"The dapple horse is called Grey Aria. He is a faithful and wise mount, and an uncanny judge of character. Aria means wisdom in our ancient tongue. Trust him. The black is called Dark Corydon. Corydon means warrior in the old language. He will carry you into battle if you need him to. He is well trained and capable, agile and swift. Either can carry you swiftly away from most any other horse in these lands so do not forget that. The other two are trained for riding, but they are young and inexperienced. Treat these beasts well and they will return the service tenfold, I guarantee you."

We sat our mounts. Andreas on Corydon and I on Aria, but the animals did the choosing. Each of us led a packhorse as we rode out through the back wall of the stable and under cover of darkness headed northwest from Behlanna toward Sandhitch. No Behlanna guard called out or tried to stop us so we plodded on as quietly as we could with four large beasts. When we were safely away we took the pace to a trot across the dark landscape. We skirted the mountain cliffs that were the north wall of the city until they gradually became rolling hills. That undulating landscape soon turned to a gradual slope that tipped away to the north in a vast span of grassland. We rode on until the sun rose over the eastern slopes and we could see the ocean. By mid-day we could see Sandhitch; a tiny cluster of shacks and shanties on the coast. We rested on the open plain overlooking the village to eat and drink and water the horses from water poured from our water skins into our cupped hands. We let them take all that was left. They had carried us far in one night. We would see to their care at a stable in town.

The ride into town was pleasant. The sea air had been tangible during the night, but now as we rode down to the coast it filled my senses. My heart raced and my spirit filled with awe at the nature of life. Often I found when I came to the sea that it had an effect on me. When I made my way back inland I would be melancholy, until once away from the salt air again I would smell the rich earth and my spirit would again be moved by nature's wonder. I'm such a mawkish fool sometimes.

The town was a mangled mass of sun baked wooden buildings and boats, cork and fishing net. In town the reek of the fish market overpowered the smell of the sea. Two ships were docked, one on either side of the main pier used for trade ships. Other smaller piers with smaller crafts jutted into the water at random spots along the wharf. There was only a hostel for lodging, a crooked building with a sagging porch and roof that must have leaked in even a small rain. The stable was no more than a row of pens with a lean-to roof and wooden troughs for food and water, but it was in good repair. The stable boy slept in one of the freshly raked and re-bedded stalls. One horse munched the new hay in the trough. He was combed and dry. So, the stable seemed to be the one well-kept place in town.

We passed the hostel and stable, not wanting to leave the horses in a lean to and went straight out to the quayside in search of Egidio. Kapit's description was no help to us. Everyman on the wharf was dark and weathered and had hair and beard in various stages of shag and grizzle. We could categorize by age, but that was as close as we could get. I let Andreas take the lead as we often do when feeling our way through the sensibilities of the local citizenry. He asked politely as to Egidio's whereabouts, and after a thorough look over from the resident a quick outstretched arm and a pointed index finger answered us. We followed his 'directions' and saw a man sitting on the deck of one of the larger fishing boats mending his nets. We waved goodbye to the 'friendly' local and rode over to the boat.

Again, I let Andreas take the lead.

"Egidio?"

Egidio did not look up. "Who wants to know?"

"Kapit sent us." Andreas flipped the medallion onto the deck. When Egidio looked up, Andreas asked in his sweetest voice: "How soon can you take us to Winter Top?"

·~· Chapter Three ·~·

I love the sea. The vast expanse of it always makes me feel like the universe belongs to me rather than I belong to the universe. I like that I am small against it but the might of it fills me and makes me feel colossal. So it was an injustice of nature that my equilibrium only operated properly on land. The vast undulating expanse made me feel like the universe had just parked in my belly and needed a way out. I was small all right— a tiny speck of retching life on a constantly bobbing boat that was itself a speck upon the water. And that speck was a day's sail from our destination and we were only two hours out from Sandhitch.

A further injustice was that Andreas who only tolerated nature felt no ill effects at all. He stood on the deck with the wind in his hair and his hands clasped behind his back taking it all in. I would have thought he looked majestic against such a backdrop, if his very presence hadn't been opposing the dip of the boat upon the water against the rise and fall of the never-ending sea. I had no time to tell him that he should stand else where for sake of my weakness before my weakness overtook me and I was again hanging over the starboard rail.

I was sure that Andreas was analyzing the potential energy he could draw from the sea and use as a spell of magic. I was equally sure that his analysis had nothing to do with making me feel better. If I had been able to speak I would have told him what a callous cad I thought he was.

I don't know how long we stayed that way, but the beast I called a partner finally came over to see about me. "Is there anything I can do?" He asked in a quiet tone.

"Uhn," I replied, which meant: "About time you heartless bastard!"

"A blanket maybe?"

I shook my head positively and groaned, which meant: "That's the least you can do after swaying in front of me all day."

He went below to the small cabin we shared with Egidio and returned quickly with not one but two blankets. He wrapped one around me and put the other on the deck so that he could sit upon it.

"Maybe you'll be better off sleeping on deck tonight where at least you'll have fresh air. I'll sleep right here in case you need me."

My partner is such a sweet man.

***

By daybreak I was feeling better. I was shaky and tired, but my stomach was settling down and my equilibrium was straightening out. I did not sleep well for obvious reasons, and Andreas did no better for looking after me. Egidio informed us that we were making good time on what he called calm seas. We would make Winter Top by mid day. Andreas and Egidio ate on the deck and we watched for land. Knowing where to look, Egidio called out first. All we saw was a white swirl of cloud, but as we came in closer we could see the mountain peaks that ringed the island. When we moved closer still, an ancient cinder cone became visible at the center of the island. It towered above the rest and the cloud that veiled the island emanated from it.

Egidio steered the ship toward the southern end of the island and found a place to anchor. We let the loading ramp out into the water, unloaded the horses, and waded together to the shore. The animals went across the sand to the grasses that grew there and ate heartily. Andreas gave them fresh water from a small cask while I looked for a way into the mountains. I followed a trail for a couple of miles and when it still looked good for as far as I could see, I returned to Andreas. We lead the horses up the trail to the point at which I had left it. The trail there opened up over a landscape of scrub and rock. We mounted and rode slowly side-by-side. The way wound through the juts of rock and over the steep sloping shoulders of the mountains. Winter Top towered above it all and the clouds were in a swirl above her. The snow swept off the clouds in veils of soft white and the air grew icy. We stopped long enough to wrap ourselves in fur-lined gear and then we moved on.

We wound up through the mountains and stopped to take in the scenery that surrounded Winter Top. We sat astride Grey Aria and Dark Corydon looking across a wide valley between the ring of mountains on which we rested and the crater called Winter Top. The stark grey lines of cold stone, black shadows, and white sky was overwhelming beautiful against the soft violet backdrop of the surrounding mountains. I'd never seen mountains so magnificent. The clouds below us in the valley swirled gradually up the sides of Winter Top and then spun in a flourish before being sucked down into the crater. In the center of the crater a tower of cloud shot up with the force of a cyclone to crash into the ceiling of the atmosphere and spread out into the cloud cover. The clouds were in turn sucked back down into the whirl of winds in the valley. The scene repeated perpetually.

We made our way down the mountain ring until we were just above the valley winds. We stayed the night there, and in the morning we made a sling for the scroll. I wore it across my left shoulder so that it hung tight against my waist just behind the sword at my right side. We left the four horses to graze in the valley.

We tied back our hair so that we could see, and tied down everything we carried, to keep it from blowing away or hindering our movement. The winds beat at us from the first moment that we broke through the swirling clouds to continue our descent into the valley and they were relentless. Even tied down everything was pulled by the wind. We allowed ourselves to be propelled by it, but as we came closer to the singular mass of Winter Top the winds grew stronger and we were at risk of being blown over. We tied together and exchanged our warm mittens for leather gloves and pickaxes to hold onto the rock as we prepared to make our ascent of Winter Top. We were battered by the wind so when at last we crawled to the edge of the crater rim and peered over we were badly bruised and beaten.

The iron rich walls of the crater were worn smooth from ages of erosive winds. The way down would be slick and treacherous; pickaxes would do little to slow a fall on so hard and smooth a surface. Fierce tempest winds tossed the clouds around the walls in a frenzied race to the central column that would toss them back into the atmosphere. I smiled at how like children at play the clouds seemed— relentlessly returning to be tossed into the sky again and again. The rush of wind was the cloud's laughter.

We were in awe of the place, and yet it filled us with fear. Any unprepared descent into the winds and the crater would be met with certain death. If we were fortunate enough to make it to the bottom intact we would be shot up into the sky. Our deaths would be the plaything of the elements, either we would be tossed about for eternity in the tempest, or flung free of their force to crash upon the rocks of the valley. We could think of no good plan, so naturally we went with a bad one.

We untied ourselves from each other, but left our gear tied down. We tied the corner of my cloak to my right wrist and Andreas's left ankle. We would slide on our backsides along the craters surface, allowing the wind to carry us toward the central whirlwind. We sat with Andreas in front of me and I wrapped my legs around him. That way he was free to concentrate on his spell and the scroll was protected, while I attempted to use my cloak as a sail. Andreas would use his new spell. He promised to name it if it worked. The idea was to borrow force from the winds to create enough counterforce against them so that we could move through the whirlwind and discover the hiding place for the scroll, grab it and get out. On our return Andreas's spell would be used again to soften the propulsion of the whirlwind, navigate to the edge of the winds, and jump clear of them, hopefully at an un-deadly height.

We shoved off moving awkwardly at first. We had to lean against the wind to avoid being turned over until I got the hang of our make shift sail. I found that I had to use my left arm as a gaff to secure the sail and capture the wind.

Andreas's leg worked just fine as a boom. The wind would suck our voices away so conversation was impossible. I could see that Andreas was carefully muttering his spell as we made our second lap around and deeper into the crater. We were picking up speed and my arms burned from the pressure the wind was putting on them. As we came closer to the column of wind I had to use all my weight against Andreas to keep us from going airborne.

Andreas's spell did not have the effect we had expected, but it was a success nonetheless. Instead of giving us a pocket in the wind we rebounded between it and the wall of the crater, which was much closer at the bottom. I didn't know how long Andreas could keep the spell going, but I did know it was all that was keeping us from certain death. I lost control of the sail and wrapped one arm around Andreas while using the other as a rudder to keep us from slamming into the rocks. Sheer strength and will kept us upright.

I saw an opening in the crater wall, and steered for it, but missed. Andreas was struggling under the elemental energy being channeled through his body, but he was still working. I watched for the opening as we were tossed about the crater and steered for it twice more as it came up, and missed twice more, but the fourth time we blew in and slammed into the back wall of what amounted to no more than a tall grotto. An old lava conduit partially revealed. There was no wind in the grotto, but it still spun ferociously just outside.

We untangled ourselves from each other and our makeshift sail. Andreas caught his breath while I inspected our surroundings. The only feature of the little cave was a huge slab of stone centered in the floor of the room. The mass of it should have been impossible for me to move, but I could not resist a try at it. When I did it slid back easily to reveal a set of stone stairs leading down to a circular room. In the center of that room was another stone slab, but upon this slab was a scroll wrapped in a finely wrought mesh net which was in turn wrapped in chains secured to the stone by an iron loop on each side.

Andreas crawled to the opening and peered down while I carefully checked the opening and then the stairs for mechanical traps. I proceeded down the stairs as I checked and arrived at the floor of the hidden room intact. It was only a few feet to the slab and the scroll but I was leery of my situation and I checked every inch of floor leading to the slab. Again I arrived safely. Certain that the slab, chains, and scroll could and would be trapped I continued, tediously checking every inch of each of them in turn. I found nothing. I was faced with the fact that there were no locks securing the chains. Each loop had been passed through several random links of the mesh net as it had been wrapped around the scroll and then the loops were passed into the stone by what must have been magical means, because there were no signs of damage to the stone or the loops. I tugged the loops by hand and pried them with a dagger, and then my spare sword, but nothing budged. I tried to untangle the scroll from the chains, but it was too thick for me to pry apart and no space was large enough to pass the scroll through. The chain and the slab of stone did not give. They were one solid piece with the stone floor.

I was out of ideas and went to rest on the stairs and to converse with Andreas. As you know by now, he had a way with the elements and I thought he might be able to manipulate the stone or the metal. Of course I wasn't asking anything he wasn't already considering. He rose and moved around me and down the stairs. I watched quietly as he walked once around the small chamber and then once around the slab. He knelt and reached out to grasp one of the loops. He pulled but nothing happened and my mind raced in search of other options, until I saw motion at the base of the loop. Andreas's muscles strained and the veins at his temples bulged, but one end of the loop eased out of the stone. Andreas let the links of chain slip off the twisted piece of metal, and then he pulled the net wrapped scroll out from the chains. He uncovered the scroll and delivered it to me, but a smile crossed his lips and he turned back. He replaced the metal net on the stone, slipped the chains back over the net, and once again his muscles strained and metal turned in his hand. He manipulated it with his mind until it was once again a loop, and then he held it to the stone and pushed. Until it was set as it was when we entered. He was flushed and sweating, but his eyes were bright and his smile was exuberant.

"I had to," he said. "I realized how vexing it would be for Polk if he does follow us." He bent to take the scroll from me again and joined me on the stairs.

The title of this composition was The One King. We knew it must be authentic. The design works of the borders were done by the same hand that had produced the Scroll we already possessed. We spent a few hours perusing the second scroll, and comparing it to the one we had, noting differences in the score. We looked long and hard to find two that after wards seemed so obvious. We found one in an octave transition. Three stanzas down the first scroll fought a great battle between cellos and mandolins, while the other was a more harmonious blend. It was a dark piece; the cellos deep toned flourishes juxtaposed with the bright lilting fingerings of the mandolin. I was reminded of minions of darkness and great warriors who sought to drive them back to the abyss.

In the first scroll; The Valkyries Lament composition, the music was epic and suspenseful and in the end triumphant. I remembered the old songs of the Montar legend. I could almost see King Montar pushing the fallen demons back behind the gate and locking the gate that had once sealed them in. In The One King the first two stanzas were identical but the third was swarming with rolling percussion crescendos. Again the old stories were recalled from my memory. I could see the trio of evil's minions, running Montar through, and locking him in chains. Then they left him to the scavengers. The legend varies about what happened next, and the music made no impression on me about it.

Father Gan thought that if we obtained this scroll, we would be able to decipher the notes that were the second key. If Polk knew the first key he could lower the seal that kept three levels of the underworld from spilling out onto the surface with mortal men.

We were sure there would be other clues, but we wanted to get back to the ship. Andreas was feeling rested and capable of another spell. He had decided to name it Wind Devil. It was an all right name, but it didn't give justice to the power it unleashed. We adjusted the sling to accommodate both scrolls, this time I hung them at my left side, and we went across the room to the entrance and the wind. Andreas began his spell and I climbed onto his back.

He took a step forward and we shot backwards to land in a heap on the floor.

I waited for Andreas to get up off of me, but as he did he was flung across the room by a creature of wind coming in from the whirlwind outside. I had heard horror stories about such things, but I never believed in them until that moment. I scrambled back quickly from the towering creature, but not fast enough. A massive hand of white cloud grabbed me around the neck and I was picked up to look the swirling white elemental straight in his stormy dark eye. I struggled, but my flailing was useless against him. His billowy softness cushioned my blows and I was too small to get my hands around him. I struggled to stay conscious, as he squeezed my neck. I could feel my heart beating in my eyes and my head ached with the pounding of it. I heard Andreas shouting something from somewhere in the small room. I remember thinking, *'Save yourself world'*. As I fought for consciousness I was thrown against the cold stone floor and I could hear Andreas still shouting. I felt a blast of searing heat and then it was raining inside the cave as I fell back into black unconsciousness.

The next thing that came to me out of the darkness was Andreas's soft voice and gentle prodding. I was alive! It took me some long moments to gather my senses before I could sit up with Andreas's help. The room was soaked and dripping with water. Andreas had improvised yet again and pulled heat from deep within the earth to blast against the creature and dissipate it into a shower of rain. He seemed none the worse for it as he checked me for injuries. My throat hurt like the worst illness I'd ever had and my eyes ached just being in my head. Other than that Andreas pronounced me fit to continue.

We were ready this time should another creature attack as we stepped out of the grotto. Could we prevent it? Could we survive attack after attack? How many were there? We could not answer any of these things, of course, so we did not dwell long on them. We chose instead to walk boldly forward. I would carry Andreas on my back and the scrolls within the sling. He would be free to cast whatever incantations or elemental manipulations he could come up with for whatever situation we faced. He climbed on and I stepped out. Another wind creature never materialized but our anticipation caused a crucial delay in our plan. We were pulled toward the swirling tower of wind. Andreas held on but I heard his words of incantation and his strained grunts as the elemental powers funneled through him. There was nothing I could do but hold onto Andreas and dear life. My feet went out from under me and we slid along on our rumps and then on our backs and then side by side.

The tip of the vortex was mere feet in front of us when I felt a tangible release of power from Andreas. He channeled it into his hands and directed it straight ahead into the swirl of clouds. This time he successfully created a seam and we passed into the vortex. He immediately put his hands down at his sides and directed the force he was calling upon behind us. I did not repeat his actions quickly enough. We shot up through the center of the vortex eye. Where Andreas rode the force he had created, I was bounced and tumbled across it. My heart raced. I was completely at the mercy of circumstance. This situation made all those previous to it fade in comparison. When we shot out of the column

Andreas snagged me out of the air, pulled me to him and wrapped himself around me. I could still feel the power emanating from his hands. He somersaulted us around in mid air to maneuver us toward the outer ring of clouds with the power he controlled. I would have screamed in fear had I not been in such awe. He was laughing with glee. There would be no living with him now that he had learned to fly.

We hit the second draft from the surrounding ring at an angle that skipped us across the top and we were free of their influence. We fell quickly, but Andreas still controlled our descent. I actually began to enjoy the sensation of flight but we were nearing the top of the mountains that surround Winter Top and we needed to find somewhere to land, before Andreas tired. I pointed out a suitable spot and he steered us toward it. It was a landing to behold, we tried to position ourselves for a smooth transition to the ground, but we each had our own ideas and we became a twisted, mangled heap, even before we hit the side of the mountain.

We sorted ourselves out, brushed ourselves off, assessed our injuries, cracked our aching joints, and danced. I danced because I was happy to be alive. Andreas danced because he was drunk with the power he had discovered in himself on that day. I was happy for him too, but I wondered if my friend would be able to keep his perspective. If he began to lose it I would have to attempt to rein him in, remembering that he wielded a weapon I could not. His ability to control the elements could kill me. I looked at him. He was frolicking—actually frolicking like a pony on an early spring day. I knew that he would be high on this for quite awhile. I knew that I would be too. We flew! I danced over to him and we frolicked together a few moments until we laughed at our own outrageousness. We settled into a walk and made our way back to the horses. When we arrived we collapsed and fell asleep.

It was night when I woke but the moons were bright, I attributed that to my brighter attitude. I judged from their phases that I had slept for the better part of two days. Andreas snored softly and I did not disturb him. Fighting the elements was exhausting for both of us, but especially Andreas. I went to check on the horses and found them sleeping nearby. It was a good thing. We had a lot of time to make up after so long a rest.

I went hunting and shot a hare. I had it prepared, wrapped in salt pork strips and on a spit before first light. The smell of it roused Andreas. I told him about the moons and he recognized our increased sense of urgency as well. We ate and broke camp. We went to the horses and saw that they got oats and took them to drink at a nearby brook. When they had their fill of both we saddled up and made our return trip as quickly as terrain and mount would allow.

Egidio was waiting as promised and we were under way shortly after boarding. I was not happy to be on a ship again, but there was nothing to do for it and I resigned myself to another agonizing voyage. I began to wish I hadn't slept so much while on the island.

While I suffered, Andreas studied the two scrolls that we had in our possession. He played each piece on his harp note-by-note, stanza-by-stanza comparing each piece that he played with the other in his mind. He was unable to crack a code that would reveal the melody of any keys, but we were more than half way back to Sandhitch when he came to me with a theory.

Andreas was well educated and he had been looking over the pictographs along the borders of the scrolls. He believed that they referred to another island amongst a cluster of islands. It was called Thunder Head. It was uncharted, but he believed that he and Egidio had collated the location from an illustration of a starlit night sky. Egidio knew the stars of course, being a sailor and we believed we had a good heading to set off on. If we were right it would be three to four days voyage on that heading. The island was formed by ancient ice flows and was rife with horned spires of rock. Andreas believed from the emotions of the music near that illustration that there was a devastating event; some sad ancient cataclysm that the rest of the world knew nothing about. He said it was as if he saw an ancient people dying in a dream as he played the music upon his harp. He believed it was some function of magic within the scroll. We discussed the images that I had seen, but dismissed until then.

Music invokes magic as simple images that all people feel when enchanted by it. It was possible that we had stumbled on a valuable tool to aid us in the deciphering of the scrolls. The element that we expected to deal with next was Earth, but after our experience on Winter Top that was the least of my fears.

If we had three scrolls we could learn the location of the master from clues within the beautifully drawn borders of each scroll. The musical keys to opening the gates were still hidden somehow within the individual scores. The gate locations were encrypted in the Master Scroll along with the words of power that could lock or unlock the Evil One.

I offered a theory, "If Polk was able to predict where the first key is then there must be something else about the scroll that the good father and his sect have been unable to extrapolate."

"Yes, I know that. Polk still needs all three scrolls to unseal the binds at the gates, when he realizes that he will be back after us for the scrolls. If he does seek the master, then the location of that must be given within each of the three scrolls, contrary to what Gan believes. He cannot free the Dark One from the binds that King Montar placed on him so long ago unless he has the words to do so, and that is only revealed in the master scroll. He cannot get to the Dark One; even if he knows the keys, unless he has the locations, and the locations are in the master. So if the Master Scroll tells us where the gates are, even though the keys are revealed in the three scrolls, the three scrolls must tell us where the master is. It would seem that we need all four scrolls, and in the end we will, but to beat Polk we may need only the three."

I acknowledged the possibility, "Then if we have the scrolls he must come to us either way, either for clues to the gates, or to open the master scroll. And while he searches for us we can unravel the key codes. Kapit or Gan will certainly be willing to sponsor us. Perhaps we can even stay in one place and let Polk come to us while under their protection."

"We already know that we must follow the scrolls to the the gates, but perhaps the scrolls, even just one can take us to the master. It seems as simple as that."

"Let's hope so." His conclusion to my half-baked theory seemed sensible. We were close to the third scroll, and from there we would go to unscramble the melodies of the keys, and perhaps even decipher the location of the master. All of that gave Polk time to worry about the master scroll. If we did not beat him to it he would still have to come to us for the gate keys, and then we would take the master from him. Andreas made financial arrangements with Egidio to take us beyond our previous arrangement. He paid him with gems from the chest provided by Kapit and it wasn't long before we were turned about and under way to Thunder Head.

I endured two additional days of misery before my body adjusted to the sea. There were still momentary lapses of balance, but they were no longer accompanied by nausea. I actually enjoyed the third day aboard and spent it on deck searching the horizon for Thunder Head. It was nearing dark when we spotted a cluster of islands off our portside. Egidio did not want to go into unfamiliar waters at night, with the risk of unseen rocks or reefs below us. We made preparation and let go the anchor. We spent the night on deck and watched the suns set on the starboard horizon. In the morning we watched the suns rise behind the islands. We were unsure which one was Thunder Head so we watched carefully as the sun lit them up. Egidio sailed around each of them at a distance that gave us a view of the entire island. We watched and waited for some glint of glass or metal, but none came—that is until high suns when we saw a large glint so sleek and tall that we had great hopes it had been manmade.

Egidio maneuvered us around the island. We watched the spot to get a bearing on it and we became certain that it was a man made obelisk. It was the same rock as the island, but the shape of it was certainly constructed. Egidio lent us his spyglass and the structure was brought in closer for our eyes to see. We could see only a portion of the top, but that was enough. Exquisite sculptures of god-like warriors crowned the pinnacle of the structure which appeared to be fluted along the entire length of it.

We made our way around again looking for a suitable landing area. Egidio slipped in masterfully between the rocks and got us close enough that we could wade in amongst the smaller rocks, but there seemed no way up. The island shot straight up out of the sea. The stone was not without handholds, but they were minimal. We considered employing Andreas's new found flying ability, but Egidio warned us off of that. He pointed out the raptors gliding on the winds, and we watched the sudden ascents and descents that they made. The birds were safe because they had wings with which to catch themselves upon the changing winds. If we shot straight up, and made it to the top we could not be certain that the wind would allow us to turn to land on the island with Andreas's still somewhat unpredictable control of his spell. We had climbed before without ropes, but this time Andreas had seen to it that we had plenty in our storage chest. We took several lengths of thin silk rope two pick-hammers and thin spikes with eyehooks for anchoring the ropes to the cliff. We put all of our weapons and armor into a leather sack that would be hoisted behind us. We wanted no odd protrusions that would jam upon the wall and make our climb even more dangerous.

We fashioned harnesses from two lengths of thick jute rope and tied it all together with a hook at the middle so that when worn, the ropes encircled our legs, ran up our backs and around our shoulders to join again at the inverted hook at our midsections. The whole contraption was uncomfortable, but it was less confining than other configurations we had tried. We made a loop in the end of the rope, slid it over the hook and tightened it. Along this loop we strung numerous spikes so they were ready as I let out the rope. We folded this length of rope and I hung it over the hook so that I could let it out as I climbed, at the end Andreas attached the leather gear bag. I put an additional coil of rope around my body and each shoulder. We guessed the cliffs at two hundred feet. We had three hundred feet of rope. If we could ascend in a generally straight up climb we would be fine, but we knew that often that was not the case and a crooked path was more usual. If we ran out of rope Andreas would have to climb up to meet me, removing the rope I had already set.

The boat rocked between two lines of rock. I was not sure that was safe, but Egidio assured me we had tied off properly. I climbed over the ship railing and let myself into the frigid waves. Andreas followed and we made our way to the base of the cliff.

I climbed about twenty feet, letting rope trail out behind me. I set a spike and made my way again. When I set the second spike Andreas began his climb. He always stayed at least two spikes behind. If one gave way we hoped the upper spikes would hold and stop a fall. We soon found that wasn't enough. We were on the second length of rope; Andreas was climbing six spikes behind me. I was about to start the third rope when the spike that Andreas was at came free and he fell. The weight took out the next three spikes until he stopped on the fourth with only two more spikes above him to hold him fast. He swung, secured by the harness, and I breathed a sigh of relief. Each spike pulled free came closer to yanking us both from the cliff to crash onto the rocks below. My relief was felt too soon; the motion of his swinging and the tension of his weight coupled with that of the gear bag strained on two more spikes and he fell again. I quickly set two more spikes on either side of the one I'd already set and wrapped what rope I could between the three spikes as swiftly as I could in an attempt to stop Andreas's momentum. I braced myself and pulled up on the rope below me in an attempt to take tension off of the spikes. One more spike went before my efforts paid off and only my hastily placed anchor remained in place.

My efforts were too late to save Andreas. He hit his head hard upon the rocks and I could see his body sag at the end of the rope. I called out several times to try to waken him, but it was useless. My heart sank. He was too far up for Egidio to be any assistance, so I would have to climb down to him. I needed to reach him quickly for my sake as well as his, but I was impeded by my lack of a mastered skill. I often dangled my life and his at the end of my fingers, gripping some thin crack or ledge, in a defiant act against gravity and death. The process seemed unending. I could not be sure what constriction was tearing into Andreas's body as he swayed to and fro with the weight of gear below him. Egidio continued to call to him from below as I made my way at a snail's pace, but Andreas just swung there.

I had gone back down another fifty feet and three spikes when I looked down and saw Andreas open his eyes. He struggled at the end of his tether and I could hear his cries of pain. I had to scream at him to break through his terrified flailing. He snapped out of his senseless fog of fear and pulled up the weight of the gear bag. His position was awkward but he was able to right himself eventually and he tied the gear off to the first length of rope and removed the constriction from himself. I still had a fifty-foot climb to get to him, but by the time I got to him he had performed some healing upon himself and pronounced that, aside from a throbbing lump on his head, he was fit to continue.

We left the gear bag attached to the first rope and Andreas hoisted it behind us as I continued ahead, finding another route up and began to set the spikes and ropes again. I used two spikes at each tie off and laced the rope around them both. This made our climb slower, but safer. We made it finally, as the sun was about to set. We pulled up our gear, and climbed down into the shelter of the rocks before outfitting ourselves. We were tired, battered and torn, from our strenuous climb and we needed rest.

Andreas was in more need than I so I took what little gear I needed to act as sentry. I checked the area to be sure Andreas would be safe and then I moved amongst the rocks to afford myself a better view of the mysterious construction and found a perch above our tiny camp and sat to watch. I could see only the violets and pinks of the suns' set, and wished that I could see them reflected on the sea. The sky eventually dimmed from blue to purple to black. The stars twinkled in and heavy moons moved slowly across the sky. The light of them allowed me to see between the rocks.

An obelisk had caused the glint of light that we had seen from the ship. Now I could barely make it out against the dark sky. I saw no light from windows or doors, no torch or lantern guttered or moved. It was too dark from that distance to see if anyone moved about without the benefit of a light source, but I watched for shadows to play upon the walls under such bright moons. No shadow showed, and still no flicker of light at window or door caught my eye, and I watched for a long while. I became drowsy and to avoid sleep I moved again about the rocks, first to check again on Andreas. He was wrapped snuggly in his sleeping roll and snoring enough to scare any animals away. I went in search of another perch with another view of the obelisk.

I found it and saw no more than I had from my other vantage point; that is until the light of morning began to make a way through the jagged angles of rock. I was nearly straight across from the point where I had watched earlier during the night, and as the sun beamed through the rocks I was allowed a view of two flights of stairs emerging from behind a wide spire of rock. The stairs emerged from the same point and they both led down in a sweeping arc as if they mirrored each other, so precise was their construction. They ended on opposite sides of what had once been a pool, or a fountain, but now it held no water at all. It was of the same fine construction as the obelisk and the stairs. I expected to see water spray forth at any second, but none came. I followed the length of the pool with my eyes, across a long courtyard to what appeared from this distance to be a wall of bronze. There were no visible holds, hinges or handles, from my line of sight. On either side of the wall was another set of wide stairs that led up to a stone niche from which a winged beast was carved. I could see that they were masterful depictions of hippogryphs.

Hippogryphs; creatures with the head and upper torso of an eagle and the hind quarters of a horse, were great and noble beasts of long ago who served only masters of honor. So, the inhabitants of this place had held the hippogryph in some esteem, I reasoned that they must have had good encounters with the beasts and must then be honorable people. The beasts were depicted with their heads bowed under a great wing laid across their faces. I was unsure what that symbolized, submission possibly. At the feet of the statues a stone porch spread between them and in the center of the porch the obelisk rose straight and true. I still saw no one about. I waited a bit longer, but when nothing changed, I made my way back to Andreas to wake him and to report what I had seen.

He had been taught that a hippogryph with head hidden under one wing meant war. If it was at rest with both wings unfurled it meant peace. So we theorized that these honorable people had been at war. Perhaps their absence indicated defeat, though the place was not sacked. We had no conclusions, just rough theories. We consulted the scrolls. The compositions showed two subtle differences that we nearly missed, but nothing made sense. We closed the scrolls, none the wiser for having looked inside. We ate cold tack and outfitted ourselves for battle, though it seemed none would come. We were still unaware of Polk's location and we had no doubt he would resurface at some time to attempt to stop us.

Our way lay amongst tall rocks with no trail. We gave up on the rope and spikes and depended upon our own strength and agility to carry us to a spot above the double stairs I had seen by dawn's light. We had done this type of climbing many times before, although this was the most difficult so far. We came over the stairs near midday and settled into a spot where we felt hidden and watched while we ate again of our hard tack and drank warm water. We still saw no one about, nor any sign of door or window. We made our way to the landing that came in just behind the great spire of stone. Together we descended to the bottom of the stairs.

The condition of the place was immaculate. No stone had fallen anywhere within the compound, how this could be after ages of disuse and no one to maintain it we did not know, but we attributed it to magic. There were no leaves to skitter through the courtyard or to fill the empty pool on this treeless isle. No wind blew this deep in the valley of stones. It was eerie and the feel of the place, put me on edge. I drew my sword. When I did an audible groan went through the very stone of the place. Andreas held my wrist and I saw in his eyes a fear I'd never seen from him before. I followed his eyes to my scabbard and I sheathed my blade. Then he nodded and understanding I drew my sword again. The place groaned again and we were taken by the sorrow of it. I replaced the blade this time without prompting and moved alone into the courtyard. "We mean no harm." I said aloud. "We have need of your knowledge and assistance in a grave matter that faces the world." I waited some sign, some word. When none came I repeated myself, shouting the words this time.

Andreas came to stand beside me. "Don't anger them." He whispered.

"Anger who? There is no one here to anger."

"Oh, but there is. This place holds great elemental power. The rocks are only a small part of it. They have force; even the building feels alive. Should we enter— it might swallow us whole. Do you not feel the greater aspect? Do you not feel— the death?"

I stood in the silence assessing Andreas's words. I felt anticipation but not unlike I'd felt at the beginning of other adventures. I was more intense of course, because there was so much more at stake. There was something though, at the back of my brain, some primal urge that was begging me to run. It was that thing that had made me draw sword. Now that I'd found it again I laid my hand upon the hilt of my best blade, but I fought the urge to draw. Was it death I felt, or just the fear of my own dying. I could not discern. Andreas though, he had a great ability with things elemental as I've said many times, and if he sensed an element of death I would respect that and let it guide my actions.

"I feel intensity." I responded at last. "I do not think my greeting would offend them though. It carries no malicious threat. It is more a plea for help really."

"It is that which frightens me. What help will death bring us without a price, and what price?"

"You speak the word death as if it is a name."

"I will not yet rule out that possibility."

"Gods." I whispered for protection.

"Yes, perhaps." Andreas said.

I looked at him long and hard. He was not fooling with me.

I sighed. "What should we do?"

"Find a way in I suppose. We're here to save the world after all. Even Death should understand that."

"Great, just bloody great. Well this is obviously over my head, as well as being dangerous; you go first." I bowed my best sweeping curtsey and he moved out into the courtyard.

The silence sucked up the sound of his footfalls. The air grew suddenly icy and our breath expelled in frosty clouds more slowly than our breathing should have allowed. The beating of my own heart seemed distant from my being. I only knew that I still existed, because I saw Andreas motion me forward. But at what level did I exist, on what plane? I stepped forward, but I felt as if I would swoon. My balance was shaky and my head swam. I fought to control myself and acclimate to the floating feel of walking in this strange place. Always it felt as if I was upon the crest of a bubble that was about to roll out from under me. Andreas spoke something to me, but his voice too was sucked up into the deafening silence.

We moved beyond the empty pool and there were three wide steps down to a porch at the foot of the bronze. These steps were repeated on either side of the pool and joined the main steps down to the porch. A wide trough, which would have once carried water, descended with the stairs at their center, but it also laid empty now. We moved down the stairs. The trough disappeared into the stone floor at the base.

The porch spanned twenty paces. Bronze squares made the wall at the back of the porch. Each was a precise six feet tall and a precisely equal measurement in width. They had been placed in three rows one atop the other to form five columns. The metal had been brushed to give it a grain and the squares had been set so that no adjoining grain ran in the same direction. There was no sign of patina, odd considering how long they had been in the sea air. I reached out to run my hand across the seams. The workmanship was tight and immaculate, even under my softest touch I could barely make them out. I traced them in search of any imperfection that might indicate a switch or wire. I found nothing and was about to have another go when Andreas tugged at my sleeve. He spoke, but remembering that we could not hear he motioned me to follow him up the set of stairs to our right. I indicated the bronze wall. "Later," he mouthed. I shrugged and followed.

We ascended the wide sweep of stairs to the porch at the feet of the hippogryph there. Andreas indicated that I should stop and stay. I obeyed, but thought what payback I might be satisfied with if I were a dog. As I watched, Andreas went about examining under the wing of the hippogryph; he had found something, and motioned for me to join him. Under the wing protected from the nonchalant observer was a long slit laid into the stone. It was not wide enough to pass through, but it was tapered; thinner on the outside and wider at the interior. An arrow slit. I turned around to calculate what shot could be gotten off from under the wing and found I could view the stairs leading to the hippogryphs feet on the opposite porch as well as the courtyard on that side. If there was a similar slit in the other hippogryph it was a well-protected niche from which to protect the entire courtyard from intruders. We crossed the vast upper porch in search of another slit in the opposite hippogryph We found it just as expected; still it offered no way in so we turned our attention to the obelisk.

We saw no obvious entrance on our walk around the obelisk. The stone structure was fluted in wide spines around the circumference and along the height of it, but the spines were too far apart and too smooth to climb, although I attempted it anyway, just to prove it to myself. At the top of the tower gargoyles depicted as guardian heroes with there hands rested upon the hilt of great swords and the heads of battleaxes looked down upon us with what seemed at once a warning gaze and then again – pleading. I went around the obelisk searching for hidden latches that might open a door into the place.

The sun was moving higher and began to seep into the courtyard between the jagged spires of protective stone. When I was through examining the obelisk the shadow of it fell across the length of the courtyard. We had found no way in. I moved across the upper porch, away from the courtyard to a spot directly behind the obelisk and looked through the tall balustrades of the wall there. A sheer wall fell into a chasm of indeterminate depth. The other side of the chasm was three hundred feet away and about one hundred feet lower than where I stood on the porch. It seemed a good defensive spot, but an arrow from this distance would be a keen shot to be sure. There was no other way onto the porch, but for the way we had come.

Andreas stood in the shadow of the obelisk with his hands stretched out to his side. He was ciphering some magical force or another. I caught his eye and indicated that I would be in the courtyard. He nodded slightly and I went back to the wall of bronze. I moved slowly across each seam, not looking, just relying on my sense of touch to indicate any imperfection. I used my eyes only to keep my place along the grid. I was in the lower right corner of the last square in the second row when I felt my index finger slide over a very slight rise in the joint of hammered bronze that sealed the squares together. I looked up to the spot and ran my finger back and forth across it. There was definitely a catch there, but I needed a better angle to see it. I climbed up the stone at the edge of the bronze wall and came to eye level with the seam. All the while I was there I felt dizzy and was sure that I would fall, but some how I found the catch again with my finger and then scrutinized it with my eyes. It was slender, only half the size of the seam and centered within it.

I braced myself and tried to pry it towards me, but it was instantly obvious to me that it was the wrong way. I braced again and pushed slowly. The catch slid in easily under my cautious touch. Below me and to the left I felt a rumble and a whoosh of air as one square popped away from the others and slid back.

I climbed down from my perch; and actually enjoyed the floating sensation it gave me. With my hand wrapped anxiously around the pommel of my sword I moved along the wall to the recessed block. It had moved in two feet. Above it on the ceiling of the recess were three perfectly matched holes at equal distances. In the floor I could see a portion of smooth stone cylinders laid across the recess; one whole cylinder and half of another. I stooped down to run my hand back and forth across the whole one. It spun slow and heavy, but smoothly under my hand. I reached across the cylinders; the whole and the half that was under the bronze. I pushed tentatively on the block, but nothing happened so I pushed firmly and it moved back revealing more rolling cylinders beneath it. I stopped and turned to fetch Andreas, but there he was standing silently behind me, his back turned to me as he protected me from any rear assault.

"Anything?" I mouthed when he glanced back to check my progress.

"Nothing," he nodded. "But you did." He pointed at the revealed opening.

"Shall I?" I mouthed.

He pointed at himself, shrugged and made a face as if to say; "You don't want me to go first?"

"Soon, very soon," I mouthed again.

I pushed the bronze block back slowly until a passage opened on either side of it. I left the block partially in the intersection and squirmed into the passage to my right. The only light was that which spilled the eight feet into the small passage vacated by the block. I looked ahead into total darkness. The air was chill and stale, like a tomb. On the other side of the block the results were the same. I wondered what would happen if I pushed the block further. Would I be able to pull it back again to seal the wall after we left? There were no handles on the block to allow it to be pulled. Around to the back of it I saw that it was partially inserted into the wall of the passage, a perfect fit all around. There was no doubt that should I push it back it would match the wall so well as to be nearly invisible. It was a perfect place to hide a passage, and now that I had partially fallen for it, I had to figure a way to pull the block back to allow me to investigate my theory. I came along one side and Andreas the other and we attempted to slide the block back into the entrance passage. Our weakened balance made the task awkward, but our determination made it work. We did not push it completely back and let the major portion of the block remain in the intersecting passage.

The passage fell into utter darkness. I fumbled in my pack for torch and cinder box. Each spark that shot off the flint was but a dim streak in the envelope of pure darkness. When the torch took, the flare of it was slow, an indication that the odd effects of time and balance still affected us inside. The light of it weakened immediately, pushed back by the darkness rather than the opposite natural effect. I laid the torch atop the block with the burning end jutting off the edge.

I examined the recess meant to accept the block. It was just large enough for the block to slip into, stone cylinders filled the floor, and three perfectly matched holes at equal distances spanned across the ceiling of the entrance to the recess. I examined the holes. They were smooth shafts perfectly drilled in the stone for about two feet up. The stone craft of the place was precise and immaculate. I had never seen such work until then, nor have I seen it since. I could not determine the purpose of the holes. I suspected they served to lock the block into place, but the back end of the block had no corresponding protrusions or mechanisms along the top and I could not at this point check the front side. I stepped cautiously into the recess. My kilter in balance made it impossible to walk or stand on the stone cylinders without bracing myself along the wall.

I moved carefully around the opening to check the outer edges for any traps or latches. Slowly and meticulously I ran the tips of my fingers along every inch of the walls concentrating along the corners between walls, floor, or ceiling. I found nothing. I moved up one sidewall and then down the other in the same manner. Still nothing. I stood in front of the back wall. I felt intimidated, a bungler in the face of such engineering. I took a deep breath, steadied my hands, and went back to work. Finally after checking all walls I found a small protrusion on the floor just in front of the back wall. After careful examination I pushed it. The first stone cylinder slid down and over to the left. More careful examination, more anxiety, but trusting my abilities; since that was all I could do, I reached down and slid the next cylinder slowly, yet firmly to the left. It went smoothly and the cylinder slid into place with a resonant clang of steel and stone. From the right side of the now vacant roller slots a thin steel plate shot out across the opening. I yanked my hand back, but not soon enough. The plate caught the ends of three fingers.

I clutched the searing appendage, and reeled around from the pain. Afraid to look, I rolled my upper body over it. I rocked and tried to breathe, until the pain subsided enough that I could make my brain move my arm and examine the damage. I had not lost any fingers, but the three middle fingers were bleeding and broken. I looked up to see Andreas moving toward me, but his attention was not on me, it was behind me. I turned and saw a dark room.

Andreas moved past me and stood at the opening. The wall that had been before us had rolled silently into the floor. I stood, still cradling my wounded hand in the other. The place was oppressive. The room revealed to us felt as if there was still a barrier between us. Andreas began to breathe short little breaths. A panic went across his face and he clutched at his armor. I reached out to touch his shoulder, but he held me at arms length with one hand and clutched his throat with the other. I loosened the straps for him. He dropped his sword and shuddered out of the armor as if it were crawling with some foul disease. He turned to run, but fell on the stone cylinders as they spun beneath him. He clambered into the main hall until he found solid ground, then he rose and ran. I grabbed up his staff-sword and armor and slid across the cylinders as if they were ice. I made the intersecting hallway in time to see Andreas running as if pursued. He gave a look over his shoulder just before he was absorbed into the darkness.

I grabbed the torch with my broken hand and ran after him, headlong into the darkness fighting the inherent imbalance of the place. He was always too far ahead of me to be able to see him, but there were no intersecting passages so I kept on. I must have pursued him for a kilometer. I wondered when he looked over his shoulder for signs of pursuit if he saw me and thought I was his enemy. I ran faster, my lungs and muscles burning, my wounded hand throbbing with the exertion.

Then there was light ahead and I could see Andreas. He was still running and checking behind him when suddenly he dropped from my sight. The passage ahead suddenly opened into a vast cavern, lit by some unnatural force deep within the mountains. I stopped at the end of the passage and looked down a vast widening stairway. Andreas was sprawled headfirst down the last three steps. Across the wide cavern another set of stairs led up to a wide, but low cave entrance. To my left yet another set led up to a massive alloy door. It was the door that seemed to light the room, but any investigation would have to wait until I knew Andreas was all right. I snuffed out the torch and went to him. He was dazed and pulled away from me.

"Andreas," I whispered, "fear not. It is me, Saeede." His eyes were not focused, perhaps from the fall. "Andreas you can not do this. I need you. Come back, come back to Saeede." I heard the whisper and so did he.

The white fog that had taken the color from his emerald eyes slipped away and his pupils shrank. He looked around at his surroundings and a whistle left his lips. When he turned to me he took my hand and pulled me to him. "My

166

faithful friend, you did not leave me." His voice spoke more of his fear than his words.

"Never." I breathed under his tight hug.

"We are not alone here. I felt a great evil beyond our comprehension in that room. Have you ever done or thought a thing so heinous that you felt the breath of the devil and prayed the Gods of light would protect you? If we cross the threshold to that room we will be in a realm, unconnected to ours." He rocked while he talked and continued to hug me. Then he suddenly pushed me back and held my hands. "We will be wholly alone, just you and me against all evil!" I winced from the pain of my broken hand within his grasp. He saw for the first time his staff-sword in my hand, and his armor across my arm, but it was my wince of pain that brought his eyes up to meet mine.

I showed him my hand and explained what had happened. He remembered when I told him, the experience at the threshold of evil had blocked it out. He set the bones and I could feel the heat of his healing touch. Then he wrapped the three fingers together so that they could not move independently, but I would be able to grip a sword if I had to. I wiped a trickle of blood from a scrape Andreas had received to his head in his fall down the stairs. After we got him comfortably back into his armor and reunited with his staff-sword we were able to continue.

The walls of the cavern were natural and rose far above us. The steps had been cut from the stone of the floor and walls. The door remained closed and was not a threat at the moment. Andreas crossed the smooth floor and climbed the stairs, angling for a look in the low cave entrance. I followed to the bottom of the stairs, but remained in the cavern.

Andreas moved like a cat staying low to the stairs as he moved closer for a better look. We waited silently, listening, and we heard a high-pitched growl from within the cave. I moved up the stairs to a position across from Andreas and slipped my bow over my head. I laid two arrows at my feet and notched two. Andreas slipped into the cave just as if he had slipped into a pool of ink. The growl came again and then another and another. Andreas was still lost to my sight, but I could sense him.

The growling came closer and we knew there was more than one beast. I drew back my bow and waited. Out of the darkness emerged the eyes of the beasts; yellow orbs reflected the light from the cavern behind us. I quickly counted eight sets of eyes and let loose my arrows at a spot just below one set. My skin crawled at the shriek that went up as the eyes fell. I grabbed and notched the arrows I had set before me, drew back aimed and fired. Another set of eyes had replaced the other when another shrill shriek went up and another set of eyes fell, to be replaced by another. I leapt from the stairs half at a time, notching two more arrows in mid air. When I hit the floor I spun, drew back the bow, and waited.

The growls came together in a crazy orchestra of guttural snarls and shrill cries. I heard two inhuman shrieks, then a yelp that was unmistakably human. I nearly dropped the bow and was about to run back in when Andreas leapt from the mouth of the cave, clearing the stairs, and landing with a tuck and roll. He was splattered with black blood and his staff-sword was dripping with it. While still in his leap a swarm of shiny black demons with fore bodies like those of a dog, but slick like the skin of a salamander, and their hind quarters those of a great lizard swarmed over the stairs like water. Andreas landed near me and scrambled to the door as he shouted for me to follow. I let loose four more volleys as I moved back toward the massive glowing door and then they were on us. I drew swords and fought my way one retreating step at a time to join Andrea's position—- backs against the door.

We fought furiously, sometimes with swords two handed, and sometimes kicking with our feet, or with our fists still wrapped around our trusted weapons. The effort to stay on our feet under the press of so great a swarm of slathering beasts was exhausting. We beat them back but they kept coming, crawling over one another to get to us. Our shouts were lost under their deafening growls. Their black tongues flicked the air like snakes; sensing for us as they moved through the horde. Blood ran thick. Our red blood mingled with the black blood of the demons causing a reaction that sent up an acrid smoke. I slipped on the mixture and was swarmed. I clawed and kicked from below while Andreas beat them off of me with swordstaff from above. He reached out his arm and I scrambled up while he flailed away in front of us. I could feel the heat of the blood mixture on my back, but I could do nothing for it, else I would certainly die.

When a hundred or more lay dead at our feet they still came. I wondered which gate of Hell Polk had beaten us to. We fought on, parched and weary until we were upon our knees at the death of the last demon. As he fell we fell too— backs against the door hard and heavy. The heat at my back had subsided as the reaction weakened, and though the sweat on my back stung at it, it seemed a clean thing so we rested and did not move for a long time.

The sight before us was awesome, and we could not speak of it, even though it spread out before us. I stared at it, trying to believe what I had just experienced. Andreas reached over and took my hand. We were both shaking with exhaustion. I looked at our hands splattered with blood and allowed my gaze to travel to my friend's face. His eyes were dull within his blackened face, and his smile was weary. I tried to offer a smile of encouragement, but I knew my own weariness had shown through.

Our weariness was deeper than the recent battle, deeper than a long overdue rest. We were becoming emotional. Andreas put his arm around me; I leaned in to his comfort and composed myself. It did me good to unload and start fresh. If he cried I am unsure of it. I heard not sob or sniffle, nor did I feel his chest heave, but his eyes were red rimmed when next I looked at him, and his smile was even more strained. With not a word spoken between us we gathered our things and stood to face the door. Our rest had only made us more worried, and so it was over.

The door before us was easily two stories tall. I could not tell what mixture of metals might have been combined to make the alloy, but it had the true color of copper, not like bronze where the color would have paled in the mix with tin. But there was no green patina to show age, the surface was bright, as if newly polished. The light that filled the chamber came from the door—how I did not know.

Andreas cast about for the forces behind the phenomenon, but he was at a loss. The face of the door was adorned with a bas-relief of two dwarf sentries facing each other, kneeling in prayer, their weapons at their feet. There was no hinge on our side so the door would open toward whatever laid beyond. No latch, handle, or knob was apparent on our side of the door either, so I took to studying the bas-relief for some device there. Andreas cast out with his mind senses, I felt about with my touch. We were there for what seemed like hours when at last I found a toggle within the folded fingers of a praying dwarf. I was half way up the door with one foot on the belt buckle of one bas-relief dwarf and the other in the crooked elbow of the other. I got a pick behind the finger and felt a tug of wire as I did. I followed the wire behind the finger and into the hand to find the origin of it. There I found another thinner wire hooked around a turning cam, a trap switch. I could not determine what the trap might be, but I was certain of the mechanism that would release it. I fed my nippers in to snip the wire thereby disabling the cam. The toggle switch could then be engaged without activating the mechanism. I alerted Andreas, held my breath and braced myself for the possibility that I could be mistaken. The wire cut smooth as butter. I felt the cam slip but I slid a steel shim in along the nipper and caught it before it fell. My breath escaped to the ragged beat of my heart. Still alive, I reached for the toggling finger and pulled. The bas-relief pushed forward. I sprang from the door expecting an undetected secondary trap, but the two praying dwarfs separated and the door behind it popped. There was an audible escape of cold stale air and then silence.

No sound came from behind the door, none from Andreas. I looked to him. He stood tense and ready, his staff-sword poised for an advance that did not come. I pulled myself up from my crouch and carefully drew my own weapons. We moved together to the opening, put our backs to the doors and turned our heads and then our bodies to get a look inside.

We looked back to each other in disbelief, shook our heads and looked again. It was what we saw, and did not hear, that struck us as surreal. A wide landing laid just the other side of the door. From it a narrowing stairway swept down into the streets of a bustling city built in the bowels of Thunder Head. Wagons lumbered along the streets pulled by mules and driven by dwarven teamsters. The glow and smoke of a huge forge filled the air at the far end of the spacious cavern. Men and women went about their chores and children played in the parks, but no sound fell upon our ears. Not one sound.

We put our shoulders to the doors, opened a space wide enough to pass through and stood together upon the landing overlooking the silent life going on below us. When we did, the heavy door, slid silently closed behind us. We only became aware of it as the bas-relief on the other side slid back into place and sent a shock wave out through the landing beneath our feet. The door was of the same glowing alloy as the other side. The light of it cast upon the landing and down the stairs. I searched every seam and hinge of the doors, or I would have, had I found any. We were locked in tight.

There was no way for us but down the stairs into a world of silence. We sheathed our weapons but the impulse to draw them was nearly irresistible. We kept our hands upon them and descended the stairs. The city was clean and orderly. Buildings were of the same precise construction as the obelisk compound on the topside of Thunder Head. The same quality construction the ancient dwarfs were noted for— the ancient, *extinct* dwarfs! My mind raced with the excitement of knowledge learned from a culture that died away and took their technology with them. Raced right passed caution, but only until the thought that they might be living dead brought back the eeriness we had experienced on the topside. My hardened demeanor broke down and I wanted to run, but Andreas clutched my shoulder and pulled me into an alley at the bottom of the stairs. His look was intense but it was not leveled at me. He was on to something, something that his sense of the elements allowed him, something I would probably never experience. Unsure of what the elements were dealing our way, he crouched and pulled me down with him.

"There is death here." I could hear him but the sound came slowly and out of sync to my ears.

"For us?"

He shook his head and tugged at his ears. He was under the same strange influence as I was. "If we choose improperly." Well, that was at once ominous and obvious. I had no verbal response, just an inquisitive look and a nervous shrug. He looked back at me with much the same response.

"This way, I think." He led us further into the alley, closer to the center of town.

We skulked in the entrance. Andreas pointed to his eyes and then the scene before us repeating the motion quickly a few times. I looked more carefully. A dwarven woman crossed the street with a child in tow, a militiaman strode by on patrol, a nobleman and merchant engaged in what seemed a heated discussion, passed very near us. I knew that dwarfs were said to have been plain folk, but there was no change of color at all in the many textures of his garments. No hint of green or brown or even black, only shades of grey. Their skin was no shade from beige to brown, but grey like the color of the stone—or the stone dead. The dead; my heart skipped and my breath caught. I surveyed our surroundings again. Grey was the dominant color—grey merchants, grey children, grey stone, but then I noticed little splashes of color: the red lettering on a shop window, the faded green of the shingle over the inn, the brown wood of a passing wagon. Aside from the grey pall backdrop of the cavern and buildings, grey was the color of the living, though they were surely the living dead.

I looked back at Andreas, he was just as he always was, emerald eyes, black silks and hair, tan skin. My hands were their usual tawny brown against the blue of my sleeve. I breathed again relieved to see our color was still alive.

We moved into the street. The militiaman was returning up our side of the street. A grey beard pulled into a braid at his chin surrounded his pallid face and his eyes were black. They looked through me as he surveyed the street and moved closer. Andreas moved back, but the dwarf's dark gaze gripped me. I was frozen–unable to move. He stepped closer and closer and then he was in my space— in me. I went cold like a sudden plunge in an icy lake. As he passed through me I was again able to move. I turned slowly as if in a dream and watched the dwarf. He glanced back over his shoulder, shuddered, but did nothing and continued on his way. In that moment another rush of cold surged through me as my hesitation allowed a youngster to run through me as she played in the street. The world swirled around me and I would have fallen had I not been paralyzed with the element of death. I watched again as the child turned back toward me, shrugged and then turned again to skip away down the street.

Suddenly I realized that sound was coming to my ears. I looked to my hands—they were paling to grey! Andreas came to me low, upon his knees and looked up into my face. He was speaking, but the sound was long and garbled. He reached for me and picked me up over his shoulder. Could I have, I would have shouted, "No!" I had allowed the death to enter me; I saw no way that he could get me out alive. I wondered if the dwarfs would accept me or if I was cursed to live out my death as an outcast.

My worry was unnecessary— Andreas moved at what seemed to be a drudging slow pace through the streets and the yards and alleys he took to avoid contact. When we stopped he sat me down against a low wall at the back of the Smithy's house. Another door, like those at the top of the stairs stood before us. This one had bas-relief of priests in death masks. The perspective was as if they had just filed through the portal beyond to kneel in supplication upon the threshold. The doors depicted in the bas-relief were made to look as if they were partially open. A masked priest stood behind each door to push the doors shut.

Andreas started a search for traps. His movements were slow but blurred as if he was— or I was out of phase. I knew it was an effect of my condition, something gone haywire in my dying brain. The cacophony of a work hammer echoed around in my skull until I covered my ears in an attempt to silence it. Andreas called my name in drawn out alarm when he saw me rocking to and fro with my hands cupped over my ears.

"Sssaaeeedaaa"

"Nnooo, Leeave mmee.

He would not, but there was no comfort for me, and so he had to go back to his task. He found nothing by hand as he was unskilled, so he went to magic. His incantation nearly drove me mad with the disorientation that it caused me. His first incantation didn't work and then the second failed.

Then a dwarf happened by and kneeled before me. "Gads, a human! Are you alone?" I understood him almost perfectly, though the words did not reach my ears in the same time that his lips formed them. I nodded affirmatively. I didn't want to give Andreas away. He reached as if to test the reality of me, but I scrambled away from him for fear of losing what was left of my life. My action caught Andreas's attention.

"What can this mean?" The Dwarf asked in a mysterious whisper. He moved closer. He seemed harmless as if he was truly concerned, but I moved further away.

"There now, young thing, I mean no harm. You must have been through some ordeal to have come to this place. You have made a long journey to be sure."

Andreas moved to intervene, but I could not allow him to fall to the same fate as I had. So I moved away. The dwarf noticed my sudden alarm, but he could not see Andreas' material form. "Hold on there little rabbit what has you so frightened?"

"Stay away. Your touch will kill me."

"What did you say?" He cocked his head, calculating the truth of my words.

"I hold no ill for you, I mean no offense. I cannot explain it, but I've been touched twice by your kind, more than touched. And each time I've been drawn closer to your condition."

"My condition? What do you know of my condition?"

I stammered in my attempt to compose a response, not helping my case at all in the dwarf's eyes. What could I say? That he was dead? I didn't think that would help my plea of sanity. If he was aware of his condition he did not seem to care. He didn't act as if he was anything other than alive, so even if he believed me I didn't want to be the bearer of that bad news. I made no response and moved further away from him. Then I spoke to Andreas and the dwarf backed two steps away from me. His wide eyes darted back and forth and he crouched into a defensive stance.

Andreas went back to his incantations and I reeled from the magic as it swirled in and out of my existence. I lay on my side wary of the dwarf but watching Andreas. Suddenly the masks upon the priests at the door were outlined in a magical light. The doors popped a seal and a rush of stale air blew by us. The dwarf saw and heard the doors, but not being able to see Andreas turned a suspicious eye to me.

"What goes here, Human?"

"I must get beyond those doors. Outside of your city, there is a world that needs my help. I attempt to stave an evil that threatens to breech the binds that hold it and spill out around the world."

"Alone?"

I decided that the only way to expedite the situation was to tell the truth. "No, not alone, but you already think me insane so I'm sure what I'm about to say will do me no good, and yet at this point no direct harm.

"My partner opened the door," On hearing this he lowered his sturdy axe, but still held it with both hands, horizontally across his body "You cannot see him, because he is alive and you— are dead. I don't know...I think I'm dead or dying and so you see me and we can speak. None of this was true until just a short time ago when I accidentally allowed one of you, and then another, to pass through me and cause this condition that keeps me precariously in two separate realities.

"Now I must go and you will do what you will."

"I will stop you, for now. Speak first with my brethren and let me alert my king. I cannot let you pass through those doors, for we are forsworn to protect what lays behind them, by sword or death, yours or mine you will not pass!"

As he spoke I rose unsteadily to my feet and moved slowly, but certainly toward the door. "Then call your brethren, my time spills from me and my people will die if we do not proceed. I must go."

The Dwarf moved to stop me, but Andreas was again at my side and pulled me hastily away from his grasp. To the dwarf it must have looked as if I leapt and spun up from the ground to land on my feet two body lengths closer to the door. He stopped, but raised his axe, aiming for a throw. Andreas grabbed my hand and yanked me toward the door. I stumbled forward, but gained my feet. Air rushed past my right temple as we made the threshold and the axe dented the bas-relief hand of the masked priest behind the right hand door.

As I looked at the hand I caught a glimpse of the magic light still around the mask of the priest. I ventured a look at the other priest and that mask too was still aglow. "The masks Andreas, we may need them. Just hold him back a few more moments." I was already working my trade, but it was made difficult by the peculiar condition of the separate time phases between this realm and mine. I heard the expulsion of magic behind me. I knew it was only a few feet, but it sounded so far away. I worked the first mask free and revealed the face of a gaunt dwarf beneath.

The next mask came more easily and another face was revealed just as another blast sounded behind me. "I have them, let's go!"

I tossed the masks through the opening of the door. Andreas ran up behind me and leaned into one of the doors to make an opening large enough to pass through.

"Go, go!" He commanded and I stumbled through the opening. I moved to push the door closed, as Andreas jumped through but my strength failed me. The dwarf was at the other side pushing against me. Andreas joined his strength to my meager attempt and quickly overpowered the dwarf. The door shut as silently as the other had. I reached up to turn the wheel that drove a bar across the door, but I was incapable, and Andreas had to do even that simple task for me.

I slumped to the floor, exhausted. Andreas came to tend to me, but there was nothing he could do. "The masks," I said, and he fetched them for me. They were much lighter than expected. They were nearly an inch thick and so could not have been made entirely of metal, woodcraft perhaps, if the quality of the work was an indication, or perhaps the material below the metal plate was an actual skull. I looked at their faces. Emaciated visages of dwarven skulls looked back. I could make out deep wrinkles running down the cheeks indicating some age. The fold of the eyelid and the sag of skin below the eye were masterfully done. Tracery of sigils and spirals decorated the faces in what I hoped were wards against evil. I turned one over and it seemed very much alive as if a cast had been made of a youngsters face. The skin was taut and there was an impression of fine hair tracing along the cheeks and forehead. Not like a dwarven beard, but like the fine hair of a child's face. Yes, a girl child's face. I turned the other mask and found the face of a boy. I flipped them back once more and realized that the masks were the aged faces of their reverse sides.

Why two masks? I wondered. Why a male and female why not one or why not two of each sex? I turned the female mask again and held it away from my face, but looked through the small eye slit. I saw the altar across the room as I would have expected, but several pillars of candles burned now at each end. When I lowered the mask again there were no candles and the altar was barely visible in the dark room.

I handed the male mask to Andreas. He examined it much as I had and held it out to look through the eyes of it. He moved forward and I followed; both of us with the masks held before us.

At the altar I scanned the stone of it through the mask while I ran a hand along the surfaces. It appeared to be just a block of stone with six candles and a wooden podium set atop it. Just this simple task exhausted me and I had to lean forward, hands upon my knees to keep my head from spinning and catch my breath.

"Rest, good friend." Andreas said as he came to help me to sit against the altar.

I thought that I heard banging upon the great doors, but I could not cry out to warn Andreas, my condition was too consuming and I fell into a fitful catatonic state.

I heard the sounds of battle and screaming as peoples of all races tried to save themselves, from a great beast upon the land, but they fell before Him. It gorged itself on the flesh of the dead left in its wake and drank their blood. With each feast He grew larger and with each growth He needed more flesh and blood. The villages and landscapes lay in ruin where He trod and it seemed He would consume the world, beast and humanoid alike. Only then would he end his relentless slaughter. At each destroyed site He pillaged through the destruction and at each site He railed with rage when He did not find the thing that He was looking for. He roared his distress in one strange word— Draghador!

I was aware of Andreas in the room with me, fussing over me as I tossed with my dream. He must have seen there was nothing he could do so he left to continue his search in the underworld of the dwarfs.

The beast consumed the land and stood upon the shore. He walked into the water for miles before it was up to His neck and He was forced to swim. He upturned ships and drank of their crews and grew larger. He did not swim long before He came to the land of the Dwarves. Their stout warriors fought with great courage but their villages and cities fell to Him. The retreating Dwarfs went into their mines leaving their mountainside homes behind. The beast was too large to follow the Dwarfs and so He beat upon the mountains bringing down great slides of rock. The entrances were forever sealed and the great Dwarven race was lost, but He could not bring down the mountains.

I was aware of a great fever upon me and Andreas put cold compresses on my face to cool me.

The beast jumped into the ocean enraged at his defeat and thrashed about for a long while. The shore land was inundated with the displaced waters. A tsunami ate away the land. When He was calmed and stood at last all that remained was a spire of rock jutting from the ocean. Bodies floated about Him in the now choppy sea. He ate and drank of their blood and was satisfied that He had won and turned away from the once vast land of the Dwarfs. His roar of "Draghador" filled my ears, but I knew not the meaning of it.

Voices called out all around me. One of them was Andreas's and his tone was calm, so I did not worry and only wondered at them before sleep came to me again.

Then I stood upon a great cliff over the ocean and I watched as a hippogryph flew over me and swooped down across the sea. The hippogryph flew out to meet the beast and raked great claws across His face taking one eye with the effort. The beast screamed out in pain, the sound of it reverberating across the lands, blasting against me as I stood watching. The hippogryph banked around coming up behind the beast and pulled a chunk of flesh from his neck. The wound gushed profusely turning the water black with his blood. The beast went down on its knees sending another wave to crash against the already broken land, but the stone withstood the force and the rebounding wave washed into the beast pushing him onto his side. As he thrashed about in the water the hippogryph swept around for another attack. The beast flung out with his great claw toward the hippogryph in a desperate attempt to defend himself. He caught the hippogryph in the chest just below the wing. The hippogryph pulled his wings in and spun away from the beast. Blood fell from the wound, the drops fell into the sea and spread. But, the hippogryph came out of his spin and spread its wings to bank and have another go at the beast. The beast was rising out of the water as the hippogryph lunged ahead with his powerful avian claws. As the beast straightened to His full height the hippogryph drove his claws deep into the beast's chest and ripped out His heart. He pulled his equine legs forward, repelled off of the slumping shoulders of the beast and gained altitude. Evil's minion went down — dead where He fell.

The hippogryph circled the beast slowly, gliding on the wind. Blood still fell from the gashes that cut the hippogryph from under-wing to belly. When it was convinced of victory it banked in ever widening circles until it passed over me again to plummet into a bowled valley surrounded by sharp spires of rock. He was weak from blood loss and he crashed into the protected valley. He tried to catch himself but his eagle talons could not stop the force behind them. He had to lower his hindquarters and the effect bounced him up and over. He tumbled across the valley and landed in a broken heap against the jagged wall.

Below the stone of the ruined land the surviving Dwarfs hauled a great ark up through the mines and out to the aerie of the hippogryph. The hippogryph lay dying. One of the dwarfs moved forward and knelt before the great creature. "Rise Philandamar, our great protector." He cried.

The hippogryph answered in a weak squawking voice. "The beast is dead Draghador; I only wish my return from the hunt had been more timely."

"You are not to blame Mar. This time was foretold, and the scroll is safe. We will build a temple for it here now and then we will retreat to the hollow of the mountain where we will make our home for eternity."

"You will be well missed among the people of the lands, good friend."

"As will you."

The dream ended and my mind fell into darkness.

I don't know for how long I remained that way, but I woke from a chill deep into me. When I finally pulled myself into the real world again my vision was blurred. Warm furs, ragged, but warm were wrapped around me, and my chill subsided. I could make out the blaze of a fire and the aroma of charred meat. I tried to lift my head to get a better look, I saw many people sitting around the fire, but I could not tell who they were or where we were. My neck shook from the effort and I fell back against the furs. I drifted back to the blackness.

Next time I became aware again Andreas was beside me kneeling over me. Someone was huddle behind him and I heard a male voice. "We must wake her it is time for you to go."

Andreas moved to nudge my shoulder, but my raspy voice cracked out at him. "I'm awake; what gives?"

"My little sunshine, must you always lay around while on the job?"

"Not if you would be kind enough to help me up."

"A bit at a time then, Love." He put an arm behind me and raised me up.

I saw the man behind him and realized from his stature that he was Dwarf. I was startled at the sight of him and pulled away pulling Andreas with me. "Don't touch him. You can have me if you must, but let him go!"

"Calm yourself woman. I have no need of your life. You can keep it." The Dwarf wore a simple wide silver circlet on his head. He was a king.

"Draghador has given us much aid in our quest." Andreas said.

"If it were not for your friend helping us to run off the subordinate of the-evil-one we would have had a different result. When my people brought you in from the temple I knew that you were the ones meant to take the scroll back to the living."

As Draghador spoke I saw his world in full color, but Andreas still cradled in my arms was as dull as the dwarfs had been when we entered this realm. I turned his face to me and saw the mask upon his face. I put a hand up to my face and felt the cold mask there. Realization came to me. "I told you we had to have them."

"You were right." Andreas said, sitting up. "They allow us to see the other side and for them to see us and communicate. We still cannot touch them, but their magic is powerful and they were able to balance your life force and bring you back from the edge.

They are ancient people and they went willingly to their deaths to protect the scroll. They made great magic to enter the underworld so that no living thing could steal the scroll. Draghador has told me great stories of their survival as you slept."

"But, someone did come to steal it. " Draghador intervened. "I can only assume that he followed you here. He had his hands upon the scroll when you came in."

185

"Polk?"

"That's right."

Andreas and Draghador were silent letting that sink into my brain.

"Did he get the scroll?"

"Your man here..." Draghador began, indicating Andreas.

I made a face behind the mask, but it was not lost. The mask had become supple and moved with me. The mask nicely enhanced one of my better looks of doubt.

Draghador looked confused. "But he called you his Sun..."

I was his sun? That was news to me.

"It's okay Draghador. She doesn't want me. I'm too civilized."

Draghador continued. "Andreas stopped him long enough for us to catch up with him." The dwarf king motioned regally to encompass the room and I looked around thoroughly for the first time since waking. A group of armed soldiers gathered near a door to my right. Another contingent of soldiers gathered together near an opening on the far side of the room. I wondered which door I had come through. In each group of soldiers there were three with stout dwarven axes and two with short recurved bows, and quivers tied to their stout legs. Between the two groups of dwarfs sat a low table. Two females and one male stood around it as if on guard. One female wore the trappings of a priestess while the other female and the male wore the trappings of wizards.

"I don't know what magic you wield." Draghador was saying to Andreas.

"Neither do I half the time," Andreas noted. "Sometimes it just comes to me and I go for it. This time I had good results. Saeede inspired it really."

"When we arrived on the scene the dead man you call Polk was pulling the scroll from the ark, "Draghador explained. It was then I realized what I thought was a table was actually a sacred ark.

"We saw Andreas mid-incantation in that door way." Draghador nodded at the door to my left, so now I knew where we had come in. "We assumed he was another enemy about to unleash on us, but his spell came off and Polk disappeared momentarily and the scroll fell back into the ark. When Polk reappeared he was insubstantial, out of phase much as you had been, but it put him in our realm and we were able to deal with him. He was no longer invincible to us."

"Did you kill him?" I asked, full of hope.

"No, the spell wore off, but our own users of magic were able to hide the scroll away from him for a short time. Andreas recast his spell and the dead man ran from it. We gave chase, but he called out ancient words and vanished. We searched all through our city and found no trace of him either physical or corporeal."

"He knows where we are Saeede; we must go from here and take the scroll with us. He will not stay away long."

"And if he waits outside? What spell do you have that will make him vulnerable to me?"

"None, yet, but I'll see what I can do."

"Is he the evil that you felt earlier?"

"No." It was Draghador who answered me. "That evil has been here for some time now. My practitioners of magic have held it off, for months. They grow weary from it. It has increased efforts to reach us in the past few days. I now suspect that is because it knew you were coming."

"O it knows alright. Does it mean that gates have been opened?" I asked, remembering the hoard of demons we fought at the gate to the city. Had they been looking for a way in too?

"It is a formidable evil." Andreas concluded, no doubt remembering the feel of it all around him in the side chamber.

We were all silent for a long time, and then Draghador spoke again.

"I have no answer to that. It could be that it is just evil that has dwelled on the surface for years and has a new purpose now, or it could be an opened gate. I have no way of knowing. For now I know that it is time for you to go, but there are still things I must show you, so that you will understand what sacrifices have been made. Perhaps you realize some of it already; on the surface. Our sacrifice is done soon, but yours whether you believe it or not, are just beginning.

"Are you well enough to walk, Lady?"

"I am. I feel remarkably well considering I was nearly dead." I felt awkward for having said that and averted my eyes from Draghador. I had no words to smooth it, a simple sorry had to suffice. The good Dwarf simply nodded with a wry smile curling his lips. Andreas helped me to my feet.

I bowed to our host. "What is it that you need to show us, Your Highness?"

"I want to show you my realm, as limited as it is." He began the tour in the room where we stood. He called it the plaza. It was a sort of antechamber between the commercial district that we had come through and the halls of government and religion. The altar in the next room; the one by which I had lost consciousness, had once been a public place. When we went back to see it I saw that it was quite a bit larger than I had realized on my first visit. Beautiful naturally occurring grottos were dotted along the three walls away from the altar and smooth stone chairs and benches were grouped around not necessarily facing the altar.

"Our people come here even now to reflect, to commune together and with the gods of our people. Our patron is Therabol the god of fortitude. He has given us great courage. He must have known we would be severely tested." Draghador released a heavy sigh.

He continued, "Come now, this way. There is much more and not much time."

We followed him back through the plaza and the cleric and wizards fell in behind us. The soldiers grouped around the ark and four dwarfs knelt to hoist it upon their shoulders by means of four foot poles in each of the lower corners. They fell in behind the practitioners of magic and the remaining guards took up the rear.

Draghador led the way. Andreas and I followed close to the king. We descended a dark gradual slope that switched back often until we stood in a fissure that rose up through the stone. Bats lined the walls of the fissure and beyond them was a faint glimmer of sunlight. We were at the root of the mountain. We stopped to give the ark bearers a rest.

Now that I paid it attention I saw that it was made of bronze hammered to the thickness of paper. Draghador assured me that the strength of the walls was equal to that of six inches of steel. It had been hammered and folded and folded and hammered one thousand times. Each fold laced with powerful enchantments of strength and durability. This made the ark light enough to be carried. The sheets of metal had been woven to give the ark the look of a basket. During the weaving process the ark was again laced with magic, but this time the spells were for bonding and protection. A flat lid of woven bronze was laid upon the top. There was no lock, but I imagined great magic had been used again to seal the top. I did not ask and Draghador did not tell. It was the ark from my dream, though my dream had not done it justice.

Draghador ordered that our procession continue. The ark was hoisted and we fell into place. We traveled along the length of the fissure for about fifty feet, glad of the faint light from above. Before us stood another set of decorated metal doors. The bas relief was of Draghador with his hand upon the heart of the hippogryph. The doors swung smoothly away from us with a slight whoosh of air.

Draghador strode through and we followed into a vast cavern that must have taken up the majority of the interior of the jagged island. The walls were iridescent with a pale green light from a covering of lichen revealing a Dwarven city that filled the great space. The layout was triangular with the narrow point at our end. This section housed the artisans, and there was a heavy scent of sulfur in the air from the smelting of metals in the area of the smiths. The odor was overwhelming and I suppressed a gag, but Draghador pressed on unaffected and the odor soon fell away. He pointed out each storefront to us; most were cut into the natural stone, or in some cases into great pillars of stalagmite. Behind these were the entrances to what was left of the mines after the cataclysmic fall of the rest of the land mass. Many of the town's citizens came to their doors or peered out windows as we passed. Excited conversation started as dwarfs gathered along our route.

At the edge of this district a garden unlike any other swept in a wide swatch across the width of the city. Clusters of prismatic crystals with smooth brilliant faces of various colors bordered the garden as if they had been cultivated and pruned. Geometric forms of crystal and gems in deeper hues bordered the paths that wound through the garden or were arranged in great shows of color around the natural stone that shot up from the bedrock. The green light played off the many facets and a show of light sprayed up upon the walls on its way toward the ceiling nearly a thousand feet above. I wondered at the value of such a place. I stopped and gaped as Draghador continued. The practitioners of magic nearly bumped into me and I trotted awkwardly ahead to catch Draghador and Andreas as they walked along a path that cut through the garden. A female dwarf sat upon a side path with her feet in front of her and an arrangement of tools on the ground between her legs. She was carefully weeding stray crystals and gems from the arrangements so carefully laid out. She put the *weeds* in a pouch propped up beside her. How could I get that job? I wondered. How could I get that pouch? In the next plot a sign was anchored to a large stone. It was in a language I could not decipher, but I imagined it said, "Do not pick the gems." Small type along the bottom probably said "by order of King Draghador" I smiled and went about my gawking.

On the other side of the garden we crossed into the religious district. A fountain of foaming seawater bubbled up and formed a sort of plaza with the garden to one side and four temples carved entirely from the natural stone arced around the other side. Each temple was unique, with intricate balconies, ornately carved entries, arches, and sweeping buttresses. Draghador indicated the patron deity of each temple. There was Therabol the god of fortitude of course, and Woldar, the god of underground places, Jertam the goddess of the sea, and Gadoon the god of protection.

We made our way around the fountain, through the buildings, and into the government district. The floor of the chasm sloped steeply up from here and each row of buildings could be seen stacked behind the others until at the back, centrally located was Draghador's residence. We climbed the ever-steepening path as it switched back and forth along the slope. Along the first switch of the road were the guild houses of the various artisans; gem cutters, all manner of smithies and jewelers, tailors, engineers, stonecutters, wainwrights, potters and coopers. On the next switch were the offices of government: Revenue, Sanitation, Maintenance, Constabulary, Agriculture, and Housing. Only the Constabulary, Sanitation, and Maintenance were operational. The others had been closed when they'd become useless after the monster sealed them in. Draghador explained how much of what we had seen had been built since their exile from their days above ground. His residence, the government buildings and the military complexes had always been there, but the rest of the caves that had once been used as food storage were now the great city of an undead race. Even in death the Dwarfs had not been idle.

The portion of the wide path we climbed next was for the military. Fine stone buildings served as barracks, offices, training gyms, and arenas. A stable and corral of fine mountain ponies seemed out of place. "What do you feed them?" I wondered.

"There is no need to worry, as there is no need of food. They are as we are—in a state of un-death, but we need no sustenance and again as I have said no need for agriculture. We once had a great land with crops enough for all and abundant hunting, but now..." His voice trailed off. "If only I could enjoy stout dark ale one more time before death takes us to our rest. Ah, well.

"We are nearly there." He said as we made the final switchback.

The pathway broadened and fanned out toward a gate surprisingly made of wood, but bound in steel. As we passed through I reached out to touch the smooth hard surface of the wood. It was cold to the touch like stone. Draghador noticed and explained that since the wood had been deprived of the elements and stood in the warmth of the dry cave for so long that the wood had become petrified and had turned to stone.

"This is indeed a wondrous place," I said. Draghador nodded with a gleam of pride in his eyes.

Once through the gate we walked along a stone causeway and arrived at the courtyard to the main entrance. Stone spires rose straight as an arrow for four stories. More twisting spires were cut into the very wall of the cavern that backed up the Dwarven Kings palace . He insisted it was just a humble dwelling. We figured humble meant extravagant in his language. Draghador gave orders to his guards and they took the ark through a private entrance. The practitioners followed them. We were met at the main entrance by the major-domo, a bent and grizzled old dwarf by the name of Mactroes. His cloudy eyes took a moment to focus on us and when they did he gasped in surprise.

"Do not gawk, Mac. Our guests are to be honored. See that the guild masters, priests and artisans are all notified of an audience here as soon as they can arrive. I will be making an important announcement to every citizen young and old. Send out the crier to every corner of the city. I have never charged you with so important a task old friend, simple as it may seem to you now." The old man's face lit up with a smile framed by his silver beard. He turned and ran fast as his tottering could take him shouting in his native tongue. The halls soon bustled with the members of Draghador's household. They stood along the great entry hall and waved and cheered as we followed Draghador. We had no teachings in their language so we knew not what they said, but they were awfully glad to see us.

We followed Draghador passed numerous arched openings that opened on comfortable parlors, a dining room, and a library. We came to a wide hallway that ran perpendicular to the one we had come down. A door stood directly before us. To either side of the door a staircase swept up and around to a balcony above the door. From the balcony the stairs joined to form one central stairway that went up another flight to another perpendicular hall. There they divided again to both sides and turned back again to climb another flight. Draghador pulled a key and unlocked the door.

We followed him down a set of stairs that mirrored those above them. We found ourselves on another balcony with still more stairs leading down from either side. A vast natural cavern spread out below us until the slope of the government district above restricted it. Spread across the cavern was a vast graveyard. Elaborate family mausoleums were interspersed with short obelisks or blocks of stone marking each grave across the whole width and breadth of the sad landscape.

"Before you span the whole of my people, each stone block indicates a body; others are the empty graves of the un-dead. The mausoleums share the same circumstance. The obelisks memorialize those who were lost in the cataclysms that sealed us here.

We were not always as you know us now, even after the disaster. We learned of our destiny long before those catastrophic events and we expected that the time of our destiny was at hand. Some thought our part had been played out. The scroll was safe and the minion of evil was dead. Others thought that though the scroll was indeed safe, the reason we were keeping it had not yet been realized and until we knew what that was we could not be sure of a fulfilled destiny.

"I set our best minds on the problem. After months of deciphering ancient scrolls they declared our destiny was still unfulfilled and worse, our time was centuries away. We had enough stores for another two seasons, three if we strictly rationed it, but after that we were lost. Any boats we had were lost in the disaster, and we dwarfs are more like stone than even we like when it comes to swimming. Our ability at climbing is even worse. Our fertile lands and forests were lost, and we used up what had been harvested in those first seasons of survival. My great hippogryph, our only means of sending for help had perished in the battle with the beast."

"I dreamed of this," I said. "I saw the battle with the beast and your hippogryph"

The sigh that Draghador released was so heavy with grief that it broke my heart. "Philandamar, a noble beast, a noble friend. We kept each other safe. Is he remembered in our history?"

I paused an uncomfortably long time, searching for the gentle words but they did not come and so I spoke the hard truth. "Your history was lost to us I'm afraid. You are more myth, than legend, but the seed of legend is now planted with us, I promise you that. My mother told stories of great battles fought in the name of right, won on the courage of great dwarfs from under the mountains. They had names like Glargadhon, and Ahlsado. I'm sorry Draghador, that your history has been lost to us. We can bring it back if you can give us the written truth" I thought that the king would be saddened, but he smiled.

"Glargadhon was my general. I will see that you leave with our histories. For now though I will tell you the rest of what befell us" He turned and walked up the stairs. His step was spryer than we'd seen it since we met. We followed in silence up the three flights as he finished his telling.

"If we were to fulfill our destiny we would need a miracle. We prayed to the gods for an answer. It was the priest of Gadoon that came to me after a vision and laid out a plan that would put us in this state. Preparations for the spell took several weeks, those wizards who were not needed during that time continued to decipher scrolls. It was fortunate that they did, as they were able to uncover more pieces to the puzzle that we faced. One thing that we learned was that our destiny was linked with that of the humans who would come for the scroll to unravel its secrets and save the world. These humans would become the next keepers of the scroll. Now here you two are; and come in search of the scrolls so that you might save the world. When the scroll passes to you we will at last go to our final resting place."

"Pardon me, your highness, if I am too bold, but why would you do that?" Andreas asked in disbelief. "You could live forever."

"There is nothing for us to live for. We are trapped on this small piece of rock with only our mundane existence to keep us entertained."

"But we could take you from here."

'To what ends? Have you already forgotten the condition that befell your friend when she made physical contact with us? Without the masks we would not see the living and this could happen again. We would still be isolated, there is no glory to that, but since my people must leave this world forever more then it will be with glory."

"Can it not be undone?" I asked anxiously.

"I am afraid our spell took as its power the essence of life from each of us." Draghador answered sadly.

"It has been thought that your race perished centuries ago. Treasure hunters looked but never found you. Your extinction remained a mystery all this time."

"Yes, but now you will return with our story and the Bards will sing our praises into the next age. Our place in history will be as protectors against evil, rather than an inexplicable disappearance."

"I respect your position, my lord, but I do so with solemn regret. Your race is a great and wondrous people. The planet hasn't been the same without you. I regret that I did not know until now."

"Well said," Andreas added. "It is only too bad that our friendship must be so short lived."

"You are too kind, though I feel the same. I wish I could be around to hear how this epic ends. There is still more that you must know, come along."

He took us to his private quarters and introduced us to his family. He had six children four boys and two girls. His oldest, Tragor was a sullen youth, robbed of his life and kingship while still a youth. He was gracious and thanked us for coming to free him from that place. The others greeted us as well and knew we were important to their day of rest, as they had come to call it, but then they went back to their play. Queen Ehnid watched after them as they frolicked and a profound sadness came over her and she nearly wept, but she was queen and the time was not now. Draghador turned her to him with both hands upon her shoulders and cupped her silken blond chin in his hand and raised her face to his. He kissed her gently then pulled her to him. They turned to face us for formal introductions. The queen bowed to us and we returned the formalities.

The four of us went together to a humble yet comfortable parlor and sat together around a cold hearth. "There are things that you must know, before you depart. To begin, there is no other way out for you, but to return the way you came. Upon the door where you retrieved the masks are three great keys; they are on the belts of the gatekeepers depicted on the door. These keys will seal the city forever as you pass through the next two doors and again at the final portal where you gained entrance. When the door is properly sealed the key will flare and melt down within the lock to seal them as well. Great magic will be released upon the turning of those keys and we will be called to our rest. The procession will begin when you turn the final key.

"Once you are away from us you may remove the mask but it won't come away easily. The magic will have created a seal, in order to make the balance between your world and ours. The bond of life to death will not be shaken easily. It will be as if the mask has become a part of you; in a sense it has. It will come away if you take your time and peel it off gradually. These masks are our gift to you; they may be of use to you again if your mission takes you to the underworld. Once this is done you may feel extraordinarily hungry or tired. You have not eaten for days and what sleep you had, Saeede," he said, "was restless and Andreas has not had sleep since then. At any rate be forewarned. You should remove the masks only when you are sure of your own safety. Have I forgotten anything Ehnid?"

"No dear, I don't believe so."

"Good then it is time we give these good warriors what they have come for."

I had never thought of us as warriors before, but I have to admit it was a title I was proud of.

Draghador rose from his seat, as did Ehnid. He took her arm and put it through his. He patted her hand twice and then left his to rest on hers. They walked back through the children's parlor and called them together. We followed without a word. He spoke their native tongue. They were saying goodbye through their tears and much hugging. We made our way quietly to the hall to give them their time privately.

"I cannot begin to imagine what pain they must be going through," I said to Andreas when we were out of earshot. "I never knew my father, but I know not what became of my mother; even still I miss them everyday."

"Well you know there is no love lost in my family. Father was a son of a bitch; in fact grandma might have been meaner than he was. Mama was too worried about her own safety to worry about me, even when the man threatened me she would not intervene for fear of the beating she would receive herself. I stayed away as much as I could. When I was twelve a jealous husband found my father with his wife and beat my father badly Mother knew what happened but stayed with him for love of money. She turned to other men for affection. She must like being beaten. My father was a raging drunk, and my mother is a stupid slut. I have no other family."

"You never told me that before."

"It's not anything to be proud of."

I put my hand on his arm for a moment. "You're turning out okay though."

"I finally have a good influence."

"Still, I can't imagine the intensity of their pain. They will lay a whole race to rest so that others may survive."

We fell into silence as we weighed the magnitude of that action.

Draghador and his family trailed out into the hall. Ehnid held the youngest in her arms; the child's face was buried in her shoulder as she tried to hide her soft sniffles. The others had red-rimmed eyes, but they carried themselves with the regal gait befitting a royal family. Tragor walked between his parents, his rightful place as heir. Other than the babe in mother's arms the others fell in line oldest to youngest. With a solemn nod from Draghador we fell into line side by side behind the children.

We followed down one flight of stairs through a colonnade lined with the dusty meeting rooms of a once prosperous time. At the end of the colonnade Draghador swung open a set of stained glass doors depicting the four gods of the dwarfs. Beyond the doors a balcony overlooked the courtyard and a cheer went up when Draghador and his family moved out. Andreas and I hung back just inside the doors to allow Draghador his final audience with his people, and— the drama of an entrance was not lost on us.

The king stood before his people giving them some time to quiet. When they did he spoke in a tone that we had not experienced before. He did not shout but his silky voice carried to every ear. His address was a strong spirit booster that soothed the fears of his people and gave them courage to face a final death. He understood their grief and shared his own, but then he spoke to them about the glory they would achieve in the halls of Klangderden, the great dwarven heaven, and in the historical tomes of great bards. He honored them for the strength they showed for millennia, for the honor of serving so great a people as king. They cheered him, hailed him, "Draghador, the Great Forever King." When the cheers subsided he turned to us and held out his hand. His family parted to allow us to move forward.

The drama was realized as a booming cheer and the banging of hammers against stone greeted us, but it was shallow, the King's speech had so moved us both that we nearly wept, for these people showed unparalleled bravery. Draghador explained our part in their great history. "Hail the Scroll Keepers," went up and was chanted throughout the crowd. Draghador raised his arms for silence.

"I have given the knowledge they need to continue their quest, and now it is time that we give them that object of the quest that has brought them to us." The ark was brought up to the balcony from side stairs and another cheer went up. The guards set it down carefully, bowed to their king and queen, and departed by way of the same stairs. Draghador ran his hand across the ark and when he found the proper spot he spread his fingers and whispered. A soft puff of air was released from under the lid and Draghador and Tragor removed it and set it aside. Draghador reached in and removed the familiar silver bound scroll of vast proportions. Great brass seals capped each end. The tooled emblem of the earth sign covered one end and the emblem for fire covered the other. In the center of the tube was the crest of Draghador's great clan. That was when I realized that this clan of Draghador had created the beautiful scrolls. They had been in this mess from the beginning!

Draghador held the scroll up for all to see. His massive arms showed no strain under the great weight of it. The crowd was remarkably quiet, only a murmur could be heard from below, but when Draghador placed the scroll in Andreas's hands the crowd erupted in great shouts and whistles. Andreas held up the scroll and the Chant of "Scroll Keeper, Scroll Keeper," went up again. I moved closer to share in the glory. Draghador removed a metal chest from the arc and placed it in my arms. "Our history." he said. Then he moved between us. Andreas cradled the scroll in his forearm. The circumference of it barely fit the nook of his arm, the length of it stretched from his furthest fingertip to his elbow. I held the chest in both arms against my chest.

"It is time for you to leave us now. We will go together into history. Take these stairs and go, you know the way. At the bottom of the stairs the practitioners will present you with a box. It is an ultra dimensional space within. It will be large enough to hold all four of the scrolls, but will be of a manageable size for you. He slipped another small scroll into Andreas's belt. "This scroll contains the word that will lock it and that which will open it. It is written in archaic. You have only one chance to read it so remember it." He turned to me then and looked deep into my eyes. "Stay well good warrior, the living needs you. You must protect Andreas" He turned back to Andreas. "And you, good warrior make your magic well. The living and this woman need you. Now go before I ask you to stay." His wry smile returned and then he bowed, we returned the formality to him and his family and moved down the stairs. The crowd broke into a song in their language. It was a bright number and many danced.

At the bottom of the stairs Andreas took the box from the practitioners and placed the scroll into it, he took the scroll from Winter Top and the one from Gan and placed them beside the other. The practitioners looked as if they wanted to hug us, but they only nodded solemnly. We made our way around the edge of the crowd, many reached out wanting to touch us. We made the first switch back and the crowd followed us to the end of that stretch singing and waving. We waved back walking backwards as we rounded the switchback until we lost site of them. Then we left the city.

The scene outside of the mysteriously glowing doors was as we had left it and the stench of the blood and decomposition of the demons was overwhelming. Draghador's practitioners worked well with metal and the light of the doors filled the chamber. The bas-relief that adorned the doors was covered with dried blood. The dwarf sentries facing each other, kneeling in prayer, and their weapons at their feet looked garish. Remembering that we had seen no latch, handle, knob, or keyhole on the door I again began to study it for some device to fit one of the remaining two keys we removed from the gatekeepers on the door to the city.

Andreas assisted with magic. Together we found a rivet head among a line of rivets that attached the bas-relief to the door. The fine alloy had the true color of copper and with some encouragement the rivet spun in its mounting and we removed it. I took the keys and compared them to the hole. They were both slender, made of the same alloy as the door and had nearly identical tines to turn the tumblers in the locks. The first one slid easily into the lock, but it would not turn. The second slipped from my fingers as it slid in. I grasped it again and turned it. The delicate key drove the lock home with a resounding boom that echoed through the chambers of the mountain. I imagined that Draghador and his people could hear it deep under the mountain; a signal that the second door had been sealed. Clan Draghador would begin their procession to their final rest.

As the booming receded the key glowed hot as if newly pulled from a forge. It melted slowly filling the hole. Only a stub of the softened metal protruded from the surface of the door, it changed shape as it cooled. A new rivet head now filled the hole. The glow of the door grew suddenly brighter and then spread to the outer edges of the doors as it grew dark in the centers. The light danced along the edges, flared once more and went out. The door was sealed and we were plunged into total darkness.

I felt for a torch from my pack. When I found one I lit it and we went out of the cavern and down the long hall. We moved slowly, battle ready. We came to the side passage where Andreas had been spooked. The block was as we had left it, partially in the entrance opening, partially in the hall.

The dark feeling from the room at the end of the side passage was still there. We knew that there was no way to immediately seal in whatever evil lurked there. The cube that blocked our exit now, would be pulled out to seal the side passage for a few moments when we left, but when we pulled the stone into the entrance to seal it the passage would be open to the rest of the under-mountain as it had been. We were confident that the magical working of metal on the gate doors to the city would be safe from the evil, and so that when we turned the key on this last portal our world too would be safe from it. Draghador and his people had accounted for every obstacle so far, so we held back our fear, but worked hurriedly none-the-less.

We forced the block back into the oppressive opening and revealed again the passage that would lead us out. We could not pull it through the entry way behind us and there was no way for us to be on the outside and place it in its proper position. I began the tedious work of finding some secret latch or alternate exit elsewhere along the passage. We were there for hours, constantly shaking off the feeling of dread that emanated from the side passage. I searched for another exit far from the passage, but it eluded me. I had no choice, but to return to that area of fear and concentrate my efforts on the exit.

We were perplexed by our situation; there had to be something. The dwarfs had millennia to prepare for this event; certainly they had not forgotten a way for us to escape the mountain. Andreas scanned about with his magic to no effect. It was up to me. I sat in the long hallway. The block now pushed partially into the oppressive side passage. What had I missed? I sat in thought, ticking off all the places that I had checked, and found no other options. The sun moved up over the mountain crags and lit the passage where I sat, that was the thing that helped us to find the mechanism.

I glimpsed a play of light on the upper inside corner of the entrance itself. I crawled to the intersection, and began my search once more. There at last I saw the edge of a tiny pressure plate just big enough for the pad of my little finger to fit on. We moved our gear into the plaza and with Andreas safely out of the mountain I pushed the pressure plate. A slab of stone in the intersection spun up slowly and pushed the block resting there into the side passage. I had to jump into the plaza to avoid being hit by the block as the slab turned once more and pushed out the length of the entry hall. We watched as it settled into place with a rumble as the mechanism screwed home. The echoes spread through the interior of the under-mountain and then were spent in the distance. There was a moment of silence. A small keyhole was obvious at the center of the square that now filled the space where the entrance had been.

I took the remaining key and solemnly placed it in the keyhole. It was of the same metal as the surface of the square. The fit was smooth and exact. I wished a blessing upon the place for the dwarves that would be at rest below. I turned the key and it flared to a molten state. A blast of magic emanated from the seam around the block and the molten metal spread out to meet it. It was the same alloy that covered the surface of the other squares. When the surface was seamlessly coated with a layer from the molten key the magic flared again, traced the edge of the block once around and went out. A series of staccato booms went out from the door, down into the depths of the mountain. Under Mountain was now safe and her people could rest.

We crawled into the concealment under the hippogryph statue's wing to rest.

***

A strong wind and heavy rain wailed outside. The sky was dark and the rain so thick that it was hard to place a time of day. I sat up awkwardly, stiff from the hard work of our foray and the cold. I wondered then what day it was and how long we had actually been in Draghador's kingdom. Andreas still slept, so I moved quietly to the box, whispered the archaic word that Andreas had taught me, and took the scrolls from the box Draghador had gifted to us. I moved out of the wind and wrapped my cloak tightly against the cold.

I compared the seals of the scrolls. The basic design of each was the same, but the elements of the designs differed. The one we had taken from Polk had sigils of Water and Air Elements tooled into the end seals. He had stolen it from the temple of Nauticus deep in the waters off of a small island near the shores of Ahnrye and it had led us to a place protected by air. The scroll we had gotten there was adorned with the seals of Air and Earth. The one we had received from the dwarfs was stamped with sigils of Earth and Fire. All four Elements were represented in an intrinsic circle—each dependent on the other for protection.

We had been investigating the murder of the purveyor, Eindal who wanted to hire us; presumably to protect his scroll from Polk. His murder had propelled us into this dire mission. Doughboy Kapit and his network of spies had first seemed as enemies when two of their own had broken into our rooms, but they had been acting without Kapit's blessing. Kapit and his men waylaid us and it was during that encounter that Kapit persuaded us, more like coerced us, to take on the adventure and procure the remaining scrolls and save the world.

We breeched Polk's defenses, obtained the scroll, and rescued Father Gan from his dungeons. We barely survived that. We battled mightily against the cloud guardian at the bottom of the chasm in the Hoary Mountains, with the wind so strong we actually flew skyward in order to escape. Had it not been for the foresight of Draghador's practitioners of magic the sheer numbers of a dwarven attack would have overpowered us had they seen us as hostile.

I laid the three scrolls out before me and turned the first one slowly to read the music stanza by stanza. I could not read the script of the title. Only Andreas understood the archaic alphabet in which that was written, but I could compare the differences in the musical passages that were relatively common between the scrolls. The melody in the first stanzas of Air and Water were the same; and I saw in my mind the cone of an active volcano protruding from the jungle canopy with a trail winding up to the crater. I searched the pictographs along the sides of those musical passages and saw one that showed a group of tropical islands. On one island there was an active volcano. A trail of lava flowed around the cone and spilled out into the field of geysers below.

Andreas continued to sleep, his constant snoring a blend with the wind that howled outside. I was so absorbed into the scrolls laid out before me that I did not see or hear Polk slip into our hiding place before he had a knife at Andreas's throat and demanded that I turn over the scrolls. I jumped to my feet and grasped the pommel of my throwing knife, but did not withdraw it as Polk pressed the knife hard against Andreas's juggler. That woke Andreas, but he lay stone still as he realized his situation.

"The scrolls, bitch. Now!" He screamed. The intensity of his voice startled me, and I jumped. I could see him smile wickedly at that even in the shadows of his hooded head.

"Move it!" he yelled again and I did, but I never took my eyes from him as I rolled the scrolls and replaced them in their tube cases, then I set them next to each other. I squatted to gather them up in my arms, and strained to stand under the combined weight of them. I crossed the short distance and stood over him until Polk took the knife from Andreas's throat and backed slowly away before standing just inside the opening. I heaved the weight of the scrolls at him.

Polk tried to deflect the force with his weapon arm, but he was unsuccessful. He fell onto the stairs below the statue and his dagger flew from his hand to clatter to the plaza below. Andreas scrambled away from the opening and I leapt to the stairs drawing my sword in mid air. Polk was an agile opponent though, and he rolled, grabbed a scroll and was on his feet running toward the plaza before I landed. He staggered as he tried to grab up another scroll, but missed and regained his footing before I could land. He was unhooded now and I saw a ghastly man, different from our first encounter back at Behlanna. He looked deathly ill, but his agility disproved that, a result of some dealing with the Dark Lord I guessed. As I braced for the impact of my long leap he was bending to retrieve his dagger. I landed, got my footing, and charged toward him. He let fly with his dagger, but I was able to dodge it. He bent to pick up another scroll, popped open at the foot of the stairs. I sprang at him, but he crouched lower and I sailed over him. He gathered up the scroll and took off at a run as I gathered myself up from the ground. I heard the sizzle of magic as it launched from Andreas's hands and watched as waves of force caught Polk in the back, but the impact only delayed his steps a moment and he was off again with a scroll in each hand. I pursued him up the stairs to the top of the crags, but he was simply too swift for me. When I emerged at the top of the island he was gone. I pursued down the most obvious trail and being unsuccessful backtracked to another more concealed way, but there was no sign of him. Amy tracks were quickly washed away by the pouring rain. Andreas joined me with all of our gear and the last of our three scrolls safely put away in the woven metal box and tucked tightly under his arm.

I shouted expletives into the air, not caring that Polk might be hearing my frustration and reveling in it. When I finished my tirade by hurling large stones into the sea below I sat down hard upon the ground to catch my breath. Andreas stood silently waiting for me.

"What scroll did he leave behind?" I asked between breaths.

Andreas took it from the box and showed it to me. I saw the sigils of Earth and Fire upon it and was relieved. "Fire."

Andreas looked quizzically.

"Stamped into the end caps." I said beginning to regain my breath.

He turned the scroll in his hands and nodded affirmatively, but was still looking at me to explain.

"I was looking at the scrolls, comparing them. Although they look very similar the sigils stamped into the metal caps are different on each scroll. The one we took from Polk in Behlanna was stamped for Water and Air. The one we took from the chasm in the Hoary Mountains was stamped for Air and Earth. Then Draghador gave us Earth and Fire. I think the second symbol indicates what element is protecting the next scroll. Polk has two scrolls now he would be able to figure that out easily enough. He will be able to reason which one we have. Now we will have to solve the puzzle and predict where we will go first. We know that it is fire and I had a vision as you did when I played the music in my head. I found an illustration much like my vision in the border art, and I think I know what region we must look in. Perhaps this is the location of the master scroll. Revealed as you said in the three scrolls. We'll see if Egidio can confirm the location when we get back to the boat."

I told Andreas about the volcanoes of the Jungle islands of Bekua. The volcanoes were renowned as the most violent in the entire world and the jungles that surrounded them were a likewise deadly environment, of unique fauna and flora left mostly unstudied by outsiders. Legends existed of explorers

211

going to study the region who never returned. Andreas knew of the region as well and we agreed that it would be a very foreboding place in which to hide a scroll.

"I'm sorry Andreas, I should have been watching, but I felt safe there. You slept for more than a day and we were unaccosted."

"No matter, I see that it could have been me in the same circumstance. Let's not waste time here any longer."

I nodded my assent and we divided our load for the climb back down the cliff. We took our time and lowered the box with the remaining scroll in it between us as we made our descent. Egidio had moved off shore, but the ship moved in closer to the rocks that surrounded the island as we made our way down the cliff face. When we stood upon the narrow shore I reached up to find the edge of the mask we had taken from the gate doors. It was a fine edge and I had to work it carefully to pull it away slowly. The supple properties of it returned to the hard properties it had before I had put it on. A thin veil of fog pulled away under it and then split as the essence of death returned to it and the essence of life returned to me. Andreas followed my lead and removed his mask. He took them both and put them in the box with the one scroll. After that was done we waded out to meet Egidio.

The ship was quiet as we climbed the ropes and set foot on the deck. Egidio was at the wheel rocking with the swells of the sea, but his rocking was ungainly. Egidio was experienced at sea; his motion should have been as one with the ship. It was the head that gave him away first.

"Trap," I whispered to Andreas, then I waved and Egidio did not return the kindness. I laid a hand upon the hilt of my sword. As I did twenty-one demonic soldiers of the dark legion stepped out of the ether and into the wet salt air around us. Wicked blades of swords, pikes, and forks were leveled at our throats. Only one among them was human— Polk. His skin was sallow and the bulging veins beneath it were black. He stood amongst his soldiers with his feet spread wide and his hands upon his hips. The pirate in him followed him even to death; or un-death as it were. His dark tattered robe snapped in the wind, the hood fluttered up against his gaunt face. He was making no attempt to conceal his face on this encounter and a grin came upon his lips slowly growing into a wide toothed smile. His pupil-less eyes seemed to suck in the light around us and I felt the same forces of death upon me as I had when we had first arrived in the plaza above King Draghador's City. Polk grinned and the force came at me. I fought that which would put me out upon the deck, but it was too quick, too powerful and I fell on my face, helpless against Polk and his minions.

When I awoke I was gratefully surprised that I was awake at all. Memory came back to me quickly and although my head pounded with sharpness behind my eyes and at the base of my skull I rolled to my knees for a look around. Andreas was at the wheel, lowering Egidio to the deck. I went to them and grateful surprise was again mine as I realized that Egidio was alive.

"How did you...?" I began to question Andreas on his luck at staying conscious. He pulled the mask that Draghador's gate had bestowed upon us, from the waist of his silk trousers and held it up for me to see. "Of course, if I'd have only thought of it," I said.

"Their force is great. It was only my experience with the elements that gave me time to draw it out and shield us from them. We would be dead now, or perhaps un-dead in service of the Dark One if not for Draghador's gift. I barely got to it myself. I was unable to save the scroll though. All that we have done are only futile acts now. We must go back and report failure to Kapit. Perhaps they have some information on the keys; perhaps a dark war has already begun."

Egidio emerged from his catatonic state. He looked slowly around, and then convinced that we were just the three of us he sat up. He was weak and shaking. I put my cloak around him and went for water for all of us. When I returned he was weeping. Andreas sat beside him, but he made no attempt to console the man, he looked even as if he might weep himself. "What is it?" I asked.

"Do you not feel the weight of it?" Egidio questioned. "What strength do you wield that protects you from the anguish that rises up within Andreas and me? What foul life have you led that this blackness does not eat at your heart?"

"Hold your tongue, fool. You do not know my life. It has been touched by darkness, you are right, but it has been a good life all in all. This darkness that you feel around your heart I feel too, but I recognize it as a residue of evil that has been laid upon me, and I fight it off with the good of me. Our situation is grim. I feel our failure deep inside. Like a knife it cuts me. It makes me shudder physically, and my soul quakes with it, but we have been played, Egi. Polk plays us even now. He planted a seed in each of us, I'm sure of that. When he saw he could not kill us he set it in the fertile stuff of our own anguish; to play with us, to see if we would fall to it—fall to him. I understand why you have succumbed, you are a fisherman with a quiet life, but

Andreas I am surprised with the ease at which you have given up."

Andreas looked away from me, ashamed at my uncovering of his weakness. He stood and raked a sleeve across his wet eyes, and then he hugged me. "I don't know what came over me, but you're right, I can fight it back. Try Egidio, you'll see."

That night as we sailed through the dark on our way back to the continent of Dinar and the river Storm, I laid alone on the main deck trying in vain to hold back the tears that streamed down the side of my face. I knew that the darkness of my spirit was a part of it, and I feared that it made me susceptible to Polk's mind numbing attack, but the awful return of the seasickness made me very sad indeed.

* * *

Deep in the land of shadows two figures as base and wicked as the stuff of shadows rendezvoused. The taller of the two hunched over the other and breathed his vile breath into his upturned face. The smaller cringed from the malicious visage of the other and would have crawled away had he not been frozen to that spot.

"What have you brought me Polqutis?"

"The three scrolls my lord."

"After all this time. What took so long? And what of the master scroll?"

"My lord, two most skilled thieves who wield weapon and magic with ease, took out my personal guard and absconded with the first scroll. I put all my resources into finding them and when I did I let them retrieve the scrolls and stole them from them."

"What great punishment did you unleash on them?"

The smaller shadow cringed again and stammered his reply, "It, it was all I could do to, to regain— possession of the scrolls. They fight like an army and the magic that one wields is powerful and difficult to oppose. I had to flee to save the scrolls."

"You are a sad excuse for a minion, Polk, but I suppose you are learning. Still you have failed to deliver the master scroll to me. Without it our master remains trapped."

"I have procured the three scrolls, as I promised that I would, now we can decipher the location of the master scroll as their time runs out. They have nothing."

The tall ones spite for his follower seeped into his tone. "Decipher them then. If I had the master now, there would be no need of the three scrolls. My master would be free to gather his legions. The gate would fall under their dark wrath and this would all be over. Instead we play a damn game of cat and mouse—so typically human.

"You disappoint me Polqutis. I give you boons and yet these mortals still live to plot and move against us again. I think that they will be more help to us than you can even dream. You are nothing to us Polq, if you cannot live up to your bargain. All of your dreams of power mean nothing to us, but we can make them real if you just deliver to us the Master Scroll. Do this, and do it soon or your life is forfeit." The threat sizzled in the atmosphere, giving it life.

Polqutis staggered from it as if he had been physically hit, but he managed a whispered reply. "I will my lord."

"There are other mortals who would jump at this chance to serve. Perhaps these two adversaries could be swayed to our ways."

"They have a reputation for good deeds, Lord."

"And yet, they know the ways of thieves. Be gone from me now Polqutis. When next I summon you be prepared for what I will demand of you."

The tall hunching shadow straightened to his full startling height. He threw back his head and laughed. The one called Polq fell to his knees and trembled. The stuff of shadows moved away, shunned him, and left him in the cold, alone. The shrill penetrating laugh faded only after his shadow had dissolved back into the surroundings.

·~· Chapter Four ·~·

We made the continent of Dinar and sailed along the coast to the mouth of the Storm. We turned up river and Egidio piloted us smoothly up the wide stream to the docks outside the western wall of the city. Andreas and I went below when we came within site of the city and Egidio guided us deftly to a pier under the shadow of the city wall. He made the claim of rare spices from the far continent of Crystalier at the behest of the merchantman Kapit. We knew that the dock master would send to Kapit for storage arrangements. At the top of the list of many spices was the entry: from the banks of the river Morte: Andreas Seed. If Egidio's name as captain wasn't enough to get Kapit's attention certainly the manifest would bring him to the docks and we would be able to talk to him in the private areas of the ship without ever setting foot in town.

We waited below for hours, but finally in the dark of night Kapit made his way to the ship accompanied by Father Gan, some dignitaries that we assumed had met Kapit's screening, and several guards. We were cramped in the small sleeping quarters of Egidio's vessel, but we made do and talked into the early hours of morning.

We told our story, with our chins to our chests, ashamed at our failure. When Andreas told those gathered the story of our entrance into Draghador's realm in detail. His words were well chosen; reverent and poetic. I knew that he was trying the phrases of an epic poem he had rambling about in his head. I interjected phrases from my own composition wherever he faltered. We had the makings of a bard song and we were proud to have such an audience for the first telling of The Forever King. When we came to the gift of the masks it was made more moving that the immortal King had bestowed such a gift on mortal man so that they may face the evil's that threatened their existence. Then we revealed the history books scribed in the hand of many of the greatest amongst the dwarven race. All those present realized the depths of sacrifice that clan Draghador had made; there was not a man amongst them who was not touched by that. When we explained, as a prologue that it was the masks that had saved us from Polk when he attacked us on our ship and took the scrolls, there were audible gasps amongst our audience. When we finished our tale exhilarated by our telling of it there was silence. Even Kapit dabbed at the corner of his eyes, but it was a guardsman from Gan's contingent that raised a glass of ale in salute.

Andreas leaned over and whispered into my ear. "We have to get that down on paper."

"Damn right." I whispered back.

It was Kapit who had kind words for our failed effort, and though he meant well it did little to sway our depression at having held victory only to have it so easily ripped away from us. Father Gan and his people set about the ship in prayer setting up blessings and protections to keep us safe from Polk and his soldiers. Then he took up with what they had been doing in our long absence.

We learned that there was a contingent of the secret sect recently arrived in Behlanna. They were housed separately, but met each day in Kapit's secret places around town, they were well guarded by Kapit's men and a few fighting cleric's of Gan's faith. They had gathered together the teachings, written and remembered, that they had carried and protected through the ages. They were attempting to piece together a possible location of the Master Scroll. The knowledge of the gate key scrolls is only written in the other gate key scrolls, but it is remembered in the hearts and minds of those who made it their lives to protect them. The acquired knowledge of each contingent was being pieced together with that from the other contingents; for each faction had protected only one scroll. Kapit's spies weighed in with their own tangible news. They knew that Polk had entered into a contract with a minion of the Dark one and that Polk was being turned to death and had been given the power to gate demons for small periods of time, but the demons would always loose strength and have to return through the gate or die forever. That explained the demons at Draghador's and again on the ship. After the debriefing they gathered together in their own circles.

We were questioned extensively for information we might have gained from our perusal of them. Andreas and I hesitated to shred Kapit's confidence and Gan's knowledge but it was time. "Sirs," I began, "we feel that there is more to the three scrolls than has been believed. Polk may only need the three scrolls to piece together the music that will unseal the binds at the gates. We believe that the location of the master is also given within them, contrary to what has always been believed. He cannot free the Dark One from the binds that King Montar placed on him unless he has the words to do so, and that is only revealed in the master scroll. He cannot get to the Dark One; even if he knows the keys, unless he has the locations of the gates, and that information must also be in the master. So if the Master Scroll tells us where the gates are, even though the keys are revealed in the three scrolls, perhaps the three scrolls tell us where the master is. If that is true than we are in a race to the master and the race is close. In the end we will need all four scrolls but to beat Polk we may need only the master for now."

Through the debriefing we were able to convince them that the master scroll lies beneath a volcano. They agreed that their research was pointing to the tropical islands of Bekua as a possible location. I am not given to clandestine religious ways. I thought they agreed only to save face in this convoluted mystery, but I was sure enough of my own ideas on the matter that I let them have their way.

Kapit took up, "Polk has all that he needs to decipher the musical keys that will unlock the master scroll. If he can also gain the location of the master scroll from them, then he has become the greatest adversary that generations of mankind have ever known. Polk has the aid of dark magic. He moves easily through the ether between life and death. He could be anywhere. He may be here and gone again, before our magic can detect him. We have placed our wards and rituals but his powers are great, they are still intact. He has not gotten to us—yet. Perhaps he needs the aid of his dark master for such things. We know he has been aided to have gotten so far."

"But we got him that far." I said in anger.

"Yes, but he does not know the location of the Master, yet. We do and that gives me great confidence. We will sail to The Bekuas as soon as we can."

I studied the faces of the learned men all around us as they absorbed the possibility, "If we have that scroll he must come to us either way, either for clues to the gates or to open the master scroll. And while he searches for his clues to the Master we will be on our way. Once we have it we can even stay in one place and let Polk come to us."

"We had wanted to follow the scrolls to the master to get to the gates, perhaps we still can. The jungles of Bekua— it seems as simple as that, but we must now watch even harder for Polk and his army of dark minions."

There was a whisper of understanding that went through the gathering and Gan spoke to silence it. "It seems even our own riddles confuse us. Perhaps that was the intent by those before us who put this into play. We will go to Bekua with all haste, but even in haste there must be preparation. Let us begin."

Andreas and I were allowed to sit with Kapit and Father Gan and the dignitaries, the members of their secret society as planning began in earnest. We were just the muscle; they were the brains and the power. They were so firm in those rolls that they were aloof. That was just fine with us they could finance us and point us in the right direction. When we got to our destination we would be in charge again. We listened for details that concerned us, until it got mundane, then we moved away from them and began to mingle with the mercs and bodyguards.

The party was beginning to heat up for them and they welcomed us to the fire. After many drinks Andreas and I were leaning against a make shift bar in the main hold taking it all in when an astonishingly beautiful couple came slowly down the stairs. They were geared up; he wore brown silks under a fitted studded leather jerkin and swashbuckler boots. Broad hard arms carried a large leather pack and a weapon belt lined with swords, daggers and a hefty axe. His hair was a dark color I'd never seen before, not red, not brown, and not even auburn, I settled for umber. His skin was dark and his muscles ripped beneath his jerkin. He was a monochromatic beauty, and my heart actually skipped a beat when he caught my eye and smiled. I glanced away, like a shy schoolgirl, but then remembering myself, I had enough presence to smile back as he crossed the room to report to Kapit.

I turned to Andreas and had to reach over to close his gaping mouth as we watched the woman who followed the man to the table. She was tall and slender, sultry in a simply cut muslin shift that showed her curves. She was muscular, but not in any way that told of great strength. She too carried a pack, but it was lighter, and smaller. This hung from the end of a mace that she had rested on her shoulder. Her hair was dark and hung in a loose ponytail down her back. She was not tan, nor pale, but was sun kissed as if having only recently spent time out of doors. Her face was thin with high cheekbones and eyes of green that matched the southern seas. Her lips were full, and when she saw me close Andreas's mouth they parted in a bright white smile. Andreas assessed his appearance and began to primp. I however was perfectly fine, not being a sloppy drunk like my friend.

We could not take our eyes from the two and we were excited that they must be the two that Kapit had mentioned would be helping us with security. There would be no need for opening lines or ice breakers and we would have a length of time in which to test the waters. I saw Kapit indicate us, and they dropped their packs behind his table and came over to us.

The big man had a quick stride and a bright smile. The woman followed gracefully. The man stopped in front of Andreas and extended his hand to him. "I am Wallace Shawn; I am here at the bequest of Master Kapit to assist you on your journeys. My friends call me Wall."

Though he shook hands with Andreas he let his eyes drift to me. My eyes were tracing along his hard torso when I heard myself say, "I can see why." My tone was a bit salacious, and hearing it aloud, outside of my thoughts surprised even me and made me aware of more than just Wallace. I saw Andreas's disapproving look, and a raised brow from the woman, but Wallace smiled and cocked an approving look my way. He did not miss a beat though and introduced the woman. "The lady is Sardon; she represents Father Gan, and comes along as healer and spiritual leader." Andreas reached to take her hand and bent to kiss it softly.

What show offs men can be, but let a woman comment on a handsome man and the room starts buzzing with derogatory remarks. I had no choice but to watch his muscles flex as he took up my gear and motioned me to a seat in a corner. I was beset with silent anticipation. I had not felt such attraction in years; not since Andreas. I would have to be careful. Being romantically involved with a partner, in the business of mercenary could be dangerous, even deadly. I tried to gather my senses, as I always had while working with Andreas, but then the man called Wall had the gall to turn and smile at me as he sat down. I was clay in his hands.

I sat and tried to find something to say, but my thoughts remained below consciousness as I looked into his eyes. Then Andreas crossed between us and took a seat next to me and Sardon sat between him and Wall.

"So," Wall began. "Tell us what we can expect on this journey. Kapit and Gan have made it clear that we take orders only from the two of you, and that our mission is one of dire importance. They have left the details for you to fill in— as you see fit of course.

"Of course," Andreas said. "Far be it for them to give any details when your life is on the line." His ire was apparent and a little "hmmph" slipped out.

"This is not the place, later, on the ship that Kapit has arranged," I offered. "Even Kapit and Gan cannot filter out everyone wishing us harm. On that ship we will have our own quarters. We can shut out listening ears, and speak in whispers. For now let's wile away a polite period of time, drink our fill and then be on our way. The ship casts off soon; at first morning tide."

We talked then about our personal histories, glory days and such. I found Wallace and Sardon both to be good company and was happy for it. The stories of their rise in their chosen professions served as a resume and I assessed that they were both experts in their fields. That was a comfort, and their aid would be well needed. The party began to slow around us and we went to Kapit and Gan to say our farewells.

It was still before the dawn as we talked and laughed, stumbled and swayed en route to our new ship. I jumped a bit when Wall lunged suddenly and came back with a wretched old thief in one hand and Sardon's purse in the other. He thrust the purse at Sardon. "Count it; your tally determines the fate of this old man."

"I only meant to take it to feed my family."

"Ha! So say you all. You are not very good at gauging your marks, old man."

"It is all here. Thank you Wall, it is all that I have."

"So you see, you were about to rob a woman of God of her meager means. Perhaps you felt she was the easiest, weakest of this group. Why in all the worlds would you mark a group with three sword fighters in it? Be glad that I am quicker than you, fool and caught you before you ran off with the good lady's coins. Now be gone." He dropped the man at our feet, who then scrambled away from us, before turning to get his feet under him in a runner's gait that gave the lie to his years.

"Old man—indeed," we all said together, and laughed at it. We made our way then with a bit more spring in our steps and arrived quickly, though not noiselessly at the ship. "I'm glad I did not have to give chase, I'm a bit in my cups. I fear he would have beaten me," Wallace said.

***

We were still awake when the sailors were called to their stations to cast off and do what sailors do to put a ship on her proper heading. We had spent the night regaling Wall and Sardon with our story starting with our entrance into Behlanna. I'm sure they didn't believe much of it then, but I knew that would change as time went on. I crawled into one of the hammocks and fell asleep to the lull of their voices, anxious to be asleep, before the sickness of the sea travel took me.

I woke not much later to the rolling and tipping of the waves of nausea in my throat. I spun out of the hammock and hit the floor with a thud. The scramble for the water bucket was without grace, but I made it in time. Sea sick and hung over, I'm just not too bright sometimes. Of course Wall and Sardon assumed hangover, but Andreas helped me to save face in the drinking derby by playing to my affliction at sea travel. Sardon quickly fixed me up with some herbs; the very scent of which began to work on me. For the rest of the trip I was sure to have a sprig of it pressed tightly under my tongue. I walked the deck, and took the sun each day. I ate with the crew and even took time to learn a bit about sailing in the few days allotted to us on the ship. Near the end of the trip I even began to find some beauty in the sea, and the odd birds and creatures that flew just above and below the surface.

On the third night we sailed through a storm, I struggled a bit but the herbs helped a great deal. The next day the wind that pushed our sails grew increasingly warm. The red and orange suns beat down to warm the saturated air to a sweltering temperature. We had watched the flora change along the island shores and mainland coasts that we passed. Trees with thick leaves as large as a man leaned out over the water. Bright flowers of colors we had never seen before grew as large as my head creating a thick blanket of undergrowth that seemed impenetrable. Egidio slipped Kapit's ship through the colorful reefs that teemed with life. Large fish jumped along side us as we made our way further south. I appreciated this all the more since I was not leaning over the rail in sheer seasick misery.

Four days out we spotted the shores of the largest island. The land sprung out of a volcanic reef. A range of volcanic cones and geysers rose up out of the island's canopy and spread out in a skyline that spewed grey steam into the atmosphere. The steam was made heavy by the mix with ash and remained trapped above the landmass. We stopped Kapit and Gan stood at the rail with Wall, Sardon, Andreas, and I; as Egidio headed around the island, staying outside of the veil of mist.

Andreas called out first, "There!" I followed his outstretched arm and fingers and I had to agree. I had explained the illustration to him on our sail back to Behlanna and so he found it. There it was right down to the slope that the lava had flowed down. The slope led around to the back of the volcano.

Egidio showed us how to wrap turbans that covered our heads except for an opening across our eyes. This would protect our lungs. With that done he sailed closer to the island and the grey mist enveloped the ship. We left the bright light of the two suns behind, and entered a place of stormy dark. The suns were only diffused orbs of pale light. Andreas and I took stations along the prow to spot out reef or stone and direct Egidio around them.

We made our way until the tide and wind would carry us no further. We could not get the ship close enough to wade in so we lowered the skiff and loaded our gear. Andreas sat upon the woven metal box that was our gift from Draghador. Sardon squeezed in next to him. Wall sat across from me. Andreas and Sardon spotted for obstacles in the water while Wall and I rowed us in to shore.

The beach was glassy black sand so fine and soft that we sank to our ankles in it. We concealed the boat in the thick foliage below a stand of leaning trees at the edge of the jungle. We had come straight in from where we had spotted the volcano that was the destination for our next stage of the quest. The foliage was thick and we had to cut our way through. We would travel southwest about fifty degrees to find the path that would lead us to the foot of the volcano. We had a compass to keep us on that heading, but we trusted our instincts more.

We floundered through the haze of ash that was settling on us like silt. Andreas followed close behind me. Sardon walked side by side with Andreas, Wallace followed close behind them. The jungle was full of unfamiliar howls and screeches that reminded us of the tales of strange and ferocious beasts. We all had weapons drawn. The thick growth was a miracle of the atmospheric conditions of the place. I used my secondary blade to hack our way through it. Andreas flipped his sword tipped staff casually. Sardon gripped her mace too tight; she was obviously not a fighter, but had the courage to join if it was asked of her. Wallace held his great axe in both hands, ready for battle if any came our way, but none did.

We found a way to the ring of hills and volcanoes that surrounded the interior of the island. Moving carefully up and around we took what foot holds the way offered or assisted one another along the way. It paid off, the way continued steeply, but it was negotiable even with our gear and the box. We climbed steadily and came out of the mist. Ash still fell, but it was like a grey snow flurry and so the light of the suns could make it through. We kept ourselves covered and took a bearing on the cone that we sought. The humidity drenched us and our already damp clothes with sweat, the ash fell upon us and soaked up the moisture making our clothes like a fine silt suit. We were off track, but not far, so we made our way inland until nightfall and then made camp.

We found firewood buried in the ash and had a nice fire going in short order. We took turns sleeping a few hours at a time, but none of us slept well. The jungle sounds did not subside during the night. In fact, the atmosphere of our location seemed to amplify and distort sound so that we were always on edge, expecting an attack from anywhere at any moment. We were undisturbed for all of our vigilance, and we were weary and sore.

Our clothes had dried over night leaving a layer of caked grey mud that crackled with every move we made. We brushed away what we could, ate a breakfast of fruit and hard tack, took our bearings on the volcano, and started out. The ash still fell and the rising suns lit it an amazing crimson. The morning air was already heavy and warm.

We climbed through the jungle and ash making slow progress on the rough terrain, through thick foliage. As the suns raised so too did the heat and the steam from out of the ground. Then suddenly as if by magic, rain fell in torrential sheets, washing away the ash that covered everything and soaking us to the bone. Massive flowers opened to drink it up, and for that time the jungle was a beautiful place, full of wondrous colors and shapes. The sounds of the jungle denizens went silent. There was only the sounds of the rain pattering the plants that grew in so close, and us hacking through them; blazing a trail toward the foot of the volcano.

We were surprised when we cut through the foliage and just on the other side was an open expanse of land dotted with pools of brightly colored mud and mineral water. The mud boiled and the water steamed. As we scanned the area geysers shot up from different pools spread out across the plain. Grey rivulets of ash-saturated rain ran off into the pools, or soaked into the soft ground.

The ground sloped up toward a range of volcanic cones some tall and steep, others squat and dome shaped. Some spewed plumes of grey ash that mingled with the rain and fell back to the ground. Other formations also dotted the landscape. They were blue-black plugs of ancient inactive volcanoes denuded by years of erosion. The grey ash that seemed to always fall here was building up in slopes at the base of these formations, a tribute to the ever-recycling effects of nature.

As we took in the primal beauty of the place, the rain suddenly stopped and the sounds of the jungle slowly came back to life as if just waking for the day. We sat upon black, porous stones that cropped up from the ground to rest and take refreshment of the cool clear water in our skins. We never took our eyes from the alien beauty before us and so we did not notice as a creature of what I can only describe as primordial, oozed its way forward from behind us.

I turned as I caught some motion in my peripheral vision. A gooey appendage with a dripping mouth orifice snaked out of a pool of black ooze and sucked in my booted foot. I don't recall the action, but my blade snickered out of its sheath and was in my hand in a flash of steel that severed the grotesque appendage cleanly. The thing did not fall away dead or wounded, instead it morphed. The appendage that had me was but a small version of the larger thing that still slithered toward us, mouth appendages flailing. Andreas had his double bladed staff weapon in hand and was attempting to slice the thing from my leg. It just oozed around the cuts, healing itself, all the while climbing further up my leg which was becoming numb, either from constriction or a brownish secretion that covered every inch of it. An appendage snapped out toward Andreas, but I cried out a warning and Wall swung his great axe off his shoulder and severed the appendage allowing Andreas to spring away safely. Sardon wielded a small mace, but it was defensive only and she stayed well away from the beast that was morphing together again.

The two pieces of the thing met and conjoined becoming one again. It was now up to my thigh, and spreading across my mid section. I hacked wildly at the thing, as the terror of being consumed gripped me. I cut through it and into myself and screamed in agony as the toxins rushed into my body, through my open blood stream. My motions slowed considerably in contrast to my racing fear. I dropped my sword and attempted to pry the thing from me with my bare hands. Wall joined my efforts, but drew back when the thing reached for him. I made very little progress as more and more mouths grabbed onto me and seeped up under the protective turban and over my chin. I clamped my mouth shut against it, but if it reached my nose I would be lost.

The next thing I knew I was in a blast of fire that Andreas shot from his hand like a child throwing a ball. The flame hit me, and the ooze creature that engulfed me, with a force that sent us flying off the rock where it had attacked me. We landed hard upon the ground my mouth was open and the wind was knocked from me. The creature entered my throat as another blast engulfed us. This time the fire flared along the surface of the thing sputtering and smoking before going out completely. I could no longer move, but I was dreadfully aware of my circumstance. I was at the mercy of the creature and Andreas's magic. I wondered darkly which one would kill me first.

The magic fire hit again and I felt the grip of the thing loosen, but it did not pull away. I could hear Andreas cursing in a tone deep in fear. He gave up on the fire and was hacking at the thing again. The creature tightened its grip on me. I felt my mind going blank and struggled to keep consciousness, even though sleep would have been merciful. Then I felt another blast of Andreas's magic— this time — harsh and sudden bitter cold. The thing released me and pulled back momentarily, but then, throwing off the pain it concentrated on me again. Andreas let go another blast that sent us rolling across the ground. We lay still, I was completely immobilized and the ooze still engulfed me. I resigned myself to death as the darkness became too much to fight.

Then there were Andreas, Wall, and Sardon beating away at the thing and it broke into chunks below their blades. They pulled the frozen thing from my head, and out of my nose and mouth. I would have gagged as the ghastly substance was pulled from deep inside of me, I felt the impulse, but my body was unable to react to it. Andreas removed what gear he could from me, breaking pieces away until the thing was removed from me completely. Then they smashed the thing into dust. He created a whirlwind that picked the dust up and took it away over the jungle and out of sight. Only then did he allow himself to turn his attention back to me.

I lay on the ground stiff as a corpse. He fell to his knees beside me to listen for my breath and heart and choked back a cry when he heard nothing. Even a blade below my nose revealed nothing to him; I could not tell him to leave it there longer. I was sure I would exhale soon. I could not speak, or move my eyes to indicate there was still life in me. I could only stare at the sky and scream inside my own head. He looked into my eyes long and hard as if to determine some life there and then he reached up and slowly lowered the lids closed. Then he took me up in his arms and held me as he cried.

I was not prepared for the intensity at which he grieved for me. He admonished himself for having not acknowledged his love for me. He begged my forgiveness for that. His emotion was so deep and his words so lovely that I was moved. I would have been sobbing had I been able to. It was torture to hear his pain and not respond, anguish to hear what I myself felt for him and be unable to affect the physical world, to reach out and touch him. He was quiet a few moments and then I heard his voice again.

"A tear? Sade, can you hear me?"

Yes, Yes!

He shook me and my eyes opened from it. I saw the world through the blear of tears that spilled out and fell numbly, down my face. He took both my hands in his. "I'm here Sade, if you can hear me squeeze my hand."

I tried, but my muscles could not react, my will could not overcome the toxins that ran through me.

He listened again for my breath turning his cheek to catch breath from either nostril or mouth. I could feel my lungs filling so slowly. I feared he would pull away again, too soon, but he stayed. "Come on, girl, come on." I heard him say, and at last my lungs filled and slowly began to compress in a slow exhale. When he was sure of what he felt he sat back and watched me. "Come on Sade, I'm here. I'm not leaving." From that point on they worked together to make a camp right there. Sardon was not pleased, fearful as she was of another attack, but Andreas laid down the law and she made no further complaints.

He talked to me the whole time. He regaled me with a report on the quality of the firewood at the edge of the trees a better quality than it had been under the moist ash. As I lay there listening to his gabble about everything and anything that he could think of to talk about I began to feel the pins and needles of life returning to my muscles. The blood was beginning to flow again. Sardon began a meal while Wall walked a small perimeter protecting our camp. Sardon brewed a pot of tea and Andreas brought a cup of the spicy brew to run the steam beneath my nose. The aroma registered and I felt as if a brittle layer around my brain fell away. Things were changing for the better but I still could not move, not a blink.

The day moved across the sky. Andreas arranged my turban to protect my face from the falling ash and gently closed my eyes again, to keep them safe for when I could open them again on my own. He continued to talk as they ate smoked fish and gritty bread and washed it all down with water. He didn't much like the fish and the gritty bread was exceptionally dry, though the best tasting he had ever had. I was honestly getting tired of hearing him go on senselessly about everything he did, but it warmed my heart to know that he did it for me.

I must have thought about opening my eyes every second since he had last closed them, the time dragged by. Andreas continued his incessant chatter and I was ready to scream when suddenly I realized my eyes had popped open and I was looking at the moon through a cloud of ash. I saw Wall pass by in one of his passes as guard. I tried to wiggle my fingers and was elated when my right index finger twitched. Things started to loosen up more quickly and soon I was able to control most of my motor skills.

"Shut up already," I was finally able to rasp.

Andreas, my friend like a brother, Andreas, maybe a lover fell over the lump of dirt he sat on in his effort to get to me.

"I'll never speak to you again, except to say this one last thing if you promise never to die on me. I've just discovered that I will not be able to go on without you."

I took his hand weakly in mine. "Go on." I wanted to hear him proclaim his love for me when he knew I could hear him.

"I am getting real tired of nursing you back to health. It gets old you know."

Close enough I thought. "I love you too you know, gods help me. We'll talk later. Now, help me up. I need to move around."

As soon as I sat up, a rush of nausea over took me and I released all the poisons of the creature in a few minutes of gut wrenching. "Still love me?" I said as I wiped spittle from my lips.

"We'll talk later," he said and walked away to fetch me some water.

We stayed close to the fire that night. We never did talk, but we lay close, glad for the comfort it gave us in that strange and eerie place.

***

In the morning we broke camp and trekked through the steaming and bubbling land between the inner volcanic range and us. The place stank of sulfur and hot mud. We moved quickly across the warm soil and made our way between two cinder cones about half as big as the imposing cone that was our destination. We stopped long enough to adjust our heading and began to climb. We moved around the eastern face of the volcano in search of the trail we expected to find there. We made a quick decision to follow the trail in the illustration around to the back of the cone.

The nearly vertical surface was very like ropes coiled together and laid side by side to cover the surface of the cone. The ash and stone cinders of past eruptions gathered in the deep crevices. Several openings along the way belched gas and ash so we did not enter. Our route would take us around to the southern face of the mountain, but we were also very near the top. We allowed that the illustration might have been a bit off, and curiosity was nagging us, so we chose to climb to the craters edge and look in. The crater was huge, and plugged. Two new cones had forced their way up from the floor of the original crater. One had a crater of its own so we knew that it had blown at least once The other was still domed, and so had not yet blown its molten contents into the air. We climbed over the lip and into the crater making our way around the two emerging cones and found yet another even smaller cone. It lay like a parasite on the shoulder of the newer un-erupted cone. It did not spew ash or belch gas but it did have a crater. No glow of orange flowed by in the depth of it. We tightened our gear, positioned our weapons, and laced each other's armor tight. With that done we shared a silent resigned look at each other, shrugged our disbelief at what we were about to do, took a deep breath, and climbed in.

We followed a narrow down sloping shaft. Assuming it was a conduit for the main volcano we expected to discover lava flow below us. But, no orange glow, foul stench or heat met our descent. When the passage turned and opened into a teardrop shaped cavern we were not surprised to see that the cavern was open at one side to a large central shaft. We were at the center of the volcano. Deep below us was the orange hot glow of magma we had been expecting. It lit the walls of the shaft. The temperature at the edge of the shaft was searing hot and smelled of sulfur. Where we stood, gazing down into the main artery of the volcano was a porch of sorts, and from that porch a wide ledge wound down into the shaft, along the inner wall. We saw no other traversable passages or pathways from that vantage point and so we took our first steps into the shaft, staying close to the outer wall the orange glow lighting our way.

We made out an opening ahead and went to it. Another passage opened up and at the far side of the cavern was another opening to another shaft like the one we had descended from outside. We moved in to investigate. We could see daylight from a vent crater above us. We were below the small cone inside the crater. The lava here was not far below us. The cavern surfaces showed signs of past eruptions, though we could not predict when those eruptions had occurred. Driplets of hardened lava hung from the roof of the cavern, and a layer of basalt coated the walls and floor between this shaft and the main shaft. The pressure of the lava flow from the main shaft would be vented off to the smaller shaft. At the time that the cone within the crater had blown its top the main shaft would have had to be full to this level as well. The other cone having its shaft at a higher level was not likely to erupt until the main shaft was nearly full and also at risk of erupting. It was the pressure below that had caused the newest cone to push up out of the old crater.

There was no traversable way around this secondary shaft. And the way we had come had ended at this cavern. We checked all along the cavern walls with torchlight then and found nothing. We went back the way we had come, and found nothing. Somewhere between beginning and end we had missed something, else we were in the wrong spot altogether. We spent hours searching up and down the ledge several times attached to ropes guided by one of us and at long last we found an opening. Andreas was having a turn on the rope and I was giving or bringing up the slack at his commands. I could not see him and so relied on his instructions to keep us both from being pulled into the chasm. I was lowering him down when he yelled stop, rather more excitedly than any other time.

"I need to go left," he called up to me. I gave him slack slowly and watched the rope move across the edge of the chasm.

"That's good there, now down a little." I pulled in the slack once then lowered him down very slowly. "There, right there!" I heard and stopped lowering him immediately. "I have a cave. It looks like it goes in about ten yards sloping down then takes a turn. Give some rope. I'm going in as far as I can."

"Are you in the cave now?" I yelled, as I tugged the rope to test the slack. There was no weight on the other end so I knew he must be, but I wanted to hear him say it, to know the communication was complete, that's how partners take care of each other, but mostly so if he fell it was his fault and not mine, that would be my argument in that case. He did not respond, but the rope began to move again so I knew he could not hear me. I stood back against the wall letting the rope out slowly. It played around the piece of black glasslike rock we used as brake as the angle and situation called for. There were a few moments of slack with no movement of the rope. I tensed ready to begin pulling him back, but then the rope began to move again. I had let out all but five feet of the rope when I felt two distinct pulls on the rope; our signal to reel in the slack. I must have brought up one hundred feet when I heard Andreas call from below again. He was back at the cave entrance and I pulled him out.

When he climbed over the rim he was singed. His cloak and loose fitting garments had holes in them from where they had caught fire and failed to spread. His hair and eyebrows were singed, the acrid odor of burnt hair still hung on him. His face was red and blistered, they would need tending, but they were not severe.

"What happened?" I asked as I gave him a hand up.

He tossed a charred length of rope on the ledge at our feet. "I'm not sure, I was moving around the bend to get a look when a blast of fire and cinders blew out of the wall at me; burned that right off me." He said indicating the rope. "I figured a trap, but the walls are full of pits and pocks, from previous eruptions and there is an orange glow that emits from them. I can't tell the source of the glow, except that it comes from behind the basalt walls."

"So it could have been a stray vein of volcanic material."

"Maybe."

We returned to the outside world, to rest and take in fresh air, as fresh as it got in that place. Sardon tended to Andreas. I made cold cheese sandwiches and then we curled up inside the small cone to watch the suns set behind the gloom of the ashen sky. It made the place beautiful for that short time. Deep shades of purples cast by suns' rays across the sky were refracted through the jungle vapors and grey ash. The sight was unmatched by any sunset I had ever seen or have seen since. I watched until the last light of day was gone, and then I pulled myself up to sit against the wall. I stretched my legs, pulled my cloak tight around me against the chill of the high elevation winds and wrapped my arms around myself. Each hand held a bare sword; ready to defend should we be molested at our rest. I found a suitable divot in the stonewall and tipped my head back into it and closed my eyes, but not my ears. Andreas and Sardon chatted softly nearby, but further down the sloping passage. Wallace took a spot closer to the opening and sat as I did ready to defend us. A soft rustling began to move through the mountain far below, a high-pitched squeal went along with it. I recognized the sound as a rush of bats but these bats were like no others. Their wingspan was easily six feet and their eyes and underbellies varied between fiery yellow and orange. Andreas threw himself over Sardon just as the fiery bats filled the passage above us. "Get down." I yelled to Wall and spread my self out on the floor in front of me with my hands over my head. We raised only our heads just enough to see them pass over us and burst from our passage into the sky.

I stood, brushed myself off and went back to my spot. "Thank you, Lovey." Andreas said as he rolled off of Sardon and curled up to go to sleep.

"Don't call me Lovey, unless you mean it." She said. She moved to a spot across from him and spread out to catch some sleep herself.

"I'll take that under consideration." He replied and the talk ended.

I rested my head back against the rock and watched the first moon rise half way up from the horizon. Sounds of the jungle drifted up soft and harmless and soon they lulled me to sleep.

I woke to sounds just outside the cone; Andreas had started a small fire and was starting on breakfast. Sardon assisted him. Wallace slept nearby. I rolled over on to the floor and allowed myself to sleep until someone came to wake me.

We ate smoked ham diced with onions and cheese stuffed into blue tubers baked soft on the stones near the fire. A cup of kaffe to wash it down and we were well energized for our work ahead. We broke camp and moved down to the ledge above the cave entrance, with our loads just a little lighter. We used the glassy rock along the edge to tie the rope around and then spiked the rope to the floor near the wall as an anchor. Being the more experienced climber I went first as always.

I checked the spikes and added more along my way, making a sort of rope and spike ladder down to the side of the cave entrance. I placed a spike inside the entrance as a handhold to aid the transition from chasm wall to passage floor. The passage was just as Andreas had described it, no one or nothing was about so I hollered up to him and he lowered the packs and the box by a rope to come down directly in front of the cave opening. I pulled the bundle to the floor and detached the rope from them. I yanked on the rope then and began pulling it into a coil as Andreas threw the other end into the chasm. He moved along the edge until he could see me and watched as the rope climbed up into a neat coil at my feet. I waved him down and he moved back to climb down along the ladder of spikes and rope.

While I waited I hoisted my gear and secured it. I went to watch as Andreas climbed. "You okay?" I asked.

"Yeah, go ahead."

"Okay watch the others then."

"You got it."

I padded quietly up the natural stone passage to the turn in the bend and then the floor was laid with flagstone, or something like it. Flat slices of dark glassy stone covered the floor. The workmanship was excellent and must have taken great skill, and time. I wondered if the dwarfs had a hand in this as well. I began the tedious chore of checking for trips and traps. I found a slightly depressed stone on the inside of the bend just at the spot I had chosen to peer around for a better look. Just above it in the wall among the pocks and pits of the natural surface was a charred opening. I saw the orange glow from many of the holes in the rock, but from that one the glow was brighter.

I crouched to get below the charred opening and then moved onto the depressed stone. Nothing happened; either we were wrong or the trap had not been reset. I thought the latter and continued my check.

From my crouched position I peered round the bend in the passage. It widened just beyond our position and took a sharp turn to head back toward the chasm we had just climbed out of. The chamber turned once more, slightly away from us, and ended with a round portal. A round door hinged on the bottom laid open into another room like a ramp.

Andreas was now beside me. Sardon and Wallace were padding up slowly behind us and we moved ahead together. I used my sword to probe the floor ahead of me and moved cautiously across the room toward the door. The rest of my team walked just behind scanning for anything or anyone that might interfere. I found two more of the fire and cinder traps, one I was able to disable, and the other barely missed as I dove aside. I do not know how many more we missed simply by benefit of our chosen route.

We came alongside the door and slipped around to the threshold to bypass another trap on our way. The threshold was chest high to me, belly high to Andreas. I moved up and peered over the rim.

Another chamber declined away from us and turned again ending at another door. Throughout the room six tall reptilian beings were perched lazily upon their snake-like tails, their hind legs crossed or dangling above the ground. So they sat with long bows at the ready, but their demeanor was casual. I call them beings, because there was intelligence about them, they were not entirely bestial, even though forked tongues darted in and out of their snakelike maws as they conversed in their language of hissing and spits. They had muscular reptilian arms covered with scales, and their hands were large reptilian like claws but with prehensile thumbs, which allowed them to grasp their weapons. Two wide curved blades crossed their backs in sheath harnesses clasped at their chests.

There was no other way for us to go. We readied our weapons and stepped up onto the door. We approached without clatter and made it half way to the first of them before we were noticed. The first to notice hissed a warning and they rocked up off of their tails with a snap. We had hoped to offer some communication, perhaps a bargain to allow us passage, but the first sound uttered was the gasp of pain from Andreas as an arrow sank deep into his shoulder. It had been fired by a snake man hidden behind a shelf of rock just the turn in the chamber. When it hit they surged upon us.

We retreated to the entrance. Andreas moved back to protect Sardon as Wallace moved up beside me. Sardon and Andreas were on the door and had a slight height advantage. Wallace and I stood side by side just before the threshold and engaged the battle. There were three on each of us and the archer on the shelf pelted us with his arrows. We yelled and landed desperate blows, but they were swift and skilled with their curved blades and we took many blows more and several arrows each. Only Sardon was spared from her protective position behind Andreas.

Wallace fought with his double bladed axe and one fell before him quickly, but another arrow pierced his shoulder and he staggered. I felled one and an arrow grazed my thigh, but failed to pierce it. I swung my sword wide and another arrow meant for me caught my blade and spun it out of my hand. The flight it took caught an unsuspecting snake man up side of his head with a crack and he went down. A fortuitous blow that tipped the odds more to our favor, but Wallace was struggling. I could hear Andreas gathering his magic. I fought fast and furious to keep them from him and off of Wallace, but an arrow pierced my upper arm, pinning it to my side. I fought on with only one arm. The snake man beat me down to my knees, and I prepared for my end, but when he rose up to unleash the strike, I found the soft underbelly and stabbed my blade into him. He died with a look of surprise on his reptilian face. I stood and turned to face another when an arrow struck me in the chest just below the clavicle. Wallace lost his footing when I moved. I had been his brace, but now he fell into me and we struggled to keep each other upright as the attack proceeded. An arrow sang by my face and sank deep into Andreas's pectoral muscle just as he was about to loose his magic. The pain of it must have been too great for he slumped and the magic sizzled away. I dropped my sword and took up his double bladed staff-sword. I could use my pinned arm as a fulcrum and was able to spin the thing handily enough to fight. I felt infuriated and that gave me an edge.

The first to go down was one that Wallace had dealt some heavy damage to. The second was not so easy. He concentrated his blows against the arrows that stuck out of me. I fought through the blinding pain; more a frenzy than a strategy but I had enough skill and strength left in me that I was finally able to slay my attacker. As he fell at my feet I heard an arrow loosed. When I turned to dive away I saw that it was Wallace who had fired it. He had made it to a bow of one of the snake men and an arrow was sailing true toward the archer above us. It sank into his throat and he fell from the shelf— dead.

Wallace fell to the ground and lay as still as if he were dead too. I turned him face up braced for the shock of his death, but was quickly elated to see his chest rise slowly with a labored breath. Still our situation was grave. I was badly wounded, and tired, Andreas was down, Sardon tended to him just out of line of the battle on the other side of the ramping door. We could not stay where we were; certainly a group of organized soldiers would have a team to relieve them.

I broke the arrow shaft that had my right arm pinned close to the fletches, and pulled my arm off of the shaft that remained. The pain was excruciating, and though I tried not to, I cried out. I bound my arm and then broke the shaft again so that it only protruded a couple of inches from my side. I stabilized it by wrapping it figure eight style and then wrapping the bandage around my mid section. I experienced pain at the site of the injury with each breath I took and that had me scared. If I extracted the faceted head I was sure that I would bleed to death. Our survival counted on getting everyone to safety and keeping us alive long enough for Andreas and Sardon to take over with their skill and a little of Andreas's magic.

I opened my leather jerkin. The arrowhead below my clavicle was sunk only a touch below the skin and so I cut it loose with my dagger and pulled it free of the chain mail shirt I wore beneath the jerkin. I packed the wound with bandage and wrapped it to my shoulder the best I could with my wounded arm. It was loose, but it would serve until I could get everyone to safety.

I pulled Wallace through the threshold and down the ramp to where Sardon was tending to Andreas. I found the carpetbag near the entrance where Andreas dropped it. I picked up our weapons and some of the arrows and stuffed them into it and laid the bag on Wallace's chest and wrapped his arms around it. Then I pulled him by the back of his armor with my good arm, while holding the bandage around the extracted arrow site tight with my wounded arm. Sardon assisted Andreas. We made it to the shaft, before I collapsed, dizzy and exhausted. I rested a few moments; tended to what injuries I could with healing unguents, and saw to Wallace as Sardon finished with Andreas.

The arrow to Wallace's shoulder was nearly through and through. I broke the shaft just below the fletching and while he was still unconscious I laid him on his side and forced the arrow through so I could then pull it out the other side. The pain of it shocked him back to awareness and he woke with a scream.

"I thought that would get your attention," I said.

"You were so right," he said through clenched teeth.

Andreas and Sardon were beside me now. Sardon had done a quick surgery on him. She had sliced the skin open and removed the arrow then slathered it with an ointment from our supplies and the pungent smell permeated the air even from under the bandage she had placed over it. They had come to see to Wallace. I used the ointment on the gash to my thigh and both sides of the wound to my upper arm and bandaged them while they did.

Andreas began an incantation and laid a finger at the point where the arrow had pierced Wallace's body. A crack of flame and sparks shot forth and traveled the length of his wound, the stench of burnt flesh filled the air. He winched against the pain but did not cry out as the magic began to mend him. Sardon tended to the rest of his wounds as Andreas turned his attention on me.

I removed my jerkin and the chain mail shirt I wore beneath it. Andreas unpacked the wound below my clavicle. The blood soaked rags came away easily and the socket that was left quickly pooled with blood and spilled over. Andreas smeared a bit of bandage with the ointment and repacked and dressed the wound. Next he tended to the most serious of my wounds, the arrow in my side. Andreas examined it and saw a bit of pink fluid, bubbling around the shaft. This indicated that I had pierced a lung. Andreas informed me that only my lung was affected and that no other vital organ had been pierced.

"We have been lucky yet again," he said sarcastically.

I was scared to death at having a lung pierced, seeing as how breathing is vital to living and all, but I simply said, "Well that's good then." I trusted that he had some way of extracting the arrowhead that would not rip my lung further.

"The magic I need to bring into play to heal you is difficult for me to gather. It is more divine than elemental. It will take great energy and tire me greatly. There is no time for rest so I may need your assistance to leave this place when I am through. Come let's get to it; remove your armor completely."

I did as I was told; first unwrapping the bandage I had used to stabilize the arrow outside of my mail shirt and then removing the jerkin. I slid my arms out of the mail shirt and Andreas held the broken shaft as I pulled the shirt slowly over my head and then slid the final chain links off along the shaft. Andreas took a blade and cut my silk shirt away from the wound. It stuck to my skin where the blood had gathered and I knew from the heat of it that the wound had already begun to fester. Andreas's surprised look did nothing to alleviate my fear. Although the blood was not discolored, the wound was swollen and the skin was black.

"This can only be from poison," he said grimly.

"What of the other wounds, why do they not fester?"

"We did well, and treated them more quickly. The unguent and cauterization stayed the advance of the poison in them."

"Luck again, I suppose?"

"Indubitably, yours however went a bit badly. Sardon I will need your aid. When I say the word you must pull the arrow out. I will be too busy with the magic to do it myself."

"But..." I said

"No questions. It will tear and be extremely painful, but as soon as it is free I will lay on the magic and the pain will leave you quickly as the wound begins to mend. The unguent will follow immediately and the poison will be become neutral, so that your body can deal with it.

"It is the same as what I did for Wallace. If I am unable to perform both spells, bury me with dignity." He actually managed a grin, but his eyes and tone were serious.

"Don't say that. You have never failed before. You are not allowed to fail now."

To Sardon he said, "If you do exactly as you are told when you are told she will have a better chance. What do you say?"

"Let's give it a try shall we?"

I braced myself. Sardon did exactly as she was told which amounted to minor surgery. I bit down on Andreas's leather gloves, as he cut down to my rib cage along the path of the arrow. Sardon pulled it until we could see the rear points of the arrowhead pressed against the lung and the muscles that surrounded it. Andreas made an X shaped incision. Gave Sardon some instructions and then began to work his magic. As the magic traced blue along the incision Sardon pulled the arrow through it. I fought a sudden wave of nausea, pain and vertigo as the broken arrow was pulled out. Andreas laid his magic long and hard into the wound. Sardon followed up by slopping unguent into the X shaped incision and all along any exposed tissue as per Andreas's instructions. I could feel the re-growth of tissue from the first seconds of the magic, and the unguent seemed to speed it along. When he was done with his magic he sewed me up. It held well, and then we slathered on more unguent before wrapping it in bandages. Andreas had held up under the task, but he was sallow and his eyes were red rimmed.

We had gone through one jar of the medicinal, and had opened another. Only one more remained after that; I hoped we would have enough to finish our quest.

There was no way that we could climb up out of the shaft to return to the surface until we had more time to heal. So Andreas and Sardon sat in the shadows just inside the entrance to the first passage and watched while Wallace and I slept.

When I woke Wallace was still sleeping quietly. Andreas and Sardon sat face to face with their heads close talking so quiet as not to wake us. I watched them a moment before I rose. They were becoming more than comrades. They touched often and their touches lingered. I rose and walked passed them to look up out of the shaft.

I could tell by the subtle light that trickled into the shaft above us that day was waxing into night. The bats made their way up and out of the shaft again. I was relieved that they had come from below us and not from within the passages where we were. I hoped that it meant we would be able to avoid them all together.

No snake men came to hunt us. That confused me, but I was getting used to that frame of mind more and more since we first arrived in Behlanna. We were safe there so we stayed two days in that passage until we were well healed and rested.

Wallace had color in his face again and I felt my strength coming back to me. We ate cold tack and drank water. Andreas saw to fresh dressing for our wounds, which were healing nicely. I helped Wallace to his feet and we both stretched to warm our muscles before continuing on. We packed the carpetbag with the remains of our foodstuffs and medicines and I went ahead to scout the caverns we had been through, to see what was the status of the snake men.

All was as we had left it. That made me uneasy. The reek of death was heavy. What purpose had the snake men served? Were they a guard that was so expendable that they had no contact with their comrades? Perhaps they had been discovered and were of no matter. If that was the case I worried about the ruthlessness of the beings. Another possibility occurred to me, perhaps they had been discovered, and were left intentionally as a ploy to make us think we were safe. I moved deeper into shadow and scanned the area again. I saw nothing alive.

I moved through the fallen bodies and searched them, looking for some clue as to what their purpose here might be. I found only pieces of the glassy black stones of no substantial value. I took them anyway; perhaps they had value to the snake men, though I doubted we would get the opportunity to bargain. That idea had nearly gotten us killed once already.

I moved through the shadows once more and made my way to the closed metal portal at the curve in the far end of the room. There were no traps or pit falls along my chosen route. I checked the door and found nothing. I listened even though I doubted I would hear anything through so thick a construction. I took the opportunity to rest, before returning to the others. My little foray had left me winded—a condition to add to my list of doubts about the success of our quest.

I joined the others and led them back to the closed portal. It had a large thick gear slightly larger than a human head in the center of it and two thick and heavy gear rails ran across it at top and bottom. The gear rails were inserted in channels that ran across the midsection of the door in opposite directions. The rails themselves were long enough to fill the channels, but only showed three quarters of their length. The remaining length was unseen, driven home into the stone doorjamb. The opposite end of each rail had a small slit in it, a keyhole of sorts.

I set to work and soon had the rails unlocked. I tried to turn the wheel, but the mechanism was too tight and heavy and the bars needed to be moved simultaneously. Andreas lent his strength to the task and soon the door was falling smoothly, but slowly toward us to create a ramp, like the door we had entered to do battle with the snake men. Andreas backed away into the shadows, and I stepped aside of the door and drew my swords, slowly and quietly. A low eerie green glow and a noxious odor emanated from the room beyond, but we waited a moment to see what might happen next. Nothing and no one came immediately through, so I ventured a peek over the threshold.

Another chamber declined slightly away from us, the length stretched out ahead of us with the door in the short side of the room opposite us. Sardon lit a torch and held it high for all of us to see inside. The stone ramp into the room gradually leveled out into a causeway that ran between two floors set at slightly higher levels. Along the higher floor to either side of us were stacks of bones carefully placed to form a long wall that divided that floor from the causeway. Behind the low wall were mounds of bones and skulls carefully stacked to form pyramids, behind those, fully reconstructed skeletons had been placed within the walls, as they would have stood in life. Some of them held hands. They were all reptilian.

We moved cautiously down the stone slope. Andreas and Sardon watched above us as Wallace and I entered back-to-back and sideways into the room. Another round portal stood at the opposite length of the room. It was what we moved toward. We had no intention of defiling the burial crypt of our vicious enemy. We came to the center of the room and no skeleton had come to take us to its world.

We made the door without incident. I did my job and when I felt it was safe Wallace helped me with the locking bars. It was good then that Andreas and Sardon had been watching our backs as the room behind us came to life. I took one look into the next room—a well-lit crypt with but a single sarcophagus and another door opposite that which we would enter. I ordered Andreas and Sardon inside. "Find out how to close this damn thing. When you know call out and we'll jump back, as soon as we're in close it!"

Andreas led Sardon across the causeway as we protected them to the new portal. When they were safely across Wallace and I stood side by side in the doorway and fought off the swarm of skeletal beings. They fell before us easily, but their number was so great that we took heavy damage as well. More and more of them rose from the stacks of bones as those around us fell. Our previous wounds made us tired, so there was nothing we could do but fend them off. Their claws tore at our flesh, and their fists bruised us well, and I felt the cold swoon of the undeath upon me. The room before us was packed with them and the room behind us was our only safe retreat. I fought through the awful sensation of distorted space and time. Wallace was beginning to be affected too. Andreas's swearing as he worked to find the mechanism sounded slow and distant. Then I felt it working beneath my feet, before he called out. Wallace and I rode the rising door as far as we could, still beating back the clutching arms of the undead guardians, until we dove off and into the room and could get the door shut.

Wallace and I sank to our knees to gather our senses as Andreas and Sardon sealed the door behind us. This new room was barely ten feet by ten feet. The sarcophagus filled most of the room with just a thin walk way all around it. I picked myself up from the ground and trudged toward the next sealed portal. As I did so the lid of the sarcophagus slid smoothly to one side and nearly landed on Wallace's feet as he walked toward the portal along that side. A bony reptilian hand clutched the sides as the occupant pulled himself up to get a look at us. I braced myself and remained with a guise of calm.

The creature was better preserved than those from the previous room; he still had skin over most of his reptilian body and his snake eyes were not shriveled out of their sockets. He looked slowly from one to the other of us, until he had taken us all in, then he set his eyes on Sardon and motioned for her to come to him. She did so at his suggestion, but not willingly. She clutched at Andrea's arm, but her mind would not obey her will to disobey the Lich. Andreas attempted to move between them but the Lich made a motion as if to brush him aside and he was flung up high against the wall. Then the thing spoke in a dry voice; raspy from disuse.

"She is the one that can help me, and in so doing may gain you access to the room beyond. Look again at that portal, there is no mechanism real or hidden that will get you through. That door will only open upon my release. Only a minion of the dying god can release me to my final rest."

"I am not a minion, I am but a priest adept, a mere mortal."

"So you say, but I sense a power in you. Is there something you are reluctant to admit?"

Sardon looked nervously to each of us as if pleading for some answer.

"I assure you I don't have any powers."

"Do not toy with me, Thing." The Lich growled. "I sense it in you and so it is there, if you have not come to terms with it, or are so weak that even you do not know of it, then you are doomed to stay here and die. I have a task I need you to do, and when it is done I will pass wholly from this shell of life and the door will open for you. You can kill me if you wish to try, but I dare say I will take at least two of you with me. Still if you kill my body my spirit will not pass as it must. It will remain trapped here in this mountain and the door will remain sealed forever. There is a gem that sits in the eye of the skull of my greatest enemy."

He didn't have to tell us, though he did, that that skull sat in the room from which we had just escaped.

"Bring me that skull and the gem within it so that I will be whole again and free to pass from this life, and the portal will be open to you."

"How must I retrieve it?"

"I am afraid that it is a condition of the curse upon me that I cannot reveal this to you. I only know that you have the power within you. It is for you to identify and control."

Sardon looked to each of us nervously. There was something about that that made me uneasy. I do not like unknowns when I am facing death, and this time when it was so literal it set me on edge. I watched her. What was this power that had eluded us? Would she recognize it in time?

The lich lay back into his sarcophagus. "I will await you," he said and flicked a finger at the portal through which we had entered his burial vault. The gear turned slowly and the door slid down to open on the room of bones. Andreas and Sardon moved back from it even as Wallace and I came forward to peer back into it. I put the undead Dwarven mask to my face. Andreas followed my lead with his mask.

It was as if we had never entered. No bones lay scattered on the floor. The low wall and pyramids had been reformed. We hoisted our weapons and moved onto the door. No sound or motion came from the room. Wallace and I moved down to the floor and looked over the skulls that we could see. The gem was obvious to us now that we were looking for it. It was in the eye of one of the fully formed skeletons embedded in the wall. Upon his large head was a gem-encrusted crown. He did not hold hands with another skeleton, presumably those were mates, but two skeletons that had been laid to rest with full battle gear flanked him. Each of these guardians had their left hand over their heart in a salute. I had no doubt that if we were to disturb the Lizard King that his two guardians would come to his aid, as would all of the bones we had just fought.

I turned then to Sardon. "I believe it is your lead."

She stepped down off of the ramping door on to the stone floor. and joined us reluctantly. She looked about and then upon spotting the gem moved towards it purposefully as if she had already identified that power the lich had declared she had. Wallace and I followed back to back again, moving sideways through the room. Andreas stayed where he was at the top of the inclined door. He could see the whole room, and all of us from there so if we should need the aid of his spells he could place them wherever the need was.

Sardon stood before the skeleton of the lizard king. She reached out a shaking hand toward the gem but a play of light jumped from her bracelet to bounce off a facet and blinked across her face. She jumped back. Wallace and I hunched into battle stance, but no motion came from any skeleton or bones. Sardon laughed nervously, removed the bracelet, and reached again. This time she got her hand around the gem, but as she did the kings hand shot out to strangle her. The two guardians stepped out of the wall with dual scimitars spinning before them.

I could hear the clatter of bones around the room gather up to destroy us.

"I don't mean to pressure you, honey, but if you don't come to terms with this power of yours we are all going to die, maybe even you first." Wallace strained to remain calm through his fear.

The swords men engaged and we did battle with them as the swarm of undead moved to surround us. I heard a crackle of magic from Andreas but it never reached us because he was involved in a fight for his own survival. The dark cold was powerful and though I wore the mask it began to take me. We were all weakened by it, only Sardon seemed to have any strength. My arms were like lead and the degree of distortion before my eyes made it difficult to land a blow, and when I did it was ineffective. The force of the undead swarm pushed against us. I heard Wallace's drawn out screams as he went down and the swarm engulfed him. I was next, but I saw Sardon reach out determined to gain the gem.

As she did I thought I saw her form change to be as one of them. We were lost and I went down under the swarm.

***

They held me. I was aware of my own dying and I fought against it. I could not affect it. No matter how I punched and tore at them they held me. My grunts and screams were silent. I could hear Andreas yelling somewhere. I tried to call out to him, but my voice never escaped my mouth. Was this to be my end; trapped below a living pile of bones? Then a sudden loud clang, like metal against stone came to my ears. I jumped. My heart was pounding and my eyes shot open. I was on the floor of the Lich's crypt and was both surprised and relieved to find we were all still alive.

Andreas and Wallace jumped up to the threshold of the newly opened portal. We had succeeded! Sardon sat in a slump against the lich's sarcophagus. Whatever she had done had caused her great strain. I got gingerly to my feet, and nearly blacked out. I shut my eyes to the pain in my head and that served to steady me. I could see that Andreas was in charge of scouting the area beyond so I went to check on Sardon. She assured me that she needed only a moment to rest and bid me go to join the others.

Andreas gave me a hug when I came up beside him, and Wallace, who seemed no worse for the wear, gave a nod and came to take my hand to help me down the ramp. I took it gratefully. My senses remained distorted and my equilibrium suffered for it.

We stood on a short landing that led to a stone bridge high up in a deep shaft. There was no opening above, and somewhere below a strong wind swirled in, pushing up through the shaft to rebound against the ceiling and push down against the up draft. Dirt and stones swirled within the winds snapping and cracking against one another to be broken into smaller pieces until more large pieces blew up from below to be broken against each other. The bridge went directly through this collision of winds and stones. There was no other way forward. We made a plan with Andreas with his magic as the key.

When Sardon was rested and my balance completely recovered we moved forward with Andreas in the middle. He moved slowly with Sardon to guide him as Wallace and I took the lead and rear respectively. Slowly he borrowed elemental strength from the winds in the shaft and let them swirl around us in a dome to repel wind and stone as we made our way across the bridge. We arrived safely to another portal and I found the familiar mechanisms and Wallace and I turned them to let the door down.

We had to push it open with some difficulty but it opened away from us and we entered into a vast low cavern. The floor of it was thick with hot mud and boiling water. The ceiling of the place was riddled with holes to the outside and sloped up toward the shaft from which we had just come. So we knew that we were somewhere along the outer edges of the volcano and the beginnings of the geyser field. There was no obvious path, just a door, barely visible at a distance and partially concealed by the natural curve of the cavern. As we took this in the floor bubbled and churned. We took a step back onto the portal door and watched helplessly as it began to rise. When it became obvious that it would continue at a steady pace we retreated and tried to pull the door shut, but it had quickly become engulfed in the stuff.

Andreas put up his enveloping shield to protect us from the winds and earthen debris that we had just left. We moved back up the bridge, toward the lich's chamber and watched as the flow of boiling mud rose higher and higher. It began to ooze through the portal like thick brown dough. Then, suddenly, it shot up and out with great force to fill the whole of the chamber and expel itself into the geyser field above. That which escaped through the open portal was caught up in the winds and soon dried to particles of dirt and dust.

We knew that if we were to get beyond the geyser chamber that we would have to move quickly, before it expelled its hot gas and mud again. Andreas left his shield up and we hurried him along. I ran ahead to the portal and gave it a quick examination for traps and was relieved to find none, but the workings were mucked up with the sludge from the expulsion of the mud several times a day. Wallace and I went to work wiping the fresh layer away from the hard crust of it that had formed over the threads and gears for years. Then we broke it away with the shafts and pommels of our weapons. As we did so the floor began to rise again. We worked at turning the gears but they would not go. The mud came up to our calves; hot and tight around our leather boots. Andreas struggled to increase the bubble to include the floor but he was straining to maintain it as it was, so he inverted it to include the floor and left it open above us. I saw the strain he was under in his face, the faraway look had turned intense, his eyes were red rimmed and veins bulged at his temples. I worked feverishly as the mud rose to my knees and began to seep into my boots. The gears turned hard and slow; I poured water over them to wash away the grit and they turned a bit better, but not fast enough. Andreas's shield was beginning to fail. The force he tried to repel was just too strong. As the mud bubbled higher the shield was weakened more. We were trapped. At any moment we were going to be thrown to the ceiling. I grabbed Sardon and Andreas and threw them face first against the wall next to the door. Then I pushed Wallace up against them, also face first and pushed myself up against them all. "Grab onto something Wall!" I yelled as I grabbed the portal door drive gear with one hand and Wallace's upper arm with the other. He understood and drove his axe head deep into the encrusted walls and held it tight with his left hand as he wrapped his right around Andreas's belt. "Sardon grab on to someone and hold on tight. Andreas, if you have anything left..." but there was no time for enchants. The floor blew. Our legs were ripped out from under us as the thick stuff ripped away from our legs. I lost my grip on the door, but not on Wallace, who struggled to keep us anchored to his axe. Sardon reached out to pull me back toward the group. Being on the outside edge of the room had kept us from the full force of the expulsion near the middle of the room. Hot mud rained down on us and we were scalded by it. We had no recourse and suffered the pain.

When it was over Wallace and I returned to the portal door. The new layer of mud served as a lubricant on the newly exposed mechanism and things turned easier. At last the door opened and we let it down into the mud of the geyser room, but the prospects on the other side seemed no more desirable than what we had just experienced.

The ceiling was lost in darkness far above an orange glow. A narrow ledge offered the only path through the narrow chamber. It ran straight ahead for about fifty yards high above the source of the glow—a flow of molten lava. The lava river flowed from underneath the geyser chamber into this narrow chamber. I saw no beings and so crouched low and climbed up and over the threshold. The heat was intense and dry, fumes seared my lungs with each breath and I felt the pain in my wounded lung once again. I retreated over the threshold and peered back into the undulating orange light. At the end of the ledge a stone bridge spanned the lava river to a dark opening in the opposite wall.

We prepared to move through the chamber. We removed the cloth we used for turbans from the carpetbag and soaked them in water. Once they were wrapped across our faces the water would block the fumes, cool the air and humidify it. I went in first, searching the way for any traps as was our normal mode of operation. I found nothing, that is, not until we came to the bridge.

A pressure plate in a near corner of the bridge was linked to a chain that traveled below the bridge and just below the top lip of the ledge. I did not know what but something strong and powerful would be unleashed upon us when the plate was depressed. I suggested that Andreas should step on that spot, so we could find out, but he would not comply— knows me too well I guess. Three more plates were staggered randomly across the stone floor of the bridge. Fortunately they were easily avoided or disarmed. Unfortunately arrows were being fired at us from some where in the dark chamber. One last pressure plate lay before us and spanned nearly the width of the bridge.

"Follow me and jump!" I yelled. I leapt across the last of the bridge, clearing the pressure plate and tucked and rolled my landing. Wallace rolled in just behind me and we crouched in shadows giving our eyes time to adjust. Sardon moved in tight behind us and Andreas moved up and laid the carpetbag on the floor before moving back beside Sardon. Wallace and I crawled up and hid behind the carpetbag. The archers took shots at our area, but we remained unhurt.

When our eyes adjusted we got a general outline of the room. It ran straight along one side until it came to an intersecting wall. Across from us, to our right, the wall curved away gradually, widening the room. Then at the widest point the wall suddenly turned sharply and the floor dropped steeply there. It was here that the archers took cover. They were reptilian of some sort, but they seemed more lizard than snake, not like the ones we had encountered in the first chamber. The dark and their cover made it hard to see just what they were. There were four of them and they had a direct line of fire. Their arrows were zeroing in on us. If we crossed to the curving wall we would be no more concealed. We drew our own bows and returned fire. My first shot flew true and took the nearest archer in the throat. Wallace let fly with two before his target went down.

The two remaining retreated down the slope of the floor behind the wall. We took that moment to cross to the wall opposite of us and staying low I skulked up quickly to peer around the sharp turn of the wall. The floor sloped steeply for nearly thirty feet. At the end of this double doors stood partially open. The doors were again made of some metal alloy, but they were not the round portals that we had seen here before, they were more like what we were used to in our lives. They were unadorned but were thick and heavy. They opened into the room beyond, and I saw no sign of the archers. I motioned for the others to join me. They stayed at the top of the slope. I started down the slope on a path that would allow me a view into the room without being at the opening. I had bow and arrows at the ready and Wallace and Andreas were likewise ready to cover me from there if it became necessary.

The room ran perpendicular to the door. It was wide and barren of life, but I could see a faint orange glow coming from the end of the room furthest from the door. I motioned to the others that I was moving up to the door. They took aim on the opening. I stayed low and got my back to the door that was opened the least and peered through the opening that was now to my right. The other door blocked my view some, but I was able to tell that the room ended after only a few feet in that direction. No living being was there, unless they were hidden behind the door. I turned my back away from the door so that I could peer around it and into the main portion of the room. The ceiling of the room was dome shaped but did not come all the way to the floor in some areas. This created natural openings in the wall just above the river of lava. I could see it spit and bubble as it flowed beneath the room. I saw no living being and so ventured a look behind the doors. We were alone.

When I looked behind the doors I discovered a low opening in the wall there. I motioned again for the others to join me.

Once we were together, I swapped my bow and arrows for my swords and bending my shoulders low stepped into the opening. It turned sharply after only a few feet and twisted and turned until it took a straight path to run along behind the room I had just left. Another opening up ahead was made obvious by the bright glow of orange that ran through the room beyond. I could make out five silhouettes of lizard beings crouched before the river with arrows knocked in bows and aimed at the opening. They had not fired so I assumed they could not see me. I turned to report back, but my partners had made their way to me and crouched just a few feet behind me.

Andreas motioned me to get behind him and I did. He gathered his magic to him. I could feel it prickle my skin as it built in power. Suddenly he let it go and it took flight up the passage. He quickly repeated the process and sent another ball of force out behind the other. The first burst from the passage hit the five archers sending three into the lava river. The two that had survived the first blast were scrambling for safety when the second blast hit and they too were deposited into the lava flow.

"Go!" Andreas ordered and I ran the length of the passage to burst into the room to put an end to any remaining resistance. Wallace was beside me and Andreas was right behind him. Four more lizard beings were running to another door. Andreas took the one in the lead with an arrow to the back. I leapt forward and blocked the retreat of the second. Wallace moved to the opening and let loose three more arrows. I heard two death cries while I dealt with the one before me. He still held his bow and would have been easy to dispatch, but I spared him in hopes there was some information we might gather from him.

The effort soon proved futile, so we left him disarmed and let him go. We gave him a head start and then pursued. He was aware of us and moved quickly, but he gave us the benefit of revealing or disarming traps that were along the way. The passage ran along the direction that the lava flowed. The heat and gases caused us to tire quickly, but we held the loose ends of our turbans over our faces and pushed on. We came to a fall of lava and watched briefly as it fell hundreds of feet churning and bubbling like a thick water fall before flowing as a river again at a lower level. The path was no more than a ledge above the flow far below, but we followed it. We had lost our unwilling guide, but soon picked him up again and made for him. We were heading away from the lava flow now and he screamed as he looked back and saw us still in pursuit. I felt it was some attempt to warn his kind hidden ahead somewhere, we increased our pace. Wallace notched an arrow as we ran.

Our quarry stopped and took a look back over his scaly shoulder, before disappearing around a stand of rock. We ran to the spot, and I peered cautiously around. A passage even more narrow than the one we were in dropped steeply away from us and back in the direction of the lava flow. The Lizard-man disappeared beneath the ceiling of a chamber below. I scrambled down first and shouted a warning as I dove over a fire ball of lava shot from a contraption that pumped the lava from the falls as it made its way deeper into the earth. I landed and jumped at the lizard-man who manned the cannon. His surprise at my acrobatics became his weakness. I ran him through before he could defend. "Now!" I yelled up to the others and Wallace jumped into the room followed by Sardon and then Andreas. The one that we had chased here fell to his knees and pleaded for mercy. Two more were frantically heaving at the gear slides of another round portal door. Wallace stopped them both dead with two well-aimed arrows.

I crouched before the pleading creature before me, my blades crossed before his throat. "Perhaps you understand us a bit better now, hey, Beast?" Beast shook his head. "So you speak my language then?" He shook his head again. "Let me hear you then. Tell me what you are doing here." Once more his head shook. "If this is a game you play, Beast, then it is a stupid one. I let you live once, to show us the way, but we are capable of finding the way on our own." He nodded again, but this time he looked me in the eye. I slid my blades against each other, close to his throat. Perhaps it was not our language that he understood, but rather our intent.

I stood up and offered my hand to help him up. He took it warily. I lead him toward the portal, but he pulled back. "What is it? Your kin seemed rather intent to open this door, why do you shy from it?" He shook his head again, this time though it was a negative action, and he pulled his claw from my hand. What ever was behind that door had a powerful effect on him. I contemplated the others who had attempted to open the door. Why two such opposite reactions, from comrades?

Andreas went up to examine the door. "It is hot." He noted. "Perhaps the flow gathers here and they would have released it to kill us."

"And themselves as well?"

"Perhaps they felt they could out run it." He moved two fingers like running legs in the direction of the steep entrance passage.

I had to agree that the supposition made some sense, "But if what is behind there is so frightening why not just run from us and leave us to it?" I asked.

I took beast by the arm and pushed him toward the door. He whimpered and fought me until I let him fall to the floor. He was no use to us, I pointed toward the exit passage and he crawled to it on his four lizard feet, and then stood like a man. He bowed once to each of us and then turned to run up the passage, on his hind legs.

The locking mechanism on the door was partially undone. We left it that way, and rested. What ever was behind that door warranted our full attention and strength. We slept in shifts near the lava cannon. When I was awake I studied the thing. A stone tube was inserted into a small hole in the wall that ran up to the back of the cannon barrel. On the side of the barrel was a large lever that from the sound of it when I pushed it forward opened something within the wall. The tube and cannon then became searing hot until I pulled the lever back and a molten ball was ejected from the business end of the cannon. The process was quick and immediate, had I not quickly expelled the lava, the contraption would have surely melted into a useless blob. Andreas was not amused by my explorations while he tried to rest, but I was happy to know how the thing worked. It might come in handy against whatever mystery waited for us behind the portal.

We passed the time without interruption. Again that seemed strange; the dwarfs and the air elemental were fiercely dedicated to the cause of protecting the scroll they had been charged with. The fact that we were after the master scroll and these reptilians had been so easily routed disturbed me. I slept in small snippets but mostly I tried to reason out what sense there could be to leaving the master scroll so loosely guarded—or were they? We had dealt with able guardians at the entrance, a multitude of undead, turbulent winds that would have dropped us into a deep chasm had it not been for Andreas's command of elemental magic, and the hot boiling mud beneath the geyser field. It hit me that we had dealt with death; what Andreas had once called the fifth element. The turbulent winds could be the element of air and the boiling mud could have been water, or earth, or perhaps both. I became certain that our next battle would be against fire. The excitement of knowing kept me awake while the others slept. Only Wallace was awake and standing watch. I relieved him and waited for them to be rested as I contemplated what might await us on the other side of the portal. Assured that our battles with death were behind us for now, I peeled the dwarven mask away slowly and returned it to tie on my belt.

During our rest we kept the cloth about our faces moist in that hot chamber, and our lungs flourished. Weakness left our bodies quickly, but the longer we stayed the more nervous I became about the chances of an ambush. We had no bearing on time so I don't know how long we stayed, but I'd guess most of a day passed before we again approached the portal. The metal was searing hot to touch. We had to don our gloves, where the thick hide of the reptilians had insulated them from the heat. We opened it and stepped aside as the door fell open smoothly. The heat from inside was oppressive and the orange glow of molten lava washed over us. We moved up the ramp created by the open door staying to the outside of the opening.

The room beyond was a vast chamber created by the fall of the lava river. A bowl burned into the mantel of the earth collected the lava. It bubbled and spit as it flowed by and fell over the lip in a slow stream. A small ledge of stone edged the lake on each side. We stepped down onto the ledge that ran along one side. We moved in with weapons drawn, but saw nothing to threaten us, aside from the lava. We looked the place over, and Andreas saw a black crystal box tucked into the stone and shadows on the opposite shore. If the scroll we sought was in that box, we had no idea how we were to obtain it.

There was no bridge, or stepping stones either natural or manmade that allowed access to the other side. I approached the edge at our side to begin a search for mechanisms, and when I did a massive disturbance occurred in the lava lake. The lava rose up in a roiling swell and lapped up onto the ledge forcing me back. Out of the surge rose a great conflagration—a beast like a dragon, but this was no creature of flesh and blood. This was a creature of fire. My mind raced. I felt defenseless against such a thing. I did not carry a shield, and my blades seemed insignificant to its great mass. I backed away from it as it grew before me in height and mass. When it had emerged fully from its fiery reservoir it strode slowly toward me.

Lava slid between the leaps of flame that were like scales covering this fire dragon's entire body. The lava dripped into the pool and sizzled before moving in dark swirls toward the lip. The beast lowered its massive head, easily the size of two merchant wagons, toward me. Lava dripped from its giant maw like the drool of a hound. Two dark eyes like pressurized steel glared at me and then he turned his head to take a measure on Andreas and the others who had backed up toward the entrance. Having determined my frightened companions no threat he turned back to me.

In the brief time that he had turned his attention from me I looked for cover. There was none. The great creature reared up and fanned its fiery wings. Little balls of flaming lava separated from the main mass of the wings and rained down on me. I dodged many of the projectiles, but those that hit were instantly, deeply agonizing. I staggered to the floor in my lurch for the door where Andreas cowered from the fear of death by this beast. All the times that I had feared my inevitable death seemed silly in the light of this great elemental force. I rolled to extinguish the flames that had caught on cloth and skin. Chunks of cinder remained imbedded in my flesh. I stood and faced the thing, in a defensive stance. If I were to die in my quest to save my world, I would not go quietly.

The beast drew in a breath and when it opened its mouth to breathe its fire upon me I leapt and rolled to come up in a crouch. The breath missed me by mere inches, but in the release of it the beast had fully extended his neck. I leapt forward and ran under it slicing my blades deep into its throat. Lava gushed from the wound and splattered me like a wound cut into flesh and blood. I leapt and rolled to extinguish the flames that caught on me again. I found my balance and got to my feet as it reared back again. I ran all out back toward the door. I was glad to see Andreas in a stance I had come to recognize. He was gathering his magic. He had only needed time to gauge what might be needed. I just hoped his calculations were correct. He kept Wallace and Sardon behind him to protect them. Wallace was ready to battle but Sardon shrank behind them.

I heard the breath and felt the blast of heat bear down on me. I crouched as a blast of magic sprang from Andreas's out stretched hands to pass just above me.

The breath and magic met in an impact that pushed me. I spun out of control and hit the wall next to the door with my back and shoulder. The air was forced from my lungs reminding me that they weren't yet thoroughly healed. I lay helpless gasping from the shock and saw that Andreas's magic now kept us safe behind a barrier of force. The danger now was how soon the expended energy would tire him. My eyes fell upon the beast. I could see the flow of lava still seeping from the wounded neck. Perhaps it could be killed after all.

When I had my breath and was certain my bones were still intact, I moved out from behind the barrier flashing my blades before me. Wallace moved out the other side and we flanked the beast. I was prepared for anything and it came in a great slap from the thick flaming tale. I jumped over the tail and lunged with my swords as I went over. The beast's tail jerked out in a reflex from the pain and hit me in the back and sent me tumbling, but I was able to withdraw my blades and run back behind the barrier. Wallace got in a swipe at the dragon's side and dodged the thing as it spun around to find him. He ran and safely joined us behind Andreas's barrier.

"Can you extinguish this thing?" I shouted above the hum of Andreas's magic.

He did not respond, but I could tell that he was considering the possibility. The protective shield began to waver with his lack of concentration and I ran out to deal what blows I could while Andreas formulated a piece of magic to save the day.

The great flaming thing lunged forward raking at me with claws of ember. I ducked the first swipe and planted a blade deep in the belly of the beast. A roar of flame blasted forth, around my stuck blade but I was saved from it as the second swiping claw; sent off course by my last attack; caught me in the edge of its arc and sent me rolling toward the lava pool. My boots began to smoke and the silk of my breeches was about to melt to my skin. I was on my belly clawing at the ground to slow my progress toward the pool. When I stopped my feet were fully over the pool. I pulled myself into a somersault and felt a blast of frigid wind as I came half way around. The beast was behind me. Andreas was in front of me, the cold wind came from his lungs and blew from his mouth. Wallace was beside him and I jumped into a defensive stance and turned to face the beast. He stood above me once again poised to strike, but his color was changing, from flaming orange to yellow to cool blue and white. I drew my spare sword from the sheath strapped to my back. The flames that were the beast slowed and then froze, and then the beast began to topple forward. I moved aside and watched the thing land. The upper body stretched out so that the nose of it landed at Andreas's feet, the belly and hind end stretched out across the pool and the tail spilled over onto the far bank.

The lava was quickly melting the carcass. I knew what I must do. I took a quick look at Andreas and then half ran, half leapt across the melting, sinking body. I landed safely on the other side. The crystal box was within my reach. I hesitated; now that I was there I was unsure of my actions.

The bridge created by the fallen beast was just small lumps of melting stone, the tail slid into the lava and was gone. I had no way back, and from what I could tell, no way forward. There was nothing to do, but go after the box; If the scroll was within it was what we were there for. What came next depended in some way upon the scroll. I had to at least examine it.

So it was that I set upon the box and after finding no traps upon it I lifted it from the ground and found not a scroll but a lever. I pulled it toward me, as it was the only way that it would move. There was a loud resounding boom when I did. Assuming a trap I had missed was about to blow up in my face, I covered my face and put my head between my knees. Nothing happened. Slowly, tentatively I uncovered, uncurled and looked around. Nothing had changed and we were still separated by the lava flow, but behind the box was an open passage. The stone that had concealed it was now leaning to one side.

I looked across to see Andreas sitting amongst the broken pieces of neck, head, and upper body of the beast; now just lumps of melting black ice. He was slumped forward and wavering in his exhaustion. Sardon was tending to him. Wallace stood defensively with his axe at the ready should another beast emerge.

I called out to him. "I have a way out from here."

He gave me a weak wave. "We'll rest first," Andreas called back. With that he lay down to sleep. I could only watch him, and hope that he regained his strength quickly. I hated that he slept so much, and at such inopportune moments. It sometimes happened when he had to twist elements into some as yet untried force of magic against some unknown awesome foe. The energy he spent that time was the most he had ever dared.

I took stock of my health, rinsing away the spent cinders that had melted into my skin with my drinking water. Though I too was feeling exhausted my mind was still intact and a little rest replenished me. I was well enough, a bit awe struck, but alert. My gear was another story. I had lost all but three arrows, during my tumble with the beast, and I had broken my bow, most likely when I had hit the wall. I was down to two swords, the other having been consumed in the fiery belly of the beast. I still had my two bandoliers of seven daggers each. I would have to throw them across the pool at anything that threatened them there. I prayed my aim would be true, and then I settled in to watch.

The fates must have rewarded us for a job well done, because we spent hours in the searing hot chamber unaccosted. When Andreas woke he was disoriented and we had to tell him what had happened.

"So we— we have it— the scroll?" He stammered as he rubbed his hands across the back of his neck.

"No, the only thing that was in the box was a lever that opened this door. See here it is." I went to it and stepped partially through so that he could see it.

A quizzical grin came to his face as the reality set in. "But we are separated. It is too far to jump and impossible to climb. I don't see what we can do. I am far to tired to bend the elements again just now, and even if I were not I have my doubts as to what I could do."

"Rest then, I will explore this way for as long as it is safe and try to find where it leads."

"You be careful, you hear me?"

"I hear you."

"Okay." He blew me a kiss, and I returned the gesture.

I watched a moment longer as they began to gather what remained of our scattered gear and repacked it into the carpetbag. Then I turned and went through the door and into a dark and narrow passage. The floor was natural stone, but smooth as if worn by traffic. The orange glow from the chamber behind lit my way for a short time until I could no longer see my way. My eyes could not adjust to such utter darkness. I rustled through my pack until I found a torch, then I struck a flint against a wall and the sparks trailed to the head of it and the flame flared up to light my way. I moved soundlessly forward. My anxiety at what might lay ahead, caused me to place each foot as gingerly as I possibly could.

I came to a great manmade stairway that wound up slowly along what must have been the outside wall of the mountain. I knew it must lead up to our next encounter in this damnable quest. I left the stairs and returned to the others stopping only to snub out the torch when the lava glow began to enter the passage once again.

When I reentered the chamber where the lava river flowed Andreas, Wallace, and Sardon were huddled close together and Andreas was explaining something to them. I stood at the edge of the lava flow as near to them as I dared to listen and not interrupt. He seemed certain that he could get them across. He had after all gained flight once in his life, and he had controlled wind more than once during this long adventure. I joined in at that point reminding him that he had borrowed his magic from an all ready existing element and that there was no wind in the chamber where we stood at that moment.

"I have considered that and though it may tire me. I believe I have enough in me to get it done. If there is air then there must be some current that brings it down under the mountain. Just because we don't see it does not mean it isn't so. I will gather it up, swirl it, and then use it as a cushion of air to glide us across the lava."

"And how quickly will you be able to move it? This stuff nearly melted my boots earlier."

The look he leveled at me was consternated, then hurt, then defiant, then triumphant. "I can do it."

"Well then what are you waiting for? Do you expect me to go on alone?" I was teasing of course, and he knew it.

"Do you have to be such a shrew? When will you ever learn to trust me?"

I knew that he was teasing as well, but I put my hands on my hips and gave him my best wounded look. "When you learn to do magic without being coached," I said.

He raised his hand toward me and grinned, then a short blast of air hit me in the face. From that blast he swirled up the air around us into a small whirlwind and then a strong vortex. It became difficult to breathe as he gathered more of the available air to him. He began to direct the wind and compress it into a small invisible platform at their feet. He stepped up on to it and Wallace and Sardon followed tentatively. They jerked back and nearly stumbled off when Andreas moved them forward, but Wallace had the presence of mind to widen his stance and grab them all together. Andreas slowed their advance slightly until he better controlled it and then increased their speed until they were safely across. Once across he deliberately released the air back to its natural state. The effect lowered them softly to the ground and Andreas bowed before me with a flourish he usually saved for dignitaries after a performance. I took a copper coin from my pouch and placed it gently in his palm and patted his hand as he took it.

"Never happy," he said.

I smiled, hugged him, and kissed his cheek. I noticed that Sardon seemed bothered by that, jealous maybe. I hugged him again. "I don't need your magic to make me happy." I said and turned to show Wallace the way to the stairs while Andreas and Sardon followed at his pace so he could regain some strength.

"That was kind of mean don't you think?" Wallace said, as I ignited my partially spent torch again.

"What?" I asked innocently.

"You know that they are interested in each other don't you. You'd be blind not to see it"

"He is my dearest friend. I love him and he makes me happy. Should I not tell him so?"

Wallace sighed, "I saw the look in your eye when Sardon looked away. You connived that last bit to put her in her place. If he is such a dear friend then shouldn't you want him to have happiness with her."

I sighed, "You are right. I did want to put her in her place, perhaps it is I who is jealous. I've had him so long to myself."

"And yet you are only friends."

"Not for lack of desire on my part."

"You are in love with him then?"

"Shush, keep your voice down."

"You are; and he doesn't know?"

"No, yes. Oh bother, just drop it okay. It will never be, so I live with it. Someday the right man will come along and make me forget all about him."

"Maybe, but how do you know when it is the right man?"

Sardon and Wallace were gaining on us. "It is just ahead." I said and the conversation was over.

At the bottom of the stairs I held the torch high as Wallace took a turn in search of traps. When the area was clear we all moved up and began the tedious process over again until we came to the top and a great arched intersection. The stairs behind us was one arm, of course, while to either side the passages curved back to follow the natural form of the mountain. We knew we were on the outside edge of the mountain's interior. So, it didn't seem to matter which way we went. If one way ended we would just come back to that spot and head the other way. We went right , with Wall searching the way for trips and traps. It took nearly an hour to reach the next intersection, because Wall had successfully disarmed two deadly traps along the way, and narrowly escaped the swinging pendulum blade of a third.

The intersection was a forked way. We had no idea which to take. "Right." Sardon suggested. "Right for righteous." It sounded good, but she shrugged her shoulders with resignation. Andreas clapped her shoulder. "One way is as good as another when you don't where you are going." So off we went to the right.

Each step was tediously slow; no one spoke as Wallace went about his business. We all listened for sounds of approach or occupation, but after a time the utter silence made our ears buzz. We allowed Wallace to choose the way, and we turned back several times when no passageway obvious or hidden presented itself.

Time meant nothing in those dark and silent passages. It could have been mere hours or a day that passed when we heard a sound. It was like an illusion at first, as if we did not experience it at all. Then as we all strained to discern it from the buzzing in our ears and then from which direction it became clear that it was real. We strained to keep it in our heads against the buzzing that would so easily slip back in and we made our way toward it.

We came to another intersection, one that turned us toward the center of the volcano. I pointed the way to Wallace and he began his routine search for traps. As I strained to keep the soft sound we had picked up in my ears, I came to realize that it now came from somewhere behind us. We had passed it. I began to check back up and beyond our transit of the passage that had brought us to that intersection. I found no egress that seemed reasonable to the location of the soft sound. The more I listened the more I thought the sound was the rising and falling of breath of a great beast. My heart jumped with excitement. I shared my conclusions with the others and we began an earnest search for a secret way that led into the attic of the volcanic stronghold.

Then, as if drawn to the spot, we each settled upon a line of runes chiseled high up on the wall in the shadows of the ceiling. There were no hidden latches of any sort, just the thin tracings of the finely chiseled runes. Sardon did not recognize them, but Andreas studied them and silently mouthed words, ruling them in or out within the context of the text. Then he clapped his hands one time and proclaimed; "I've got it! It is the ancient arcane, not the one used by so many today. The power here comes from the elements; this phrase calls upon all of them to protect the passage beyond. If I mispronounce even a syllable we may all end right here. I have not spoken this language, I have only heard it and I was not much more than a boy. An old wizard tried to teach me the old ways against my parent's wishes. I can hear the sounds in my head, but I have never spoken them."

"Surely your magic must call upon some form of these words to call upon the elements." Sardon stated.

"In some way, yes, but I speak my own words, whatever seems logical to the force I call upon."

"We have no choice but to let you try. I will take the others back up the passage. If you should fail, then the rest of us must try another way," Wallace said. He was becoming comfortable in his role of protector.

"No," I said. "That is unacceptable. Andreas and I are a team I will not leave him. He may need me."

Wallace sighed and put a hand upon my shoulder. "Why are you being so short-sighted? Do you not see that if Andreas should perish that it would leave only you to decipher the scores once we have them? You have complained to me what a daunting task it will be. No, we cannot risk you both. I do not mean to be so callous, but should Andreas fail, and perish, then you must survive."

"He is right." Andreas said firmly, "I will go alone. If I fail it will do no good to lose you. Saeede, you must survive to retrieve and decipher the scores."

Sardon spoke then, "What is all this talk of failure? Would you send the man to his task with doubt on his mind?

I for one believe you can do it. You know the words in your head; let your tongue form them. Do not be afraid."

"But there is a cadence to enchants such as these, if my accent is wrong, if..."

Sardon, put her hands on Andreas's forearm. "Call upon the ancients, call upon your old wizard, call upon your own magic. You are strong with it. It has not failed you so far. Fear not Andreas, you will do well, and we will be here to greet you when you have finished."

Andreas took her hands in his. "Well I'd better not fail then, had I?"

"You won't."

Andreas scrutinized her face. He was looking for the truth of her conviction, behind her eyes. She did not look away from him until he cast his eyes to the rest of us. He turned at last to me. We knew each other well enough to read each other without a word. He was frightened, but courage, and no doubt Sardon's words bolstered him. Still he was resigned to his fate; he understood the value of what he must do. He saw in my eyes the same reservations, and the well of tears that lay upon my lower eyelids. There was no room for adaptation here, and that was his biggest advantage in nearly every challenge we had faced up to now. The loss of this dear friend would kill me. We both knew I would be lost in the world without him, that his sacrifice would be mine too, but his sacrifice would end, mine would endure. I wanted to hold him, but the emotion that generated between us was almost unbearable. He nodded. I nodded. We knew each other's minds and that was enough. We moved back up the passage and Andreas remained. "I hope he will be okay." Sardon whispered to no one in particular.

"But you said…" Wallace began.

"He needed to hear it," was all she said.

I stood at the end of the passage watching him as the others took cover around the corner. He turned to study the runes. When he was ready he glanced back to see we were safely tucked away, he motioned me back, then he stretched his arms out to his side and threw his head back. I peered around the corner. He stayed that way a few moments mouthing something silently. Perhaps he was calling on his Grandfather as Sardon had advised. He hesitated, and then he spoke the words aloud. His voice quaked but the words were loud and clear. Wallace pulled me back around the corner and the words stopped. There was a crack and a boom, and a rush of air, and dust and fine shards of stone found us even around the corner. I moved to the corridor, but Wallace was quite strong and held me back against the wall.

When the dust settled he let me go. I scrambled around the corner but stopped short to see Andreas coated in the fine grey stone dust. He was leaning against the wall his knees buckled so that he looked like a sitting stone man. His arms were still outstretched in the position I had last seen them. I began to move slowly, apprehensively, toward him. Then I saw his arms move slowly and he pushed away from the wall. He was alive! He moved slowly at first, awkwardly, as he began to dance. He looked like a stone man dancing a jig.

I laughed and ran to him so we could dance together. Wallace came to join us and then Sardon, only Sardon did not dance. She stood before the glowing portal that swirled within the wall. We were all aware of it, but life was too good not to celebrate it at that moment. Still her singular action brought us all gradually back to the reality at hand.

We gathered our things and passed through the portal. I took a torch from Wallace and I went first, then the others followed, with Andreas being last. As he passed through the portal shimmered away and there was solid stone in its place once again.

We stood in a natural stone passage. The air was warm and humid. I held my hand up for quiet and we all cast about to pick up the sound that had brought us here. It was ahead and to our right. "Right for righteous," I whispered.

Wallace and I moved together along the passage. It declined steeply and turned gradually to circle the volcano's core. We checked and double-checked, but we found nothing until we came to an opening in the right hand wall of the passage. The air from the passage was even warmer than the rest of the passage and the stink that came from it was reptilian. I went to the ground and crawled on my belly and elbows to the opening and peered inside.

Stretched out as far as I could see in either direction was a cavern filled with a lake of steaming water made white with the minerals dissolved in it. Islands of white stone dotted the lake. The islands were actually stalactites and stalagmites that had joined together creating pillars of the white stone that stretched up and supported the ceiling. The soft rise and fall that I thought had been the breath of a beast was the rush and hiss of the water steaming in the lake. One island near the center of the lake was larger than the others. What caught my eye was the gold mound that rose up out of it — not white, but gold. I traced the outline with my eyes— there she was; another dragon. White steam rose from her nostrils as she breathed and it was pulled away by a breeze that passed through at the upper reaches of the room.

"It must be here." I whispered.

I crawled backwards the few feet to where the others waited and described what I saw. We could not formulate a plan. There were too many variables. The only thing we knew for sure was that we had to convince a dragon not to eat us so that we could also convince it to give up a scroll of relic magnificence. In the end we settled on a no secrets one for all approach and stepped slowly to the cavern entrance together. The Dragon lifted her head from the ground and peered at us from that low stance. She made no move toward us and so we advanced slowly toward her. The water was shallow and hot. The bottom was a slick surface of white mud that sucked at our feet as we moved. As we came closer she raised her head more and more until we had to look up to see her face.

She was easily the size of the ship that had brought us to this land. Her head was the size of a house and her tail wrapped around her great paws, like a preening cat. Each claw was the size of a tall man. The tips were pointed and the edges were serrated. Her scales were the color of purest gold with a line of color like molten lava along the edge of each one. Her mouth parted slightly and we could see her great gleaming teeth and black forked tongue. The steam of her breath created a cloud above us. Her eyes watched us curiously, and there was intelligence in her gaze.

She made no move toward us, but we were not unaware of the advantage she had on us. If she chose to lash out at us with her great maw open she could swallow whole any one or perhaps all of us before we could move to prevent it. Wallace's hand went impulsively to his axe and she gave him a warning look that made him snatch his hand back. We stopped before her and she brought her great snout down to breathe us in, her tongue flicking out to taste emotions, perhaps even our perceptions. She gazed long at Sardon and sniffed hard at Andreas and myself. Then she drew up to her full height, her scales tinkling together like wind chimes. She was a most beautiful, yet fearsome beast. She cocked her head a few times reasoning us out and then she spoke. Her grasp of the language was perfect, her accent guttural with a slight hiss to it. It too was beautiful.

"Vhhat brings-s-s you heare;" She searched for a word to call us and settled on; "mortals-s-s?"

Andreas swallowed hard and moved forward. "A great crisis threatens the world, Great One. We but seek your wisdom on the matter and in the end, favor."

"G-rant you fafvor or g-rant a fafvor? Do not bandy words-s-s with me. You will likely lose-s-s."

"Excuse me Great One. I mean no disrespect. It is only that I am awed by you."

The dragon stood silent a long moment and then she seemed to smile as she said; "You halve way about you. Are a poli-tich-ian?"

"No, No, God no, a diplomat of sorts, I am a traveling minstrel, by choice, but fate has dealt me into a game and now I serve mankind as well. There are but a few of us who serve to protect Mankind against the rise of evil. It is that rising that we seek to discuss with you this day."

"Your tone of voice is grave. I s-s-shall delay hew no more. Pray, tell me vhhat this-s great crisis-s is-s-s?"

Andreas began his narrative, introducing each of as our part was played in the story. At each introduction the great head came before that one and went about the sensory testing once again. Andreas waited respectfully each time. Only when the great Beast seemed satisfied did she continue again. It was long in the telling. Andreas spared no bit of history or needed detail, all of that he built up to our voyage to the Jungles of Bekua, and from there our descent into the realm of the great gold dragon.

"You har trusting of me to tell all of this-s, Mor-tal. Why s-should I not devour you hall now? My exis-stence will not be chang-ed by good or evil. I vhhill remain here perhaps-s until they both pass-s from this earth and I vhhill live vhhith neutral-it-y at last."

"I do not think you would do that. You know the importance of what I speak; else you would not be here in this place. If I judge my surroundings correctly you are the final guardian of the Master Scroll and you know that for us to have come seeking you that the world is in grave need of it.

"S-so fate has chos-sen wisely. You show great promise. Are you hall so geefted?"

"I assure you that we are. Our masters have chosen wisely."

"The S-scroll Dominus-s-s, s-so this-s is-s the fa-vor that you ask hat last. You ask from me nothing less-s than power over the Lhord hof Darkness-s-s, a most powerful hightem, s-surely you not expect that I just turn it h-over to you."

"Of course not Great one, but we beseech you to use care when determining your bargain. Our quest is urgent. We have no time for gallivanting around the world in search of treasure for your horde."

"Hew insult me, Mortal. I recognize-s your plight, and I believe I have s-solution. Three riddles, one for heach of the three key scrolls-s that will open for hew the Dark Ones-s Kingdom. If hew answer all of riddles-s correct I vhhill turn over the S-scroll. S-should you meess-s but one riddle— one hof hew, one hof my choos-sing mus-st s-stay vhhith me in s-servitude until the death, or I die wheech-hever comes firs-st. Of course I would retain poss-sess-sion of the s-scroll as vhhell."

"That is unacceptable Great One."

"Damn right!" Wallace nearly shouted, but thought better of it and reduced his voice to an angry whisper.

I had taken a step forward; when Andreas stopped any further outburst with a steel eye leveled at each of us. "Let me handle this!" he whispered through clenched teeth.

"S-sh-urely, hay bit hof enter–tain-imient hafter hall thes-se ages-s is-s but s-small dalliance. Hew s-say your ques-st is ur-a-gent. This-s would s-send hew on yhour vhhay; that is-s if hew riddle correct-a-ly."

"Great One each of us plays a part in this group; surely your assessment of us has told you that."

"There is-s one hof hew that can be dispens-sed vhhith."

"No Great One there is not; Saeede and I must decipher the scores of the key scrolls and whatever is contained in Scroll Dominus, Wallace is our protector, Sardon is our Healer and spiritual guide, and when the time comes all of those things are sure to come into play."

"There is-s one hof hew that can be dispens-sed vhhith."

Andreas sighed, a heavy heave that left his shoulders drooping. "Who then—who is it that will not be missed amongst this group."

"Hann excel-i-ent Riddle, s-shall vhhe s-start vhhith that?"

Andreas hung his head, he was being beaten and he knew it. "I must confer with my group before we continue with this dangerous game."

"Certain-i-ly, take hewr time, but do not forget hewr third option. Hew may leave vhhith no consee-quence; ohf course-s the s-scroll vhhould remain vhhith me."

Andreas nodded and turned to gather us together.

"This is not going well," Andreas said. "We should just kill her now and be done with it."

"And then what? Search the rest of our days for the scroll?" I asked angrily. My patience was wearing thin.

"Perhaps I could find a way to scry for it."

"Perhaps, perhaps not."

"I think we should play along and then if we lose we kill her." Wallace offered.

Andreas thought playing the riddle game was sensible. "Chances are that we would win, though a riddle challenge is serious business. The winner and loser are bound to the agreement made over the riddle. The riddle cannot be impossible to answer. If the answer is obviously true once stated, it is a valid answer even though it may not be the answer the riddler expected.

"When one person or group challenges another to a riddling contest and the challenge is accepted, the participants are bound to the results. If the loser of a riddle contest does not honor the bargain, the offended party will be granted some retribution to the dishonorable party. Any consequence may be chosen by the offended party short of death. It is said that when a riddle contest takes place in a place of power, the injured party may call for God to intercede. I'd say this location falls into that category. If

God decides the infraction is heinous enough He may rule that death is a fair consequence, which would depend on the weight of the bargain agreed upon. Any party that cheats in a riddle contest instantly loses and suffers the consequences of the bargain."

"None of this really matters though does it?" I asked, without awaiting an answer I pushed on. "We are bound to this quest and the scroll is bound to the quest. We must have it and none of us are willing to leave anyone behind in servitude to a dragon. What does that even mean? The bargain that we must make is to know the location of the scroll, and for each correct riddle answered she must give us a clue to that location, in case we should fail this game overall, we may still have a chance at it."

"Good idea." Wallace agreed and the others nodded their agreement.

Andreas went on, "If we lose full out. I intend that the bargain states that I be the one to stay behind."

"No." Sardon gasped.

"Over my dead body." Wallace announced.

Andreas and I looked at each other, considering the possibilities. I caved in first. "No absolutely not, we will need your magic through this.

"No we play the game to win and if in the end we lose— we steal the scroll, or kill her for it, we will face whatever curse Gan's forgiving god should place upon us. I think He would be on our side though. The dragon plays frivolously with the fate of the world."

"So I will make our bargain to include the clues to the scroll location for each right answer. That gives me room to haggle, she will expect it. In the end we will kill her if we lose?"

"Only if an immediate opportunity to take the scroll has not been presented first. Look to Andreas or myself for the lead move when the time comes. Just be ready for anything," I said.

"Do we start the riddle with who would stay behind then?"

"No, we don't want her thinking that way."

Andreas turned back and we stood side by side as he haggled with the dragon. The dragon enjoyed the process and proved to be a shrewd negotiator. As the negotiation went along the great beast moved slowly toward us until her neck curved down toward us and her great head hung just above and in front of Andreas. My brave friend stood his ground and spoke with only a slight quiver in his voice. I found myself sizing up the girth of the great neck and wondered how many swings of my sword it would take to penetrate the golden scales to get through the meat and to the spinal column. I ceased my assessment when I felt her cold eyes stray to me.

In the end we had a short list of rules. There would be three riddles, the first two were for the rite to continue, if they were lost the game was over and we must leave—of course we had no intention of honoring that if we lost. If we won the dragon would give us one clue about the location of the scroll for each of the first two riddles if we answered correctly. The final riddle was for the scroll itself. If we lost we would be expected to leave, of course we wouldn't. If we won the dragon would surrender the scroll to us.

The dragon did not move from her spot, but drew her head up slightly so that we had to tilt ours back to look at her face. We were all nervous, but Sardon was visibly shaking. Andreas took her hand and smiled sweetly at her. She moved closer to him and he took a half step to his side, a move that put her shoulder behind his so that he could step in front of her if things went badly. At the same moment Wallace and I each took an instinctive step closer together. The whole thing was smooth and appeared to be a casual reaction, a coming at ease after a tense negotiation.

The dragon looked at each of us. "Har hew ready? S-shall vhhe bee-gin?"

Andreas was our leader for this and he answered aloud for us. "Aye, we are." We nodded our silent agreements in unison.

"Vhhell then here i-ss the first— Tell me, vhhere hall great kings-s of Crys-stalier vhhere crowned."

We conferred. The kings were not all crowned at the same location, each was coroneted at his family's holdings, so there came only one logical answer, but it seemed too easy and so we did not trust it, but by the rules if the answer is obviously true once stated, it is a valid answer. We turned to face the dragon.

"On the head, of course." Andreas answered.

"Ahh, goot, that vhhas too eeasy, hay test to vhharm hew up."

"You owe us a clue to the location of the scroll."

"Yes-s, yes-s-s, let's-s see, s-simple yet obs-scure, hay ha-right prop-hare clue. Alright then, hew vhhill find key in bowels-s hof a fiery fur-nace."

The dragon said no more about it and moved on to consideration of her next riddle. "Vhhell, let's-s s-see, anhother r-eeddle, more deeff-i-cult this-s time." She was silent a few moments and then; "Oh hyes, here is-s one for hew—hand I vhhill eeven geeve hew part of answer. Two grandmothers, vhhith their two granddaughters-s. Two hussbands-s, vhhith their two wives-s. Two fathers-s, vhhith their two daughters-s-s. Two mothers-s, vhhith their two sons-s. Two maidens-s, vhhith their two mothers. Two sisters, vhhith their two brothers. Only seex in hall born legeet-e-mat, clear from incest. Explain how this-s may be."

The dragon looked pleased with herself and I for one had no idea what the answer might be. I turned to join my companions to riddle it out. We took some time and the dragon chided us, trying to get us to admit defeat. But, we had not negotiated a time restraint and when Andreas pointed that out the dragon pulled back and waited although she flicked and thumped her tail incessantly, an obvious ploy to distract us. Andreas knelt down in the centre of our huddle and scribbled a very short family tree in the silt with his finger.

"Yes, yes that must be it!" and he explained it to us. We all nodded, though dubiously and broke the huddle. Andreas stood and faced the dragon. His answer was clear and confident. "Two widows each had a son, and each widow married the son of the other, and then each had a daughter."

The dragon drew back and cocked a golden eye at him. "Ex-x-xcellent, I ham impress-ed. My task becomes-s more deeff-i-cult, let me see..." Her voice trailed off as she fell into thought. "Hof course; here is-s one just mint for hew!

"You owe us another clue, Great One." Andreas reminded her carefully.

"Oh yes-s, yes-s, that. Hew hare s-so vhhorried about these clues-s. Hew hare s-so determined a group. Let me s-see then... hof course, here hew go then— you will go through great lengths-s to receive the s-scroll."

"That is no clue!" I retorted.

"Hew doubt me!?" The beast literally fumed, great puffs of steam spewed from her nostrils and the sides of her mouth. She levelled her neck and her gaze at me. "Do not. I ham bound to this-s game has are hew. I cannot ch-eat hew." She cocked her head as she moved back to a position before Andreas, so that one golden eye watched me a moment longer. She flicked her forked tongue once and then turned her attention again to Andreas.

"Four bro-thers-s vhhere born into this-s vhhorld together. The first runs-s hand nev-air wearies-s. The s-second drinks-s but is-s always-s thirs-sty, the third eats-s but is-s nev-air full, hand the fourth sings-s hay s-song that can nev-air be written. Tell me, a who hare these brothers-s?"

We moved again into our huddle. "Wallace was agitated; Sardon was silent, considering the words of the riddle. Andreas asked the dragon if she would repeat herself.

She hesitated, but then said, "Oh very vhhell, vhhat harm can vhhe do hat this-s point? Four bro-thers-s vhhere born into this-s vhhorld together. The first runs-s hand nev-air wearies-s. The s-second drinks-s but is-s always-s thirs-sty, the third eats-s but is-s nev-air full, hand the fourth sings-s hay s-song that can nev-air be written. Tell me, a who hare these brothers-s?"

Andreas and I looked into each other's eyes, and we knew that we knew the answer! A riddle just for us! I was the first to speak it aloud. "Water, Earth, Fire and Wind, in that order. That's the answer!"

"Absolutely," he replied, "and so it is just for us."

We turned and stood side by side again to deliver our answer. We had won, and none of us feared the dragon any longer. We would have our prize, and deal a blow to our enemy! But, the dragon had moved away from us, back into the caverns where she had rested when first we entered. But, she was not resting. She stood proudly with her back to the wall and her tail flicked menacingly along the floor on her left. Her wings were pulled back as if to protect her sides. Her great fore claws were spread wide in a powerful stance, but her neck drooped, and her head hung low. Her demeanor was not one of defeat, but one of fear or sorrow. We stood in our line, ready to answer, but the sight of her confused us and we did not speak it.

Andreas recovered and spoke. "Great One we are ready to answer your riddle and receive our prize. Are you prepared to hear it?"

"I vhhill hear it."

"Are you not well, Great One? Is there something we can do?" Sardon the healer, sweet Sardon, always compassionate.

The Dragon reeled on her. "No-thing!" she wailed. "My end his-s near hand there is-s no-thing hew can do. Let me hear answer so that vhhe complete the s-strictures-s of this s-sacred game."

"Water, Earth, Fire and Wind, in that order. That is our answer!"

"You are cor-rect. Con-grat-ulations-s-s." The dragon's tone was not sincere. She fell into silence. A long time went by and we became impatient. She must have sensed it for she gave out a long steamy sigh and then spoke again. "I ham afraid that I cannot give to hew the scroll. Whhuld hif I coult."

"What! Andreas roared. "You just said that you could not cheat us!"

"And I vhhill not. Hew vhhill half your s-scroll, but fate rules-s that hew must take hit from me. If hew vhhant at last to possess-s hit, hew must kill me firs-s-t."

We looked at each other, confused by this turn. We had planned all along to kill her if need be, but now, to have her propose the idea felt unreasonable.

"You knew this all along." I did not question, but stated what now seemed obvious.

The great dragon nodded agreement.

"Did you let us win?"

"No, indeed not, that vhhould half made mockery of hew and hyour purpose, hand me and my purpose. Hew hare meant to have hit, and hew s-shall. If you keell me for it. I smelt my death on hew when fir-sst hew entered into my place."

The thought of her sacrificing herself to us made no sense. "Say that we do kill you, how will we know the location of the key?"

"You have the clues— to one last riddle it seems."

And I knew the answer. "It is inside of you, but how?"

"When firs-st I agreed to guard this-s s-scroll I s-swallowed hit to keep hit s-safe. Anyone what dared to fight me would loose, I thought, but on the off chance I s-should

299

los-se I want scroll well hidden. Then I needed test, to de-termine s-suitable replacement for mys-self has the guardian hand s-so riddle game became that tes-st, I have never been beaten even amongs-st dragons-s-s. It vhhould take s-someone s-shrewd to beat me. I have been waiting long time for s-someone to get pass-sed traps-s hand guard-ians-s before me. Mos-st himpressive don't hew think?"

We nodded our agreement.

"Now for final test. If hew keel me your tes-st is-s done, hew s-shall have s-scroll hand I s-shall be releas-sed from this-s long exis-stence hand pain hof battles-s to come. I vhhish there vhhas another vhhay, but s-scroll has become lodged in my gizzard, s-so there is-s no other way. Your magic cannot hurt me; it vhhill only make me s-stronger. I cannot s-spit it out."

I was angry at this turn in events, another delay, but the beast was noble in her intent and I found that I no longer wanted to kill her.

"The bowels of a fiery furnace." Andreas nearly whispered. Awe was in his tone.

"You will cut through great lengths." Wallace said, with a similar tone.

I moved toward the dragon and she reared back. I stopped. "Is there no other way?"

"You understand s-sacrifice, hew have given much to this-s caus-se."

I nodded, and said nothing.

"Then do not attempt to s-sway me from vhhat mus-st be done."

"What must we do?"

"Hew know that already, hand I tire hof repeating, just let me go vhhith honour."

Andreas and I felt the pain and the dedication that the dragon held. We knew her fear. We had felt it many times in battle together protecting each other, while attempting to make some good in our world.

"You shall have it Great One." I moved forward and drew my swords.

Andreas came to my side. His right hand was over his heart; in his left he held his staff swords.

Tears filled our eyes as she once more cocked her head to assess us with one golden eye. She reared back, taking in a great breath. Andreas took his hand from his heart and met the force of her fiery breath with a force of magic that repelled the fire from us. Wallace ran up at our backs and waited, with dual axes to join us in battle. I took a quick glance back to see Sardon invoking a prayer. The blessing was not for us, but for the dragon.

The breath dissipated and the three of us charged in. The beast fought well, as if determined not to die, knowing the whole time that she must. We took great injuries, but in the end she was vanquished.

Andreas and Sardon both said a prayer over her carcass. I stood reverently and Wallace walked the length of her; weapons at the ready as if expecting her to rise up again. Sardon walked amongst us and tended our wounds as we stood dumbfounded. I saw the tears in her eyes as well when she tended me.

She went then to perform death rites on the dragon. When she was done Andreas found a soft spot below the great breastbone of the beast and between seams of the scales. He sliced her open delicately, as if he tried not to hurt her. He wretched as her entrails spilled, but he went about his grim task and found a scroll case lodged in a fold of tissue just at the top of one stomach. He cut it out the stomach and hot molten spilled out at his feet. He jumped back, but managed to maintain his hold on the disembowelled gut, with only a smattering of burns to his boots. He removed The Scroll gingerly, for it still glowed as if from a blacksmith's forge, and let it fall into a small pool of water on the cavern floor. It sputtered and hissed, for a long while. Even when he thought it would be cool enough to take up in his hand he had to flip it back and forth from palm to palm to avoid burning himself. Sardon, came to him with a bit of bandage cloth and he placed it there as she held it out for us all to see.

It was a work of art. The barrel of the case shaft was of rare obsidion. The metal base cap and crowning standard was dymium of the purest grade. Dymium is a rare silvery, metal that glistens in raw form. When it is worked it shines and it is lighter than iron but just as hard. I would love to have a suit of armor made rom it. The end cap was finely filigreed and the standard was the likeness of the great dragon we had just slain. The craftsmanship was exquisite, worked in amongst the flames coming from her mouth and nostrils were arcanic runes. Andreas examined them, but he dared not speak them until he knew for certain what they said.

"It is hard to believe that we have actually obtained the scroll." Sardon's voice was barely above an awed whisper. "We should return quickly."

"All the appropriate rites were given to her. We will take from her what we need and leave her to the elements. Sardon is right we should hurry." Andreas agreed.

"What can we take from her?"

Sardon spoke up. "The blood of a dragon is a powerful base for an elixir that can heal great wounds. The scales are said to make sturdy shields, and if ground into a paste they are a base for an elixir that can protect from the influences of magic."

"Can the bones do anything, or the claws, or teeth?" Wallace wanted to know.

"Not that I know." Sardon replied.

"Good then I will do some of my own collecting."

I watched as Sardon collected the steaming blood into glass vials. Wallace collected a few scales, but when he raised his sword to amputate a claw I yelled at him to stop. I could not stand to see the noble beast disfigured. It was a heinous thing to leave so noble a creature without a proper burial.

"You are right, of course, Lady. Forgive me," he said. I nodded and we all moved slowly back to our gear and gathered it up again.

We moved slowly from the caverns. Each of us stopped at the exit and turned back with our own thoughts, and bid the dragon farewell. So it was that even with our prize in hand we travelled wearily out of the cave labyrinth by a route that brought us high up in the mountain. I felt the kiss of a breeze upon my face and knew that I was nearly out of the volcano. With my swords sheathed and the scroll secured under my left arm I ran ahead anxious to be away from the oppressive stone. Once there I stopped for a peek outside before I ventured out.

The setting suns showed red and orange behind the veil of ash and steam. The air was heavy with it as always. I wrapped the tattered remains of my turban about my head and face and emerged from a parasitic cone near the top of the volcano, the place that must have been the great dragon's eyrie. Bones of various animals littered the stone shelf and there was no traversable way down. Only a flying creature could have made it to this spot.

None of us relished the thought of traveling through the jungle at night. We cleared the bones and gathered wood from what scrub trees we could find to make a camp in the rim of the dragon's porch. Then, while Andreas retold the story of how the two of us had escaped from the chasm deep in Winter Top we rested and ate. Andreas had learned to fly that day, and I knew he intended to do it again.

When the story was done we each took our turn at the watch while the others slept. I took first watch, and kept the scroll with me. When it was my turn to sleep I laid the scroll down to be my pillow, put my swords upon the ground, and laid down to sleep. We slept more that night than we had since our arrival on the island. When morning came sunlight barely reached us through the incessant haze. We stretched to limber ourselves from the deep sleep we had. We were all highly excited to be back to the ship, but first we had to make our way down.

Andreas flew us all safely down to a clearing among some trees, we took a few moments for Sardon and Wallace to gather their wits again then we moved out through the geyser fields toward the ring of jungle, and beyond that, our waiting ship.

We came out of the heights and as we crossed toward the jungle the thought of the smothering ooze that had nearly taken my life a few days ago spurred me into a trot. I drew weapon and took a tighter grip on the scroll.

We pushed through to the black sand beach not far from the stand of leaning trees where we had concealed the boat. It was just as we had left it. I placed the scroll in the bottom of the skiff and pulled the vessel out of hiding. Together we muscled it to the edge of the water. The suns passed through the veil of ash and were well on their way to the dusk horizon when we climbed back up on deck. The boat was hoisted aboard neatly and stowed away. Word of our return had been called down to Kapit and Gan and they were there to meet us. They did not ask aloud so I nodded once to affirm our success and they turned to lead us down to the captain's quarters.

Egidio had graciously allowed Kapit and Gan to share his quarters and he just as graciously stayed topside when we all went below. Andreas and I saluted him as he passed and he nodded his acknowledgement. He was a good captain and a good man and he trusted us. He did not know all that we had done, but after his encounter with Polk at Thunderhead he had a pretty good idea what was at stake. He was involved and proud of it, but it was not easy for a captain to give over his crew and the ship he was commissioned without full knowledge of why he was giving them over. I made a mental note to bring that up to the others if Egidio continued to serve us.

I hoisted our burden from out of the box where Andreas had properly put it, and placed it on the thick oaken table that served as desk and table to the captain. Andreas sat down upon the Dwarven box. He was thinking, running over what we knew in his head and latching on to the first threads of a plan. When he needed something clarified or wanted an opinion, we talked about it. I allowed my gaze to fall upon him from time to time. He was still the most beautiful man I had ever laid eyes on. He caught my gaze once, before I could turn it aside and he smiled that disarming smile of his. It was always that way for me when he smiled. Sardon turned away from us, a look of anger coming across her face. Kapit and Gan asked us about our adventure on the island. We retold it all, but aside from Andreas's occasional questions about what the future held there was no solid planning talk. That would be saved for the safety of Kapit's compound.

·~· Chapter Five ·~·

We were given a suite in Kapit's holdings and conferences began the next day to discover a way to unlock Scroll Dominus without the musical keys. Wallace and Sardon stayed with us. One night, while the others slept I held The Scroll called Dominus close to me. Firestorm had been taken from us by Polk aboard Egidio's ship only hours after he had successfully robbed us of the Earth Scroll, called The Mountain King and the one called Valkyries' Lament. I was contemplating again the puzzle that had been set before us.

Earth had protected Fire, or was it Death? I decided on Death for my purposes; after all the great Dwarfs had given their lives for the scroll. We had gained The Mountain King in the whirlwinds of the highest peak of the Hoary Mountains on Winter Top Island. Air had protected Earth. Valkyries Lament representing the element of air had once been locked away in the temple of Nauticus deep in a dangerous part of the sea. Air was protected by Water. Only the secret brotherhood of priests knew the location until Polk somehow deciphered the location and was able to steal it. It was that scroll that we got back from him in the dungeons beneath the Palace in Behlanna. In the process we saved Father Gan, and delivered a young man, to his parents, but too late for he had suffered from a death by torture. Firestorm came to us through Draghador under his mountain on Thunderhead. Earth and Death protected Fire.

Dominus could not be opened— not until we regained the Three Scrolls and learned the scores that were the keys that would magically unlock it. Dominus held the secrets to the locations of the entrances to the nine gates of hell. The unscrambling of those scrolls would be most difficult. It wouldn't be like deciphering a code of words or numbers. We would have to play through all three scores and note differences or perhaps they'd only be nuances. I hoped they would be chaotic obvious transitions, but I didn't hold out much luck for that.

Andreas and I had each studied hard over the scrolls for the time we had them in our possession; hearing each instrument alone and ensemble, but only in our heads. Andreas had drummed out the soft nuances of the rapid beat in sections of the scrolls, attempting to compare the differences in sections of the scores that were relatively common between them. All that we knew for sure was that the melodies in Air and Fire were the same; but composed in opposite ranges.

If we successfully regained possession of them we would need time to compare the scores to pull out the differences and rescore those. We would have to memorize each rescored section and then play them all together in our minds. Only then would we be able to determine any code that was hidden within them. Kapit's intelligence network was responsible for the procuring of instruments that we did not own.

In the mornings Andreas, Wallace, Sardon, and myself would sit in on the conference of faction representatives.

They conferred long and hard putting together separate histories in an attempt to reveal the locations of the gates. At night we were engaged in music lessons. It took weeks to even have all the instruments we needed in our possession. Then we would have to teach ourselves how to play them before we could teach the others and decipher their meaning within the scores. Sardon and Wallace were our students so we could increase the instruments in our ensemble and better play the scores.

Kapit had spies spread across many kingdoms, watching and waiting for any signs that would indicate Polk had successfully breeched a Gate of Three. Gan's people watched for signs of possessions of souls within the general population.

All of these urgent things were on my mind, and everything Andreas and I had been through, so I could not sleep. I sat up that night going over them all hoping for some clue that would allow me to open the scroll.

If the three scrolls were the keys to open Scroll Dominus, then there had to be a mechanism of some kind hidden, somewhere. If I could find it perhaps I could release it manually. The scroll tugged at my curiosity. I held it at arm's length and examined the metal tube and the large end caps that held the scroll shut tight. All the elemental figures that we had endured were represented in the inlays and embossing. Water, Air, Earth, and Death all held spots on each end cap, but Fire was depicted as licks of flame tracing around each symbol and along all edges of the metal. I knew that meant fire protected the scroll. I turned it over and over in my hands looking for some seam or protrusion, even a slight depression that might indicate a mechanism.

As I turned the scroll forth and back, end over end, round and round I became slowly aware of a shift in weight. At first I attributed this to the scroll itself moving within the tube, but there was something more. The shift sloshed ever so slightly as I moved the tube end to end. I could not reason how the scroll would be protected by fire, while in a liquid, or how the scroll could survive for centuries if submerged. So the liquid must have been sealed away from the scroll, perhaps in an internal sleeve around the inside of the case. The liquid was flammable, I was sure of that— it had to be. If I did not open the scroll properly, I expected there would be a conflagration, which must destroy the scroll and perhaps even me.

None of this was enough to deter me. I was confident in my abilities and set to the task of finding the mechanism that would unlock the case and put the scroll into my hands. I was growing weary of the process when my unfocused eye caught the slightest imperfection. Of course I lost it again when with renewed energy I refocused and tried to find the thing again. But I was so weary and my eyes began to fail me again, that is until I realized that in my unfocused sight I could see the lines within the licks of flames, the lines that revealed a puzzle lock. I could not focus or un-focus long enough to keep my eyes on them. Then a thought came to me and I went to get my mask that I had received in Draghador's kingdom. I reasoned that this scroll might be protected by all the elements even death and if death protected the scroll, perhaps it was in the element of death that the great talents of the smiths in Draghador's kingdom of dead had produced the puzzle. I returned to the scroll and put the mask on. There were the lines as plain as day. I studied them long and hard before I made my first pull of the sliding metal pieces. I heard a click, but no liquid was released.

I went to wake Andreas. He should be a part of this. I remembered to remove my mask so I would not startle him and I quickly explained. He grabbed his own mask from the carpetbag and went back with me to the table and the scroll.

We put on the masks. I made a turn of two pieces in opposite directions and felt them slip into place with another click, this one louder and we jumped and stepped back, even with the rod held at arm's length and my body stretched back. Nothing happened and I continued to examine the lines within the flames which were now misaligned by the pieces already shifted. This made the puzzling more difficult, but together we deciphered the correct move. This time I felt something move in both ends of the scroll under each cap. Our last move had released a series of internal pins under each end cap. I had to turn each of them as if it was travelling through a maze. I could not see it and so I had to feel my way. It took hours, but at last I made my way through the maze lock. I turned the tube slowly and my eyes widened as the scroll caps came loose in my hands and our hope was revealed. I tipped the case and the scroll came into my hand. The scroll called Dominus.

We stood in stark awed silence.

By the time the light began to seep in around the curtains Andreas and I had already deciphered two gate locations, the first was an insane asylum near the Cheoa dam in a land half way around the world. It was a cold dry place called KoMan and the Asylum was on the outskirts of a large city by the same name, known to breed evil ways.

The second was a prison on the Continent of Crystalier far to the south. The Prison was filled with the most heinous of criminal and was located far from any city. We believed it to be a city in its own right, an oppressive building with walls and towers carved from the mountain itself and strongly fortified with guards and soldiers.

We were working on the third and were analyzing our thoughts about it when Wallace came into the room. He stood nearby and as the reality of what laid out before him came clear to his waking brain he let out a slow shrill whistle. Sardon soon joined us and her normal demeanor changed. She became anxious and paced the floor as she watched us.

The third gate was in a den of thieves in the slums of the evil city of Pyritia, named for the forge that separates sulfur from the iron in pyrite to obtain iron for weapon manufacturing. The industrious workers there had turned a once small mine into a thriving mining and smelting industry. The skies there were said to always be yellow from the smoke of sulfur released from the forges as a byproduct of the separation process and the people were blue from the oxidants in the air. Under the city is a great factory for just such uses. Also under the city was a great network of played out mines that had become the den of thieves and in them, somewhere stood one of the three gates.

Three gates each led to three more. It seemed that they might be near each other in groups of three; around a central location. We took our information to the conference in hopes that our information would be consistent with theirs and we could confirm the gate locations.

What had promised to be a long tedious conference took on the air of celebration. The three factions of the sect that had faithfully, even blindly, protected the scrolls allowed themselves a moment in time to take a breath. They loosened their grip on their providence and hugged and laughed like they had never done before. Kapit had a large breakfast brought in as he would have anyway, but mead and wine was added and imbibed liberally. I was hugged and kissed and patted until I was tired of it, but I endured. A storm brewed outside and darkened the day, but spirits were bright within the conference room.

We all agreed that the gates were grouped in sets of three, but we could only agree on the location of one. So we got down to the business of planning our next trip; to the prison in Crystalier. We would need a ship and a loyal crew. I brought up my concern that Egidio was being asked too much for a small fisherman, but he had played along and brought us safely to each location that we had asked of him. I thought that he should know more, so that he knew what was at stake and was in or out at his own discretion. It was agreed upon and Kapit sent for him, by secret ways and means of course.

After that I became weary from my sleepless night and a bit of honey mead. I struggled through the meeting but made it through. When it was done all I knew was that we sailed for Crystalier and the city of Mareese in two days. I retired early. I knew that Andreas would see to our needs and comforts for the trip.

The storm that had been brewing during the day churned closer and fiercer as I slept. Until even surrounded by Kapit's enclave, the walls of our suite rocked with the fury of the wind. It woke me several times, but I rolled over and pulled the pillow around my head. I regained sleep and dreamed or at least I thought I did.

I was playing before a court of nobles. The piece was peculiar with eerie crescendos. I knew it from what we had learned from the scrolls At each crescendo the wind picked up and rattled at the shutters and whistled through the doors. The crowd was not much pleased at my performance and jeered me, but I was compelled to continue and show them something new for their stale tastes. Each gust of wind added an eerie crescendo to the all ready peculiar music and a feeling of uneasiness went through my gathered audience. The lord of the castle bade me stop and I obeyed, though reluctantly. I drained my flute and wiped it down before setting it in its case upon a chair.

When I looked up again Sardon and Andreas were across the now empty room in an affectionate embrace. They had become quite close and I forced myself to work my way through my initial jealousy. Wallace had turned his attentions my way, and I was more than interested. I gave him an alluring look as he entered from a far door and I made my exit to return to my room.

When I passed through the room I had no bearing on my surroundings. I was in a palace I had never been to before. I wandered until I was so weary that any bed would do. I found an empty bedchamber and slumped exhausted onto the fur-covered bed. The wind beat against the building for a long time. The old wood creaked and moaned, the shutters clacked, and the doors shook. The wind howled and I was frightened even in my dream. The fury of nature was nothing to be scoffed at. If the roof remained above our heads that night I would be most grateful to the Mother of Nature.

I woke, or I thought I did, to the incessant thumping of my shutters banging against the window of my room in Kapit's enclave. The storm and wind had blown heavy snow in upon the floor and bed. The fur drape that had held back the winds tore down the rod that held it and the whole thing banged and flapped wildly against the walls. I jumped from the bed pulling the heavy covers with me and made for the window but I stopped short when I noticed a dark form lurking in the window alcove. I had no weapons in this room, save for the dagger I left beneath the mattress. We had all grown comfortable in Kapit's care and most of our things were locked up in a chest beneath the basement stairs.

"Who are you?" I asked in a shaken voice that had been meant to be loud enough to be heard in the next rooms but it was muffled by the wind and something else.

"The one you want." The reply came in an unearthly voice. The sound of it terrified me and I found that I was frozen from the moment of his speaking; unable to react— the words repeating in a whisper upon the wind. The shadowy form moved toward me and I saw that it was Wallace. I could not move as he reached out to caress my face. His touch chilled me more than the winter wind that swirled around me. Winter , wind? Somewhere in my mind I knew this was not the season, but the thought was snatched away and I did not care.

Wallace took me in his embrace and I went willingly. He kissed me long and hard and I shared his passion. When I drew back to rub my hand across his strong face I saw for the first time what he was—and was not. He was not Wallace. He was possessed.

I knew absolutely that Wallace was not present in his own body but that some dark force had possessed him; the force of the Dark One himself or a minion? I could not be sure. His face came close to mine again. He knew that I had discovered him. Black swirling pools were Wallace's eyes now and they considered me with a deep and dark intelligence. The breath that fell upon my face was not warm, but burnt me with absolute cold. A grin caught the corners of Wallace's lips, but the smile that spread across his once beautiful face was lecherous. A pointed black tongue parted the lips that I had so willing kissed just short moments earlier. The evil that possessed Wallace slowly licked his soft pink human lips. His intent was obvious and I screamed. I know that I did but the sound fell into the swirl of wind and was lost. My terror was not wholly my own. Much of it was being willed upon me by the power within Wallace. I fought it back with my own will like a great hammer against a steel wall—it would not crumble. Then the thing in Wallace spoke to me again, his cold breath falling upon my breast.

"Do not fight so, Pretty. It will only tire you and make you weak."

I was tired but at the word weak my will sagged. I could not fight him and the strong arms of Wallace picked me up and put me upon the bed. I suddenly wanted him to have me; as I had wanted Wallace, and Andreas. I tore at his clothing with heated desire to touch and be touched. I was amazed that I could move and appalled at what I was doing. Inside I screamed again, but this time it was silent all of its own—

trapped behind the thing that now possessed us both, locked within a dream I could not break.

He tore away my nightclothes and slowly, meticulously tasted my flesh with his black tongue. My body was uncontrollably aroused, but my trapped spirit was painfully horrified. I willed myself to fight him, but his strength was inhuman and I could not win. I don't know what time it was when he left me, but I still remember every awful moment of the encounter. I woke suddenly, sick and cold. Snow fell softly within my room and a pile had gathered up around me. It was stained red with blood. My body, the torn bedclothes, and the bed itself were sticky from it. I thought I knew what had happened, and I began to wretch uncontrollably. I soon found that my assumption of rape had been wrong. When I rolled and fell from the bed to go to the window I stumbled upon the cold dead body of sweet Wallace. The pommel of the dagger I kept hidden below the mattress still protruded from just below his breastbone. It had been forced upward to pierce his heart. It was his blood and it pooled out around him. I slipped in it as I kneeled beside him. This time my scream did not go silent.

Andreas was in the room in seconds and Sardon was right behind. I cradled Wallace in my arms and rocked him until I could not breathe. Sardon covered us with a fur and Andreas went to close the window. I was inconsolable and incoherent, a condition that was foreign to me. There were no words for the magnitude and mass of emotions that I felt. I had killed a loyal and trusted friend! I recognized the turn of the knife in Wallace's chest. It was one of my moves. The devil had set the scene, but I had played it out, somehow in my dark desperation to rid of the demon in us; I had played it out! This I could not remember.

Sardon went out and returned with one of her concoctions. I slapped it away. The cup broke in a corner and the brew splattered across the walls and seeped in at the edge of the blood pool. I would not be drugged. I would not have my emotions played with again.

Sardon and Andreas moved away from me. Andreas was investigating the scene and Sardon whispered something to him before leaving again. Andreas came back to sit quietly beside me and rubbed my back. It was sometime before I calmed down. I stopped rocking but I could not let go of Wallace.

Sardon returned with Father Gan. The priest moved to me and put his hands upon my shoulders. "You have to let go sometime, Saeede. I will help you." His eyes never left mine as he moved his hands down my arms and helped me to ease Wallace to the floor. "Come now, come away from here and tell us what has happened."

I shuddered visibly at the thought of it. They took it for the cold of the room and wrapped me tighter in the fur. Andreas helped me to my feet and caught me as my knees buckled under me. I was as weak as a baby. I leaned against Andreas and Father Gan took my other arm and they led me from the room. Sardon had built a fire in the parlor and pulled a chair over near it. They sat me there but the fire would not warm me. I began to shake from cold, sickness, weakness, and shock.

"We must warm her quickly. Sardon draw a bath. Heat it to warm but not too hot." Father Gan ordered his student.

"That will take too long to draw the water and heat it. While you do that I have another way." He went away and returned with two glasses of brandy. I drank them but they did nothing for me; the chill only deepened and I quaked from it.

Andreas stripped down to his britches. He unwrapped me and scooped my naked, blood caked body into his arms. He moved close to the open fire and held me next to his warm skin while rubbing his hands quickly back and forth to create frictional heat across my skin. But, I was so consumed with shivers that I could not feel it. "Wrap us up Father," Andreas ordered.

Father Gan averted his eyes from me as he draped the fur over us and went to retrieve another. Sardon had closed my bedroom door and recruited Sorrell and Argus to help her tote water and they soon had the tub filled. Andreas tried to rub warmth into my extremities but they would not warm. The first words that I put together to make any sense were, "Better make the water hot."

Andreas took me to the tub. Sardon unwrapped us and he placed me into the water. Sardon gently wiped the blood from me as I shivered. Shock had certainly set in, but these shivers were beyond even that. Father Gan brought me another brandy bashfully served from the door and passed on to Sardon who placed it in my shaking hands.

I ordered more heat on the water. Sardon was hesitant when she tested what was in the tub but she stoked the fire anyway and at last I began to feel some warmth. Some but not enough, I have never, even to this day felt wholly warm again. I forced myself to stay in the blood dyed water trying to warm myself, even though it sickened me. When that became futile I dressed in clothes that Sardon had warmed near the fire and wrapped myself immediately after in a fur. Then I went to sit in the chair by the fire. Another brandy and I felt nearly normal. Gan had sent for Kapit and he came in with two other men at that time. Gan went to meet them and the four of them went into my room. They had come for Wallace's body, and an explanation was owed. I gathered my wits, for what was sure to be an interrogation. I motioned for Andreas and he came to me. "Please do not leave my side old friend. This will be more gruesome than any tale we have ever told. Our dear friend is dead by an evil that may still reside here, maybe in me."

"God's Sade, no. How do you know?"

"I do not know. I will tell it all, but only once. Gather the others."

"Sardon, will you fetch Kapit and the father?" Andreas asked. She did so and they came to gather round me in silence. Andreas sat upon the arm of the chair beside me and Sardon stood just behind us both. Kapit pulled up a stool and plopped his large body onto it with his arms crossed tightly across his chest. Father Gan leaned against the mantle, being careful not to block the heat from me.

"Take your time," Andreas said.

I took a deep breath and began. It was horrible to relive it so fresh in my mind. I became physically ill at the telling of it and had to retreat to the bath to be rid of it. I sobbed and shuddered and cringed at the memories and at one point I found that I had subliminally hugged myself. I rocked and cried uncontrollably until I thought I would die from it. Sardon stroked my hair to comfort me and Andreas took my hand, but Father Gan and Kapit said nor did anything. When the men that had come to tend to Wallace took him from our suite I felt a stab of guilt that caused me to gulp for air and caused real pain in my heart. I knew logically that this was not my fault, but emotionally I could not remove myself from it. The emotion seemed illogical to me. Not that I did not feel remorse, but that the emotions were foreign to me. I felt as if I was a stranger in my own skin. Logic would get me through most things and I was always able to swallow my emotions before. This was a bit of insanity, I was sure of it, but kept it to myself.

"Finish your telling, dear." Kapit said in a sad a voice, "and then we will go and pay our respects."

I did finish at last but I was emotionally and physically spent. Gan was calm, but Kapit was agitated. I was not sure he believed me. We went out together to a room where Wallace had been laid out. Father Gan anointed the body and said his priest words over him. Kapit stood in silence, but a tear streamed down each cheek. Sardon stood silently and did not cry. I did not know she possessed such strength. I cried openly.

Andreas spoke, "Though we did not know you long, you were a brother at arms, a friend and trusted companion. You were well loved and you will be well missed." His words were perfect, so I did not have to speak, though I don't think I'd have been able. I knelt beside the bed and took his cold hand in mine, still crying, unable to control myself. The company stood in silence over me, until Andreas came and brought me to my feet.

"He's gone now, Sade, and you need to rest. You can have my room."

I allowed myself to be ushered away, but I did not think I would ever sleep again. It frightened me to even think of it. Andreas helped me into bed. Sardon covered me well and put warm stones all around me, because I still shivered from the chill I had taken. Andreas kissed my forehead and looked deep into my eyes. I saw a sorrow in him that I had never seen before.

"We'll be right outside," he said. As they moved to leave I asked them to keep the door open.

I laid there a long time listening to the hushed conversation between Kapit, Gan, Andreas, and Sardon. I gathered enough to fear for my life. It was possible that I might be possessed, though Father Gan thought it more likely that I was marked. It was obvious that the evil, whatever— whoever it was could have killed me and had chosen not to. Why he had used me to take Wallace's life was a mystery to them as well. Kapit had recently received runners from surveillance posts around the realm. Something had gotten past them. Several of his people had suddenly committed suicide, were found dead or had been murdered by others who had gone mad. He needed to figure out what, how and where before we proceeded much further. If there was one there might be more. It was obvious without hearing their telling that one had gotten to Wallace and through him to me.

Andreas suggested that they put whatever influence they had over the prince into play to convince him to put military into defensive positions around the city. Neither Gan nor Kapit liked that idea, but they knew Andreas was right. Convincing Prince Duadan without revealing their hand would be impossible, and they had hoped to keep him in the dark. If they could convince him and gain his trust and bond of secrecy they would feel better about it. I fought sleep, wanting to know more, but their hushed voices lulled me to sleep.

I slept, but woke often to fleeting haunts by dark dreams that I could make no sense of. I went to stand before the fire sulky and silent. Kapit and Gan were gone. My room had been cleaned and refurnished, and Wallace had been removed from the house. Sardon brought me a bowl of thick stew and a bit of bread, but I had no appetite so it sat after only a few bites taken.

I was deep in thought, uncertain what I— what we must do next, unsure of how much more I could take. Still, I felt a deep need to avenge Wallace, and an equally deep need of revenge for myself. What if I was marked? Marked for what; and why?

Andreas came to stand near me. He had a fur bundled in his arms. "You still shiver. Put this around you."

I did as I was told. "What do we do now, Andreas?"

There was silence as he contemplated, and so I filled the silence with my questions. "Did that demon find us because I removed the scroll? Was he a guardian we overlooked? The wind was so much a part of it; and the snow." I looked out the window into a courtyard of blooming flowers. "I think this was just the knock on the door. What has he come for? Who is he? He said he was the one I want. What does that mean? The Dark One himself then?

"I heard you all talking earlier, what did Father Gan mean that I might be marked? How, why me? With the powers he held over me, I am certainly no threat." Then I stopped short, a gasp of sorrow caught at my breath. So there it was, the thing that most frightened me in all of this. I held no threat. I had become useless to our cause. But, then I wondered, "Does that mean that you do threaten him?" Andreas leveled a confused look at me. "What, with your command of elements. If he had wanted to kill someone why didn't he just slip in on Sardon and have her seduce you? You would have been willing."

"Saeede; a little tact please. Are you so distraught that you really do not believe you are a threat to him? You killed what you perceived to be him. You were out of it when the killing happened. How do you know that the devil did not kill Wallace when he was through with him? Perhaps all he wanted was to make a mess of your head. It would be some advantage to him to take you out of the game. Maybe this is the thing that made those others go mad. Thing is— he didn't account for us being mad already.

"If he meant to attack us as an enemy then why kill Wallace, when it could have been you? It seems that you would be the strongest against that type of attack. Why not eliminate you while you were vulnerable? Perhaps all he wanted was you. Perhaps he fancies you."

"That's not funny!"

"I did not intend it to be."

Now I was silent. Even that awful thing needed to be considered.

"Perhaps we'll know more when Kapit gathers more intelligence. But in the meantime you are going to brood over this aren't you?"

"I can think of nothing else. I wonder if Wallace was aware of the possession as I was, and unable to fight it. If he knew it was wrong as I did. It was the most awful thing I've ever known. To be so aware, so intensely aware of every emotion, and sensation you have ever had, and to know that it was not of your making. I fought with every ounce of my will, and it was not enough. I hope that he was unaware so that somehow he died in peace. Had I broken through, Wallace might be alive now."

"And you dead."

"That would be preferable to this cold. It wraps around my heart as if to strangle it."

"You have always been cold hearted." Andreas's tone was joking, the kind of banter we had often shared.

I turned away from him. "Perhaps that is what the demon liked about me."

"Oh, Sade. I'm sorry. I only long to see you smile."

"I know, friend. I only wonder if I ever will again. It is as if the whole thing was meant to steal away my joy and leave me alone with this incessant cold. I have to move on from here but I feel so responsible for Wallace's death. I cannot separate myself from it."

"Have you not considered that you did regain control at some time if only briefly?"

"If I had been in control I would not have harmed Wallace in anyway. How do I avenge him, when the thing that killed him has absolute control over me? How do I avenge myself?"

"We continue on. We are getting too close or the thing wouldn't have bothered with us. It only seeks to frighten us off."

"Dominus has been a great help, but it will never be complete without the Three Scores, and now each move we make maybe watched. We may suffer more attacks . This whole thing feels like just another sick joke of the gods.

Maybe the music isn't actually the key. Maybe the real battle is between the masters of heaven and hell, and we are just pawns in the game, but whose pawns? Maybe the world as as we know it is about to end. That will be good, 'cause this world reeks wicked. If the joke loving good guys win? Will that be better? Maybe..." My voice had gotten shrill and Andreas called me on it.

"Sade, madness, remember it is one of the side effects here. You are sounding a bit crazy. I only point it out because I love you. Take a breath and think."

"I can't think."

"Alright then, let me do it for you. We have no keys, but we do know where one of the gates are and you and I know the other two even if they don't. So if we get to them we can attempt to unlock them. You know amongst Kapit's people they are saying you must be the greatest thief ever, to have undone a lock protected not just by the four elements, but by the gods as well. Gan's people have set about looking through their scriptures for some clue to a chosen one sent to unlock the scroll."

I humphed at that—me chosen—*ha*.

"We leave tomorrow night at first high tide, under cloak of darkness. We head for Crystalier. We will go to the prison and find the gate. If the Gods are jokers they will surely show it then."

I considered and then reconsidered. If my opinion of the Gods was accurate it had merit. My instincts told me he was right, of course. I didn't trust my instincts much at that moment. Still I trusted Andreas and that gave me a playing field I was familiar with and a way to work out the darkness that was strangling me. "What if we're wrong? We don't know where to take the fight then."

"We aren't wrong!"

"And when we get there, what then?"

"We go in and make sure the gates are locked tight behind us, and if we find them open we hunt down whatever has escaped."

"And if we fail?"

"Then we improvise."

"Improvise? With the fate of the world?"

Andreas shrugged and his look was pained. I was reminded that he was living on frayed nerves as well. "Kapit and Gan have sent their best runners on the best horses to the southern province of Plano and the capital at Ahnrye. They are meeting with Prince Duadan now to co-ordinate the support of the armies and plan the defenses of our three biggest cities. Before we leave the continent we will meet with King Dune himself so that we can speak with him first hand and he can call on kingdoms around the globe to prepare them."

Sardon who had been busy replenishing her stock of herbals and listening all the while joined in. "You aren't serious are you?"

"I believe that we are." Andreas replied.

"You don't have to go." I offered.

"But I must go. I am bound to assist you."

I stood looking at her, reassessing. She was a quiet person; a gentle woman. She had not had to test her fighting abilities. She was thin, not muscular. It said a lot for her that her reasons for going were made from loyalty. It showed courage. Having her along as a trained healer was reason enough to bring her along. "Of course you must go then Sardon, but the way will be rugged and fraught with perils. If you become afraid we will not be able to turn back. If you become hurt you will not be coddled. We will press on, even to death if that is what must be. If you are called upon to fight you must fight. Will you be able to live with these conditions?"

"Knowing that my dear friends faced them and needed me I could not live with myself if I stayed behind."

"I will be proud to have you join us then." I said. My voice choked with emotion. I hated that. I had always considered uncontrolled emotion to be a weakness. I would be glad, no ecstatic when this was over. "Then we must prepare. We have much to discuss!"

Andreas moved to Sardon and put his arm around her. Sardon gave Andreas an annoyed look that did not get passed me. Was there trouble in paradise? "By the way, if you have any lover's quarrels while we're out there. I'll unleash hell upon you myself."

·~· Chapter Six ·~·

We spent that day and evening cloistered away in our little house, surrounded by Kapit's enclave. We checked our gear and packed, and speculated on different scenarios, and what each of us must do as part of the team if a scenario presented itself. During that evening Father Gan performed blessings on my old room, and then moved into Wallace's room. Andreas and Sardon slipped quietly into Sardon's room and I slept in Andreas's. Kapit was there too, but he insisted that the big chair in the parlor was enough for him so my room remained empty. None of this really mattered, as sleep was but a short respite between trains of thought and frenzied planning. Messengers came and went at all hours.

In the first light of morning we buried Wallace at a private site within the enclave. The rest of the day was hard to focus on, but we forced ourselves and told each other he would have wanted it that way.

We had just returned from Wallace's funeral when word came to Kapit from his spy within the palace. Several of the Scorpion guard had suddenly left the city. The prince ordered them banished. Kapit was furious, to banish a suspected enemy was dangerous. He ordered the messenger to take a mixed party of guild members only and track them down. He wanted to know exactly what they were doing. They took some carrier birds with them and left the enclave within the hour.

329

"I must see to this, Father will you join me?"

The two left Sardon, Andreas and I worried, but we fell back into our tasks. Andreas and I were checking off the last of our equipment needed for this undertaking, and Sardon was asleep on the divan when Kapit and Gan returned.

"We must leave, now. Those men were not ordered away. They were chased. They botched an attempt on Prince Duadan. It appears several of the Scorpion are loyal only to Polk and they attempted a coup.

"I have more word from the streets that several guards were asking around about you two, and father Gan's name and mine were heard in places that make no sense. Duadan has his hands full sorting out his loyal subjects. He will be no protection for us. I assured him of our loyalties, and then assured him that we must leave. I put my best people in charge and sent him some of my spies to help him get his house in order. Pack everything, I have a wagon waiting outside. The tide is still low but rising, we will be off as soon as Egidio can make it happen. He has been alerted and makes the ship ready.

We packed hastily. The trunk from below the stairs was opened and our weapons distributed. There was no time to sort through Wallace's things so Andreas put them carefully away for another time and placed the trunk on the wagon beside our carpetbag. Even Kapit helped as best he could. Sardon, Andreas, and myself hid inside the covered wagon while two more of Kapit's men dressed as warehousers drove us to the docks. We stole aboard amongst the hub-bub of a loading ship and slipped below, unseen by most of the crew, and anyone watching from the docks. Kapit and Gan would follow. Kapit was not a stranger to the docks, but chose to go by coach so he would not be seen in transit. They watched the docks from his coach and boarded the ship just as Egidio gave his orders that took us away from the pier and into the wide river.

We sailed night and day with the swift water and made Ahnrye by the second morning. It was soon obvious that Kapit's network had been hard at work. More supplies were brought in for the long voyage across the sea. Kapit saw to a kitchen and food supplies enough to get us to Crystalier. Father Gan gave Sardon a list of things and told her who to talk to. She was the least recognizable of the group, but when she left Kapit sent two of his men to watch over her. She returned shortly after with a large leather sack for Gan. Kapit left us for a time to hear reports from all of his men in the capital and then we were allowed to leave. Kapit led us out. Seven armored soldiers met us on the pier.

These were not Kapit's men. These were knights of the realm, each with their own standard emblazoned on a colored tabard. A tall middle-aged man wearing the finest of chain mail and thick, well-worn high leather boots moved with the swagger of an experienced soldier. He gave the orders and they were carried out. We were quickly flanked by two of his men on each side and two behind. Kapit called him Eucharist. I could only guess that he was a soldier of the church, his men called him Sir.

We were led from the wharf to the city. The outer buildings were built right up against the defensive walls. The trade district was just inside the walls, a neat and bustling place with well kept shops. Colorful tents and awnings of the traveling merchants dotted the avenue. People moved aside respectfully and waved as we went by. Eucharist and his knights waved in return and so did we.

The way to Dune's castle was only two turns to a main causeway that took us up to the main gate. We were waved in and soon sat at a long table together awaiting the arrival of the High King of Dinar. We were not made to wait long. King Dune entered the room with the grace engrained in someone of his station. He was a tall and husky man who kept his white hair and beard close-cropped. The white hair contrasted nicely with his tan and weathered skin. His face was calm and the lines of age and weather made him pleasant to look at. His eyes were blue and shined clear and deep but his expression was unreadable. His scent was musky, but there was a fruity aroma to it. I assumed it was some sweet oil from his bath. Everything about him seemed to contrast another aspect. Even when Kapit rose to pull out a chair for him the king opted to stand and surveyed the group his men had escorted to him.

"I have sent for my religious counsel. He should be here at any moment." Dune announced, and as if on cue a man in white robes came into the chamber. He was still straightening his robe and brushing out the wrinkles when Gan stood and bowed to the man. He quickly finished his primping and returned the gesture.

Dune introduced us to his High Priest, Chalcedon. Chalcedon was a tall lanky man with a humble bearing but a ready smile that was complimented by round sun kissed cheeks. His hair was silver and cut in the style of a pious leader of God's men. He wore cotton robes and leather sandals. He was slightly rumpled, as if he had dressed quickly straight from bed.

Dune made introductions of our military escort. They all had names that could be associated with the Dying God's church, Crozier the Gold, Cruet the Green, Rood the Black, Vigil the Rose, Viaticum the Purple, Pyx the Red, and their leader, Eucharist the White.

When Kapit finished our introductions Dune looked deep into the eyes of each of us, while Chalcedon presented himself with a handshake and a nod. I noticed when I took his hand that his nails were left dirty with soil from the earth and the sweet smell of grapes clung to him. So he was a workingman of God, I liked that about him. When he came side to side with King Dune they bowed to each other and Chalcedon stood beside him, a gesture of unity.

"I have heard the messages of your runners, Kapit. I trust that now you will give me all the details." The two men looked eye to eye, and then exchanged a smile. Kapit stood and turned with a sweep of his hand to include us all. "Your Majesty, this is the company you have been hearing about. Now that proper introductions have been made you will know all that we can tell you."

"Let's get on with it then. I am anxious to see if what you tell me will make up for dragging me so early from my bed and my warm wife."

"We will do our best. I'm sorry about the hasty nature of our arrival, but it could not be helped." Kapit continued, "Perhaps if you each give us a brief on what you know we can tie things together more quickly."

"Well from the communiqués that I have received and the meetings your people have been so insistent on lately;" Dune began, "and the conversations I've had with Father Chalcedon we know that there is an evil about to spill out upon the world that we have never seen in our lives and only read about in the ancient holy words. We know that you are in possession of an item that will banish that evil back to the abyss if they should escape. I do not know if you have yet completed the riddles or as one communiqué suggested if the riddles were just annoyances placed in your way. For my part I have discovered that my son has been a poor example to my people. He has been a womanizing cad, no more than a slaver who has allowed his realm to be a pawn in the Dark One's game. I have sent my own prime minister, Strom, with a contingent of my own troops and a few members of my household to pull him back. It is not unusual for him to visit other realms and I want the people to know that I am still in charge and that I will not tolerate a careless indulgent brat of a man-child to ruin all that I have lived and fought for. He is my son, my representative, I cannot allow him to blacken my name, and so I sent a letter along to remove Duadan from power, for now. He will take his orders from Strom but he will appear to be in charge until I have a suitable replacement. When the time is right I will put Duadane in command of a unit of men and we will deploy him to the front, wherever that will be. He is a good soldier, perhaps I have left him idle for too long. Strom is a proven and trusted friend I will leave him in charge for now.

"All of this may sound good, but it has caused some unrest in the city. Polk's mercenaries that remained in the palace have been removed from their duties and imprisoned until I can preside over their trials. Those who believed they still had some power committed crimes against the people and the crown. We routed most of them, but there have been insurgencies. We have lost citizens and a few men, but we have gained citizen militia and things are coming under control. That is all I have to offer for now. Brother Chalcedon do you have anything to add?"

"Only that we are calling our Paladins home from their pilgrimages. We have one hundred spread across the world. The seven that are here with us now are those that remain to protect our church here. It will take about another month to have them all together. They will remain in service to the church, but where they are deployed depends upon your report so I am anxious to hear what you have to say."

Kapit who had become our spokesman by default began, "We have done much with little, and events draw us to an end game, but we are too few. For all that has transpired there is still far to go, but we believe we have come up with a plan that will buy us time and perhaps rid us of Polk." He launched into our strategy naming each location of one of the three main gates to levels of Hell. "We know that Polk has the three keys to the gates and it appears that he has succeeded at opening at least one of them. We have wide spread reports of bands of demons sweeping out of the darkness to take down villages. They leave with the citizens in tow as cursed soldiers, cannon fodder to their dark swarm.

"We will need you to coordinate with the rulers of these lands to stand against these hordes. Meanwhile we infiltrate through the gates, fighting back what we can to lock them behind the gate, but ultimately that is not our goal. We go after the Dark One. We have in Saeede one of the greatest rogues of all time. It was she who unlocked the scroll when none of us thought it could be done without the other scrolls. She brought us to the knowledge of Scroll Dominus. Andreas is perhaps the only man who controls the elements so adeptly. It is this aspect of him that has gotten us to this point. Still we are not strong enough. We need might; we need men to help us fight our way into the depths of Hell. To us, and our mission this is the most important thing. You have such men as have been trained in the ways of battle."

Dune sighed, "When I read your first communiqué I sent my own people out to confirm or deny your reports. I have already received several confirmations. I have sent my own communiqués to the rulers of these lands and they have begun taking measures to defend their lands. I sent orders to my Duke, Mediwin in Plano to begin reinforcing his defenses until I can get men to him. I fear for him. I have had no response. Whether he received the message or not, this does not bode well. I await word on that matter, from another rider. My man Strom should have arrived in Behlanna and I have sent word to him of this so that they may prepare for battle if it comes to them. Already my human resources are being stretched thin.

"I have only these seven men that I can send with you. They are Paladins, all. I have more soldiers but none to spare when an entire country is at stake.

"What more can you tell me?"

"We have a ship with a trusted captain and crew all of my choosing, but though they are willing and loyal they are untrained at naval warfare. Is there anything that can be done for us there? I do not anticipate an attack at sea, but I do not like our chances if I am wrong."

"I have but one ship to spare. I can give you her captain and crew but I will need them back. I will draft a letter to Diony in Mareese the capitol city of the Larol Province on Crystalier. They are known for their navy. I will request that she give what aid she can in this regard. She is new to the throne, and young, a champion of her people. She threw down the oppressive overlord who ruled before her. We have communicated often, so I think I know her. Her means are small, but if she has a way she will give it gladly."

"How will Egidio feel about being replaced?" I wondered aloud.

"Perhaps his time of service has run its course. He will not know the waters where we are going. I will see that he is handsomely rewarded." Kapit said.

"Perhaps I can find him a place in my navy if he wants to stay in the fight. We will need all the able and willing that we can find. We'll send for him. If you vouch for him, Kapit I will make him welcome." Dune offered.

"I will; he is a solid character and deserves our gratitude."

King Dune pulled a bell cord and a faint chime was heard from a nearby room. Moments later a young pageboy entered and received orders from his king to bring the man called Egidio from the ship just arrived from Behlanna.

"While we wait I'll have you shown to rooms. You will stay under my protection tonight. I will alert the Captain of the Silver Dawn. The craft is one of the sleekest boats on the water in these parts and her armaments are tested. Her captain is an experienced sailor and I have used him often to run my messengers across the seas. He has only just returned, in fact. We can meet again for the morning meal and we will finalize our plans."

Dune pulled the bell cord, twice this time and a plump young woman bustled into the room a short time later.

"Your Highness?" She said and gave a proper curtsey.

"We will have guests for the day. They will be leaving on the morrow. I'd say we would need two or three rooms. Some of you can double up, can't you?" We nodded. "Good, once you are settled in please return here and I'll see that you are properly dined. If there is anything you need from the ship please let Katya here know and she will see that it is done. Until then there are other matters of government that demand my attention."

We stood to follow Katya out, but Kapit stayed behind and I saw him tug discreetly at Father Gan's sleeve to stall him as well. No words were spoken, but I was sure there was an important matter Kapit did not want the rest of us to know just yet. Espionage must be a difficult business to gain friends and respect in, but he seemed to have both. I put the incident out of my head. Whatever it was I trusted Kapit had his reasons and would let us know his mind when the time was right.

Katya led us through the austere hallways and up a flight of stairs at the back of the palace. Katya pointed out the room where Kapit and Gan would be staying. She led Andreas to a room of his own and Sardon and I were put together. We were three rooms clustered together. Kapit and Gan were across the hall from the other two rooms, which were side-by-side and adjoining. Katya lit candles and removed dust covers in each room, before she allowed us to enter. She piled the dust covers on the floor outside each room to be retrieved later by another chambermaid.

"I'll send up someone to see to your needs if you'd like."

"I just want some sleep before breakfast." I said. "The last few days have been without much of that for me."

"I'm not very tired Andreas," Sardon said. "What do you say we take a tour of the city?"

"That sounds nice. Some fresh air will do me good. I've been feeling cooped up lately. Don't worry about our things Katya we'll bring them."

"O thank you sir. If there is nothing else then."

"No, nothing. Thank you."

"I'll see that water is brought in for your basins." Then Katya bowed and went off down the stairs. I was concerned about Sardon and Andreas going on tour. They might be known. He assured me he would check with Kapit and Dune. I was relieved and went into my room for some much needed sleep.

I slept soundly for several hours until I heard a door open and saw Sardon slip through the door from Andrea's room half dressed. She held her clothes in a bundle before her in one arm and carried her pack in the other. I closed my eyes not wanting to be put in an awkward position. She and Andreas were falling in love, if they wanted to have relations before marriage I was not one to judge. She went to the washbasin and bathed.

I was surprised that the water had been brought in without my knowing. I was a light sleeper in the best of times, when I was on my guard as I was I could normally hear a pin drop while I slept. Perhaps it was the comfortable surroundings, but I promised myself I'd be more careful. I tossed and stretched and lounged in the bed, happy for the quiet time. When I heard Sardon rustling with her clothes I chose that time to open my eyes and wake up to her. I acted surprised to see her.

"I didn't hear you come in. Did you have a nice tour?"

"We did, Dune arranged a carriage for us. The city is like so many others in some ways, but they have a beautiful park near the wharfs. We went down and watched the ships and the gulls. It was nice. We only got back a few minutes ago. You've been asleep for hours. Andreas has your things in that carpetbag he always carries. He brought your instruments too, so that you can play for your supper, as he says it."

"It is customary when given hospitality that a minstrel plays to show their appreciation. I do not like to think any harm would come from that now, still these are suspicious times. If anyone suspects that it is us."

"You are not the only man and women minstrel team in all the lands you know."

"No? Name another."

"Well, I don't know their names right off, but I've seen them."

"Minstrels, not musical troupes, are you certain."

"Do you have such disdain for musical troupes? You say the words as if they are poison on your tongue."

"You judge my tone wrongly. No, I am sure that their dreams are to be minstrels one day. It is just that it takes more than travel to tell a story in song meant for a king's court. It takes adventure and a feel for intrigue. If they do it well and are recognized they may become bards and sit at the side of kings. That is my hope, to some day sit in comfort, my future cared for, and sing of the adventures that were my life and those of my king. Better that our adventures were heroic. Right now my life and my songs are full of possibilities." I paused, remembering the point. "You still have not named another duo of minstrels that are a man and woman team."

"Is it so important?"

"Just a curiosity really. I've never heard tell, and I think I'd be in a position to hear. Don't you?" I found that I was angry with her. I had set my unwarranted jealousy aside, I was certain of that. Something about this conversation made me edgy I tried to find exactly what. "Perhaps we should not play."

"Your business has made you so cautious that you have lost your joy for life. You should let your guard down a little— have some fun. Maybe it will shake you loose of that dark cloud you've got yourself under."

I was enraged at Sardon's rash assessment of my nature. Any joy that was left had been violently ripped away at Wallace's death. If my guard was up it was perfectly understandable. Had she slept through the whole trip to the Bekua islands? Dark cloud? What did she know of dark clouds? Mine was an insidious cold thing that seeped into my very bones, and from there into my heart and soul. I had to fight to push it back every minute of the day. Staying in my head and in the game was a chore that exhausted me.

I stood by the side of the bed seething and she knew it, but she made no attempt at apology and just went on choosing a proper cleric's shift to wear down to dinner. At that moment a rap came at the door. I went to answer it. It was Andreas. I let him in without word or gesture, just turned my back and returned to flop down on the bed.

"Get up on the wrong side of the bed?" He asked me and dropped the carpetbag beside the bed.

"Wish I hadn't got up at all."

"Well it's time that you do. Katya has announced that breakfast will be served promptly."

"Great."

"What's with you?"

I stole a look at Sardon that did not go unnoticed by either of them, but I pushed passed it. "Still upset about Wallace I guess, the cold still nags at me, I'm deadly tired. I want to rest. I want this all to go away."

"Come on, get dressed, a good meal will do you good. We'll wait in my room."

"Ya, okay." They left together and I dragged myself away from the bed. I washed and pulled on my best gown. It was wrinkled, but it fit like a second skin, so that was barely noticeable. I brushed my hair and pulled it back in a loose twist at my neck. I felt like crap, and it showed in my eyes, but I was still a fox. It lifted my spirits and I went to Andreas's room.

I did not knock, and wished I had. I found them in a compromising position. They scrambled for decorum and I stumbled on words. I settled for; "I'll see you downstairs."

When I arrived King Dune was there as were Kapit and Gan. Gan seemed distressed, but when I asked him out of concern he assured me he was just tired and a bit afraid for the future. "I can identify with that," I said, and moved on. I greeted Dune who introduced me to our new captain who had arrived with Egidio. The Captain's name was Octavio. His golden hair was slicked back into a tail at the nape of his neck. He was strong, tall and thin. His blue eyes assessed me favorably, I smiled, and he smiled. Andreas was right, a good meal would do me good.

Andreas and Sardon arrived separately; Andreas first. Dune introduced him to Captain Octavio. They chatted a few moments and then Andreas came to me when Sardon entered. "You look great." He eyed me approvingly and did not notice when Sardon greeted Father Gan. Gan received her embrace, but not with his usual enthusiasm for his beloved student.

Wine was served and we mingled awhile. Andreas and I went to talk with Egidio and found out that he had been taken on as Octavio's first mate. We toasted to that and Sardon drifted over to Andreas's side to see what the excitement was about. Eucharist entered the room and after greeting his King and master came to join us. The rest of his Paladins did not join us. He acted as their leader and so he represented them to the king this day. Kapit, Dune, Gan, and Chalcedon stood together near the hearth and exchanged administrative anecdotes. We were feeling the warmth of the wine when our meal was served. There was a tender roast of venison brought up from his larder and fresh picked spring fruit steamed to perfection, and warm bread just pulled from the ovens and sweet butter to lather on it. We ate well of the King's fare and when the meal was cleared we sat back and began the talks that were our final preparations for our voyage to Crystalier.

"Then we must make a solid plan," Dune said.

So we stayed in that room until we hammered out a plan we all agreed to. Brother Chalcedon would lend us seven Paladins to sail with us. King Dune added five of his own men, archers, in addition to the scorpions already fitted to the ship. With all the extra men and horses to be loaded, many of us would be sleeping on the decks. Dune informed us that the horses were being loaded throughout the day in a piecemeal fashion so that one or two horses at a time would be overlooked in the bustle of men and gear coming and going. Arms and armor were being handled much the same way, so that no one would arrive on the ship in armor and would likely be taken for crew by anyone who might be observing.

Kapit already had in his possession several letters of introduction to the kings in realms we expected to pass through. "Octavio will wait for you to report back to him after you meet with Governor Diony in Mareese. It will be the last report I have from you for some time I fear, but I will know how and when you are on your way to the prison. All of this will be difficult and you must know that you will be acting on your own most of the time. Dune will remain here and oversee intelligence. We spent some time overnight coordinating intelligence forces and so he will watch over us as best he can through that. Still there will be gaps and so we will be alone much of the time. When we can, we will send messages along our way. This will help to fill the gaps, at least for a time and I will do what I can to keep the other kingdoms informed so that they can move to assist or at least to keep your way clear."

When all was said and done Dune requested that we play for his private audience. I went up and retrieved our carpetbag. When I returned we began to play for the first time our epic bard song. We had never composed anything as wonderful before. It was rough at first as we each played out our own ideas in solo, back and forth, but we soon melded the two works nicely and we awed even ourselves as we moved into a duet. When we finished there was no immediate applause, but comments of awesome and beautiful were whispered. Dune stood and came to us with his arms outstretched. We stood to greet the lord of the house with a bow and curtsy, but he grabbed us to him and hugged us robustly,

"You have honored my house, with this. We have not had such beautiful song ever in this place. I thank you for allowing us to be a part of its creation."

"The honor is ours m'lord." I said. "It is a song about ancient kings meant for kings to hear. It is still incomplete, but we each have been itching to play aloud what has been in our hearts for some time now."

"I request then that when it is complete you return and play it for my entire household to hear."

"For the honor of your hospitality my lord it will be so."

He inclined his head to me and I curtsied for him. He inclined his head then to Andreas who bowed. "We will drink then to the ancient kings before we retire."

We rejoined the table and stiff liquor was served around. We drank to more than ancient kings. We drank to our blessings, to our new captain, and his new first mate, to King Dune and his leadership and to Chalcedon and his Paladins. We drank to Kapit and Gan; their brotherhoods and their protection. We drank to us and to our next mission. By then we were all ready to eat again.

Our final plans had been made over the midday meal. I drank much so I excused myself and went to my room. I was glad for the intoxication. It had warmed me some and I knew I would sleep.

"Shall we wake you for dinner?" Dune inquired.

The day had gone so long I had forgotten the time. "Will there be drinking?" I asked with a mischievous tone.

"If you desire it." Dune replied with an equally mischievous smile.

"Then you may wake me." I took up my instruments, bowed, and left the room.

I slept until a young chambermaid, who was making a washbasin ready awakened me. I had slept in my clothes and she gently asked if there was some other thing that she could lay out for me. My head throbbed with a hangover. I waggled my finger at the carpetbag and she went to it to find an appropriate gown.

"I can take hot rocks to this and take out the wrinkles for you, if you want."

"Is there time?"

"Yes, lady."

"Then, yes, please do." She took the gown and went out leaving me to my misery.

I sat up slowly and the pounding at the top of my head increased. I sat still until it subsided, then I stood and undressed. I went to the washbasin and splashed water on my face and then over my head. It did me no good so I gave up and submerged my head. I washed and dumped the dirty water out a window that over looked the backside of the castle wall. I put my head out and poured the contents of the filling pitcher over my head. When I turned back to the room the chambermaid had returned with my pressed gown. I was a soggy, naked mess, with my hair all around my face. I flipped my head and my hair was out of the way. She stood with her eyes averted and the gown folded neatly over her arms. I wrapped myself in a towel and asked her to put the gown on the bed.

"Will there be anything else?" She asked as she spread the gown out for my approval.

"If there is anything that you can do for a bad head and a deep chill I would be grateful."

"Are you unwell, lady?"

"In more ways than one I'm afraid."

"I'll see what I can do."

"Thank you. Do you by chance know where my partners are?"

She stood with a quizzical look on her face.

"The one called Andreas, and the lady Sardon."

She hesitated.

"What is it? Are they safe?"

"O yes, quite, but they have tongues wagging amongst the household," she said in an amused way.

I knew the answer, nut I found myself asking; "Why is that?"

"They have had a *busy* day."

"Ya, they have that new love thing goin' on. It always seems to energize those involved."

"We should all have such energy, m'lady." The maiden giggled and blushed.

"Great."

"Don't be embarrassed lady. We were admiring their exuberance," she smiled.

I returned the smile, "Is that what you call it?"

"Mam?"

"Never mind. How soon until dinner?"

"About an hour."

"Well I better get ready then."

"Will you need assistance?"

"No but when you return with that elixir I asked for you can fasten my buttons."

"As you wish m'lady," she turned to leave.

"It's Saeede."

"M'lady?"

"My name, call me Saeede. I am not noble born."

"But your bearing…"

"I have been around, that is all. Call me Saeede"

"As you wish."

She left and I dressed. The elixir she brought was warming, but the taste was sharp and medicinal. It cured my head and relieved the chill for a time, but by dinner the chill had returned. I wrapped myself in a shawl and went down to join the others. I couldn't resist a playful rap on Andreas and Sardon's' door as I passed.

When I arrived everyone was seated except Sardon and Andreas who were absent. Father Gan stood and pulled out a chair for me to sit next to him. When he was seated he leaned in close to me and whispered. "Please excuse me, Saeede, but are you un-well?"

"Do I look as bad as I feel?"

"Enough to concern me. Others here are suffering hangovers, but you look absolutely sallow."

"Just a chill. Perhaps I'm coming down with something."

"The same chill you've felt since the Dark One attacked you and killed Wallace?"

I didn't want to admit it, to acknowledge that the Dark One had left me plagued, but I knew it was better for others in my group to know. "It seems so, Father. I haven't completely shaken it, though I try."

"I will confer with Father Chalcedon. There are rituals to combat possessions."

"Possessions!?!" I said the word a bit loud and those near us turned to us. I lowered my voice and they returned to their own conversations, all except Kapit who looked me over intently. I watched his face as I spoke to Gan. "Do you think truly that is what affects me? I hear no voices, I have no thoughts of killing my compatriots."

"There are ways to possess that allow you to be reachable when the possessor desires to find you. I believe this is what has happened to you. If I'm right that could put all of us in jeopardy. We will meet with Chalcedon and see what can be done."

Just then Andreas and Sardon entered arm in arm. Dune, Kapit, Gan, and Chalcedon all had unabashed looks of disdain on their faces. Sardon did not seem to notice, but Andreas had and looked to me for some clue as to why. I gave a discreet unknowing shrug. They moved round the table to the only empty seats, which were between Eucharist and myself. Andreas pulled out the chair next to Eucharist for Sardon, but she slid in next to me. It seemed obvious that she wanted to separate Andreas from me. Perhaps she still hadn't forgiven me my jealousy. Several eyebrows were raised by her action, but nothing was said and dinner was being brought in.

We ate and when dinner was through we sat back for casual conversation. I sipped lightly on a fine brandy to warm myself, but didn't want to incur another hangover. Gan stood and went to speak quietly with Chalcedon. The conversation was obviously about me as they watched me carefully during their talk. Gan returned to me and Chalcedon leaned over to Kapit and Dune and relayed the conversation to them. None of this did anything to sooth my fears of my situation.

When the three had finished their talk Chalcedon stood to say a blessing for our group and our mission. After it was said Dune stood and made his rounds to wish us all well and excuse himself. The party broke up after that. Sardon and Andreas said good night and went for a walk on the parapet under the moonlight. Eucharist went to his men and would lead them to the ship that night. Kapit offered his company to escort me to my room. I inclined my head to accept, but remembered that Gan had wanted to meet with me. Kapit must have read my thoughts; he said, "Perhaps you will accompany me first to Chalcedon's chapel here in the keep." I inclined my head again.

Gan and Chalcedon were just ahead of us in the hall walking casually as they conversed. They went into the chapel and the door swung closed quietly behind them. When we entered they were nowhere in sight. Kapit lead me to a door behind the altar and down a short flight of stairs. We were in the chapel basement. Another door stood open just ahead and a pale light flickered from within. Chalcedon came out of that door.

"Go right in. I only have to lock the basement door. I'll be right back."

Inside the room was a stone slab on a stone pedestal in the center of the room. The floor around it was only a few feet wide and a narrow walkway led from the door to the pedestal. On the floor near the slab was a wooden table and on it were religious items neatly arranged. The rest of the floor that edged along the walls was a shallow pit of wax lit by hundreds of burning wicks and additional candles shoved into the soft wax. Gan put out his hand to me, fear gripped me suddenly, but I went to him.

"Be not afraid, Saeede. We will call upon God to rid you of your possession. Father Chalcedon has far more experience with exorcisms than I. I will assist. We will not leave you, fear not."

Chalcedon returned and locked then barred the door of this small chamber as well. He came to me and without a word lifted me and gently laid me out upon the slab. Then he went to the table and checked the arrangement of the items laid out there. Laid beside them all was a purple priest stole and a white linen alb.

The room went silent as we waited for Father Chalcedon to don his alb and purple stole. He came to me then and made the sign of his god over me. He removed the stole from his neck, kissed it and placed it around my neck; the whole while he spoke ancient words over me. As he did the chill in me began to increase so that I shivered uncontrollably. Gan explained that was the demon being agitated. Chalcedon placed his right hand on my forehead and Gan put his over that. The touch was warm at first but grew to a searing pain. I writhed beneath it and Kapit came to hold me down. Gan removed his hand, but Chalcedon's remained as he instructed Gan to place a tome of prayer upon my chest. The weight of it was enough to suffocate me and I fought for breath. Chalcedon launched into fervent prayer and Gan's voice joined his. By now I was convulsing uncontrollably. Kapit laid across my legs and Gan stood at my head with his hands tight against my shoulders to hold me down. Chalcedon waved his church relics over me and spoke more ancient words. The chill intensified and with it grew my fear. I was now utterly convinced that somehow I had been laced with an evil, but I felt no presence of a possessing spirit. Chalcedon proceeded through the ritual and I fought to stay aware of it, but my physical being was taking over and the pain of the frigid chill grew so as to burn me with its cold. I screamed out from it. I wanted Chalcedon to stop, but I could not form the word. My mind was a swirling explosion of excruciating pain. Chalcedon grabbed relic after relic and spent prayer after prayer on me, but the chill, now magnified never left me. He fought on determined to rid me of my demon. I fought on determined to scream out that there was no one there, but the words would not come. Time passed and all this frenzy moved to a higher and higher climax until at last, mercifully Chalcedon collapsed under the spending of so much energy. Kapit went to him. Father Gan stayed with me as the chill subsided to its normal intensity and my mind swirled to a manageable swoon. I passed out.

When I awoke I was on the ship, it was daylight and we were sailing. It was early the next day and I was informed that we had been smuggled out of Dune's castle in the dark of night. When I asked Gan about the success of the exorcism I was sad to hear that it had failed because I was not possessed— I was cursed. They had tried all they knew to do for me before we left Dune's care and nothing had worked. The curse could not be reversed by any means that they knew though they tried against hope. The nature of the evil that had been called upon me was unknown. Chalcedon and Gan felt as if a deadly seed had taken in me. I had a mission. If that mission did not succeed it could mean my life. It was only a matter of time and the seed would take over me; when or where no one could tell. I was doomed. My mood was dark and I was left alone to deal with my fate.

I wandered onto the deck, but no one approached me—not even Andreas. I saw him move toward me, but Sardon kept him back, allowing me time to absorb my situation for myself. I was grateful to her for it. I could not face my friend with my inevitable death, not yet, not then. I turned from him and went to the prow and looked out over the sea. We were sailing smooth, the ship cut slick through the water and the seasickness did not bother me greatly. It seemed only moments that I stood there trying to comprehend my plight and searching my mind for some means by which to fight it.

Darkness was upon us when Andreas came to stand silently beside me. He put his arm around me and I leaned in to put my head on his chest. He hugged me close and I cried and sobbed into the wind. I was dying and there was no medicine that would be able to relieve me when the chill became a frigid cold that could not be broken. I was dying and on the way to Hell. The thought was ludicrous and I smiled despite it all. It was enough that I let out a little laugh. So I shared the thought with my dear Andreas and we stood at the rail laughing and crying together. When we were exhausted we went below and joined the others for dinner in the galley.

Kapit broke that awkward silence that accompanied our entrance by coming to me and putting his hands on my shoulders. "My dear girl," he said. "If ever there is something, anything I can do, you have only to ask."

"Thank you Kapit, I know. Thank You, it means a lot to me."

Gan joined in, "We will not give up looking for a solution."

"I know you did all you knew to do Gan. I think the solution is in me somehow, or with the Dark One. We are on the path that I need to follow now."

Eucharist joined. "We will see you safely along, I swear."

"I am honored by your commitment to my safety, Sir. I welcome your protection. I think you will be well tested, as we all have been and will be still. Yes, Sir, your protection is well needed and wholly welcome."

We looked eye to eye assessing each other's words and commitment. It was strong and true. We shared a silent moment and a nod of affirming trust.

I was in good company; it lent me fortitude. I looked around me at the group we had gathered and smiled. My mood remained somber, but it was somewhat lightened. I moved to sit amongst them and Andreas sat beside me away from Sardon who was across the table from us. It gave me some comfort, and Sardon swallowed her pride about it. We sat together exchanging stories and laughs as Octavio and Egidio sailed us swiftly toward the city of Mareese.

The next day we finished the ongoing preparation of defenses along the ship rails and in the masts as we sailed on. By morning we would be leaving Dinar behind and sailing into the open sea. We kept a watch for approaching ships expecting Polk to be on our tail. We were unescorted and if

Polk did move on us we would have to battle him. A black sailed dhow appeared just off the horizon. She mirrored our course and then would veer to move in closer. She never turned broadside to us but moved in and let us pass. Then she would turn back and skim the horizon again. We had every confidence that our arch adversary was following us and wanted us to know it.

On our last expected day at sea we were all together again at the midday meal in the galley. The fresh fish were grilled to perfection. Our moods were tense and tempers were short. Kapit had Jac, our cook, roll out a keg of rum to ease our stress. We all partook but moderately. We would sail into Mareese the next day with the morning tide. We made plans for our meeting with the Governor and sat there through the evening meal. I went to my quarters and spent the night curled up close to the stove. Everyone else stayed late topside enjoying the balmy breeze of the late summer.

I slept reasonably well. I needed the sleep no doubt, but what was most surprising to me was that the chill had not kept me tossing and turning all night. I did not know what that meant. I was becoming too used to it. I changed clothes and went above. The Wharf gates, two white towers marking either side of the Mareesian harbor gleamed in the morning sun. I looked for the black sailed ship but could make nothing out.

Andreas and Sardon stood close together at the taffrail watching out over the stern at the foamy trail that we made through the green waters of the sea. I went to them and they greeted me heartily. I stood away from the rail afraid that the sight of the moving water would bring on my seasickness.

"How soon before we dock?" I asked.

"Several hours, Octavio is in line after several waiting ships."

"I actually slept the night through."

"And then some," Sardon joined. "Perhaps you are on the mend."

I paused a moment and gauged the chill that had gripped me since the night of my possession. It seemed as it always had. I was disappointed, but I wanted to seem optimistic so I replied, "Perhaps you are right. We'll see."

"Do you think that Kapit and Gan are ready for what will play out here?"

"Kapit assures us that he has trusted men here. He will brief them and send them ahead with word to the Governor. We have our letter of introduction from Dune."

"I know all that, I was speaking of after, when we move on the prison? What if Polk has spies in this capital? Is Kapit sure he will be able to outsmart them? Let's hope he doesn't have to outrun them."

"You know as well as I that Kapit holds great pride for his network, and as odd as the man may seem to us his people seem to love him. I think that he will be safe. He will be well guarded I'm sure."

"Well watched is what worries me."

"It worries us all, but there is nothing for it now. We can only put the plan into play and be ready for anything from there on."

"You are right, of course. I just grow tired of this game."

Andreas simply sighed and nodded his agreement. Sardon slipped her arm through his and moved closer. I knew then that my old jealousy had died. I was happy for my old friend. He had found someone to care for him and love him. He reached an arm around her and pulled her to him. She leaned back against him and he kissed her head. They stood at the rail in that embrace watching out to sea. My old friend had found someone he could care for and love as well. I bid them adieu, but I doubt they heard me, they were probably glad to be rid of me. I went to the galley in search of food.

Kapit was there enjoying his favorite smoke of Black Dragon. The small area was filled with the blue smoke and it seemed to be intoxicating in itself. I took a seat across from him near the galley stove. He offered and this time I joined him willingly. I took a long drag on the sweet herb and felt it fill my lungs. Then I exhaled slowly, watching the smoke rise from my mouth and nostrils to mingle with what hung under the beams. As I did I felt my body relax and my mind release. I handed the pipe back to Kapit and leaned against the bench back watching again as the smoke rose from his exhale and entwined with mine. *'Odd how we are so entwined as is the smoke,'* I thought to myself. My mind wandered through events since the day we had first stepped foot in Behlanna. What had we missed along the way? What mistakes had we made that could give Polk and his Master the advantage? Who could we trust? Could we trust each and everyman within our party now? We had been careful, but all who acted in support of us were aware of our plan. Had that been wise? Should we have kept them removed from the final plan; to know only what we wanted them to know?

At some point Jac had placed a plate of food before me. I was brought back to reality by Kapit's hand upon mine. "Saeede, are you alright?" I looked at him bleary eyed. "You don't partake of the weed often do you? I should have known it would be too strong for you, what with your condition and all."

"Condition? No it is just too early in the day for me I suppose. Condition— what condition?" I teased.

He pushed my breakfast plate toward me—a change of subject. "You should eat before it goes cold."

I was angry with him for pointing out my weakness. I hated weakness and he knew that. How dare he throw it in my face like that? I stabbed at my hash and took a large bite of it. What was my problem? Perhaps that one puff of dragon had made me paranoid. I looked up at Kapit and behind him Jac. They were both regarding me with some concern.

I brushed it off. "Good food, Jac. Thanks for saving me some." He nodded and went back to his cleaning. Kapit though, still regarded me openly. I tried to ignore him, but it set me off and I became awkward.

"Alright, Kapit, I'm fine. You were right. Your brand of weed is too much for me so early." His look did not change. "Really, I'm fine. Now get over it because we need to talk."

That seemed to make him feel better about me and he leaned in to listen. I went over with him again my concerns about Polk having his own intelligence agents in place in Mareese. What he said did nothing to alleviate my initial concerns, but I felt better knowing he had the same concerns and had addressed them long ago. He told me things that had been talked about in detail during other planning sessions that I had been unable to attend. It was just always assumed that he had things well in control. He would be checking on those details when we landed in Mareese. He invited me to go along and see just how things worked on his end. I gratefully accepted. When he took my hand as a symbol of trust he drew me near and whispered in a malicious tone. "If ever I find that you took actions against me your life will be forfeit."

I felt fear of him again as I had at our first meeting, but I held my wits and whispered my response. "If I ever give you reason to distrust me then my life will already be forfeit."

We stayed that way looking eye to eye, until he let go of me and nodded. He went back to his pipe and I finished my meal before going out to the deck for fresh air to clear my head of Kapit's smoke.

We arrived in Mareese five hours after my talk with Kapit. The sea remained calm, but the sky grew overcast. We saw no sign of the black sailed ship. We docked and Egidio saw to arrangements with the harbormaster. Our party of dignitaries, Andreas, Gan, Kapit, Eucharist and I disembarked. We followed Kapit and Gan to the wharf tower. Kapit handed a clerk there a sealed letter and the man left the building without a word; no doubt our courier to the new Governor.

Yellow leafs had just begun to fall from the trees that lined the clean cobbled ways of the white washed tiered city. We walked up through the steep winding ways and stopped at a warehouse where we met with a man Kapit called Ali. Ali was the purveyor of the general goods warehouse. I'm certain Ali was just a cover name. He was a jovial sort. The kind of person you expected to be behind the operations of a sale business. When we got to his office in a back room surrounded by stacks of bales and crates he was all business and deferred to Kapit. They had been expecting us and had been watching with all care for signs of counter intelligence players within the city. They had identified three suspected characters and would know their reactions to our arrival. Ali had already alerted Kapit's people in the castle when our ship arrived.

Kapit gave Ali a brief of our itinerary and instructed him to fill a list of supplies for the ship personally and deliver them as soon as possible to the ship. "I think they will need more of this." Kapit said as he jotted a note on the list and handed it to Ali. "When you report to me on the ship I will expect to know the movements of the suspected spies, and I want to know their whereabouts up to the last possible moment of your report. Who do you have assigned to them?"

Ali hesitated. He was reluctant to report with strangers in the room. Kapit gave him permission, assuring him that we were trusted allies and at any rate we would not be out of his sight for anytime during our stay in Mareese. So Ali gave three names; which I remembered in case I needed to recall them later, hoping I wouldn't have to. Each name was paired with a location but two were obviously in the city so I assumed the third was in the castle.

Our business with Ali ended quickly. We did not dally there and went directly up to the house of the Governor.

The Governor's home was well guarded by citizen soldiers. They had been notified of our arrival and once the guards at the gate ultimately inspected our letter of introduction we were given instructions on where to present ourselves within the courtyard. We found the side door at the end of the crushed gravel path and spoke to the guard there— the one with the scarlet sash around his waist, as instructed and we were led inside by Scarlet himself. The interior of the home was in disarray. Trunks and crates lined the walls or were stacked in the center of several open rooms that we passed along the way. Several servants went about opening and removing contents to place them as instructed by an impeccably dressed young woman who stood in the hall between rooms calling out to those in the rooms, and crossing off a list as they answered back that the item was found and properly placed.

As we were led through the hall the woman moved aside and greeted us with, "Welcome to Mareese, the city of light. Pardon our dust. Lady Diony is delayed for a moment. I am Catrine. If you need for anything ask for me. I will see to it."

Scarlet Scarf did not stop as she spoke and so Kapit called back our "thank you" and we continued on. We were taken to a well-appointed office and Scarlet Scarf offered us seats in the plush upholstered chairs set alongside and in front of the desk. Behind the heavy desk a tall open window with the shutters thrown open looked out over a newly painted balcony. A dying fire glowed in the hearth. Scarlet stoked the coals and added a log from the nearby stack before announcing; "The Governor will be right with you," and removed himself with a bow.

We waited in silence. There was nothing else to say amongst us. We weren't kept long when a young woman with premature white hair entered and looked us over with striking violet eyes. "I'm sorry to have kept you waiting on such an urgent matter. I was going over King Dune's letter and seeing to some things that I might do to assist you." She couldn't have been past twenty years of age, if that, but her bearing was beyond her years.

She crossed to her desk, followed by Scarlet. He was strong and dark, brooding as he stood behind her with his hands resting on the pommels of the swords he wore at each side. He was introduced as Brynal, The Lord Protector. We were not sure what she needed protecting from, and we did not ask. "So then, Dune informs me that you are in need in of soldiers. Which one of you is Kapit?"

Kapit raised his hand.

"I know your people here, Kapit. I am sure you know that we are rebuilding our city as well as our government and defenses. Our small army is still being trained, and though they are doing well they are untried, still if you are willing there is a way. I might be able to help you if you are willing to take on experienced mercenaries that we currently hold in our dungeons. You see, I feel that in light of the dire mission that Dune has explained to me I would be foolish to deplete loyal, if untried guards in loan to you. The mercenaries that we hold were loyal to the overlord who was overthrown here just this year. They have been sentenced to life in prison for crimes against the people. You know that already, what you don't know is that I am willing to let you have as many as agree to go with you. If they serve you well and honorably I will relinquish their sentences and only banish them from this realm.

Kapit and Gan looked incredulous, but then Kapit's face softened and he turned to Eucharist. "They would be under your charge, Lord Paladin. What say you?"

"I would want to know the charges against them and meet the curs first before I could fully know my mind on it."

"That seems wise." Kapit agreed. He turned back to the governor. "Can that be arranged?"

"Absolutely. I expected as much and I have the list of charges with me. Brynal has ordered the prisoners be brought up to a large common area we have for them." She pulled a roll of paper sheets from the drape of her sleeve and set them on the blotter in front of her.

"I can bring you to them at any time, but before I do we must have a plan for their transfer that will have the best chance at maintaining the security of my people."

"Do you have something in mind?"

"I do. My city has many underground passages; some are large enough to transport wagons and men. I propose that we designate a meeting point. I will have some of my most trusted officers escort the willing prisoners underground. You and yours will leave by boat and it will seem as if no agreements have been made between us. I wish that we could be more proud and open with even this small gesture, but my defenses are not what they should be, and I do not wish to bring the wrath of the devil down upon these people as they are just recovering from our own evil."

"Our own ship is to return to Ahnrye. We had hoped to purchase a ship here to be ready for the next leg of our quest. Our plan was to make it look as if we were aboard the ship we came in on and were returning to our lives in Ahnrye."

"Or we could divert it elsewhere, as if our voyage was continuing." Andreas suggested.

"But Dune requested that we return the ship to him."

"Yes, but his concern was to be prepared for the coming of the devil's army." I joined. "If we can play a bit of cat and mouse with the devil's black masted spy ship. Wouldn't that keep the devil guessing as to where to send his army?"

Kapit thought for a time then leaned in close to Gan and then Eucharist to confer on the idea.

"I will send ahead to Dune that his ship has been diverted to God's Head. I will make up some instance and there will be no mention of your aid to us, Diony; in case the message be intercepted. We will board the ship as it is being loaded and smuggle ourselves away just as quickly. I'm sure that we can make some arrangements for that between us. We will join your caravan of prisoners and be on our way from here as soon as possible, before our ship has even sailed."

Diony lifted the papers from the blotter, and held them up. "Shall I read them aloud or would you rather look over them yourselves?"

Kapit pulled his massive form up from his chair and held out his hand. "By your leave, Lady I think we'll get more from it if we read it ourselves." The young governor handed them over with a polite bow of her head. Kapit scanned the pages and then passed them to Eucharist. As Eucharist looked them over Kapit informed the rest of us. "Treason on all counts, accessory to murder, civil misconduct, vicious assault—have I left anything out, Lady?"

"Hijacking, depravity, looting; it took us several days to round them all up and restore order. They were nothing more than paid henchmen to our overlord, an evil man. They had been allowed their way with the citizens of this city for so long that they were furious when it was pulled away from them. They lashed out, first under orders of the overlord, and then after he fell they tried to regain control so as not to lose the life they had known for so long.

Kapit looked to Eucharist who nodded and rolled the papers.

"We are ready, Governor Diony." Kapit announced.

Diony came from around the desk and led the way. Protector Brynal ushered us out and closed the door behind us. He joined us, trotting up to take a place beside Eucharist.

"How many men do you plan to take?" Brynal asked the Paladin.

"As many as will agree to my terms."

"I'm sure the Governor has a few terms of her own, don't you Diony?"

Diony who walked just ahead of them beside Kapit and Gan spoke over her shoulder. "If these people need them and are willing to take them on, my only condition is that they serve well and honorably for all of the time that they are needed, however long that may be. Once they leave here their fate is up to the ruling of these same people. If they fail at them in any way I want only to be notified. If any prisoner who fails at this ever returns here their sentence will convert back and start again from that day that we return him to our cells. If they agree to that first then they can hear what ever conditions are offered by these people."

She turned back to her conversation with Kapit and Gan, which it turned out, was all about the fine points of our intent. She was being careful. She did not want to hand down a death sentence to these criminals, but it was her only means by which to help us and to rid her coffers of a burden during a time when the city was rebuilding. She chose her words carefully. Trying to protect her people and herself from what was their weakness—the rule of an untried and perhaps reluctant young ruler over a timid and untried population and militia guard. She was wise that was certain and when we arrived at the hall to the common area she had stated well her concerns to Kapit and Gan and was confident about turning the men over to us.

The door to the common room was guarded by two stout men of middle years with large fearsome axes. They stood tall when we approached and one opened the door while the other bowed to the governor. We passed through into a large room with trestle tables down the middle. The prisoners sat at the tables and guards lined the walls all along the room. The prisoners were not happy at seeing the governor and shouted their discontent in expletives that could only have come from deep hatred.

Diony sighed and moved a bit ahead of our group. The door closed behind us and a heavy lock could be heard to secure the door tight. The shouts continued.

"Hold your tongues, all of you." Diony's voice was unexpectedly strong above the din. "I have come to offer you freedom." The din stopped short, but as quickly took up again with disbelief and untrusting comments hurled at her. She shrugged. "If you are uninterested then." She turned around as if to leave, turning Kapit and Gan by the arm as she did. The din stopped and a confused whisper went through the room as Eucharist and Brynal turned aside to allow them passage.

"We'll hear you," came a single voice.

Diony stopped, turned, and graciously allowed Kapit and Gan to return to their places before moving ahead of them.

"That would be wise. These people are in need of soldiers. Since you have left this city in dire need of the same, and since I cannot trust you to take a position amongst the new guard I have offered them your services, on a strictly voluntary basis of course. If you agree to their terms, and mine I will see that the personal effects you came to us with are returned to you. To a man this means you would be armed and armored. My terms are that you serve these men well and with honor for all of the time that they will need you. If that is done to their satisfaction, I will release you of your sentence here, with only one addendum. You will never return here, if you do I will convert your sentence from the time that we return you to our cells. If you agree and do not serve to their satisfaction then they may return you to us for safe keeping until such time as you cease to breathe. In any case you will always be wanted men in the realms of Mareese. Once they lay out their terms for you and you agree to them you are free of this place and under their control. I think you can see that if you agree to fight for them you have a chance to rebuild, an opportunity I am glad to offer you. But, succeed or fail you will never be allowed in Mareese again. If you have family here it will be for you to contact them and make arrangements for them. You will have the opportunity before you reach your destination with these good people. What say you?"

The room was quiet with disbelief for only a moment. The prisoners leaned in close across the table conferring amongst themselves. Then one head popped up and asked; "What be this dire mission you mean to send us on?"

Diony responded. "This will only be known when you first agree to my terms. If you can do that then I will turn this discussion over to them."

There were angry grumbles and dirty looks directed at Diony over that but she stood still with her head high and the

367

prisoners returned to their conference. There was a show of hands amongst them and we did not see one man who did not join it. One man stood from the table and moved forward. The guards along the wall moved into offensive stances and he stayed his place.

"If we agree to the terms of Governor Diony as they are put before us, what guarantee do we have that she will honor her part?"

Diony held out her hand to Brynal who pulled a sealed scroll tube from his belt. She handed it to Kapit. "Please sir, read this, then if you feel it is fairly presented I will deliver it to these men for them to sign. I will put my signature and seal upon it in the end and we will have a contract for these men."

Kapit took the scroll and unsealed it. He looked upon Diony and nodded respectfully. He was beginning to appreciate her style. He read the scroll slowly being certain that there was nothing that could harm any of the three involved parties in the future. "I find this to be in order." He declared to all those gathered there. Diony took the unfurled scroll from him and went to the man who stood beside the other prisoners seated at their tables. Protector Brynal started and went to his weapon, but stayed his action. He was visibly nervous and ready to pounce should any man make a move toward his charge.

Diony stood face to face with the prisoner as he read the scroll with the same care that Kapit had given it. The other prisoners waited anxiously for his proclamation. "It is in order, just as she spoke it to us now. I will sign this, but only to hear what it is that the strangers have in store for us. If then I do not feel good about it I will return to my cell, and be glad of another day." Diony produced a quill and a small vial of ink from the purse at her side and handed it to the prisoner. He signed and passed the document around to his men to sign it in their turn. Diony followed the document, being sure that all who wanted to sign it had the opportunity. Brynal followed her. No man refused to sign and the open scroll was returned to Diony. She set it on the table before taking the pen and ink. Then she spoke aloud what she wrote, "Signed on this day by all prisoners of the Legend Destiny Uprising and witnessed by Governor Diony and Company." She added her signature and the date and proclaimed the matter done. She sprinkled salt across the document to aid the drying and blew across it until she was satisfied that it was safe then rolled the scroll and returned to her place with us.

"Who will speak for you Kapit?" she asked.

"I will begin," he replied.

Diony did not introduce him. Kapit stepped forward and paced before us gathering his thoughts before he spoke. Then he turned and addressed the prisoners who waited quietly for him. "I have no concern for your passed crimes, though I trust in Governor Diony's wisdom and I am certain that you have each been fairly tried." He paused there to give a moment for the prisoners to react or dispute him, but none did. He glanced at Diony and smiled before he continued. "My concern is that while you are under my command you commit no further crimes to anyone within my command or to anyone we may encounter along the way. I will not tolerate it and my justice will not come with a trial of your peers. Our mission is dire and as such must remain a guarded secret and so I will not reveal it until you have signed on with me." Grumbles of cheat and scoundrel went through the prisoners. Kapit held up his hand to quiet them before continuing. "I can tell you that you will face hardships you have never imagined. We will battle evils you have only seen in your darkest dreams. Your skills and mettle will be well tested. You can go from convict to hero in the minds of the people. In the end you will have equal share of the plunders, divided amongst those who are skilled—or lucky enough to survive. You will be the main force, a hammer on the gates of our enemy, a diversion to our true cause. Your time of service is indeterminable, but you will be as well cared for as any army can be. I will see to your room and board, though often your room will be the cold hard ground. I also expect that you serve well and with honor. If you do this under dire conditions then you will be free. Only Mareese will remain exempt from your wanderings, as final punishment for your crimes against this fair city and the people who live here.

"You will fall under the direct command of our Lord Paladin who will speak to you now."

Kapit returned to stand beside Diony and Eucharist moved forward. "I am not a man of words." He began. "I am a man of God and I fight for him. With that I hope you can gather that this mission is of a holy nature. Judging from the charges you have been convicted of I can gather that you are *not* men of God. That is unfortunate, but cannot be helped — for now. Under my command you will take daily meditations with myself and our priest if events allow for it. If this turns you against this matter then I hope the time you spend in your cell will lead you to enlightenment, but I doubt it will. Under my command you will train each morning after meditations and each night before retiring, if events allow for it. You may think of yourselves as warriors now, and I will not deny that you have some expertise. But, I dare say, that you have gone soft during your service to a sluggard of a man who was apathetic toward the practice of virtue, to say the least. Under my command you will be expected to conduct yourselves in the manner of a gentleman at all times. Any misconduct will fall under my judgment first and then if I am unsatisfied I will turn you over to Master Kapit to do as he sees fit. At that time I will be done with you and your fate will be out of my hands. So you see this trial to your freedom will be most difficult for you. Not only will you face unknown dangers along the lines that Kapit described, but you must also remake yourselves into acceptable human beings, men amongst men so to speak. If you feel that you can stand up to that then stand and be counted."

There was another conference amongst the prisoners in which the standing man leaned in close, a knee upon a bench. There was some arguing, but in the end, in their own time, each man stood and faced us. Kapit produced a scroll of his own, but his paper was empty. He scrawled a title with Diony's pen. "Eucharist's Army" it said and he went to sit at the table. "Form a line." He said to them. "And sign your name legibly here so that we may have a roll call."

Brynal and Eucharist saw to the order of the men so that no prisoner could slip through the cracks and disobey the contract with Diony and the city of Mareese. Diony compared the signatures to those on her document, being sure that no man could default on her demands. With this done Diony sealed the document with wax and press. Eucharist called the men into formation and looked them over closely.

371

Diony gave some orders to the men outside the door and a short time later a knock came on that same door. Diony spoke again to the guards outside and then came forward.

"Your personal effects will be delivered to a staging area as soon as they can be gathered together. Messengers will be provided for you to notify your families. They can stay in this city if they desire to do so, as long as they remain lawful. When you have all made your contacts you will be escorted to the staging area. At that time you are released from my control and fall under the command of these people. Good luck and God speed to you all.

"Come to me before you leave here, please Kapit." She said this and left the room. Brynal remained behind to see that his lady's interests were kept.

***

Brynal the Protector carefully chose passages the soldiers would have already known from their service with the overlord; passages that were well guarded in the everyday security of the city. If the prisoner soldiers sought to return by these routes, intent on revenge they would be discovered and properly dispatched. The passages had been built long ago for the movement of goods and troops.

Kapit and Diony met long into the night while the prisoners, now soldiers, were being led through the underground passages. Kapit and Diony saw to the movement of supplies that would be needed to sustain a small army and a network for communication. On the latter point Kapit was surprised to know how well Diony had put together a small, but efficient intelligence network in a short amount of time. In so doing she was well aware of his intents and actions in her city. She was curious as to why he felt it necessary to spy on them.

"Dear girl, I only seek to stay abreast of happenings in the great capitals of our world. I must say that your recent participation in world events had me scrambling for information. I knew the overlord was agitated, expectant of some move against him. He kept himself well protected and spoke almost exclusively to his Lord Wizard. Until you entered the scene we were in the dark. You came on the scene like a skyrocket, but then you disappeared and when you reappeared it was fireworks again. I think I will have to put a man in your house just for entertainment."

"The woman you have in my house is doing just fine thank you." Diony's tone carried a warning and Kapit noted it well. "I have no reservations in giving you information, Kapit. All you need do is have the woman, Cheoah, I believe, ask. I have hopes that the events that we have just shared will be the beginnings of a long mutually beneficial relationship."

"Well then let me invite you to have a trusted emissary come to my city when this is done and I will set them up with contacts."

Diony smiled. "I am certain it would not be to our benefit at this time to reveal all of our contacts to you, just as I am sure that you would rather not reveal all of your contacts to me, just yet."

Kapit's annoyance flashed across his face. Though she hadn't actually admitted to it he knew and was surprised to know that Diony already had contacts in his city that he was unaware of. He would have to take that matter up via messenger immediately. He answered Diony with calm voice. "As you wish, Lady. I am confident that you will do well with security here. I look forward to working with you"

"Let's return to more immediate matters, shall we?"

"Yes, I am anxious to get things underway."

"As you know I want to offer as much help in this matter as we can. The actions I have taken up to this point; though within my realm of power will have people talking tomorrow. You know that I cannot guarantee the silence of so many citizen guards and soldiers. I have my network and yours on alert for anyone who would take this information to those who mean us harm. Since neither of us have been successful at discovering our enemies base of operations that may prove difficult. Until we actually follow someone back to a base we are in a grey area. If it comes to that it may be too late to stop the delivery of their message. At that time we can watch their actions and attempt to stop their advance. That is all that I see in our favor on this point at this time. Do you agree?"

"Sadly, reluctantly, yes I agree."

"So there is nothing else that can be done at this time?"

"We must have messengers that are known to us both. We should have a password or signal that will allow us to send others if the need arises. We will keep each other well aware of events. I will contact Dune and tell him of your willingness to help and of your limited means to do so. I am sure if there is aid that he can send that he will."

"On that matter I have already sent messengers to my fellows in Jour, and Coastello to alert them of the situation on our soil. Jour is a large city, Theod is the Mayor there. They have a militia as we do, but it is better trained and more experienced. Coastello is nothing more than a fishing town, but they have many seaworthy ships and able sailors that we may be able to call upon. I have asked them to gather those who are willing to take special training. There is one man, Tourabain in his stronghold, called Ge who I have called upon to train them. He is a great man and has been a champion of justice in his past. He is capable in military strategy as well as diplomacy and intelligence. I have a man that sits on my council for such matters who was one of his trusted men. I have no doubt that we will have the co-operation of all parties. I hope that it will be enough. Your telling of this tragedy has me more than a little frightened. Though we are of limited means you will find my people resilient and full of heart. We will be there when you need us."

So the allegiance was made and details were finalized. Kapit left Diony and returned to Gan and Eucharist at the entrance to the tunnels. Diony returned to her office and saw to a communiqué to Captain Octavio and another to Dune to be delivered by Octavio. She arranged a shipment of sundry goods, a sampling of her cities great tradesmen to be loaded onto the ship. She could not pass up an opportunity to promote her cities trades. When her task was complete three of her most trusted spies went under disguise as a soldier, priest, and fat tradesman. They boarded Dune's ship with the letters composed by Diony and Kapit. The ship would return to Dune via God's Head as Kapit wanted and Diony's people would report to Dune on the recent developments and serve as Diony's messengers there when Dune needed them.

Brynal and two trusted men escorted Kapit, Gan, and Eucharist. Their way beneath the city ended when they arrived at a mountain cave in a range of mountains that paralleled a main cause way. They looked out across the mountains and into Larol Pass where they would stop to rest and test the mettle of their men.

They would move through the Larol Mountains into the vast desert East of Vale where they were forced to cross the open road twice then skirt the mountains where the two arms met and head south along the Vales until they could turn up into the mountains to find the sheer edge overlooking the blazing sands where stood Endar Prison.

·~· Chapter Seven ·~·

Diony had provided a supply wagons and tents to Kapit's army. When he met with us in Larol Pass we appeared to be an organized unit. This of course was credit to Eucharist's command. The tents were grouped in neat rows to form a square keeping the men close together. The larger command tent, and quarters for Kapit, Father Gan and Eucharist flanked the other tents with openings centered on the wide center aisle between the tents. The tents nearest the command tent housed Eucharist's own men and Andreas in a tent of his own, next to a tent for Sardon and me. Eucharist's men walked the perimeter of the camp and guarded the tents of their leaders. We could enjoy the luxury of cook fires now, they would not be allowed on our trek across the open desert.

In the valley of the pass we were concealed from the road. The way through to the desert was likewise concealed from the road and broad enough to accommodate our large numbers. Eucharist's scouts were certain we had not yet been detected. We had one more crossing before Endar Prison. Once we left the pass we would turn west and skirt the mountains. We would take it in the dead of night and head south along the Vale Mountains, out of Arai.

We traveled well and set up camp in the Vales north of the prison to begin surveillance of the area before the first light of morning. Eucharist was allowed several days to train and assess his troops. Scouts were sent ahead to find a suitable area to camp and to watch the routines at the prison. When the army was ready to leave, Eucharist had chosen three leaders from among the prisoners one for every one hundred men. He put them in a tent together and they were given all the respects of his own guards. In return they were to train their men and keep them on task and see to it that they attended daily prayer and exercise. Eucharist ordered his Paladins to mingle freely with the men and forge what bonds they could.

On the third evening when they were breaking camp to move out of the pass unity was emerging amongst the men. They were a smart looking troop as they moved in rank and file order. We moved to the southeastern tip of the pass and made our way to a shoulder of two mountains and the source of the great-unnamed river that emptied into the Solit Sea far to their north.

The desert air was cooling pleasantly as they waited for the sun to set before continuing west to the road in the cool of the night. The soil at the base of the mountains was still warm from the constant touch of day's sun. We rested and waited. The conscripted soldiers were allowed to remove armor to cool down from the climb. Eucharist saw that we were given plenty of water from the wagon, and that our stores were replenished from the cool mountain stream that was the source of the river.

We moved out under a half moon that lit our way a bit too much for Eucharist's liking, but we crossed the road with the knowledge and aid of scouts and went undetected again. We advanced quickly south and were intercepted by advance scouts who took us up into the mountains again. The way was slow and now Eucharist was glad of the moons light, although now he found it lacking. The place the scouts had found was large enough and traversable enough to bring the wagons all the way in.

Eucharist was given a tour of the area. It was a long, narrow furrow at the southern edge of the desert. The eastern access was rocky, but sloping and wide. Two men were placed there, atop either side of the slope as watchers. To the north the mountain walls were sheer and high, but there was a way up and Eucharist placed two more watchers at the top there. The west was closed off and stepped down in elevation to the wall at the south. Another man was posted on the west wall. The south wall was not as steep, but no less jagged. They made their way up through the rocks there to a concealed edge that looked out over a smaller ravine where Endar Prison stood.

Two men were placed there and Eucharist stayed with them. The prison gorge is deep and closes in around the building. The building became part of the walls as if it grew right up out of the ground in the southwest corner of the ravine. A high curved wall formed the boundary of a small yard. Atop the gate large shards of glass and stone were set right into the wall. A heavy wooden beamed door bound with darkening iron was the only entrance they could see. The scouts had looked for others but found none. A natural spring had spawned an oasis on the edge of the ravine. It spilled over the eastern wall of the ravine and sloughed across the small yard inside the prison gates, barely flowing. Barred openings along the buildings foundation did nothing to keep the water from spilling in at several locations. Weathered guards in dark, weathered armor walked the walls at regular intervals. Two stood stationary at either side of the entrance gate and two stood on the roof above the door. No one had ever escaped the prison without being quickly apprehended, and then they did not live to see the prison again. Eucharist remained there watching for a long time. The activity at the prison did not seem out of the ordinary for a prison. While Eucharist watched the rest of us set up camp and gathered into groups.

I sat with Andreas and Sardon and a few of Eucharist's Paladins. We were to be the clandestine force. Our job was to gain access to the prison, discover the hidden gate that led to the depths of hell, sneak in, find the Dark One — hopefully still chained fast, kill him, and return to a safe new world. We were to do all of this without any denizens from Hell knowing that we had passed through— all of this without allowing Hell's denizens to spill out into our world. Eucharist's Paladins would give us holy protection, but even that had limits against a horde of frenzied demons. Sardon was our healer. Andreas our magician; I was the spy, the operative, the thief. I had been the one to break the code that brought us to this place now. What had been thought impossible, I had done. Now together, we would walk through the gates and step over the line of reality and into the dark that we hid from as children and buried deep in our adult psyches. Vicious evil would greet us and tear at our souls. I shivered at the thought and at my own deep chill and moved closer to the fire.

So many trials had brought us there, at that time, with those people. We knew our mutual fate would mean the death of one, or perhaps all of us. I wished for a way to save them all from it. I knew that I must go, it was the only way to be rid of the curse upon me. I found myself plotting a way to leave them all behind and go it alone.

By night's end all seven of the Paladins had gathered with us. Only Eucharist was not present. He remained on watch with several of his new soldiers. Kapit and Gan joined us briefly, with words of encouragement, but they were awkward and soon left us again. That silent bond that we forged that night felt stronger than any I had ever felt before. We knew our chances were slim, but we absolutely trusted each other. We shook hands or hugged and went to bed early. We would move on the prison the next night so the morning promised a day of strategies and trainings and we all needed to be alert for them. I shivered with my malady, but I was becoming used to it.

I had become resigned to the worries of our mission and so I no longer fretted every unforeseen detail. The thought of entering the prison alone was compelling though, and I found I could not sleep. Certainly my chances of being detected were much less. Andreas was capable of getting them through traps and locked doors, and if that failed he could back it up with magic where I could not. I lay on my cot burrowed deep in several blankets and gazed into the dark. I was contemplating how I could sneak through the camp undetected when Sardon rose quietly from her bed. She padded toward me and I closed my eyes, but I tensed defensively. When she was convinced I was asleep she moved soundlessly to the opening in the tent. She lifted the flap only slightly so that she could peer outside. When her way was clear she slipped out.

I rose and quickly put on my boots, slipped on my chain mail armor, then grabbed my remaining gear. I lifted the flap to peer out and I saw her slink around the back side of the tents. I noted the positions of the guards and when my way was clear I slipped out and made my way to intercept her without alerting them. Perhaps she was just relieving herself, but her movements were meant to keep her hidden. I wanted to know what she was up to.

I should have alerted the guards, but I was so used to working alone. Even in tandem with Andreas I was often working ahead of him finding a safe way through whatever obstacles blocked our way. This felt no different.

I kept my distance and remained in the shadows of the camp when she moved into the cover of rocks that surrounded it. She was not very good and I saw her bobbing about for cover several times. When she had the distance I moved from my shadows and ran the gap to the cover of the stones and trees. She was moving up the rise to the west of camp. I belted on my swords and hoisted my pack then as I watched. She made the top and slipped over the other side. Then I moved again.

When I made the top I lay down upon the ground and peered over so that I could be hidden while I spotted for her again. When I saw her, my heart jumped. She was not alone, nor was she with a friend. Dark minions surrounded her. I was about to call out to her when I realized that I had been wrong. She *was* with friends, just not any of ours. She was conversing with a hooded being, too tall to be a man to large to be a demon. I called him Minion. It was not Polk, but had the same bearing as he had when we met upon that ship. He was escorted by four trollish men; ugly, misshapen, muscular men of great strength.

I wanted to call out for help, but it became unnecessary as Eucharist and ten of his men burst into the tiny clearing and attacked. Two men pulled Sardon away. She fought them and one of the Trolls came to her aid. Together they killed two of our soldiers. I jumped over the rise and slid down the loose stone to enter the fray at the rear of Eucharist's attack. The trolls were fierce fighters, and the minion launched balls of flame at our feet. I saw a soldier losing ground and slid in behind his attacker. We nearly had him beaten when he turned and ran. His speed defied his size. I looked at the soldier who stood stunned, so I was the one who gave chase. I overtook the beast on another rise as he stooped to catch his breath. I did not slow or worry about stealth, I just ran at him and ran him through before he could react. He fell dead upon my sword.

I stopped a few moments to catch my breath and then looked back down the rise to the battle. The minion was gone, but the trolls were dead or dying upon the ground. I counted five of our soldiers down. I could not hear what was said, but Eucharist grabbed Sardon himself and wrestled her clawing and kicking back to camp. The others followed each with a dead man over their shoulders. Eucharist and the man I had helped scanned the area of the rise where I stood. When Eucharist looked my way, something came over me and I hid. Why? I do not know, but when I did I realized that moment was my best chance to gain the prison. Right then, before they had a chance to increase their guards.

I moved out keeping just over the rise and made my way. I heard the distant commotion from the camp as Sardon was returned to them—as prisoner now.

***

Kapit and Gan ran as best either of them could toward the sound of the commotion. Kapit— running; this had to be a dire event. Andreas dressed quickly and made his way to the end of camp, pushing through the gather of off duty soldiers and arrived to see Eucharist throw a bound Sardon to the ground at Gan's feet.

Gan spoke not a word. His expression showed a deep emotional pain. Kapit put an arm around him to steady him. Andreas strode into the circle at that point, saw Sardon and went to move toward her.

"Stay your place." Eucharist boomed so that to a man they all jumped.

The gathered went silent, all inquiries cut off by Eucharist's command. The Paladin captain moved to Gan. "I am sorry, Father," he spoke now in a most gentle tone. "As you suspected from that night in Ahnrye she has made her contact with our enemies. She left camp and we followed. They know now that we are here. We lost six men in our attempt to stop her. They were expecting her of that I am sure. They were conversing when we caught up with her. She was well protected and they fought to keep her. We fought through but her contact eluded us with dark magic. We must prepare to defend in case the prison makes a move on us. Though I suggest we attack as soon as possible. Has Saeede returned yet?"

They were silent at that; no one in camp knew that I had gone.

"She was there, saved one of my men and gave chase to his attacker. We did not see her after. I will send a party to search for her."

He stood silent a moment and watched a tear stream down Gan's cheek. He placed a hand upon the Father's shoulder. "I am sorry, Father. We must move on the prison, without Sardon and it seems without Saeede. This is dismal for our plan to fall to shreds now. Our time is now. I believe I know a way to get Andreas and the Paladins inside during an attack."

Gan nodded once but never took his eyes from Sardon.

Eucharist ordered two men to bring Sardon to the command tent. His captains took charge of their troops then and the camp was quickly a bustle of activity. Kapit and Gan turned to follow Eucharist back to the command tent. Andreas stood alone. Cruet went to him. "Come on friend, let us see what this is all about."

He was disconnected from awareness, his mind was spinning and he allowed himself to be lead away. Cruet told me much later that Andreas seemed incapable of speech at that moment and only muttered, "What just happened?"

Eucharist stood before the command table. Sardon was on her knees beside him. Her accompanying guards stood closely behind her with swords drawn to her back. Kapit stood on the opposite side of the table with Gan seated beside him. Kapit was grilling Eucharist with questions about the last night's events. Eucharist answered each with full detail.

Sardon had slipped from her tent and made her way around the camp. She slipped by the posted guards, unaware that she was being followed by Eucharist's men. A detail I had not even been aware of. If any had seen me they must have thought I was on a like mission. One of Eucharist's seven Paladins, was able to make contact with one of the parameter guards and that guard alerted Eucharist, Kapit, and

Gan. Eucharist took ten of the criminal soldiers and led them on the chase himself. I learned later that they found the Paladin on the path, stuck full of arrows. He was dead. From there they picked up Sardon's fleeing trail. She had been joined by two more just after putting the first rise behind her. Soon after Eucharist and his men ambushed her and her comrades and lost men, but they fought through and recaptured Sardon as she was quickly relaying our plan. Eucharist claimed that he heard her himself. He admitted that they came upon the meeting place suddenly, a hidden pit among the rocks. They were engaged almost immediately. The man that Sardon had reported to tried to protect Sardon, but when he was unable to he escaped and Sardon was captured. They looked for me from that spot, but feared a retributive strike and so made their way back without manning a search. Eucharist ordered a retreat and they returned with Sardon in tow.

It did not look good for Sardon as Kapit turned his questions on her. Sardon raised her head proudly and denied none of it. In the end she proclaimed her undying allegiance to the Dark Lord. When she was lead from the tent so that Kapit might decide how best to kill her, she looked once at Andreas and spat on him. My strong unflappable friend shook and remained silent. Cruet put an arm across his back. When he did Andreas reared back and shouted out his rage. When his shout expired from his lungs he allowed himself to sag forward and cry silently. Eucharist witnessed this and then went silently from the tent. Kapit flopped down hard into his seat and rubbed his hands over his eyes as a heavy sigh escaped him. Gan stood and went to Andreas. "I grieve with you, my son. Let us sit together and decide what must be done next."

Andreas gathered himself and went to a place at the table. As he sat Kapit stood and went to leave the tent, but he stopped and addressed Andreas from the entry. "My heart is heavy for you, Andreas—friend. That makes my task now that much heavier. I hope you can understand what I must do. I know that you loved her."

Andreas raised his eyes to meet Kapit's. They watched each other a moment as if accessing a strangers intentions. Andreas nodded once and said, "I do, and I did." Kapit returned the nod and then left the tent. "God's help me. Do I still love her?" he whispered.

Andreas took time to gather his thoughts. Cruet poured him a tall whiskey and he sipped in silence until at last he spoke. "Such a fool I was."

"We all were." Gan replied. "What about me? She studied amongst us for years. She was one of my best students—my most trusted."

"When did you first suspect her?" Andreas wanted to know.

"Back in Ahnrye. When we sent her on those early morning errands to gather the things I would need in my clerical pursuits as we traveled. Kapit sent two men to keep her safe. Neither of us thought she would be a danger herself. When she returned we all went about our business none the wiser. Kapit went to hear his reports from his people about the city. When he returned he came to me and reported that Sardon had veered from her list of tasks and met with a man known to be disreputable; a suspected spy, but for whom was not known. Kapit's men became suspicious and hid themselves well to watch. She spoke briefly to the man, who nodded and then she slipped him a folded paper. He gave her a small pouch. The man slipped away and was gone from sight. She looked around about her, before looking into the pouch. She pulled a small note from it, read it, and then replaced it in the pouch. She hefted the pouch as if to test its weight. We believe there were coins, a payment perhaps for some information in that pouch. She finished her errands then, but before returning to us she went to the river bridge, took the paper from her pouch, tore it to pieces, and set them adrift in the river. Kapit's men did not approach her, since they knew not the nature of her errands. Their orders were to keep her safe. They were certain to mention the meeting in their report and the details came out under Kapit's questioning."

Meanwhile outside Eucharist gave the soldiers orders and sent them to their posts with a reminder to be battle ready. He chose the five men who had survived the battle to capture Sardon to go in search of me. After that was done he returned to the tent and held a briefing attended by Andreas, Kapit and Gan, and Crozier the Gold. They were also put on alert. Eucharist handed his command of the Paladins to Crozier. Eucharist showed them the placement of his troops. The focus of the Paladins was now to keep Andreas safe and protected. They were to make preparations and be ready to move on the prison at a moment's notice. With the absence of Sardon as healer the job was given to the Paladin with the most training and experience with the healing arts on the battlefield; Cruet the Green. My job; as I knew it would, fell to Andreas. When there were no questions he went back to his men. Eucharist appeared a short time later, striding toward the ridge over the prison. He strapped a mighty great sword to his back as he moved with purpose through the camp. He stopped here and there to speak with leaders amongst the soldiers gained from Mareese, or he shouted orders as he passed. The camp was nearly empty after his passing, as his army had gone off to defend the camp and perhaps the world from what was expected to emerge from the walls of that sinister prison. Three guards were left at the camp, one for the sole purpose of running messages back and forth. With gear secured the Paladin Guard that once had been meant to be my escort, sat around the central fire with Kapit and Gan.

I knew of no search party looking for me, but I expected one and so my movements to stay concealed were two fold important. I was slow in my progress toward the prison. The thought crossed my mind that they would think me traitor as well. I dwelled on it only long enough to reason that in the end they would know I did it to protect them.

Back in camp they passed the evening in near silence. Over a meal of cold camp stew Kapit breeched the possibility of my treason.

"Never!" My staunch friend railed at the thought.

"I hope so, for all our sakes, but why else would she leave us at so crucial a moment in the plan, and at the same moment as a confessed traitor?"

Andreas had no answer.

After some time he pulled my good harp from the carpetbag and diddled a tune. I heard the soft plying come to me on the breeze. My heart ached. I missed my friend. Later I heard him play upon his wooden flute. I sat a moment to listen and rest. The full sad tones came to me and I was filled with a kind of remorse. I was sad to leave them all behind, but convinced that what I must do led toward the greater success.

The flute stopped a moment and then began again joined by a set of trilling pipes. They were playing Soldier's Lament. It was an old tune about the parting of lovers when the man is called to war. It sounded sweet and clear in the night air. Who ever played along with Andreas was well practiced. The two instruments played a fine harmony and I took a moment more just to listen. A beautiful tenor joined in on the lyrics. I found myself smiling. I longed to pull my childhood harp, the only one I had with me, always it was with me and play along, but I knew that would give me away and I could not allow that. I could only imagine a soft underlying hush of strings beneath the woodwinds. It struck me that what they played was appropriate accompaniment to what I was about to do so I moved on. The music faded from me as I moved further from the camp. It was then that I felt the loneliness; complete and utter aloneness.

Then it came, a harsh interruption— a shout from the steep face of rock to my north and west followed by a clash of steel on steel. I heard a shout from camp "They are on us!" I ran to where I knew the desert ravine would be. Dark mutants of man, like beasts... unholy things, spilled out of the gates and flowed up and over the ravine walls. I had to move or I would surely be discovered. I crouched and ran along the rim to a place above the prison near the back, but still along the side. There was no way down from there. If I could make the roof and move along the back where the building joined the mountain while the rooftop guards attention was on the horde spilling out beneath them, then I might be able to get down into the space between the prison and the opposite ravine wall where the water pooled in at the foundation of the building. I checked the guards and they were intent on the scene beneath them. I wasted no time and leaped from edge to ledge until I could make the final leap to the roof not far below me. I picked myself up and pressed against the mountain. I was unnoticed and ran to the far edge of the roof. There were no gates on the wall below me so no horde was there.

I looked again to the guards. They remained enthralled by the scene that now played out across the top of the ridged ravine walls. Eucharist and his men were holding the high ground and had an advantage with the sheer sides that delayed the ascent of the dark horde. They were no longer humans, but still humanoid. Whatever had befallen them was a malignant and insidious evil. The weight of our mission suddenly strangled me and the mental block I had on my cursed chill faltered. I stopped short, uncontrolled, my knees buckled and I fell off the roof to the ground splashing into the shallow water that gathered there. It was icy cold, made so by the constant shadow there. Instinct took over and I rolled up against the building and pulled my legs up close so that I fit into the well of a barred foundation opening where the water spilled into the building. I stayed there unmoving for a long time. I could not see the roof so I did not know if the guards came to check what had created the splash, or if they had even heard it. When after a long time I was not accosted I uncurled myself and looked about me.

One small room sat empty and dark beyond that small opening. It reeked of mold and mildew. A wooden door blocked further access to the interior and it was certainly swollen with moisture. The water flowed freely under the door and left a thick carpet of algae on the stone floor of the room. I saw no light and heard no sound from the area.

I watched Andreas and the Paladins climb down the southern ridge of the camp and move southeast across a broad plateau, leaving the battle behind them. They were moving toward my position via a thin branch of the plateau. I was sure they had not yet seen me, but it would not be long before they did.

I was drenched and the chill of the water was like ice against me, and my fight for control against my own chill faltered even more. It was difficult to breathe and the chill shook me uncontrollably. now, I demanded of myself. I set my mind to regaining control of my body. When I had I looked for a place to hide. I spotted a dark crack in the surface of the ravine wall. I looked for Andreas and the Paladins, but they were nowhere in sight. They had to be on the plateau above me.

I hesitated no longer and made for the fissure. Once safely away I waited for Andreas and his troop to make their move. I wrapped my arms around myself and rubbed my body to warm it. It had no effect and I fought hard against the cold that threatened to overwhelm me.

I heard the hushed voices of Cruet and Andreas above me and to my left. I moved to the back of the fissure; only a couple more feet, but the shadow was completely over me there. Their voices were distorted by distance, stone, and my fight with the chill. They were discussing what had transpired so far with the main battle. A mass of horde had broken away from the main group and took a route up the cliffs that would bring them to Eucharist's left flank.

"This is not good." Crozier observed. "We have to get in and fast. If Eucharist cannot hold them and they turn back on us— I hate to think of it."

Andreas replied, "I do not think they will be turning back; though you are right that we need to get in fast, but only so that they are unaware of us. I think I see a way. Follow me." With that Andreas turned and ran ahead. No one questioned or waited. I heard them move further to my left; closer to the back of the prison. I moved forward, keeping myself in the fissure just enough that I could remain hidden and still see the court yard. When Andreas peered over the edge I saw him. He could see that the water from the falls to the west of the prison flowed through below them. They searched for a way down and when Pyx called out he had only to point and they made their way with Andreas once again in the lead.

They moved along the southern rim of the gorge, sloshed through the flow of water above the court yard, and moved back toward the prison. They were concealed from my view, for a time, by a curve in the cliff face. When they emerged they were very close to the prison wall. I could see that the armed guards, like the mutants I now called trolls, on the roof and at the gate were unaware of any presence in the gully courtyard. Their attention was fully on the battle raging in the cliffs before them.

Andreas motioned and Cruet moved up and crouched beside him and just in front of Crozier. I could not hear them, but soon after they were climbing down into the gully court yard. They had a chosen a corner between building and mountain. They could climb wall or cliff or both at once as it suited them and they were all over in less than a minute.

They stepped nearly soundless into the flow of water which was broader here, backed up against the wall until it could find some hole in the foundation, which was submerged beneath the surface. I could see the shape of the window at ground level. The guards on the roof paid no mind to them, and I saw no others in my area of the yard or on the cliff above them. I stayed and watched as they made their way single file to the window well that I had hidden in after my fall. Andreas led them. He had no choice but to lay down in the water to get his face close enough to be able to see the interior beyond.

He twisted at the bars in their sodden mortar and they came away easily. I watched as they removed their packs and hung them on Crozier's long staff to keep them out of water. Then they went in one by one and Crozier knelt to pass in each pack through the open window, and then his staff before sliding in behind them. I saw the bars put back and twisted into the mortar until they stayed. Then they were gone completely from my sight.

So away I went. I ran to the prison wall and approached the window from the opposite direction. I did not pass before it, but crouched low against the wall and listened. I quaked from the chill and had to hold my swords to keep them from jingling and giving me away. I fought to ignore the chill, to control it. There was more at stake than my discomfort and my private quest to remove the curse.

I could hear their hushed voices, but I could not make out their words. Suddenly the room went quiet. There was only the sound of the slow running water. Then I heard a low creak and a moan like an old door opening and a splash. A swarm of insects scurried out of the window and skittered across the water or up the prison wall and me. I fought my repulsion and stayed still, to not give myself away to my friends or the guards above me. Below me they stomped and swatted at the crawling things frantically. The sound of retreating insects rustled across all surfaces. When all was settled again I ventured a peek and found the room empty. The door was fallen in and formed a sort of bridge across the sunken threshold.

I listened until I heard them move out from the next room and then I tugged at the bars They came away easily and I set them on the ground next to the window. I removed my pack and set it on top of them, and then I lowered myself in. I reached back and pulled my pack toward the window, bringing the bars with it. I retrieved them all, and replaced the bars again. There was little left to hold them, and I expected they would give way from the flow of water. I only hoped they would hold long enough to hide our passage.

The walls and floor of the room were alive with algae, moss, and insects. I moved ahead pushing my feet slowly through the water so I would not splash. I peered through the doorway opening, being careful not to step on the door in case it would make noise. Just like the floor and walls the door was alive with moss and insects. The wood was swollen from the water, but the insects were worming their way in and out of it. It looked as if it would crumble to the touch. There was no one in the next room.

I stepped over the door and into a broad anteroom. The moisture affected most of the area but one area near a door was dry. The contents of the flooded rooms were stacked up along a wall there. It had recently been moved by Andreas and his troop. The silt and algae around it had not yet settled back. One door stood where the stacks must have been. It was not fully closed. I listened and when I was satisfied of my safety I looked out to an empty hall, but I could hear shouts and movement in one direction. I could not tell if the shouts were from Andreas and his men or otherwise. I saw no one and so I moved ahead.

I came upon them two halls in. They were crouched low in a dark shadow of the wall and watched Andreas ahead of them peering into a great hall. I could hear the shouts, but there was more. There was movement of men—armored men from the sound of it, and anguished moans and cries.

They turned away from the opening then and made their way down the length of the hall and away from me. I tucked into the shadows, but Pyx at the back of the line stopped and peered in my direction. He took three tentative steps, but then hurried on by the group he moved on, but continued to watch over his shoulder until they moved out of the hall by another door.

I moved to where Andreas had been looking out into the great room. It was filled with all manner of men turned to evil mutants. Three tiers of cells climbed to the ceiling on all four walls save for an access that led deeper into the bowels of the prison. From that opening came more men turned demon. Weapons of all kinds were heaped in one far corner and armor in another. The beings eddied around, between the piles, geared themselves, and then made their way to a man at the far end of the room from me. The man incanted ceaselessly and when the beings drew near him they became agitated and roiled together anxious to draw the blood of normal men.

In the cells moans and cries were nearly lost in the commotion below, but I heard them and I looked up to see what was there. In these cells the prisoners were still human. Emaciated bony hands clutched at the bars of several cells. Sunken eyes watched the scene below. One poor soul hung from the bars with hands and feet and wailed his distress. Insanity had taken him. Was it the incantations, or his witness of the cruel mutations, or his own suffering? I could not tell. I drew back before I was discovered. There was no way through there.

I made my way the only way that was open to me; away from the noise, and on the trail of my friends. Heavy desperation hung over me. What I had just seen was being unleashed upon Eucharist and his army. Andreas and his men went deeper into the halls of the enemy. I was to have been a part of that task, the reason that Eucharist fought was to allow us time to find the gate to hell, breech it and find a way to slay the Dark Lord that reigned there. I knew— I was told, that I must slay him or my curse would never be released. I wanted to save my friends that battle, that and I wanted to be sure that it was I who made the kill. Alone I could guarantee that the Dark Lord engaged with me and no other. But was I wrong? Could I really slay him with out their aid? I began to doubt my ways and I nearly began to run to catch up to them. I could explain it so that they would understand. I longed for the comfort of their numbers, but I stayed put. I reason now that it was some compulsion that made me do that; the work of the curse calling for me I presumed. Whenever the thought of rejoining them came to me I would freeze, afraid to act on any decision that would have a reunion as its result.

So I resigned myself to my plan and told myself that it was my instincts that stayed me. I remained behind them, stalking them, letting them clear my way into the lower recesses of the prison. We moved away from the staging area of the devil's army and went in search of our goal. It was hard to believe that a hell gate had not been breeched. Surely there was evil enough that human servants of The Dark One could easily brandish the power I had witnessed. The priest I had seen was only one example. I was certain there must be more.

Along our way we passed safely through three more areas where cell boxes were stacked one atop the other. A system of wooden scaffolds had been built to allow access to the prisoners. The condition of the prisoners varied from healthy to near death. We saw only priests attending them and they were enraptured by the words they incanted endlessly— mindlessly it seemed.

The troop moved through quickly. The prisoners saw them and they did not call out, but there were whispered pleas for help and words of encouragement. The Paladins said prayers as they passed them; for the deliverance of the prisoners and for their own forgiveness for leaving them. I waited as the troop passed from my sight. I had to; as four heavily armed and armored guards, moved through toward the front of the prison. "At last," one said. "At last we have come to the day of our salvation. My contract is up at last. If I survive this battle I am a free man."

"Aye," said another. "Let us be to it then." The four moved off at a run pulling weapons to brandish them wildly as they yelped and hollered along their way. I ran then to the hall way that Andreas and the Paladins had turned into. I did not see them. From around another corner came a flow of more demon-men and women. They moved in concert, shuffling mindlessly. My heart nearly stopped as I jumped back into the cell room, vulnerable to detection from all angles. The demons turned again and went to some unknown place perhaps in some support capacity. When they moved on, and it seemed no more would follow I moved ahead again to survey the area.

The way was clear. Only two corridors split the walls of the corridor that I stood in. The one was the one the demons had just turned into and the other was where they had come from. That corridor intersected and ran left to right I moved forward not knowing which way Andreas had led his men. I heard nothing, but the chants and wails from the cell room behind me. I knew I did not stand a chance alone against the demons that had passed through so I moved to the opposite intersecting hallway and moved into it. It ran the full width of the prison and branched out again in both directions along the outer wall. Not far ahead, between my position and the outer wall, it took another turn. I went there and found a set of narrow stone steps leading down as far as the eye could see into darkness. I did not see or hear any sign of Andreas and the Paladins.

Old habits kicked in and I checked the stairs for traps all along the way, but there were none. After a long descent I stepped out onto a damp stone and earthen floor of a man made catacombs. I moved along the wall of hand cut niches. Decayed remains of thousands, were piled two or three corpses high.

I was well into the vast area when I heard guttural voices off to one side. I moved to hide behind a buttress and waited, listening, trying to decipher the language. They came closer, they spoke brokenly, but it was the the familiar language. As they came closer to me I saw Crozier emerge from behind a sarcophagus and point in the direction from which the hoardlings had come. Andreas and the rest of the Paladins also emerged from hiding and they moved out. When the monsters had moved past me I moved as quickly as stealth would allow and hid again at the sound of guttural voices approaching.

Two mutants passed too close to Crozier who raised his crooked staff and came down on their temples with two swift raps that incapacitated them both with barely a sound. He tossed them up into vacant spaces in two nearby niches.

I followed at a distance as Andreas led them through the catacombs to another steep stairway down. I gave them time to get further ahead and then I made my way. The stairs switched back flight after flight. I could not see them ahead of me, but a guttering candle moving down ahead of me made me aware of their location. I made my way at the outer edge of that light. When it stopped moving, I stopped.

My legs burned from the climb down, and down as if it would never end until suddenly it switched back and the landing opened up to a small ledge. The light stopped and so did I. A great dark iron gate blocked us from the edge. A low hum emanated from beyond the gate. As my ears became accustomed the hum became discernable, not as a hum, but as a communal wail. The sound of it wracked through to our souls, the hopelessness, the pain, and the wretchedness ripped at the fiber of our beings. Crozier began his prayers of blessings and protection. The inner strength of the great Paladins was tested and they stood firmly as tears rolled down their cheeks and suppressed sobs lurched in their shoulders. Andreas, who was less pious than they were, simply held his ears against it until Crozier's prayers eased his discomfort. The power of that prayer did not reach me. That little undecorated gate was a barrier to Hell. It seemed unreal.. The force of evil and sheer pain that emanated from it seemed too much for such a ordinary gate. I braced against the granite, reeled from the onslaught of cold dismay, and swooned.

·~· Chapter Eight ·~·

Eucharist fought bravely. His army of Mareesian prisoners, the old soldiers of the overthrown overlord did not break when they saw the evil that spilled from Endar Prison. They had been warned and these mutants of man did not seem as bad as what they had expected. The battle came to them in the early hours of night and they fought with torch and sword, axe and arrow. The dark horde was falling to them, but they were in danger of being flanked. The Paladin Commander saw his small spearhead force make their way across the plateau and into the prison gorge. They were minus two. Sardon was captured. Where I had gone and why he could not know. He was worried and saddened by my absence, but there was nothing to be done for it, now that the battle was on them. A swarm of horde came through the rocks at their right flank and he lost sight of Andreas and his Paladin escort.

His forces split and they were pushed back. The horde gained the rim, but Eucharist and his troops fought in retreat. He caught one last look at his small advance troop as they slipped into a side window into the prison basement. Eucharist's troops were surrounded in the furrow that had been their camp. They fought and were losing, when the horde lost interest and streamed away from the battle and into the wilds. Eucharist pursued and they slayed many, but their numbers were too small by then to deal a blow to such masses. Eucharist gathered his men and they saw to the dead and wounded. The shrieks of the horde kept them on edge as they sounded in the distance or nearby as they passed out of the prison. Eucharist set a guard of his strongest men and they dug graves until morning was full up in the sky. Skirmishes broke out through the remaining hours of night and Eucharist lost three more men. When the dead were buried and the wounded put in the wagon or supported by able bodied men they moved out. It was nearly noon by then.

They numbered ninety from the original three hundred. They returned by their same route and watched at the road, but this time their goal was not to conceal their movement, but to waylay the monsters that had escaped them. The road was empty for the time. Eucharist chose four healthy men and sent them together to Jour to report there and have fresh messengers sent to Ge. Diony would send to Coastello as soon as he returned to report to her. Eucharist blessed the four and watched until they were out of sight, then he turned the remainder of his dwindling troop onto the road anxious to be back to Mareese.

The miles clicked by slowly, the convict soldiers were out of shape and Eucharist had no choice, but to rest them or lose them to infirmity, or mutiny. They had fought well and honored their contract so far, but they would be needed again and their loyalty was still a fragile commodity.

It was nearly dark again when they came to the city gates and Eucharist announced his troop to the guards there. The young militia man at the wall hesitated and Eucharist had to convince him to consult with a superior. Long moments passed, and the top of the wall filled with bowmen, but then the sounds of galloping horsemen and shouts came to them.

Diony's man, Ray MacVen looked down from the wall at them and made the order for the gate to be opened. Ray met Eucharist with a horse for him and wagons were arriving to take the men to the stronghold. Brynal took charge of them as Eucharist was led away to speak to Diony.

Diony was already pacing her office when he arrived. Eucharist did not wait for formalities, but launched into a full report. She shook more and more as his report went on, and collapsed into her chair with the weight of the news by the time his report was complete.

"I have runners ready to go and a ship to send to Coastello. Our cities are prepared to fight, but the outlands remain unprotected. I have asked the city fathers to prepare to take in these citizens. I will send to them that now is the time. Will you stay to help me send a detailed report as quickly as possible?"

"Of course I will."

It was not long before Diony laid down her pen and turned the parchment for Eucharist to add his signature to hers.

Brynal returned at this time. "I have the men in a common area at the academy. They are being fed and have beds in which to rest. The Elders are seeing to their wounds. They are well contained there, with the illusion of freedom for now, until you advise me otherwise."

"They all fulfilled their contracts, but we will have need of them again. I respect the contract you have put them to, Diony, but we should talk about how to ease it some. We will both have need of their loyalty before this is over."

"Then we will discuss it, but first you need food and rest. Come I will see to it myself."

They all arrived at the kitchen when the final cleanup from the day's work was just about finished. Diony dismissed the workers with a feel of comradery and assured them that she would see to the cleanup of any mess they made and that the kitchen would be spotless when they arrived in the morning. She and Brynal went about the kitchen and soon had a buffet of cold beef, yams, garden vegetables, and sweet bread. Diony made up sandwiches while Brynal sliced and heated the potatoes in a skillet. Eucharist sensed something more to their relationship, but said nothing of it.

When his plate was ready Diony set it before him and Brynal followed up with a frothy mug of red ale. Eucharist ate with gusto. Diony waited until his plate was nearly clear and she had refilled his mug before starting the conversation.

"So tell me; what you think we should do for the convict soldiers?"

"Giving them some sense of freedom was a good start. Still I will need access to them and we will need to train and drill amongst your city militia so that when the time comes to defend the city we will understand our role."

"I believe I can solve your first concerns with little problem, but I must stay to my part of the contract. We have an old outpost at the intersection of the roads from Ge and Jour."

"I have seen this place. It is in need of repair."

"I have had crews there for several days. We have spent hours going through the overlord's things and found some hidden ledgers and a substantial amount of hidden money. My city is not prepared for a war and so I am taking the money to remedy that. The dwellings there are much improved now, though the outer walls and gates still need reinforcing. You could stay there with your men and train in exchange for an agreement that you will patrol the areas around us. I want to be fair so I will also send you staff to see to the daily meals and the final repairs."

"Your intent is duly noted and appreciated. If you can see to the repairs I think I can hold the men to our contract for sometime more, since they are being well cared for. I will see that they know it is your benevolence that puts a roof over their heads and meals in their bellies."

"I thank you for that. Do you think that I will need to see to a wage for them at sometime?"

"Not if you stick to your contract. Keep your money, Lady. If this goes on for a long time I will ask Kapit to see to their wages. If they continue to serve well and enter into war, it may be right that we compensate them."

"I will let the work men know to expect you, let me know if there is else you need."

"What have you done to see to the protection of the city itself?"

"I have started a hometown defense. I am training any and all that want it in Self Defense and Swordsmanship. We do this under pretense of never falling to tyranny again. With your message the time has come to tell them more. I am seeing to armaments in strategic locations and we have a defense and shelter plan as well as an evacuation plan in place, but have yet to test either. I don't want to put too much on these people at once."

"For now it is good that they learn to fight."

At that moment Kapit and Gan entered the room. "I knew that you would want to confer with Eucharist. I am sorry to have wakened you."

"Do not be concerned dear girl, you were right to do so of course. Pray tell, Eucharist, what goes?" Father Gan came to his Paladin leader and shook his hand.

"It has begun. We were attacked. The enemy is not mortal man, or at least they are no longer men. They came in droves. I lost many men. I saw Andreas go inside with the Paladins. Saeede, is still lost to us. She knew the plan; my hope is that she will be capable of her own journey, and find some way into the prison. Perhaps she will be able to reunite with Andreas and our Paladins. We fought on, but the enemy scattered after a time, as if they lost interest in us. We know not why. We hunted what we could and encountered a few on our return here. We lost several more men. We are only eighty-two men now.

"That's over two-thirds gone!"

"How are the men taking it?"

"There is sorrow, but when they saw the enemy I believe that they put aside old grievances in the face of something they knew could change their world forever if they did not fight against it. They fought well and hard. I believe that I have a force that could be special if trained properly. Diony and I were discussing just that when you came in and we have made arrangements. What we need now is some guidance from you and your tribunal.

"What became of Sardon? Is she imprisoned here?"

Gan sat down heavily in the nearest chair. "She is for now." The kitchen went silent for sometime.

Kapit paced the kitchen, deep in thought, but it was Gan who spoke first. "There are reports by all means from all of our brethren that their people and lands have been plagued by demons that eat their livestock— as well as their children. They take the weak minded easily into their fold, and torture those who do not go willingly. Women are being raped, and we know not what will be the offspring of that. Villages burn—sometimes from loss of the battle, other times as a means of some diversion, or for escape and preservation. Even then the demon plague hunts them and few survive. This news has only just reached us, Diony.

"You had better prepare your physicians and soldiers for a mass influx of refugees in the next few days as word spreads of this dire news. Make ready what accommodations you have. The time has come for you to report to your citizens what has transpired while you kept them in the dark."

"Watch how you speak, father. Do not say it as if she has had no regard for her people. For certainly she has, and not just for their physical safety, but for their hearts and souls as well." Brynal was furious and he stood up to speak over the father.

"I meant no insult, sir," Father Gan whispered.

Diony put her hand upon her lord protector's arm. "Thank you for your support, but the father speaks a thing that is also true. I have been afraid that this would come upon us, before our people were fully healed from the woes Overlord Kaedl heaved upon us. Many will think that I did keep them in the dark, yet another woe that I am left to mend for this city and her people. I will find a way."

"He does not understand our ways and our people. I will not have you talked to in such a way."

The lady and her protector shared a long look and soon the protector moved away from Father Gan. "See that a proclamation goes out through the town criers. I will address the citizens at day break and we will see that Father Gan's concerns are assuaged. See that all the council comes to me before so that I can brief them and they will be present for the address. Will any of you join me?"

"We will all attend." Kapit announced. "I think we should meet your council as well, you may face some anger there as well. We can speak to the urgency of the matter and lend you credence. I am grateful for and sympathetic to your position."

"For now there is much we must all see to I am sure." Diony said. "Eucharist, would you accompany me as I go to my commanders and I will give you a tour of our defenses? I would value your input on anything in either of those departments. Your experience will help our people."

"I would be happy to."

"Brynal when you have seen to the criers and the council find Ray MacVen and join us."

"I'll pick him up on the way, Milady."

"Well then if there is nothing else." Diony looked to each man present and when no words were spoken she turned Eucharist by the arm and he followed her out. The others dispersed to their own duties, to be done before the address of the council and the citizens.

·~· Chapter Nine ·~·

I walked through a dream landscape. Stark trees and bramble bushes stood against a deep purple sky. Low lying fog swept across the ground. I felt cold fingers of it wrap around my legs and ankles, but each time I struggled to free myself the fingers withdrew. They teased at my hands and throat. I thrashed at them but they were relentless. I could not convince myself to waken and so dread built in me. I needed to find a way out. I sensed it was my only way to survive this place, not to wake, but to metaphysically exit by some yet undiscovered means. I became aware of distant voices crying out to me, but from where, what direction? I could not tell. I stumbled through the fog until I came to a broken road. I had no way of knowing which direction to travel along so I chose and went that way. After awhile I saw a dark form traveling along ahead of me, in the same direction. The sight of it filled me with dread and I stopped to gain some focus through the fog. My sudden realization of who and what this was nearly caused my heart to stop. I fell to my knees, clutching at my chest and struggling for air. When I did he came toward me riding atop the fog. He willed me to look at him and I could not disobey.

"Sweet Saeede, at last we meet face to face."

His face was a roiling mass of darkness, wind, and plasmic explosions, much like a thunderstorm that springs up at dusk and lights the clouds with static explosions. His eyes were oily black and reflected the low light of our surroundings. He had a snout like a dog and his black tongue slid across his sharp teeth to lick lasciviously across his black lips. He wore a hood, but it rose above his head oddly as if suspended there.

My face was a stricken piece of white flesh, frozen in an expression of fear. I felt my icy tears trail down my cold skin.

"Don't be afraid. You have traveled so far and through such adversity to see me. At last you are here. Come take my hand."

His hand revealed from beneath a shawl of diaphanous leather reached for me. It was like the claw of a rat, but I longed to touch it, to feel the power that must reside there. As his arm extended toward me I saw the diaphanous leather was a membrane that connected his arm and legs and would unfurl along his sides to act as a wing much like a bat. This repulsed me and I drew back my hand.

My hand—my hand was a weak, shaking, useless appendage against this beast. I felt for my weapons; there they were, steel comfort, if only I was strong enough to wield them. I had great doubt of that.

The action offended the beast and he made a move toward me, but when I fell back to scramble away he stopped and spoke softly to me instead. "Do not fear me. I want only the best for you. Why do you cower from me when I can offer you so much?"

Suddenly I heard my mother's words repeated to me so often; "Fear no evil," she would say. "Fear no evil." I said to myself. "Fear no evil," I whispered. "You do not want what is best for me. You killed my friend, and used me to do it.

Since then I am cursed with a plague of cold. Now you come to me to make an offer— an offer of what?"

"You are a fiery thing, amongst a sea of mundane beings. You walk the line between light and dark; good and evil every day with an ease unknown to the mundane masses. I have watched you since you left your mother's womb. She would have none of me either, but she was not strong enough to resist me in the end. I know that you have wondered about her disappearance many times."

"She went away to save me from persecution."

"No, she gave herself to me to keep you from me. You were the one I wanted. Though you never knew it, you are my child. Your mother's ways made you curious about the dark, about me. That was fortunate. So you are my child. Your mother was my concubine. I needed a vessel by which to conceive and ensorcel you. She was a naive dabbler in magic on a path for knowledge, delving deep into ritual meditations that she was not performing correctly. I brought her to me and seduced her for my means. Soon after she realized who I was, she discovered that she was pregnant and moved outside the city. She did all that she could think of that would cause her to miscarry. She began to dabble in herbals with the same intent, but fell upon information that might actually save you and so put her energy into that. It seems she had some good success there; I have tried to reach you for a long time. Ironic isn't it that you come to me anyway? Do you know that she nearly died in the birth of you? Even I cannot live forever and I need an heir. I have several to choose from, but you are my favorite. You fascinate me."

"So you offer up your kingdom to me?"

"I do. I can take you there now. All you must do is renounce your worldly existence and recognize me as your lord and father. I will teach you all that you must know, then when I move to my death you will be the ruler of all that lies above and below the earth."

"How will I rule what lies above? That realm belongs to man."

He laughed, like a father amused by a babe's innocent observation. "You are of man, and demon. Have you never felt the stirring in you? No matter, you will come to embrace both. Who better to rule over both? You have walked proud between both realms since you embarked on your life of adventure. You have been fair and just in most things. Those are traits for any good ruler—to uphold what is lawful."

"You forget that I have seen what you do to men. I have seen them demonized. It was only mentally, emotionally before, but today I have seen the complete transformation. Why must you turn them into monsters?"

"Monsters?" Again he laughed in that fatherly way. "Those are the dredges of your society. Their transformation is the sentence they pay for their crimes. They have become what they embraced."

"And so what crime did you commit that shackled you with such an appearance?"

He was silent a moment considering me, and his answer. Then he laughed again, a robust rolling thing that shook the ground upon which we stood. "You are irreverent. You do not fear me do you?"

"I fight my fear. I have gotten good at it. This adventure I believe I have perfected the art. You haven't answered my question."

"I get results with this form, when my subjects fear me they respond favorably. I can take on any form I choose." To prove it he changed in size and form to become a handsome man. "This is how your mother saw me. I had favorable results with this form when I was allowed to roam the earth. Women found me handsome and I very much enjoyed them. I will enjoy you very much too, over and over again until Death takes me to Her realm."

Now I was silent, his spell was beginning to work on me and I never saw when he cast it. I felt myself yearn for his touch as I had the night of Wallace's death. I wanted him and I felt myself move toward him, reach for him. He moved to me and took me in his arms. His embrace was warm, his kiss hot and passionate. I kissed him back and warmed my chill on his hot skin. He kissed my neck, my chest. He thought he had me and relaxed his spell. Then I came back to myself. I pushed away, but he held me tight. I clawed, kicked, screamed.

It was the scream that freed me. The terror of our first encounter back in Behlanna rushed back on me and I broke free from him. I fought my way back from his shadow realm, stumbling head long through the grasping fog. The sharp trees tore at me and I spun away from one to avoid a gash to my eye. I fell and when I landed I found myself back on the landing with Andreas and the Paladins. I should say, more accurately that I found myself back on the landing observing myself in Andreas's arms, while the Paladins gathered around us— them.

"Is she alright?" Rood asked.

"Does she look alright?" Crozier retorted. "Can't you see?"

Andreas patted my cheeks, the universal signal for I have no idea what to do. "Come on girl, there is no time for you to slack off now." I could hear fear in his voice. Considering the situation I know that they were all rightfully afraid for me and our chance of success. Andreas pushed a strand of hair off my forehead and kissed me there.

"Kissed by a frog," my conscious self whispered.

"Kissed by a frog," he said. "Kissed by a frog—come on princess."

I knew not which of me was reality and which was dream. I reasoned that since the me I watched was asleep or unconscious that she must be real and dreaming me. I waited for her to awaken, but she did not. Andreas hung his head and I saw his shoulders shake as if he was crying. He held my body—my body? He held it close and kissed my forehead before he laid me gently down.

Crozier and all of the Paladins took an unconscious step back. "Did she say anything to you?"

Andreas only shook his head, and then said, "We cannot leave her in this place. She'll be discovered and turned into one of them, or worse, they'll baptize her in their fires and we'll never be able to save her soul."

I barely heard Crozier say that they could spare no one to return me. "The way back is fraught with all evil as you well know. One or two alone with a body to carry would have little chance of success. If they make it out of the prison we are now behind enemy lines and their chances of making it through that seem slimmer still. We can consecrate the body so that if she is found they will be repelled, at the least; they will not be able to turn her.

They were all silent for a moment and I was glad of it. The thought of being turned sent a chill through me to match that which I was already fighting. I shuddered at the feeling of the dark one's own touch upon me. My chill deepened and a tear ran down my face. My chill— it was still real to me and so I reasoned *I* must be the real one. The dark one had pulled a switch. The Saeede in Andreas's arms was a simulacrum, a trick to convince them I was dead and so I had failed them, and been beaten by the Dark Lord. So if ever we met again they would doubt and renounce me.

Andreas turned away from them and walked a few paces toward me as I watched. He was deep in thought. I reached out, instinctively to touch him; to comfort him. My hand rested gently on his shoulder he shuddered and stepped back as he looked up. I thought he saw me there. He peered into the darkness as if to make me out, but then shook his head to clear it and turned back to Crozier.

"As it must be;" he started, "but we will carry her far enough so that we can hide her away. Then you will consecrate the ground there as well. Perhaps it will keep them away."

He went to where my body lay, pulled me up, and wrapped a fur around me. Before he hoisted me into his arms he kissed my cheek. He handed me over to Pyx and then turned his attention back to the gate.

"Well let's see to this gate then," he offered and went about searching it for tricks, traps and snares. Andreas found several traps and tested Cruet's healing skills each time. The last put a gash across his right palm that would not stop

417

bleeding—there was no blade, but a force that caused it. Cruet packed it and wrapped his hand like a club. Only the tips of his fingers were any good and that was no good for the job. He fumbled with the lock, a great big thing of precision gears and tumblers.

Perhaps I could affect the real world as I had when I touched his shoulder. I went to the lock and examined it over Andreas's shoulder. If I could be Andreas right hand and I worked my picks against his we might get the last tumbler to fall. I reached over him and my plan worked. The black gate opened without a whisper or a squeak and the dreadful moaning stopped which was a great weight off the Paladins' souls.

"I feel her." Andreas whispered. "I swear I do."

Crozier said a prayer and they passed through the gate. Crozier took the lead and they began their further descent into the dark reaches of the underworld. Andreas took my body from Pyx and Pyx took up the rear guard. When I tried to step in behind Pyx, they were gone from me. I stood again in the fog and the chill within me joined with the chill that surrounded me.

·~· Chapter Ten ·~·

A horn sounded from the outpost where Eucharist and his men guarded the crossroads and the wilds beyond. They engaged the enemy but there were too many and they broke through their lines. On the walls of Mareese the sounds of battle came to the militia there like a slow moving storm rolling thunder in the distance. The first scream within Mareese came well into the night. The guards on the walls thought it was a demon dog at first, but when it came again they recognized the human terror in it. Mareese was about to be tested by the dark of evil.

Another scream hit the night; a piercing jagged thing that split the soul and chilled the blood. A howl and a snarl followed and it was answered by many more from all directions. Shouts rang out on the north side of the city as dark hoardling things crawled out of the sea and gained access to the wharf where there were no protective walls. The clash of battle rang across the night air. On the walls tried and untried soldiers waited unseeing for the battle to reach them. A thunder of battle would roll in the streets and recede and when it would be heard again it was closer to the walled section of the city each time. The skirmishes soon spread out along the walls. Eucharist and his men rode in from the outpost beating down the horde where they could, but his men were tired and the horde too many. The black beasts ran through his forces and crawled up the walls to engage the militia there.

The brave souls of Mareese fought hard for their lives, family, freedom, their souls, and Mareese itself. Many of the brave fell, but many more of the hoardlings fell before their passionate attacks. Mareese held and in the first hours of dawn the surviving horde spilled back over the walls and were pursued or slain as they tried to escape. The academy bell rang three low tones to call her citizen soldiers back to the walls. It rang again and again throughout the day once for each of the fallen as they were counted.

Diony was among the wounded, but her hurts were easily bound and she returned to her duties amongst her people with praises and gratitude. She grieved with the families of the lost. When all of this was done, she met with her advisors; among them now were Kapit, and Father Gan.

The meeting was short. They were cut off from their allies and could not expect help. Their allies fought their own battles with the horde. They knew what must be done and they went about it with great haste and intent. Materials for more catapults were hauled atop the walls and construction began. Large kettles were brought up and placed on braziers between the catapults. Some were filled with oil; others were filled with scrap iron and flack from the forges and tended by the apprentices of the Blacksmith trades. When the slow melting dirty stuff was molten they banked the braziers just to keep the stuff hot and liquid. The catapults rose up on the walls quickly and by evening they were complete and all manner of stone and junk was being stacked up as ammunition for them.

Eucharist spent this time realigning his troops to make the best of what they had. His prisoner-soldiers held a broken line around the city. Diony ordered all ships out to sea and those that had armaments held a line along the coast so that they could support the battle from there.

As night fell the howls began again and the storm of battle rolled again toward the great city.

***

"O, Polqutis, my favored one. You have brought me the keys at last. Yet our triumph is incomplete. You have brought back my lovely Sardonius, at least you have been good for that. I wish I could see their surprise when they discover that the one who occupies their prison cell is nothing but a phantom now. Her return pleases me, but joy is denied me. My master reviles me and I must receive his displeasure, though it is you who brings him down on me."

The one known as Polk to man fell to his knees as Polqutis before the harsh eye of his master, the Dark One's minion. "My Lord Master, I have done all that you have asked of me. I have failed only in one thing. I can still bring you the girl, Saeede. When her partner rose and fought like a beast from heaven against us. The mask upon his face lit so bright as to sear our eyes. We had to retreat or we would all have been lost."

"Had you only brought me the girl, if only that before you ran like a coward. If only that then I could spare you now." The minion grabbed the throat of Polqutis and the cold of his touch spread and froze the man to death. He pulled his hand from the futile frozen grip of his victim. When he turned from Polqutis his shape changed from human to a whirling dark shape that was like a man, but his black eyes in their sockets were the only discernible feature.

He reached a hand out to a beautiful women standing nearby. She went willingly to his arms and laid her fair head upon his chest. He stroked her hair. "You have never done anything in all these years to disappoint me Sardonius. You have fulfilled all that we have asked. If the master will allow it I will take you as my own, as my reward for service. If we can bring him Saeede— perhaps then he will grant me this. He desires her greatly."

"Fear not my darling. She is weak and awkward. The cold is upon her. Even Polqutis said that she quaked with it as they came near her. I just love that it was the undeath enchantments of those vile dwarfs that made her so susceptible to his subliminal touch. We will make her Malisgalar's. She cannot withstand another encounter, and now we have the keys. Malisgalar himself can take her."

The two devils tossed their heads back in cacophonous laughter and walked away from Polqutis.

They had not seen me lying in the fog. I watched as they disappeared into it and then I drug myself across the frosty ground to where Polk, Polqutis, stood frozen and dead. I shuddered from cold, fear, and disgust as I used his body to pull myself up and leaned against him until I was sure that my feet would not go out from under me. Then I went in search of Sardonius and the dark minion that she accompanied. I knew that they would lead me to the Dark One and that I alone was meant to slay him.

Where ever Andreas and our Paladins were I knew that they would no longer be looking me. They had my body, or at least an illusion of it, perhaps that was a Phantom as well.

Some subliminal message cast upon them by The Dark One. My course was being laid by Malisgalar himself and if I was right about that then the beast no longer slept. He had not been sleeping at all, but casting out his evil from within his prison, casting it out with the sheer power of his mind. If I was wrong then I was trapped within the monsters dream, and waking him would be my only way out.

I took a deep breath of the frosty air. When I exhaled there was no warm cloud of breath. That realization spoke of my imminent death. I remembered the mask that hung at my belt, a gift from the dwarfs to protect me from undeath. What harm or good it would do now I did not know, but I put it on, for whatever protection it would give.

I stepped forward in the direction that Minion and Sardon had gone. Distant sounds came to my ears, but I could not sort them. Direction was impossible to determine. The further I moved into the fog the more my senses became muddled. If I found my prey it would be by circumstance and no good ability of mine. I drew my swords and moved in the direction that I hoped would take me to my quest.

I chose rightly. I smiled and thanked the god's for circumstance. There before me was a great river; broad and smooth it flowed; black under the fog that rose up from it. Across the river a tangle of towers rose from the fog. They too were black. Orange light shone from the windows. I walked the shore in both directions in search of a boat, I only found the tell tale scrapings of one recently cast off into the river.

I tested the water. Its chill was greater than what flowed through me, but warmer than the air around me. A river so broad would flow for miles. I might never find a way across and my time for success was becoming limited. I had my doubts, but swimming was the quickest option. I had no choice. I sheathed my swords and strapped them to my thighs, waded in, and pointed myself toward the towers. I pushed my pack before me as I swam slow and steady. The current took me, but I let it. There was not else to do. I sneered and cursed at circumstance then. An hour later I was still struggling for the far shore. My chill now matched the water. My teeth chattered, my mind wandered, and my heart barely beat. Each stroke was a labor of sheer will. I wanted sleep. I no longer cared if the water took me. I was tired of fighting. Death would be a welcome respite from my struggle.

***

In a reality not so far removed from my own, Andreas and the Paladins trekked deeper into the abyss. They had their mission. Secure the nine gates so that no more evil could spill out upon the world. Once that was done they would turn to their search for the dark lord. If they had to meet him and kill him without me it would be so.

I knew that my fate was secondary to the common good. I doubted that we would ever meet again. A lump came to my throat and the stress of emotion made my head ache. We all had the same mission— kill The Dark One. They were to have been my support so that I could deal the death blow. Now my life force was slipping steadily away from me, and they believed I was already dead. I believed that I was slowly becoming a wraith drifting further into undeath.

It reasoned out during our crazy adventure that the dark one was my father. He had tricked my mother and they conceived me. She hid it from me and since it had been told to me I had never admitted aloud to believing that it was true. I had not wanted to accept that my mother was the black witch the town folk had said she was. I wished I had her with me so that she could explain it all to me. Since she disappeared years ago that was unlikely so I just remained quiet about it, but nothing else made sense. Nothing. I once again resolved myself to the task of killing the evil that had spawned me when my mind drifted into darkness.

***

I was surprised to find myself regaining consciousness in a tangle of bush that hung over a low bank in the river. My legs were still in the water; bobbing behind me still caught in the current. Strength was no part of me. The branches were all that held me. I pulled upon them and thanks to buoyancy I made a little progress, but it was a long time before I had all of me on solid ground. I don't know for how long I slept after that, but I woke to the sound of wolves. Least I thought it was wolves. I raised my head wearily to have a look around, but I saw nothing but black— black ground, black sky, black river, and black trees. I was convinced that if there were eyes watching me that they would be black as well and so virtually invisible. I rolled my pack and struggled to sit against it. I knew that my torches would be soaked and useless, so I rummaged in the dark for some smoked meat. The foul water had gotten into it and I spit out the horrid taste of it. Perhaps the wolves would be interested if I encountered them.

***

Treaties were made amongst the great rulers of Dinar and Crystalier as more and more reports came of wicked beasts taking over entire cities and using the citizens as slaves, concubines, and worse. Black sailed ships appeared on the horizons of all majors cities and Dark armies swept down out of the mountains and into the plains. Mankind pulled common folk into the protective walls of cities and sent soldiers out to face the enemy. Many were no more than frightened but determined citizens. Duadan left Strom in charge of Behlanna with an official proclamation and led a troop of Calvary and infantry out of the city to join with King Dune's men to form a barrier around the northern half of their island continent. Duadan's control arced from the Barrier Mountains south and east of Behlanna to Sandhitch, Dune would control Sandhitch to Ahnrye and east to the coast. Duke Midewin's forces would fill the gap along the eastern strands. Dune put ships out to patrol the coast and to support the land troops if the need presented itself. They were no warships, only ketches and schooners fitted with scorpions and small catapults. The ships were meant to serve as runners to report movement of enemy ships or move in to engage in the event of an enemy landing. The war ships had been deployed to the three coastal cities and the Northern and Southern Outlooks. The Outlooks were little more than rustic strongholds built up around stone towers situated on high points of land that gave wide views of the coastal shores and the seas stretched out beyond. Swift horses and experienced messengers were deployed at each of these posts and the three cities. Word spread from merchant ships that dark horde had taken the city of Coastello and that Mareese was holding with battles taking place at several locations around the city.

The horde became known as goblin soldiers. Man like creatures with grey to green skin, bulging black eyes and sharp-toothed mouths with dark, sometimes forked tongues. They fought with a frenzied focus and were said to move through fire with ease. Lanced Calvary on swift blue dragons began to appear, often leading the way into the cities, but Mareese with her many tiers and elevated vantage points had cut into their numbers considerably. The dead of our world were being scooped up and placed on ships to be reincarnated as goblins. It was not unheard of for kin to face goblin kin in battle. When the mortal kin was victorious there was grief and anguish. When the goblin-kin won there was blood letting and victory cries.

As reports came in and military strategies were made and remade Kapit and Gan, poured over copious amounts of religious writings searching for some verification as to the location of the remaining gates. Messages were coming in from fronts in several locations and they were at last able to correlate the information. If they could put armies in those places and stay the flow of exodus from the dark realm civilization might yet survive. They made preparations and gathered men from Brother Chalcedon's Paladins and Kapit's varied forces. They hoped to buy our mission time. They did not know that we were so close to failure soon after our foray into the prison began.

***

Andreas fought well into the depths of the abyss. They found eight gates and sealed them with prayer, music, and magic. Down and down they wound their way through stone of earth in search of the ninth. What they found instead was an opening to a dark and grotesque landscape. They had burned my phantom body under protest from Andreas, but in the end he saw the right of it. My death had already taken me out of the picture as far as he knew. He swallowed his grief and began to plan a way without me.

The dark of the day was falling into darker night. Further travel would be foolish, but they had no means for fire and so sat huddled close in the darkness. They did not sleep for fear that the howling; screeching creatures would swarm down and kill them all. They fought off three attacks in the night. The dark things coming at them like specters of a nightmare. The battles were clumsy frantic bids for survival, and survive they did, but their wounds were great inflamed rips in flesh. Andreas and Cruet did all they could to heal them. Viaticum prayed for their souls and gave thanks for their deliverance from death. Their wounds burned as they moved forward toward the dark opening once again.

When the dim light of morning came they agreed to move off along the rim of dark cliffs that surround the land. They moved along it in hopes of finding the final gate, until the vast dark of the night in that place forced them to stop again. That night they were undisturbed and even slept in two hour shifts.

In the morning they moved along the cliffs again and after some time they discovered a dark opening. The closer they came, the fouler, and more prevalent the creatures became. The soldiers fought bravely, though they were soon only five. Only Andreas, Crozier, Viaticum, Pym, and Rood, were left to face the evil scourge. They burned the bodies of their brethren and sent them to their god so that they would not have to rest eternally in that wicked place. When they gained the gate and fought to seal it again they were only three— Andreas, Crozier and Viaticum. They moved from the gate with Rood in Viaticum's arms, and Pym was carried by Crozier. They built a pyre from the strangled thorn trees that grew over everything in the area. They placed the bodies upon it and Andreas set it aflame with a wisp of magic. Cruet and Viaticum said ritual words as the fire spread and caught upon the bodies. Andreas continued to feed the fire and when the bodies were being consumed the living fell exhausted to the ground.

As they rested dark fell again . In the distance they espied a faint shape; a formation of rock or perhaps a tower. When the dim light came again they would make their way to it. They started a watch fire and set watch, but they could not sleep. With their task nearly complete their hearts and minds turned to the Dark One. To soothe their nerves and perhaps to protect themselves from stray beasts they pulled their instruments and began to play.

***

The night creatures did not take me as I slept at the river bank. I opened my eyes reluctantly to a grey sky of dim light. The tower was not far, but it seemed to take forever for me to reach the shallow marsh that surrounded the low tor on which the towers were built. I circumnavigated to an upward sloping causeway that lead between two towers. High above me I could make out dark forms walking along the parapets. I quickly tucked myself up against the causeway and moved toward the foundation of the towers walls. The causeway shielded me from sight, but now I was forced to climb the high end of it to get a look between the towers.

I made the short climb with great effort, and remained prone upon the ground only turning my head to see between the towers and into the walls of what I hoped was The Dark One's fortress. There was no one about at ground level that I could see. I crawled upon my belly to a place just inside and around to the right of the nearest tower. My pack weighed on me like a great stone. I talked myself out of leaving it behind where I rested in the shadows, catching my breath.

Across the damp courtyard an arched entry stood open in the corner between two wings of the main building. It was open and I felt it beckoning me in. I reached down into my dwindled reserve of strength and moved out. Weapons drawn and battle ready I slinked through shadow and climbed the three low stairs before the entrance. The light inside was from candles placed in four corners of a square vestibule. Two doors gave access to the inner rooms. One was shut, and dark above its threshold. The other was open and the orange glow of candles lit the room beyond. Open and beckoning me in; I moved to it. Inside a great black stone stairway led up along the outer wall. There were no other doors or windows so I took a candle from a sconce and moved up the stairs. A hall way stretched out before me. Doors lined its length, but only one was open. I went to it. My father was lighting my way to him.

Inside was a vast room, part library, part parlor. The room was well lit with candles and lanthorns. I saw no other doors or windows, but a spiral staircase of wrought iron led to a balcony that held rows of shelves packed with dusty books and scrolls. I climbed the stairs and walked along the end of the rows. I could see between them that another room filled a space at the other end. The light was bright there; I could see instruments of music, along the walls and on tables there. I moved slowly toward it down the last row of shelves. I saw another open door, ahead and on another wall another door, but it was closed. I stood just inside the rows surveying the room before I would enter in to it. The sight that met my eyes was inconceivable. It filled me with a rush of emotion. At the site of my mother netted and chained, crucified to a high rafter, I fell to my knees.

She saw me, but did not speak. She did not have to. I saw terror and deepest sorrow in her eyes. I rose and took a step toward her. A hooked fisherman's net was wrapped completely around her, the hooks piercing her if she moved at all. Her chains were tight around her wrists and the net that enveloped her, then wrapped loosely around her arms and body and the beam to hold her there and weigh her down. The pressure on her upper body must have been immense.

I stopped and took another look around. I could discern no immediate threat. I moved to the door and looked out. It opened to a balcony looking out over the bizarre landscape of the Dark One's realm. There seemed no threat in that. I closed the door and returned my attention to my mother.

My mother— so long ago lost to me, now here before me. Malisgalar said she had come to him to keep me from him. I believe Malisgalar had taken her from me. Had he wanted me so badly he had only to let me know that and I'd have come directly; to save her. This insane game with the scrolls was unnecessary. It didn't matter. If he was my father I was dark spawn. Somehow that gave me strength. What powers had I inherited that my mother had kept from me? What could I call forth to save her now? Nothing, sadly as I tried to release her with powers like I had seen Andreas use. Nothing worked. I growled out my anger and frustration. The room filled with force. Papers flew from out of the nearest shelves; a pan pipe flew from its table and hit the rafter not far from my mother's head. A great harp tipped and scraped against the wall before leaning precariously there. All the candles within the room blew out. Only the hooded lanterns gave off light now. The surprise of it sat me down hard upon the ground. I heard my mother gasp and then weep.

I had to save her. The urgency of the situation was dire. I was frightened. How long had she hung there I could not be sure. Her breath was already labored and her weeping would only speed the suffocation. I pulled rope from my pack and then flipped it high to sail over the rafter. I pulled the two ends together and began my climb.

When I was perched safely on the rafter the balcony door flew open and a great wind tossed me off. A stench of fire, death, and sulfur burned my nose and throat making its way to my lungs. The remaining lights within the room guttered and then went out.

I fumbled to stand and draw my weapons. Not sure of my direction, I turned slowly swinging my weapons to find my adversary. But, this was no foe of flesh and blood. Out of the dark a roiling face loomed toward me.

"You cannot have her. She does not belong to you! You have gone astray. She is not why you have come, or have you forgotten me?"

As quickly as the thing had come it was gone, but I remembered it. It was the voice of the apparition that had proclaimed to be my father. It was the breath of the thing that took me in Kapit's house. I would never forget that reeking breath. This belonged to that which made me kill Wallace. Somewhere in this twisted palace was the living entity that had controlled me —If my mother's presence had not been enough I knew for certain then that I had made my way to the right place. The rope from the rafters fell across my shoulder. My mother's head hung low against her chest. She still breathed, but barely.

I flipped the rope again and climbed quickly to the rafter. I hesitated a moment there, waiting for the dark face to return, but it did not. I quickly wrapped the rope around my mother, to pull the weight off her lungs and tied her to the rafter. Blood oozed from her wounds where the hooks had bitten in. I pulled at the chains, in an attempt to lower her, but they only entangled her more tightly. My panic at being unable to free her released an involuntary growl and the force came from me to do my bidding. The chains popped free. I untied the rope and lowered her slowly to the floor and then I jumped down, rolled, and went to her. I removed the net slowly undoing those that had pierced her skin and turned the hooks away from her. When she was free of it I rubbed her weakened limbs to get her blood flowing again. She stirred and looked up at me. Her shaking hand came up to take mine. She could not speak. I realized then with horror and rage that her tongue had been cut out. She kissed my hand and then held it to her cheek.

I had no water and food from my pack to give her. It had all been spoiled in the river.

"Where must I go mother? The entire world depends on me to kill him. Is it true that he is my father? She hung her head from me and wept again, but she shook her head. *Yes.* I sat back speechless, though I already knew it was true that I was devil spawn. I watched her as she wept—ashamed. I could not fault her, or hate her. She had taught me all I knew, loved me, and protected me. I put my hand against her

433

face and wiped her tears. She reached for me and pulled me close. I was again in the embrace of the only person who had ever loved me. It was my time to weep and she stroked my hair as I did. I was a child again, and her love gave me hope, and determination. I did not know how, but I would not let my father take my mother from me again. I could not leave her. I let her rest and looked through the books and scrolls while she did. Nothing offered me any insight. So I browsed the instruments. Andreas had all of good our instruments in the carpetbag. I gathered an ornately carved lyre, and a kaval made of black horn with a pearl mouth end. I felt justified in taking them, due to the nature of my business here. There might come a time I would need to play. I only carried one other instrument with me. The harp I played as a child, but it was not of good quality, no more than a keepsake. I put the lyre in a small sack tied to the back of my belt. The kaval tucked in nicely to my sword belt at my left hip.

I went back to see to Mother. She was a hindrance, but I couldn't leave her behind. I pulled her to her feet, and helped her to walk back to the vestibule and the only other door that would bring me closer to Malisgalar.

I stood before it daunted, afraid to move, and afraid not to. Mother leaned on me. As weak as I felt, I had to be strong. I could not let her see me dying. I called upon my courage, tested the door, then swung it open. This corridor stretched out as far as I could see with doors and intersections all along it. Afraid to move and afraid not to I stepped in. Mother followed with her hand upon my shoulder. I wondered what she thought of me; wounded, bedraggled; bristling with weapons. Did see remember the little girl that played the harp upon her hearth, or did she see a desperate woman crazed by fate. I longed so much for that hearth and harp and the warm smile of the woman who so loved me then. When this evil was over I hoped she could love me still.

Overwhelming grief hit me at the thought of losing her again. When it did that roiling force with a face rushed down the corridor at us.

"I said you cannot have her!" It screamed. I pushed Mother back through the door and stood in the opening braced for the impact.

"She is mine!" I screamed back, and raised my weapons.

My sword swept down across the brow of the force and ripped a gash in the smoky thing. Fire exploded from it and I was thrown back against Mother. Shards of fire and brimstone rained down on us. I grabbed Mother and rolled away from it, until I could gain my feet and drag her back into the hall we had come from, across the room, and out of range. She was patting fire from my hair as I patted it from her skirt. The look we shared was so full of emotions that all we could do was stare into each other's eyes watching them change with each new one felt.

Then I felt a whisper in my ear. "Come Saeede, I want your life. You seek my death. Let us have this out. Come to me. You can bring your ignorant bitch mother, but in the end she will only watch you die."

That moment I realized a thing about that place. My emotions were feeding it. I was nearly primal from all that had befallen me and now here with my mother everything I had suppressed for years was rushing to the surface. I was like a beacon. He could feel me.

I explained it to Mother, and then I pulled the harp I had kept for all those years packed away in my backpack. It always made me smile to think of those lost days in my child hood home in the woods, making music. Those days were the best days of my life, filled with joy. What would this place do with joy? I hoped it would repulse, and so offer some level of protection. I tuned it and strummed it once, twice more, melody, song, joy.

My blades hung in their thongs and scabbards. My weapon was my little wooden harp. I started to feel the music and a sway made its way into my stride. Behind me mother shuffled the dance she had done so often in the yard as I played upon the porch. My spirit came back to me a bit. We moved this way, boldly, in defiance of the dark all around us, all inside me. Nothing came to us or taunted our minds as we meandered through the doors and corridors trying to find a route to Malisgalar.

When at last we found him our brief joy was crushed. We had entered a vast cavern. He paced along the edge of a low stone shelf. He was awake and I was not a part of a dream. So was I dead or alive, was mother alive or a phantom? Behind him a sundered stone throne wrapped in broken chains leaned on its broken feet. When he sensed our entrance he turned slowly and smiled. Black teeth shined behind black lips.

Sardon moved out from behind a natural pillar of stone and just behind her was the minion I had seen her with when I had arrived at this place. For the first time I saw fully the face of him—he was the one— he had controlled me. Sheer panic took over in me. 'Could he do it again? Would he try? How would I counter that?' I had no idea.

My mind raced with all that I must do. With all that I did not know to do. I knew I could not win against them all. I swept my arm back to put Mother behind me. I put the little harp down slowly on the ground. When I stood again I saw that Sardon and Malisgalar's minion had come closer. I drew two swords and prayed.

Sardon came toward me first, suddenly charging. I fought her off and though she fought much better than I expected, she soon laid dying at my feet. This so enraged her concubine demon, that he spat fire at me, but he did not charge. He came easily into my mind and I was overwhelmed with a sudden need to kill Mother. My body turned to her, but my soul raged against it. My sword came up and she cowered. I shook with the effort to control my muscles. The demon bore down harder on my mind and I nearly swung the blade down upon my mother's neck. The growl was fighting to release, pushing against the control that the beast had on me. The blade was now set at my mother's throat. My muscles tensed to push the blade and pierce her windpipe.

The growl that came at last was a bestial thing that echoed through the cavern. "Rawwerrrllll-ahhhh!"

Mother fell in a heap, but I saw her breathe. I turned to the demon. Shock was upon him. "So, even minion demons know fear then." I said as I strode forward. We fought long and he would have had me, but for the low growl I teased upon him in my twisted humor. He fell back and I leapt upon him, slashing his throat with both blades. Dark blood spilt out on the stone and etched into the surface. Acrid smoke rose up and stung my eyes. I returned to Mother, and waited.

Malisgalar paced again. I heard a sound like marching, from beyond the cavern. Then demons like those that had swarmed us at Draghador's Mountain home came up and over the stone shelf and ran toward us.

I was done for. Malisgalar would live to rule the earth. I gambled one last look at him. He stood arrogantly with his arms crossed at his chest a content smile across his shiny black face. Then the swarm was upon me. I tried to keep thoughts of victory, strength, and courage in my mind, in an attempt to remain in the battle. It was for naught. The cold that I learned to suppress was suddenly dominant in me again and worked against me. I growled, and even though a few of the dark dogs faltered others swarmed over them to take their places. I was on my knees, barely keeping my swords up; when I became aware of music far off in the distance. The music was that of the scrolls. I fought on with a flow of renewed strength. Somewhere not too far off Andreas and the Paladins played. I was certain that I recognized Andrea's touch upon the cittern.

I fought on and I was soaked by the burning blood of the beasts. Malisgalar threw balls of force upon me that exploded in cold that joined with the cold within me. I know not how I remained in the fight. I credited the mask, the music, and sheer will to survive. The last dogs fell as Malisgalar turned to me.

I was in distress with only a trace of stamina left to sustain me. I pulled the kaval from my belt and put it to my lips. I played with my left hand to join the song of the distant music.

Malisgalar fell back but summoned his will and pushed toward me. I played all that I could until he struck me and the kaval flew from my lips and was lost somewhere behind me.

I swung with one sword as I drew the second and spun round and ducked to avoid his raking claw. When I came around his other claw was raking up at me and I had to fall back to avoid that hit. I must have frustrated him because he rained down forces of the elements upon me. Each time I was close enough to strike I would fall or reel away from fire, or ice, stone, or wind. I began to hum the missing piece of the movement that was being played outside. Then suddenly a harp, the old harp from my youth joined in as Mother attempted the tune that I had hummed, the missing harmony to Andreas's cittern.

A quake of stone emanated from the broken throne as it began to move back together The chains reformed and lashed out to pull Malisgalar back. He stumbled and was dragged across the stones away from me.

The music filled me with courage and hope. It was eerie, yet beautiful. I gave chase as Malisgalar was pulled away scrambling for a hold. He got it at last on the pillar from which Sardon had emerged. Still the chains pulled mightily at him. He struggled. I stood over him. I brought both blades up to pierce his black heart. He raised one hand to unleash some element upon me, but I was swift. The blades sank deep, chinking the stone beneath him. He raged at his death, and the fire in his gut spewed from his mouth like vomit. I jumped away from it.

I pulled the kaval flute from my belt. I did not want to be left out of this song. We played on as he died. He held so tightly to the pillar in his attempt to survive that it cracked and gave way. The chains drug him back into the chair and bound him tight.

We played on a few moments, tentatively, afraid that if we stopped he would spring on us again. Mother was the first to stop. She walked slowly past me to go up to him. Each step was a struggle, but when she was near enough and sure that he was dead she spat upon him three times. That was when I stopped playing.

I went to where the beast, my father sat in dead repose. I reached for my blades, to pull them out, but Mother stayed my hand.

"Best they stay?" I said. That was all. Above us the ceiling gave a frightening crack I grabbed mother and pushed her back toward the only opening I knew. Behind us the stone shelf fell away and the ceiling cracked again. Now I felt a tremor beneath my feet. Rubble and dust spewed toward us and cracked the floor beneath us.

"Run!" I screeched, as unnecessary as that was. Stone fell all round us cutting and buffering us against other crumbling walls. We pressed on pulling and pushing each other to safety. The courtyard lay just ahead. We made it out but encountered three beasts fleeing down the ramp. When we were on flat ground they turned on us. I pushed mother ahead and spun between her and them. When I did I saw the towers slowly imploding. The rubble rolled toward us. I was frozen by the sight, and furious that my victory was so short lived.

The beasts read my expression, turned to see the falling tower and then ran away. I turned to find mother and rush her to safety, but it was too late. A chunk of tower bounced near me and took me off my feet. I flew, tumbling in mid air the whole while.

***

I heard someone call my name. I woke. Every nerve that carried pain now carried it to the extreme. Then I heard a voice again. Andreas's voice!

"How do I know what can be believed?" Andreas asked.

"I do not know," Crozier replied.

I opened my eyes to see them leaning over me.

"About time you showed up." I rasped.

Wha?" Andreas gaped, dumbfounded. "I…You…how?"

"Not now Andreas, Later. Just get me out of here."

"How do I know it is you?"

"Of course it's me. Who…" Then I remembered. It was not going to be easy to convince him, not after he held my dead body thing.

"You said you felt me with you. I can't explain it, but I was there with you and my dead body, but I couldn't have been dead because here I am alive, well barely anyway. I thought I might be a figment of Malisgalar's dream, but when I found him he wasn't sleeping."

"You found him!?" This time Andreas and the paladins all spoke in unison.

"Yes, but you knew that, you played for me, to make him vulnerable."

"No, we played for ourselves, because we were vulnerable. Do you mean to tell me that you killed him?" Andreas asked.

"I did. We did."

"Prove this so we will know it is true. That you are true and real."

"Help me then."

He helped me to sit. Hot pain shot through my back. Perhaps it was broken. I waited for it to subside and then slipped from the rock to test my legs. The pain came again, but my legs moved and held me. I walked gingerly and Mother came for me to lean on.

"Have you all met my mother?" I asked as way of introduction.

"Wha? How?" Andreas was sometimes a contradiction to his educated ways.

"It's a long story I'll tell you on the way."

Mother and I led them back to the fallen tower, and made our way carefully over the rubble. The general form of the foundation was apparent and we were able to make our way through the rubble to where the cavern entrance had been. A slide of rock had fallen into it and we were able to clear it enough that we could squeeze through. It was dark except for the dim light seeping through the gap and from another larger one that was hidden from view by a jut of rock. I knew that must have been where I had heard the music from. It must lead outside.

I pointed to where Malisgalar would be and they found him there with my swords still in his throat. Andreas looked to me and to my swords. He went to remove them, but Crozier stayed his hand. "It is better that they stay where they are," he said.

I moved to find the other opening and looked out at the dim light of the twisted landscape. It was over, but we were still trapped in that god forsaken place. I leaned against the entrance of the cave that looked out. I was feeling odd, and knew if I did not sit I would faint. Mother was there for me, but it was Andreas who picked me up and carried me back to the rock where they had found me.

"I am so sorry to have doubted you, but with all the trickery I had to be sure."

"I know."

Andreas curled me up close as he carried me like a baby. When we came to the rock he set me down and held me in an embrace that nearly knocked me out. "You did it, you dark little witchling."

"We did it," I corrected, "We all did it."

"Yes."

Andreas laid me back down and went to make a litter to carry me. Crozier dressed our wounds. Viaticum stood guard. I lay on the lump of stone drifting in and out of fitful sleep. I was awakened at one point, by a shudder of earth and the crumbling of stone. I raised my head to see Andreas with his body bent and his hands thrust out as he had released some force upon the cave. The hill that had been Malisgalar's shelter was no more than a crater now. Crozier and Viaticum went about it and the tower remains with holy water, salt, and consecrating prayers. I drifted off again in the comfort that the Dark Lord was forever dead.

At some point I was placed upon the litter. That simple thing caused my fitfulness to relax and I slipped into a deep exhausted sleep. It was over—and somehow I was still—we were still alive!

I remember only two things about our climb out of that wicked abyss. Once during the clash of a battle, I saw my mother bent over me in a protective stance. A dome of shimmering light enveloped us. I was sure that she had conjured it up, her face was contorted in the effort it spent her. I saw beyond her Andreas and the Paladins fighting off a swarm of flying demons. The dome would flicker and snap its energy when one would try to swoop down on us. Mother would grunt but the dome held and the creature would fall. I remember wondering who she was; who she really was. I could not rise to the battle and sleep took me again.

When next I woke we were in the halls of the prison. I had opened my eyes to see the buttressed walls and ceilings. We were not moving. Mother sat upon the ground next to me and rubbed her soft hand across my head. I turned my heavy head and she smiled up at me. I thought I must be dreaming to have her there. I took her hand, because I could not speak through a flood of emotion that sprang up unexpectedly. Embarrassed, I looked away and saw the stacks of cages and the catwalks that accessed them. Andreas went about opening locks with picks or magic, which ever worked best. Crozier went before him, praying and laying hands upon the poor souls within. I could not see Viaticum and I prayed we had not lost him too. I watched for awhile and savored the caress of my mother's hand until sleep over took me again.

***

When I woke at last from the fatigue that had overwhelmed me I found myself in a tent. A drone of voices came to me but as I listened I began to sort them. Andreas, Crozier, another I was unsure of, and then Viaticum. I was at once glad to hear his voice and sad to remember that the other Paladins were all lost. I lay there a bit longer listening while I gauged the strength within me and realized the cold that had gripped me since the night of Wallace's death had softened to a mere shiver. Poor Wallace, so many good people had been lost to the evil. I was stricken with grief and found that I could not restrain the sobs that welled up from within. I covered my face with a pillow and fought desperately to quiet my pain as it forced its way out of me at last. It must have been hours that I anguished, but at last I fell asleep, exhausted once again.

When next I woke it was to the warmth of the sun as it beat down upon the canvas roof of the tent. I heard voices again nearby, but I did not recognize them. I sat up; my back was deeply bruised, but not broken. The tent was sparsely furnished, but I found my things in a stack at the end of my pallet. I dressed, gingerly for the aches and bruises were greater than I realized.

At the tent flap I took a deep breath before I pulled it back, not knowing what I might find beyond it. I was glad to find a fair day. The clouds drifted slowly across a cerulean blue sky. The air was soft, and a gentle breeze brought a light touch of warmth to kiss across my skin. I breathed it in as I looked out across a military encampment. I was up on a rise and could see the soldiers tents set up neatly in their rows. Wagons and horses formed a half circle at the edges of the camp furthest from me. Soldiers went about their duties and several bowed to me as I stood half out of the tent taking in the scene. I smiled and bowed awkwardly in return.

Beyond the wagons hot fires burned in a battlefield where some epic battle must have raged not long ago. Dark and twisted bodies of demons and devil spawn were being thrown upon the fires. The fallen soldiers were being placed upon carts that when full were brought to a place where a mass grave was being dug. Crozier, Viaticum, Eucharist and my mother moved about giving blessings and anointment to all of the dead. I was saddened by the sight, but the fact that I stood within a camp of my own kind heartened me. Our side had had a victory here.

Near the far end of camp a group of soldiers mingled while they went about the tasks of maintaining their gear. Their laughter came to me on the breeze, and I was glad for it.

I took several steps out of the tent and turned to see what lay behind me. Near to me, mine was one of four large tents, set upon the rise to watch the battle unfold in the fields below. Behind these tents a smithy and a cook tent stood side by side, beyond that forest sloped up to meet the mountain further on. A faint scent of ocean mingled with the breeze, but I saw no glimmer of water from any direction.

The voices I had heard on my waking were from the tent to the left of mine. I moved toward it and my head spun, but only enough to make my walk interesting. Two soldiers stood guard there but let me pass and held back the tent flap as I did. A meeting was in progress, and not wanting to interrupt I took a seat at the back. I did not recognize the speaker, who was addressing the panel at the back of the tent, but I saw many people on panel and in the audience that I did. Andreas sat in the audience with Father Gan. Kapit, and Diony sat on the panel as did her chief of Security, Ray MacVen. Diony seemed to notice me and gave me a long look over as I sat alone in the back, but she made no mention of it.

The speaker was a soldier, one of Dune's men from across the sea. Why on earth was he so far from home, I wondered. I leaned forward to hear him better. He had been sent to bring home the Paladins and lay them to rest as heroes amongst their people. It was Kapit who informed them that they had received proper religious heroes' rites on their fields of battle and that to protect their souls the surviving Paladins had given them a burial by fire. The man understood, but was anxious to reunite with the surviving Paladins. Diony informed him that they were needed to complete the work of sanctifying the ground of what she called the last great battle. Then she directed him to the place where they could be found. He thanked the panel and left the tent.

Andreas saw me as he watched the soldier leave and came to me. Kapit and Gan saw me too and Kapit opened his mouth to announce me, but I shook my head no and he sat back. Andreas put out his hand to me and I took it. He helped me to my feet and led me from the tent. We went back to the tent I had been placed in and he sat me on a stool near my cot.

"I have much to tell you, but I don't know where to start."

"Start with: is it over?"

"In large part it is, though small skirmishes still flair up in the outer regions. We have scout troops out in all the lands. Our fear is that we will never really know if and when they have all been vanquished."

"Where are we now?"

"In the grasslands north of the prison, south of Mareese. We came out of the main gate of the prison and two great fire demons blocked our way. Fortunately their attention was on a great battle raging on the plateaus above them. We nearly made it up to the plateau when one of them spotted us. You were in and out of consciousness, and we were lifting you up the same cliff we descended when we gained entrance to the place, when a ball of fire blasted against the rock near your head. Do you remember?"

I tried to access the memory. I saw an orange ball arcing toward me and remembered a string of shouted expletives and a fall of about twenty feet. "I thought it was just another thread of nightmare. I believe I hit my head on the way down." I rubbed my head and found the sore spot. "Yes I did, it knocked me cold didn't it?"

"It did."

"What is happening? Is it over?"

"It is over, for the most part. There are still skirmishes throughout the lands as I said. I don't think we will ever beat them back completely. There is talk of a celebration in Mareese. The people there fought bravely, but they lost many. There will be a memorial and then to turn things around Diony wants to have a festival; a day of honor she calls it. She wants her people to be proud of what they did; to give them a spot to move forward from. We are to be honored guests. We must go I suppose, but I have never wanted to be so far from civilization, ever."

"That is saying a lot coming from you."

"We really should go, It would inspire the people to see you there for sure. After what you have been through I understand that you are tired, but it has been a long dark year. A festival might cheer you."

I sighed, resigned to the better good. I would go, and Andreas knew it. Perhaps it would cheer me, but I made him promise that as soon as we would not be missed we would slip away. He made the promise happily.

Outside of our tent the sounds of people leaving the meeting came to us and then shortly after Diony, Kaedl and

Father Gan came in to my tent. They had only come to give me greetings and did not stay long, saying that I needed to rest. We were to ride to Mareese the very next day.

Andreas kissed my forehead and left with the others. "I will tell your good mam that you have revived."

I smiled, "Tell her when she returns. I am exhausted and I will sleep until then."

***

Mother did not wake me upon her return. When I woke again it was to the shouts of men, the creaking of wagons and the clomp of horses hoofs. When I opened my eyes there was mother sitting cross legged on the cot across from me.

I could tell from the light in the tent that it was morning. She had watched me all through the night and wiped a tear from her cheek when she saw my eyes open. She came to me then and sat at the edge of my bed looking down at me. Her soft grey eyes gazing at me with such warmth melted anything that I had left to hold myself together. The final strain of exhaustion snapped and it seemed as if all the emotions of my life time splashed over me. Tears welled up in my eyes as I gazed back at the mother I had grieved for, for so long. My throat caught and broke and as she reached to pull me up into her embrace I lost the control. Control—it was laughable just how little I had left. I hated myself for it, but the stroke of her loving hand upon my back allowed me to surrender to it. The sorrow came in waves of sobs and then quiet snuffling until the reality of all that had happened came again to my heart and I was off again in uncontrollable sobs. I have great pride in myself though that I was able to quiet the sounds by sheer will or my mother's shoulder.

I don't know how long I let the fear, and anger seep away from me. I told her everything that had happened since she sent me away. She cried with me. Mother sent two messengers from the tent with a steely gaze, and then no one else came again. It was nearly noon when I forced myself to regain decorum. I had a headache that pounded every inch of my cranium and behind my eyes. My back and abdomen hurt from the strain and I knew I looked a sight.

Mother went to her basin and filled it with herbs and cool water. She rinsed a cloth in it and washed my face. Then I repeatedly rinsed the cloth and compressed it to my eyes. As I did mother combed my hair as she did when I was but a girl. I reveled in the nurturing. I knew from the sounds outside that the business of breaking camp must be nearing an end, and that Diony and Eucharist would want to be getting underway. Mother agreed with a nod of her head. I undressed and washed in the herb water. Then I gathered my silks, my remaining weapons and armor, and mother helped me to dress. I placed the silk sash she had given me only a few short years ago around her neck and kissed her cheek. Those short years had seemed like forever ago. She touched my cheek and then we turned together without a word and went outside.

Andreas saw us and turned the hitching of a wagon to a two horsed harness over to a nearby livery boy. He came to us and I noticed an impish smile upon his face. Mother tensed; I sensed she did not like my friend.

"I think she thinks I will cause you pain."

"What did you do?"

"Nothing, I swear."

"Then what did you say?"

"This is vicious accusery! I am nothing if not a gentleman."

I crossed my arms.

"Well I think she might have overheard me calling you..." He looked at Mother and leaned in to whisper to me. "...a dark little witchling."

I laughed a little. "Always the charmer," I said to him. "That is just the type of comment that would set her off you buffoon." Andreas shrugged and attempted a shy smile. Mother and I were not fooled, but it warmed my heart to see my friend at least attempting to fawn. "It's okay Mother. He is a good guy just clumsy around beautiful women."

Then he moved to Mother. He took her hand, to kiss it, but she pulled away. He looked at me, again dumbfounded. His charm rarely failed.

"My apologies madam," he said graciously. "It is just that I'm so happy to see her, and alive at that. Each time since we found you in that dark place I am reminded of how lucky and happy I am to have my good friend here with me again. Our friendship is a lighthearted one, we jest more than anything."

She gave him a scrupulous look, bowed and then went to help Crozier where he was loading wounded into a wagon.

"She hates me."

"Does that bother you?"

"Immensely. You are like a sister to me. My own parents cast me out. When I knew it to be your mother I was amazed and then gladdened that I might have some relationship with her as you have told me you have had."

"I am like a sister?"

"Of course, you knew that."

"Aye." Of course I had always hoped for more, but it was not to be with him.

"They cut out her tongue, Andre. She had a voice like an angel; she used to sing when I played. She is doing her best to communicate with her eyes; perhaps we just do not understand her yet. I'll talk to her and explain you to her, if that is even possible. Still, I'm not sure about that look she just gave you. I'd be careful if I was you.

"Come on I'm feeling better, Mother and I had a long talk. I am anxious to get on with the rest of my life."

He bowed dramatically, like a courtesan and allowed me to pass, and then he trotted up alongside me and put my arm through his. We looked a haughty pair as he gave me a tour of the grounds and then helped me to mount Grey Daria. The mare that Kapit had gifted to me was anxious to be off and I gave her rein. We flew down the camp road and into the valley where the last of the evil dead were being burned. I turned her wide and back toward Mareese. Andreas joined me soon enough on Dark Corydon and we raced side by side, giving all control to the great animals we had the privilege to ride. I laughed loud and mighty. I was filled again with the joy of life. When the horses tired we let them find their pace as we turned them back toward camp. The first of the wagons were being pulled onto the camp road, while the last of the tents were being brought down, and packed into the last of the wagons when we returned. My mother and Father Gan rode together near the center of the line. What a match; witch and priest. She saw me and I waved. "Hail great Mother!" I yelled.

She laughed aloud and I joined her, so happy was I to hear that she could still do that. I turned my mount aside and

Andreas and I stayed our mounts as the procession passed. We hailed all our friends as they passed us by and cheered the soldiers who had fought the great battle against the evil. Laughter and song went up throughout the ranks. Of all that had happened I think that was our greatest moment to stay and cheer all those who had supported our dark task. When the camp was empty we clasped hands and hugged across the gap between our mounts. Then we raced off to join Eucharist, Diony, and her man Brynal at the front of the procession back to Mareese.

Fini

About the Author

Nance Bulow Morgan has been a photojournalist and worked in the print industry for three decades. A native of Northern Illinois, Bulow Morgan now resides in the Sandhills of North Carolina.

She has published a book of prose and a fantasy novel, Legend Destiny, that has become the spring board for a series titled The Minstrels' Tale Mysteries. Minstrels' Gambit is the first in that series!

Other Books by Nance Bulow-Morgan
Legend Destiny
Voyage: A Book of Prose

To be Released Spring 2014
Minstrels' Covenant

Current Projects
Minstrels' Prize

www.ingramcontent.com/pod-product-compliance
Lightning Source LLC
Chambersburg PA
CBHW051432260626
47162CB00001B/53